HER RECKLESS REVENGE

THE SAXONS OF HYRSTOW

C.A. FRAY

Also by C.A. Fray

The Saxons of Hyrstow Trilogy:
His Viking Captive
His Saxon Wife

Editor: Tracey Barski

Cover Design: Okay Creations

Published by: CF Publishing

*To every woman who has been considered a villain simply
because she prioritized herself.*

A NOTE TO THE READER

Thank you for choosing to read Her Reckless Revenge. This book contains scenes of gory violence, on page death, animal violence including the stabbing of a horse, discussion of sexual assault (off-page), onlookers in the consummation of a marriage, open discussion of sex work/being a mistress, and scenes where a character experiences panic attacks. I hope that I have treated these topics with the care they deserve. Please be aware of these topics if you choose to read further.

THE SAXONS OF HYRSTOW BOOK THREE

HER RECKLESS REVENGE

C.A. FRAY

PROLOGUE

Grahame

Northumbria

Late summer 788 AD

He ran up the hill feeling as if his heart was about to burst. It was nearly sundown. Despite his father's protest that he remain for supper after he'd been gone for a week, Grahame ran across his family's land, his legs eating up the space between him and the girl he loved. Adara.

Love.

It was a bright, shiny feeling in his chest. His grin shone with it as he topped the hill and looked down to the small homestead nestled in the basin of the slope. It was a sturdy home, large, with solid wood planks and a thickly thatched roof. Smoke curled from the chimney while animals grazed in a fenced area to the right of the house. It was his first time laying eyes on Adara's cousin's home, the place she had lived the entire summer. Adara had always ventured to him since he was busy shepherding.

Excitement spurred Grahame onward. He knew Adara would be happy to see him. They'd parted on bad terms, with Adara begging him not to go. She had feared for his safety, and rightly so. He had followed his friends, Ridley and Branton, to a small outpost to the southeast, not far from their home village of Hyrstow. In it were the men that killed Ridley's parents in a vicious raid seven years prior.

Grahame shuddered beneath the fading sun. The bloodshed had been swift and merciless. Ridley had shown a side of himself Grahame didn't want to see again. Though Grahame had wielded a sword, his blade was not the one to carry out the deaths. He had kept his promise to Adara to remain safe. To come back to her.

Adara. She was of noble birth yet there *had* to be a way they could be together.

Despite his only being ten and four years, he considered himself a man. He would take over his father's sheep one day. Though of lesser status, his father and mother's business was starting to grow. Adara's father would perhaps be amenable to marriage if Grahame could prove his worth.

Confidence brimming, Grahame clenched his hand into a fist and knocked on the house's door.

A slight young woman with hair the color of ripe wheat answered. She could not have been much older than Grahame and Adara. Grahame smiled wide. She must have been Adara's cousin, Cecilia, of whom Adara had shared many stories.

"I have come to call on Adara," he said. He couldn't help the way his chest puffed out. Adara would be so happy to see him. She would forget their argument, he was sure of it.

The woman's gaze trailed from his too-long golden curls to his simple tunic to the slight hole in the knee of his trousers. Grahame tried not to fidget. He'd changed his travel dusted clothing before coming, though he wished he'd had something finer. No matter. Adara cared little over his attire.

"She is not here," the young woman said, not unkindly.

That couldn't be right. Adara was to remain with her cousin for the rest of the summer. Three more weeks stood between them and her summons. Grahame tried again.

"My name is—"

"Grahame," she supplied, "from over the hill and yonder."

Grahame felt his smile slip a fraction.

"She's told you of me," he replied slowly. He hadn't considered an outcome where Adara was not waiting for him. He tried to make himself look trustworthy by propping his hands on his hips. Perhaps she was still angry and instructed her cousin to turn him away.

"Please, I understand she was angry with me but if you'll just let me see her."

The woman's light eyebrows rose for a moment, though her mouth did not curl with surprise. She began to shut the door. Grahame's hands shot out in a gesture for her to halt.

"No, no, please. Please. I am here to see Adara. I had to help my friend and I have come to let her know of my success and my safety. I just need to see her."

The pleading in his tone must have been cause for pity because the woman opened the door wide, sighing. She turned to the room inside, gesturing with a hand to show it empty.

"She is gone. Her father's men came to collect her the day after you left."

Horror hollowed out Grahame's belly.

"Gone?"

The woman nodded, biting her lip. Her shoulders slouched with the loss. "Adara didn't go without a fight. Scratched one of them across the face."

A hollow feeling dug into his gut, scrounged upward into his chest.

"She's not here?"

The woman crossed her arms. "Do you have trouble hearing? She's been taken back to her father's keep. Going to be married off, as was always planned. Count yourselves lucky you were not here when they took her so that there was no contestation of her purity. Now, I have things to do today, so..."

Grahame tried to swallow and found he couldn't. Nor could he suck in enough air.

"You look a bit green. D' you want to sit down for a spell?"

Grahame could only nod as he was guided into the tidy home. A small fire crackled in a hearth to the right. It was bracketed by a large table and a set of fur-lined chairs. A woven rug softened Grahame's footsteps.

"I'm Cecilia, Adara's cousin. She would be happy to know you came back well. She was worried sick over the risk you were taking for your friend."

Cecilia pushed him into a sturdy chair then bustled over to the fire. She scooped a ladle of broth into a ceramic mug and brought it to him. Grahame accepted it though he did not drink. He simply stared at the liquid, his entire being empty.

"I should have stayed," he muttered.

"No, like I said, it was good you were not here. She would have fought to stay harder."

"I would have fought for her to stay, too." The words were wooden.

Cecilia clapped her hands. "Ach, I am sorry to not be full of sympathy, but you both are young. Too young."

"Yet she is of age to marry?" he challenged. Ire struck like a flint to flame inside him. He knew it was misplaced, knew that Cecilia was being hospitable, yet could not help his annoyance with her assessment.

Cecilia's mouth pressed into a wobbly line. She eased into the chair beside his, lashes fluttering to dispel the sheen that overtook her eyes.

"Soon. Her betrothed is Lord Clayton. The marriage will be held when her father and Clayton see fit. She is my friend as well as my cousin. I have been grieving the loss of her presence this week. I fear once she is married I shall not see her again. So, forgive me, Grahame, if I am harsh. You are a shepherd, and she is the earl's daughter. There is nothing to be done for it."

Grahame felt as if a giant boulder had been tied around his waist and thrown into a lake. There was no coming back. No telling Adara he succeeded, no seeing her again. Grahame felt his heart crack.

"Oh no," he moaned into his hand. "How far is it to her father's keep? Perhaps—"

Cecilia grasped his arm to keep him from rising. Her face had contorted into a worried scowl.

"Do not go to her. The earl is not kind. You would sign your death warrant if you appeared asking to see her."

"What if I do not care? I need to see her one last time."

Cecilia gave his arm a good shake.

"Stop thinking of yourself. It would not only be bad for you. Her father would ensure Adara suffered for the misdeed of grousing around with a shepherd."

The truth settled along Grahame's bones like a too-heavy blanket. He was suddenly overcome with regret. It made the backs of his eyes prickle. He pinched the bridge of his nose.

"It will be alright," Cecilia's tone softened. Her pity

and the sure hand on his shoulder made him want to vomit.

"I—I will go. Thank you for your kindness."

He passed the mug of untouched broth into Cecilia's waiting hand before he rushed from the room. Hot tears streamed down his cheeks as he ran back the way he came.

CHAPTER

ONE

Grahame

Summer 796 AD

Never in his life had Grahame Shepherd witnessed someone fall completely apart. His friend and chieftain, Ridley, was on his knees in the dirt, his glazed stare fixed on the hacked-off length of blonde hair in his hand. The proof that his wife, Yrsa, had been taken against her will.

"Ridley," Grahame said, trying to keep his tone even.

Ridley was a warrior, a leader. There was no reason for him to be crumbling. They needed to *go*. Helplessness itched at Grahame's spine. He crumpled the piece of parchment in his hand. The words inked on the page were found with Yrsa's hair and accused Ridley of some "egregious debt" owed to Lady Adara Clayton of Guston.

Adara.

9

The name rattled around in Grahame's mind, threatening to drive him mad. No. He wouldn't allow it. His friends needed him. Resolute, Grahame shoved the name of the girl he once knew to a familiar compartment in the back of his mind.

"Ridley," Grahame said, a demand.

Still, his friend sat in the dirt, dazed eyes fixed on the strands of yellow hair he clutched. As if that would bring her back. Had it been only moments ago that they had been partaking in tug of war and drink? The sun had gazed down at them with the love of a mother as the village prepared for a feast.

"How could they have taken her?" Branton challenged.

Grahame's gaze ripped to his brother-in-law who scanned the huts bordering Hyrstow's hall, in front of which Ridley knelt. He'd drawn his pregnant wife, Emma, to him, his large hand secured firmly about her waist.

Branton's voice was strained as he continued. "Earlier, Merthe said she couldn't find Yrsa. We need to go. Check on the children. There could be raiders. They could be infiltrating..."

"There aren't."

There was no reason for Grahame to think raiders would spare the village after Clayton had ordered it ransacked only weeks prior, but Grahame knew Adara. Or, rather, he thought he did. The girl he'd known in his youth had been cunning. There was no world in which she would try the same thing twice if the first time did not garner the desired result. Which, apparently, was the capture of Yrsa.

When Branton speared him with a look full of disbelief, Grahame elaborated.

"She took Yrsa. It says so in the letter which also commands me to Clayton House. What debt is she referring to, Rid?" Grahame held up the parchment.

"Ridley?" Branton stepped forward and shook Ridley's shoulder with a meaty hand. A tear streaked down Ridley's cheek as his shoulder was pushed back and forth.

"I couldn't keep her safe." The words grated up Ridley's throat.

The high sun was too warm on Grahame's neck. He felt like he couldn't take a full breath. The village couldn't handle another blow. They needed to *do* something.

Footsteps on the dirt path behind them hinted at others gathering. Grahame's hands went clammy.

"Mother?" Merthe, Emma's daughter strode up, her mouth pulled downward. Only when Emma opened her arms to Merthe and wrapped her in a bone-crushing hug did Branton release his wife.

"Merthe, Yrsa has been taken. We don't know much, but I need you to come with me and gather the children."

"What?" Merthe asked, eyes wide. "Why?"

"I will go with you," Branton said. "We'll bring everyone to the hall this time. Put others on alert."

Grahame rubbed at his jaw, recently shaved in anticipation of summer's heat. He understood Branton's protective instincts when it came to his family; he'd lost his first wife, Grahame's sister, Freda, the year prior, and just as his new marriage to Emma was forming, the village was raided while Branton was gone. It was a miracle Emma and Yrsa had fought off some of the raiders and saved the children. Grahame did not begrudge Branton for angling himself behind Emma as she turned to follow Merthe back to their hut, but he wished he was not the only one to think on how they were to get Yrsa back. The Viking woman was like a sister to him.

"We have to do something, Rid," Grahame infused a bit of steel into the name. Urgency churned his gut. Grahame wasn't a decision-maker. He was the joker, the friend, the man there for a good time, though not a long one. He most certainly did not know what action to take when his friend was staring at the ground like a simpleton.

"What's gone on?" Thomas Thatcher came from their right, tension lining his shoulders.

Grahame ignored him. They didn't have *time* for this.

"Is that hair?" someone said.

"Ridley," Grahame said. He squeezed Ridley's shoulder.

Footsteps neared, kicking up dust in the path. Others crowded.

Grahame gritted his teeth against the panic blooming behind his breastbone. Dropping to a crouch, he clasped the back of Ridley's neck, tight enough to hurt, and pulled him close.

"Ridley," he hissed. His friend's golden eyes darted to him, the only indication he'd heard. "We may be able to catch them. We must move swiftly."

"I didn't protect her. She..."

"She would have fought, Rid."

When Ridley merely nodded, brash, untethered anger slipped against the careful restraint Grahame kept on it. A decision had to be made. He leaned forward to hiss in his friend's ear.

"Whatever this is, this sorrow or guilt, bury it. They could have Yrsa tied, dragging behind a horse, or worse, stabbed and bleeding out in a cage for all we know."

The images he painted must have been enough because Ridley shoved upward with a roar that echoed among the huts. Pure, unadulterated murder shone in his eyes. Grahame blew out a thankful breath as he braced a hand on his knee to rise.

"Thomas," Ridley commanded, stalking toward the other man, "Yrsa's been taken. Gather whomever you can, any weapons, horses. We go after her. *Now.*"

Relief poured through Grahame. He would follow Ridley to the end of the earth to find Yrsa. Lady Wolf, as he affectionately started calling her when she joined their lives, had become family. Amid others telling him he needed to settle down, Yrsa was a grounding point in his life. She never bothered him about his lack of wife or luck that he would inherit his father's wealthy sheep farm.

Grahame ran inside the men's hall to the heavy war chest that stood against the far timbered wall. He cracked the ornately carved lid, hefting it upward. Grahame's hands met with the handle of a short sword, an ax, and a mace. He dragged out all three.

He tripped as he stood, the weapons in his arms jostling.

"Goddamnit!" he snarled.

Adara had done this. The knobby-kneed girl he'd met one dreary morning while tending to his father's sheep. The same girl who had come back day after day, watching, then pestering him with her idle chatter. She'd been pale and haunted, her eyes too big for her head, nose too round. She'd delighted in his speech—different from her noble dialect—and his ability to call the lambs to him. As she ran her hands over the little beasts, her laugh made the sky sparkle. Now, as a woman, a lady of a warring territory, she'd taken one of the few people in his life he truly cared for.

Grahame dumped the weapons at the feet of the men assembled. Ridley, Thomas, Awolf Tanner, Aeon Smith whose wife was slain in the last raid, Sam Sawyer, Murhed Butcher and others stood in a circle near the hall's door. Some were glassy-eyed with drink from the day's festivities, others were demanding answers or offering to stay behind to protect the village. Ridley doled out orders while Grahame disappeared inside the hall once again. If he kept moving, they could get to Yrsa in time. If he kept moving, they would bring her back and the only harm done to her would be a haircut. If he kept moving...

"Let's go!" Ridley shouted from outside.

Arms laden with more weapons, he returned to the group, passing the steel to awaiting hands. Horses had been gathered, their direction settled upon. At last, Grahame reached for the remaining weapon on the ground.

Ridley barely looked at him, but offered over his shoulder, "Can you pull that thing?"

Grahame bit back the thread of annoyance that shot through him as he picked up the bow. He may not have been known for his prowess on the battlefield but he deserved some credit. He'd done the required combat training Ridley put the men through, albeit not well.

"Yes."

"Good."

His chief threw himself upon his horse, galloping away as fast as it would carry him. Grahame clambered up on the awaiting mare that had been brought 'round. He wasn't sure if he could aim well but would do his damnedest to try.

In the short bursts of time he'd known Adara Clayton, she'd wreaked havoc on his life. At fourteen, they'd spent a summer together. His heart had been torn asunder when she'd been taken home. He didn't know for sure if she was behind the most recent raid or if it was an order given by her sickly husband. Either way, she would have known of it. The final straw, she'd captured Yrsa. He was through with her antics. Revenge was a red haze that swallowed him whole.

Adara

Ulrich plodded dutifully through the dense forest, his magnificent black coat shiny with perspiration. Her mount did not balk at Adara's demands, only ran when she spurred him and halted when she jerked the reins. She allowed herself a rare show of affection as she ran a hand over his shoulder, though she fenced her murmurs of gratitude inside her head. Only Hagan, her trusted guard, had heard her comfort the animal. She would not allow others to see her softer side. There was difficulty enough being a woman, let alone a widow.

Adara checked over her shoulder to the proud, blonde woman in tow behind her horse. Two of Adara's men, Thorhild and Leon, followed on horseback. Together they were a small but mighty force, stealthy enough to steal a woman without commotion. It was what she should have done in the first place. Though, if a glare could kill, Adara would have been dead ten times over.

When they'd taken her, Hagan had cut the woman's hair at Adara's command. The golden hank had been left at the village for Ridley Ward, chieftain of Hyrstow. Adara was dejected to find that the cut strands favorably framed the point of the woman's chin while the remaining, marred with dirt, hung limply over her left shoulder. A deep, purple bruise bloomed on the left side of her lip. Adara abhorred it. She did not condone violence against women, yet this one did not go easy with them.

Adara frowned and turned forward in her saddle. Splinters of the high sun shot through the dark green leaves overhead. Summer heat bled through her fine blue cloak. An idyllic day, yet every rustle, each far off swish of branches, caused Adara's shoulders to tighten.

"You needn't have come," Hagan said from beside her. Towering in his saddle, he'd dropped back from the lead to speak with her. Adara tightened her grip on the reins before replying.

"I do not require your advice."

Hagan pursed his lips, silver mail glinting in the dappled light as they wove between trees. It was heavy, she knew, as she wore her own version. Hagan had insisted she wear it, citing he would not help with her mission if she didn't help herself. Adara squashed the small part of her that warmed to think he cared.

"Indeed. However, I would like to inquire, if I may," he said, his deep timbre low so the others would not overhear.

Adara kept her eyes on the deer path they traversed. She didn't want to discuss her reasons for taking Ridley Ward's wife. Adara had been told what to do, where to go, and who to spend time with her entire life. Only in the past two months, after her husband Elvin's death, had she been free to do as she pleased. She knew her men did not understand her grudge against Hyrstow. Knew that they likely spoke of her mad hunger to harm the village while drinking ale in the kitchens of her house.

"Get on with it," she said, the words clipped.

Hagan hesitated, something rare, so she turned to look up into his rough face. The long-healed scar that ran from his left temple to his mouth puckered with his frown.

"These past months, you've trained as if you're being sent to war. Today, you made it clear you were to accompany us on this task despite me advising I can carry out your wishes. Do you not trust me? Do you not think me a worthy fighter if the need arises?"

Adara forced her eyes to stop their roll before it started. It was a skill she was rather good at. Something honed with years of practice from being the daughter of a terrifying man then married to a cruel one.

Of course, this was about the fragile egos of dangerous men.

"I trust you to carry out my wishes. However, I wished to accompany today's dealings for reasons of my own."

"My lady, if I may, being privy to—"

"You may not," she said, authority ringing in her tone. "You are my guard. I have my reasons for wanting to look upon Hyrstow and the filth who dwell there. I do not have to explain them to you or anybody else."

Hagan tucked his chin to his chest in acceptance. It shrank his form for a heartbeat though it did not weaken it. Something in Adara softened. She wished she could have confessed why she had to set eyes on Hyrstow. Though torturing herself by looking for the man who'd broken her heart all those years ago sounded too pathetic a reason to voice aloud.

"I understand, my lady. Apologies."

A familiar self-loathing churned Adara's middle as Hagan offered a quick nod before trotting forward. The man had been her faithful guard for years, since her arrival at Clayton House eight winters ago. Close to her age and willing to prove himself despite the derogatory nature of his position, they had struck up as close a friendship as one could between a lady and a guard. With a sigh, Adara opened her mouth to offer a conciliatory remark but a pained male cry from behind cut the air.

Adara twisted on her horse, her hand sliding over the handle of the custom-made short sword on her belt.

The woman had slipped her bonds. Behind where she should have been, Leon held a palm to his leg.

"She struck me with a rock!"

"How did she get a rock?" Thorhild snarled as he scrambled off his horse, his face contorted in anger beneath his mop of shaggy blond hair.

Leon straightened, despite his grimace of pain. He ran into the woods.

How had she escaped?

Adara growled low in her throat, throwing a leg over her horse to dismount. Hagan raised a hand to stop her.

"My lady, you must remain horsed. We will catch her. She cannot be far."

"She is my bounty; I shall ensure she remains so!" Adara snarked back.

With her sword in hand, she dropped to the ground on light feet. To her right, behind the cover of an impossibly large oak, a man squealed in pain. Sounds of a struggle echoed through the bush. Hagan gave chase. Thor looked back at Adara for a heartbeat then ran to the tree to recapture the wild woman. He and Hagan rounded the leaf laden tree on both sides, each coming round the other side without the captive.

"Leon is down," Hagan said, panting. He shrugged off his shield, shoving it into her hands. "Take this. Get on your horse."

Adara lifted her chin as she gripped the thick leather at the back of the wide wooden shield. Her knees nearly buckled with the strength it took to hold the thing up. "I can take care of myself. *Get her.*"

Thor and Hagan ran past the oak, separating from one another to cover more ground. Adara clutched her weapons, rage spilling through her at the woman's audacity. Ridley's bride would pay. They would all pay for what Adara had had to endure.

A rustling behind her had Adara turning. Unbothered, Ulrich nosed the long grass that sprung up in tufts beside the path. Only yearling trees and dense bush lay past his swishing tail. However, the sounds of the men crashing through the wilderness echoed through the forest.

Was it a pounding drum in the distance? Or was that the thrum of her heart?

The snap of a twig caused her teeth to clench. A deep curse from Thor boomed through the trees. The hair on Adara's neck stood on end.

Still, thunder rumbled the ground. Hooves, as if an entire army had come.

Fear seized her, but only for a moment. She was not one to dwell on prospects when a course of action could be taken. Crouching low, Adara discarded the shield and moved between the horses, clutching her sword in her right hand. She turned her steps into a whisper as she'd learned to do to avoid her husband, proceeding in the opposite direction of the men. It led her closer to the sound of the incoming horses but Adara suspected the chieftain of Hyrstow's wife to be cunning. If the men didn't catch her, she wouldn't remain where they could.

Ducking down, Adara moved around a dense bush. She drew a deep breath through her nose to calm the wild beating of her heart. She would not allow the woman to escape. Ridley's wife was the key to Adara's revenge. The only way to avenge the only person she'd ever cared for.

Not true.

The words echoed through her mind like a stern older sister.

Adara gritted her teeth and stood. Walking toe to heel, she was near-silent as she moved over hard-packed dirt and sticks covered in moss. Green and brown grasses cushioned her steps as she moved east, toward the fields that she remembered all too well.

Something cold and sharp settled along her throat. Adara went perfectly still.

"I shall spill your blood upon my boots, you cunt."

"Colorful language," Adara sneered.

The woman's chest pressed her back. She dug her knee into Adara's thigh with such force it nearly caused Adara to drive her neck forward onto the blade.

"You should kill me," Adara suggested, her mind entering the calm space of nothing she retreated to when necessary. It dulled everything, even the feel of the sharp edge on her skin.

"I've killed one of your men. The others are looking in the wrong direction. Now, tell me. What do you want with Hyrstow?"

"Ah," Adara said, "who said I wanted anything to do with Hyrstow?"

The woman gripped Adara's upper arm, her grasp merciless. The thunder of hooves grew. Adara willed herself to look at the situation as if she wasn't in death's clutches. She thought of where her men were, whoever was coming, and how long it would take for them to arrive. Not long.

"Your death will be enough for me," the blonde woman snarled. She pressed the tip of the blade into Adara's throat. Pain bloomed beneath her chin.

"Fine. Your husband."

The woman behind her stilled. Adara went on. "He took something from me. Something very precious. You might as well kill me and get the war started because I will not stop until he has suffered as I have."

"War?" came the response. It was uncertain enough that Adara grinned.

The hooves halted. Footfalls crashed toward them from the right.

"Indeed. I am Lady Clayton of Guston. Daughter to the Earl of Bernira. You spill my blood on your territory, and my house, along with my father's, will rain wreckage down upon your pathetic little village such as you have never seen."

"We've seen plenty," Ridley's wife hissed.

Adara infused a smirk into her words. She kept her gaze on Ulrich. The beast had raised his head and stared at her with one glassy eye.

"I wish to distress Ridley Ward. Make him suffer. It was the intent of the raid weeks ago and your capture. I will not harm you more than necessary. If he believes you are captured, he will suffer, will he not?"

The woman did not speak. The hesitation was enough for Adara to press on. "He is likely coming for you right now, am I right? Is that the reason you stall?"

A growl of impatience, though the blade at Adara's neck loosened just enough to make her confident.

"Did you know I have a rather large house? Nothing like an earl's keep but a stronghold in itself. In my employ is an excellent dungeon master. He delights in using his tools to ensure maximum pain. I can promise to not turn you over to him, but if you kill me, my men will raze your village to the ground. Your husband's life is to be forfeit."

Crashing sounded from the south coupled with Hagan's hoarse shout: "My lady!"

He came into view, tall and broad and as furious as she'd ever seen him. A scratch marred his cheek as if a tree had whipped him in the face.

Behind them, someone yelled, "Yrsa!"

Sweat slicked Adara's underarms. She was out of time. She tried to keep her tone level as she spoke.

"It sounds as if your people have found us. Let it be known that my men's only order is to kill your Ridley. They are prepared to die to do so. If you do not come with me now, you sacrifice him for a cause that you know nothing about."

Yrsa's grip on her arm lessened.

"You swear not to harm him if I go with you?"

Adara grinned. "For now."

It seemed to be enough. The heat of the woman left Adara's back, the knife falling away. Adara turned, allowing her cold smile to grow.

"Drop your weapon."

Breaths sawed from the woman. Rage lived in her

dark blue eyes along with something else, something touched by fear. Ignoring the sounds of footsteps on both sides of them, Adara extended her blade, ensuring Yrsa understood she was captive again.

"Get on my horse. Now."

Yrsa smashed her lips together, striding to the horse. Adara followed, mounting behind the woman whose shoulders sagged a little as she settled.

Triumph sang in Adara's bones. She angled her short sword at Yrsa's side—a blow that would cause her to bleed out within moments if she chose to move.

"Hagan, let's go," she commanded, taking hold of Ulrich's reins.

Hagan ran for his mount, swinging himself up into his saddle. Leon had gotten himself killed and God knew where Thorhild was. So long as she and Hagan made it to the open plain, they could outrun Hyrstow's people. Adara scanned behind her to ensure she wouldn't receive a dagger to the back when her gaze clashed with the greenest eyes she thought she'd never see again.

CHAPTER

THREE

Grahame

Grahame fought the urge to retch. After racing over his father's lands, a shout in the forest bordering the fields alerted them to Yrsa's location. Thorns and low lying brush had clawed at Grahame's trousers as he ran through the woods, frantically trying to see through the greenery for a glimpse of Yrsa's blonde hair or the men who took her. Somehow, he had picked the right direction when the others fanned out. His arms shaking with the strain of having the bow drawn and ready, he'd found Yrsa holding a woman at knifepoint. The sight had frozen Grahame to the spot.

Raven hair spilled over a slate-blue cloak. Only the curve of her cheek was visible but Grahame knew the softness of it in his marrow.

Adara Clayton. Her letter had not been coerced by a dying husband to wreak havoc on Hyrstow. *She'd* taken part in Yrsa's capture.

The last shred of hope he'd been holding deep in his chest cleaved inward.

The women appeared to be talking. Why? Red stained Yrsa's leg and forearms. Grahame could only pray she wasn't wounded. He inhaled sharply as Yrsa stepped away from the other woman and mounted a large, black horse. Was she going *with* Adara? His shoulders quaked from holding the bowstring at the ready, yet he could not bring himself to release the arrow.

"Grahame, shoot the horse! Stop them!" Ridley's voice came from far behind his left shoulder. Too far back.

When Adara turned at the sound of Ridley's rage-filled voice, Grahame's hard-won grip on the bowstring faltered. Tongue stuck to the roof of his mouth, he stared dumbly as she moved to the horse, quickly settling behind Yrsa.

She looked different. Of course she did. Last time he saw her, she was fourteen, with tears streaming down her cheeks into her wide pink lips. The woman before him had eyes like a storm, which were narrowed in incredulity at him. Her pillowed lips were pinched together in displeasure, yet her straight back betrayed her noble lineage. The sword held ready to bury in Yrsa's side made him want to vomit.

His Adara, all grown up and ready for bloodshed.

He couldn't take his eyes off her. Couldn't breathe

past the knot of emotion that had formed in his throat. Breathing would remind him that this was real, that she truly would harm those he cared for. That Adara was no longer the girl he knew. Perhaps she never was.

"Grahame!" Ridley was nearly on him now, panic leaching into his tone.

Adara didn't wait. Her lip curled in a snarl and she flicked the reins, surging through the trees on a beast as black as a demon. Her cloak and midnight hair flowed behind her like the devil's banner. A huge man in chainmail followed on his own horse. A third man shot from the bush to bring up the rear, staggering to his horse, shouting at it to move while he was mid-mount.

Grahame loosed the arrow at the third man's back. It merely scored along the plated armour of his shoulder as he disappeared through the trees. Grahame's hands trembled as he brought the bow down.

"Damn it!" Ridley raged as he came upon Grahame. "Why did you wait?"

Ridley shoved him, hard. Grahame stumbled back.

"You could have shot the animal twice in the time it took you to stand there and stare. Could have made it harder to get away!"

Before Grahame could steady himself, Ridley whirled, racing back to their horses left abandoned in the field past the trees. They didn't think they'd be able to ride in the tree-filled terrain and now they would pay for their follied judgement.

Grahame's head felt as if it would float away. He went to one knee in the dirt, bracing a hand on the ground as his stomach churned. Bile climbed his throat, emptying onto the bracken in front of him as he tried to reconcile what he'd witnessed.

Adara had done it all. It hadn't been her husband who had ordered the raid on Hyrstow. No, Adara had shown up in the forest and spoken with Yrsa and Emma weeks beforehand, gleaning information from them without revealing anything about herself. Emma had said she'd seen the same woman at the raid. Grahame had suspected, but to have it confirmed—to know that *she* was the one to take Yrsa, to bring hell upon his people...

He heaved again. There was the crashing of feet through the bush and Thomas's voice beside him.

"Ridley went after them alone. Get up; we must go."

Grahame nodded, wiping the spit from his mouth with the back of his hand. He stood on weak legs, loathing himself for being so useless. It was a familiar feeling as of late. Twigs scraped at their knees as they ran back to the horses, converging with Sam and Murhed.

"Ridley's gone off," Murhed said, his heavy copper brows a deep 'V' overtop his eyes. Sam panted beside the butcher, holding his side as if he'd run from Guston and back.

"We know."

They mounted, galloping in the direction of Guston and, after the better part of an hour, caught up with Ridley's horse. It had stopped at a crossroads, the man atop bent over. As they neared, Grahame could make out ragged sobs. The others hesitated, unsure of how to proceed. Grahame guided his mare closer. A crying man didn't scare him. He'd dealt with Branton's unruly emotions after Freda passed.

Ridley's gaze was fixed on the horizon as he spoke.

"They're gone. I didn't even see them. They must have taken another way but..."

"C'mon, Rid. Let us head back. Regroup."

Grahame was amazed he could force the words out. Ridley turned to point a finger at him.

"*You.*" The fury that laced Ridley's tone nearly made Grahame's bowels turn to water. "We could have had her. You were there first. You could have done *something.*"

Grahame opened his mouth to let Ridley know the same thoughts rattled in his head, but he was cut off by Ridley readying to spur his horse toward Guston.

"We will proceed to Clayton House."

"Rid, we can't."

"Why not?" Ridley snarled.

Grahame offered a small shrug. He tried to grin but his mouth wouldn't reach for it.

"Yrsa had a knife on Lady Clayton in the woods. She *had* her, Rid. For some reason, just when I got there, she let the woman go and went with her."

The ruddy color of rage leaked from Ridley's face.

"I couldn't believe it at first. It was why I did not shoot. I have to believe Yrsa knows what she's doing if she went with the woman."

In the distance, Murhed made a scoffing sound. Grahame felt the urge to hit him. The butcher had never believed Yrsa to be true to Hyrstow. Part of a Viking raid on the village two summers ago, she became Ridley's captive then his wife. Some felt her allegiance to Hyrstow shaky. Grahame didn't have time to chastise him. Not with Ridley so close to the edge.

"Went with her? Are they in league together?" Sam dared to ask. The words were said through white lips.

"No." Grahame's tone had enough steel in it that Sam appeared properly cowed by his answer.

"There is something more to it. She was covered in blood." Grahame turned to Ridley, whose face had turned ashen.

Hastily, Grahame added, "Not hers. Something the other woman said swayed her. And we have to trust Yrsa's decision enough not to go barrelling into a trap or worse."

Ridley stared at him long and hard, his hands twitching on the reins as if his hold on them was the only thing preventing him from strangling Grahame. For his part, Grahame tried not to flinch. It wasn't as difficult as it used to be. He could withstand Ridley's displeasure, even his scorn. He'd always been looked upon as the younger brother, the charming man with loose morals. Other people's judgement didn't carry the sting it used to. They would judge no matter the cause.

Ridley broke his stare and gave one final look in the direction he thought his wife to be. The set in his bearded jaw, the stubborn line of his back was a gift, for it told Grahame he was thinking like a knight again, not a devastated husband. Finally, Ridley turned his horse back the way they'd come.

"We will return to Hyrstow and regroup. I will send a herald to the earl alerting him to this act of war. Grahame, you will ride with me and tell me why someone from Bernira territory would steal my wife and accept you in exchange."

THE RIDE BACK WAS SOMBER. Ridley went directly to the hall, presumably to find Æleck, the village herald, while the others dispersed to their homes with various bids to keep in touch about the next course of action. Grahame licked his dry lips as he contemplated going to Branton's to check on his nieces and nephew rather than face Ridley's wrath, though he knew prolonging the inevitable would only make it harder.

In the hall, Ridley sat like a king in one of the great fur-lined chairs before the roaring central fire.

"Tell me everything you know about Lady Clayton."

"I knew her when we were young."

Grahame kept his tone even as he approached. Ridley's fingers were curled around the carved wooden armrests, his foot tapping the ground. Needing to do something with his hands, Grahame clasped the back of a chair across from his friend.

"How?"

A sigh rattled loose from Grahame. He moved 'round to the chair beside Ridley's, indicating with an eyebrow a silent question as to whether or not he would be permitted to sit. Ridley waved a hand in a gesture of acceptance.

"Do you remember the girl I used to run around with?"

"You'll have to be more forthcoming. You've spent time with a lot of women. I am not one to remember them all."

"Fair enough," Grahame said, though he covered his wince with a nod. Shifting in his seat, he bumped the side of his fist up and down against the armrest.

"She is the Earl of Bernira's daughter."

"What?" Ridley's bark was as sharp as he'd ever heard it.

"We were fourteen. She was simply Adara back then. Her father had sent her to live with her cousin. We came across one another one day and...she would shepherd with me sometimes. It was just before you and I and Bran went after the men that killed your parents."

"And?"

Grahame swiped a hand over his mouth as he fixed his gaze on the fire's dancing flames. He tried to swallow around the pebble in his throat.

"And she was of high station so she went back, was married off."

"And?" Ridley pressed, leaning forward in his seat.

"And that's all I knew of her. Until she approached Yrsa and Emma in the woods."

Ridley straightened, his entire being sharpening.

"You knew it was her?"

"I didn't know. I suspected. From their description, she had dark hair, was dressed finely, and came from the direction of my land which is the same direction as Guston. Adara would have known the terrain from the time we spent together. Then Emma saw the same woman when Hyrstow was ransacked and Branton confirmed the bandits had heard the raid on us to be Guston's revenge. It lined up."

Ridley drew his thumb over his bottom lip in thought. Grahame wished for a mug of ale but didn't dare move. Not when he'd failed his chieftain so thoroughly.

"And the letter? What debt does she speak of?"

Grahame's head shot up, his gaze honing on Ridley. "You don't know?"

"No. Do you?"

"No! Why would I know?" Grahame spread his hands. He thought, surely, Ridley knew of the debt Adara claimed he owed.

"Because you know the woman who stole my wife!" Ridley shouted. His big hands banged the chair's armrest.

Grahame closed his eyes. An ache had begun low in his head, one that grew brighter with the knowledge of his friend's disappointment in him. When he opened them, Ridley had settled back in his chair, hands steepled against his mouth. Words of excuse drenched Grahame's tongue.

"I swear I didn't know she would do this. I admit to knowing her before. But that is all. We have had no contact since she was sent away. I was devastated to learn she'd had a role in the raid but I thought, perhaps, her husband ordered it. He had been sick, and I didn't expect a woman to…"

"He'd been sick?"

Grahame gulped. He'd not intended to reveal how he had kept track of Adara over the years. It was to be his secret, his own dastardly embarrassment. He scratched the back of his neck.

"I pay one of the cooks at her keep to keep me abreast of her dealings. She sends word through travellers when she can. We're on the outside of town, near the territory. Folks were too happy to stop to relay a simple message for payment."

Ridley arched a brow, a look of incredulity written on his face.

"How long have you been doing *that*?"

Grahame ran his hand over his head then down the front of his warming face, wishing he didn't sound like such a meddlesome bastard. The words out loud painted him as a madman, one unable to accept the marriage of a woman he knew in his youth.

"A few years. My Pa, he sold some wool to a man that told us his wife worked at Clayton House. After they supped, I followed him outside to ask after Lady Clayton. The man must have been smarter than I because he proposed the deal. I took it. Eventually he died, but his wife kept up the messages, sending them when she could. I sent back payment, at first having no idea how it would even get to her. It must have." Grahame shrugged, wishing the motion would loosen his shoulders.

Ridley leaned forward, elbows to his knees, his gaze locked on Grahame. He waited.

"The Adara I knew wouldn't do this, Rid. I have no idea why she's running around the countryside, taking women. Especially women like Yrsa who can defend themselves. It was a shock for me to see her today with Yrsa's knife on her, then for Yrsa to go with her...it does not make sense. I'm as confused as you."

Grahame's voice hollowed out. Coming upon the women, seeing Yrsa's blade on Adara, had frozen Grahame to the spot. It was all he could do to remain rooted rather than obey the part of him that screamed to lurch forward, to steal Yrsa's knife away from Adara's throat.

Ridley leaned back, his lips forming a line as he thought over Grahame's confession. Finally, he said, "You love her?"

"Who? Yrsa? Of course. Lady Wolf has grown to be a sister to me. I want her back."

Ridley shook his head with an upraised hand. "Clayton. You had a bond with her when you were a young man. You are calling her Adara, for Christ's sake. You kept abreast of her dealings."

The shaking of Grahame's head had Ridley halting his speech. There may have been a time when he would have devoured Adara's affection whole but that time had passed. He had simply been shocked to see her.

"No, Rid." Grahame offered his friend a crooked smile. "As you all say, I love women. I have heard her husband is an old prick and her father worse. I wanted to check up on her."

Branton's entrance into the hall forced Grahame's mouth closed. He could tell himself all the lies he wanted, but Ridley only stared at him as if he were a stranger. His golden eyes tracked Grahame, as if he were little more than a traitor. It was more than Grahame could bear without Branton's scorn added to the pile. He cowered in his seat, locking his gaze on his hands.

"The village is still secure. No raiders," Branton said. He thumbed the top of his hatchet where it was slung into his belt as he came to stand between their chairs. His scowl laid heavy within his beard. If he and Ridley were to have a brooding contest, Grahame knew who would win.

"Thank you," Ridley nodded. Grahame wished he was on the other end of those words rather than sitting square on the side of Ridley's ire.

Ridley briefly filled Branton in on what Grahame had told him, to which Branton responded with surprise. Grahame didn't bother telling Rid that Bran knew some of it already. He didn't need to stir up discord between the two friends. He was used to being on the blunt end of things between the three of them. Younger by two years, Grahame sowed his wild oats when he could, and had more wealth than both. No matter their bond, those things kept him a bit separate no matter how desperately he wished it not to be so. When finished, Ridley turned back to Grahame.

"I need you to get word to the cook right away. She

needs to watch out for Yrsa. I've dispatched two heralds, one to the Clayton keep and one to Lachlan. So help me, I will bring war to Bernira's doorstep if Yrsa is harmed."

Grahame lifted his hands in a gesture of helplessness. Raids and spats between villages were one thing, but a war between earldoms another.

"It doesn't work that way, Rid. She sends me word with travellers when she sees fit. It's someone different every time since her husband died."

Ridley stood, shoulders squared, fists flexing as if the motion would keep him steady. He was a man of action and there was nothing to be done. Not until a herald from the Clayton keep was sent their way or Grahame fulfilled the demands in the letter.

The letter.

In it, Adara had said he could be exchanged for Yrsa's life. A sliver of hope cut through the despair clouding his mind. Grahame jumped from his seat.

"I will go, as ordered."

Branton's head snapped in his direction, a question written in his frown.

"Of course, I will go. An exchange for a debt, right? I do not know what debt Clayton speaks of but I will surrender myself for Yrsa."

FOUR

Adara

"You cannot think they won't come for her." Hagan chewed a roll as he paced the great room.

The space wasn't as grand as the hall in her father's stone keep but it still boasted timber walls and four windows, two on each side of the grand fireplace, made of skin so thinly stretched that on a sunny day light soared in. When her husband, Elvin, was alive, the extravagance of them was something on which he prided himself, despite the need for tapestries to cover the thin skins in the winter months. Now, the dusky light of the setting sun mixed with the lit iron sconces to cast the great room in a cozy glow. Adara set her gaze on Hagan as she leaned back in her chair at the long dining table, satisfied in a manner she hadn't experienced in God knew how long.

"Of course they will come for her. That is the point." She drank deeply from her brass goblet. A fine mead, one Elvin had been saving for a special occasion. She relished its honey-oak flavour.

Hagan shook his head, his dark hair whipping around his eyes. He stalked to the table, choosing a fresh bun from the wooden bowl. The frown he'd donned since leaving the keep that morning hadn't waned an inch.

"If you only told me why," he said before he stuffed the remainder of the roll into his mouth and grabbed his own goblet of mead from above his place setting at her left. It was long enough to seat twelve men, though a good many years had passed since it had seen that many.

"I've told you why."

"Indeed, I know you wish to wreak havoc on Ridley Ward and we have done so. I want to know *why* that bowman didn't shoot. Why you wrote a note ordering another man from Hyrstow in exchange for our prisoner, who bit me when I threw her in the dungeon, by the way."

Adara itched her nose to cover her grin. She'd known Ridley Ward's bride to be a warrior. It had been written in the deft way she handled her knife when Adara had encountered her months ago, washing in the woods with another woman. Her skills during Adara's raid on Hyrstow had been valuable—she defended the village too well. The men Adara sent hadn't been able to capture her, as was intended. It made her curious, however, that Yrsa appeared to be Viking. She spoke strangely and had the airs of the northerners that had come to plunder parts of Northumbria's coastline.

Hagan's long, impatient sigh caused her to prop both elbows on the table and clasp them overtop her nearly finished plate. The quail had been cooked to perfection. Adara would have to thank Cook later.

"Who was he?" Hagan pressed, dark brow tenting in question.

Adara tried to work up some saliva to soothe her dry mouth.

Grahame.

The name sliced through her, straight at her heart. Before the warm blanket of memory could wrap around her, she thought of a fist clasping the name and crushing it between fingers. There was no room for the cut of heartbreak she felt when she thought of her fourteenth year.

"The man who couldn't kill me and the one I ordered sent here are one and the same."

Hagan's dark eyes went round, his mouth dropping open. The scratch he'd received in the forest somehow enhanced his brutishly handsome face. Adara hated that men appeared better with age. It had certainly been true of Grahame.

His eyes had been round as he'd leveled the bow at her, their emerald depths startling in their brilliance. What she hadn't anticipated was his height or the breadth of his shoulders. Grahame had been tall and spindly as a youth. With no other reference than his peach-fuzz covered face and lanky frame, Adara had carried the image of him in her mind, aging it as she did. It had been impossible to imagine how he would be as a man. Adara found it obnoxious how sultry his lips looked, even pressed into a line of concentration. Or the fact that his hair was still like burnished gold and carried a curl women would dream of having.

"*That* was Grahame Shepherd? Why didn't we just take him in the forest?"

Hagan placed both fists, knuckles-down, on either side of his half-finished meal. The back of Adara's neck prickled beneath his glower. A reaction she was prone to when questioned by men. She raised her chin to combat the feeling, reminding herself that she need not cower to any man but one. And her father was miles away.

"It was. And if Ridley's bride hadn't been poised to kill me and Grahame ready to deliver an arrow to my back, I would have stopped to take him as well. Thankfully, she had enough sense to listen to me, so I can still get both things I want."

"Which are?" Hagan drew out the words as his glare nailed Adara to her seat. Her own eyes narrowed in response. As her most trusted, he was allowed to pepper her with his thoughts, though there was a limit.

"Oh, you're back!"

The female voice that carried through the room caused Hagan to straighten. Adara smirked into her goblet.

"Yes, hello. Back we are," Adara confirmed, downing the dregs of her drink before pouring herself another glass.

Adara's closest friend, Muretta, strolled through the door from the house's lifeline, the hall that ran between the great room on the house's east side to the bedrooms on the west. To the south, the front entrance stood sentinel.

"Everything went well, I assume?" Muretta came to stand beside Adara, her ringed hand skimming lightly over the tabletop. Hagan's gaze traveled from her pert nose to her rosy mouth to her hand's movements as if anywhere it chose to settle was lewd. Adara rolled her eyes at him.

"Other than one of our men being killed by Ridley's bride as she tried to escape, everything went to plan," Adara said.

"His name was Leon," Hagan muttered, shooting her a glare.

"Why should I bother to remember the name of a man who failed me?" Adara shot back.

Of course, she knew the man's name. Leon had come to them before winter, one of a tenant's many sons. He wished to make a name for himself and was eager to help in the stables, the kitchen, anywhere that would have him. She stood, anger coursing through her at Hagan's impudence. She hated to admit it, but too many of her men had died on her watch. Guilt was a slimy thing in her belly but, as their leader, none of them needed to know that.

"Careful, my lady. You are sounding rather like your dead husband," Muretta's singsong voice scratched at her like nails on metal.

Her friend plucked an apple from the bowl at the table's center. Adara made her face impassive. Muretta shrugged as she bit into the fruit, ignoring Adara's surliness. Instead, she ran a hand down the front of her rich green gown, grinning at Hagan as she chewed. The look they shared was conspiratorial. As if to say they were unbothered by Adara's moods.

"I am going to bed," Adara declared, goblet in hand. That made her like her late husband as well, but she couldn't bring herself to care. "You two enjoy each other."

She left amid awkward denials of wanting anything more than others' company. Adara didn't begrudge Hagan and Muretta their lies. Elvin had been in the ground a mere two months. Though lingering glances had been exchanged between Hagan and her husband's mistress for years, Adara knew they would not jump into one another's beds the moment Elvin passed.

Rather than retire to her room, Adara continued to the door at the end of the hall. Large, metal hinges creaked as she unlocked it and swung it open. A mouth of blackness greeted her, the stairs downward like rotten teeth. Adara hesitated. She wasn't one for dark, cramped places. She'd spent enough time in the shadowy corners of her father's keep trying to avoid his men. No sounds echoed from below.

After a moment, she shook out her shoulders, grabbing the lit torch in the sconce outside the door. The flame flickered, making the narrow descent feel a little less like a coffin. At the bottom, two cells carved from dirt and barred with iron greeted her. The ceiling was low, hugging Adara too close, but she withstood it. Adara could hear Yrsa breathing. Holding the torch closer to the metal bars, she found Ridley's wife sitting on her haunches, her eyes cast to the floor.

A sneer decorated Adara's top lip. Yrsa likely kept her gaze downcast because she was trying to convey meekness. Or the sharp light of the torch hurt after being left for so many hours in complete darkness. Whichever it was, Adara told herself she didn't care. She told herself that the begrudging respect that bloomed for Yrsa's sacrifice did not exist. That the wife of her enemy was a fool for giving herself up willingly.

The two women remained breathing in silence for longer than was comfortable though neither broke. After a while Yrsa sat on her bottom, her head falling back against the dirt wall, one leg stretched out in front of her. Elbow on her upraised knee, she finally looked Adara in the eye. No snarl nipped at her lips, nor pleading sprang from her throat. It was as if she stared through to Adara's soul, had deemed it rotten, and had passed her judgement.

Let her. Adara's soul was no longer something she worried over. She served only herself, not some overseer or promise of greatness to come.

Without a word, Adara spun on her heel and made her way up the shallow steps, leaving Yrsa in darkness once again. Frustration with herself nibbled its way through her chest. The whole point of her revenge was to alleviate the constant ache she felt at the loss of her cousin. Yet, even with Ridley Ward's wife in the dungeon, peace would not come. Adara told herself it was because she hadn't yet witnessed his suffering. At the top of the stairs, she retrieved the goblet she'd left on the floor and slung back the contents. It helped ease the scorn she felt for herself for leaving a woman in the cold dungeon.

Muretta was right. She was just like Elvin. Perhaps she always had been. Like often called to like. He'd been cruel and selfish and bold. Same as her father. It didn't matter that Adara's plan for Ridley Ward was borne of anguish. Her actions hurt people all the same. Adding Grahame to the mix had been a last minute, self-serving decision. Indeed, it solved the problem of her father's most recent missive; however Adara could have chosen anyone. She did not need to drag Grahame into her life. It was a ruthless, desperate move.

Elvin had taught her well, it seemed.

Grahame

Grahame awoke at dawn. He'd had a fitful sleep, unable to lose himself in the luxurious comfort of his down-filled mattress. All grown up, images of Adara haunted him. The cut of her cheeks was different than when she'd been a girl—they'd become like the rounded tops of bells—while her too-wide mouth had filled into a sensuous pout.

Desire simmered in him like a lingering slap across a cheek. He should not have had any thoughts of her other than how much he loathed what she'd become. Even the hate in her steel-colored eyes was not enough to cool the shock of seeing her again. When thoughts of Adara became too much, he knifed upward to ready himself for the day.

He'd offered to be exchanged for Yrsa, and the herald had returned from the Clayton's with an agreement of terms. Though he had no inkling of Ridley's supposed debt, he would make it right.

Grahame lit a candle. He pulled on a wheat-colored tunic that he knew made his brassy hair seem brighter, and paired it with a belt dyed with lavender he wore at special gatherings. Dark brown trousers went on beneath the tunic while leather boots finished his dress.

Grahame wasn't one to shy away from fine things. With excellent grazing land and the smooth manner in which his mother spun the wool, his family had done well in recent years. The wealth didn't matter much to Grahame other than giving him a sense of comfort. If anything, his family's wealth was something that set him apart from others in Hyrstow. Indeed, Grahame's loose way with women was the main reason men applauded him while women admonished him, but he managed with that well enough. A pretty face and a grin went a long way. However, his family's income was another reason for them to joke on his behalf. No matter. He prided himself on looking good, and on a day that felt like a funeral, he wanted to look his best.

Hurrying, he packed several pieces of clothing into a cloth bag he could sling along his back. There was no way to know what Adara wanted with him or how long she would keep him. Would it be for days? A week? Would she deliver some punishment she felt he deserved? Or had Yrsa received that punishment already?

His middle churned as all the terrible tortures that

could befall Yrsa flitted through his mind. And whatever Grahame was thinking, he imagined Ridley's thoughts to be worse. With a sigh, he tightened the bag, rotating his head to release the sense of unease that had locked around his neck.

He was to see Adara. After eight years of heartbreak and wonder over her wellbeing, he was to enter her home. As what? Friend or foe? Whatever her motives were, Grahame hated that he did not know this version of her after knowing the other so well.

In the main living area, his mother, Fiona, stood by the hearth's crackling fire. Herbs dangled above her head as she stirred an iron pot of something simmering over the flames.

"Couldn't sleep," she offered with a wan smile. "Here, sit. Have something to eat."

Something inside Grahame crumbled at the slouch in his mother's proud shoulders. She'd lost her daughter the year prior and now had to send off her son. Grahame crossed the spacious living area, rounding the chairs made of leather and wood that his father had bought at market years ago when they started earning reliable coin. Grahame scooped the bowl of pottage from his mother's hand, placing it on the table before enveloping her in a hug. She welcomed it, pressing her nose into his chest, shaking with the tears she tried to hold back.

"I'll be alright, Ma," he said gruffly into her kerchief.

Like always, she smelled of lanolin and broth, woodsmoke and thyme. Most boys wanted to leave home to find a bride, to make something of themselves on their own. It was another thing that made Grahame odd. He loved his parents and was loath to leave them. Staying in the men's hall held a certain sense of freedom sometimes, but his mother had never tried to clip his wings, and therefore, he always came back to her.

To have to leave and not know when—or if—he would return was a special kind of torture. One he turned inward to kindle the roiling hate he was cultivating for Adara.

"I have to believe it will be." She sniffed, releasing him as she tipped her head back to look at him. "Otherwise, I will have nothing left."

"Ma," Grahame chided, shaking his head as he offered a grin to bolster her spirits. His heart already felt shredded, and it was merely morning. "I'll be back to bother you before you know it. You'll be begging Clayton to take me back."

She stepped out of his embrace to smack him playfully on the arm. "Watch your words."

Grahame chuckled as he pulled a stool from beneath the sturdy wood table.

"What is it you're on about?" Wilfred's voice came from his bedroom.

His father sauntered into the living area, a brittle smile pasted across his mouth. He ran his fingers through his white hair, unruly curls similar to Grahame's flopping forward as soon as his hand came away. Grahame nudged him with his shoulder as he passed to sit at the table.

"I was just saying I can't wait to come back and take

over this poor excuse of a sheep farm you're running," Grahame volleyed before stuffing a spoonful of pottage into his mouth.

Breakfast passed in much the same manner; affectionate jabs amid slurps of warm food. Everyone's smiles were a little too wide, their eyes a little too watery. When they finished, Grahame accepted the bread, cheese, ale, and apples his mother had packed for his journey. He joked that she had sent enough to feed an army, though it didn't land well. Fiona's mouth pinched downward, her hands clutching her apron. He gave her another hug, but it was interrupted by a loud knock. Wilfred opened the door to find Branton on the threshold, his dark features dressed in a frown.

"Good morn'," he said.

His son, Neil, stood behind him, trying to see past Branton's broad shoulder into his grandparents' home. Behind, a group of men on horseback shifted in their saddles.

"I brought Neil to keep you both company," Bran said, a gentle grin weaving its way up his mouth.

Grahame's shoulders came down from around his ears. The distraction of a grandchild was a gift.

"Wonderful," Fiona said, stepping forward as Wilfred moved back to allow the boy to enter.

Neil accepted his grandmother's embrace dutifully. A small child no longer, Neil towered over his grandmother by a handspan.

"Indeed." Grahame gave his nephew's shoulder a hearty pat as he followed Wilfred outside.

Clouds the color of dirty wool hung close to the tree-tops that bordered the valley to the southwest. Past the yard's gate, Ridley, clad in metal, sat atop his horse. Chainmail, gauntlets, a helmet—only his mouth, pressed into a line, was visible. It pained Grahame to see the tension on the reins. He knew the only reason Ridley wasn't trying to break down the doors of Clayton House was because both Branton and Grahame had spent the previous two nights convincing him to be smart and wait for news from the herald. Branton stayed with Ridley overnight to ensure he did not race to the keep and put Yrsa or himself in jeopardy. It also ensured Grahame could have one last sleep in his home.

"Hello," Grahame said as he approached Ridley.

His friend nodded. The slits in his helmet revealed shadowed eyes, weary with fatigue.

"Did ya get any sleep?" Grahame asked, taking the reins of the horse Wilf held out to him.

Ridley gave a nearly imperceptible nod.

Knowing he wouldn't be able to impart much on the road or at the Clayton's, Grahame patted Ridley's knee. "We'll get her back. She'll be alright."

The sound that keened from Ridley was halfway between a groan and a sigh, as if thoughts of what Yrsa was enduring were too much to bear. There was no way of knowing how she fared other than to trust the herald's message of her safe keeping. All Grahame could do was pray that the girl he once knew was still 'Dara, a girl who'd once asked him to save a dragonfly tangled in a spider's web.

When he turned away, Wilf was waiting, arms outstretched. His father would not accompany the party. He had to tend the sheep. And Grahame was not convinced his father wouldn't do something stupid on his behalf.

"See you in a while, old man," Grahame said, embracing his father and clapping him about the shoulders.

"Good, son," was the gruff reply.

His Pa made to step away as Branton came through the gate, but Grahame held on just a little longer, taking in his father's sheepskin and woodsmoke scent. Life was always balanced on the edge of a knife, however, Grahame felt the potential loss sharpen the longer he held onto the man who'd taught him the value of it.

When Ridley turned his horse in preparation to leave, Grahame let his father go. Bran came up and slung an arm about his shoulder, pulling him into a crisp, hard hug. Bran also would not accompany the party to Clayton's. Instead, he would remain in Hyrstow, guarding Emma, their children, and the rest of the village. The two did not speak as they released one another. It wasn't needed. Though related through marriage, they were brothers in bond, Grahame having witnessed some of Branton's darkest moments and pulling him back from the brink.

Grahame followed Ridley's horse down the hill to meet up with the other men. There were not many. His friends Sam, Awolf, Murhed, plus Geoff Wagner and Robert Lister. He told himself he wouldn't look back at his parents, that it was not goodbye. He would help free Yrsa. While doing so, somehow he would find out about Adara's vendetta against Ridley and change her mind. Or end her. Never in his life had Grahame been relied upon in such a manner, but he would do these things for his friends.

As his horse neared the bottom of the hill, he cast a glance over his shoulder to find his parents and nephew staring at him, their features filled with sorrow, as if they knew something he did not.

Grahame

A blanket of rain soaked the party as they made their way to the meeting point on the grassy lawn south of Clayton House. Clever of Adara to order them to her rather than meeting on neutral ground. Though, with the ongoing conflict between the earldoms of Deircia and Bernira, no place was neutral. At the behest of their earl, Ridley's reclamation of the land between Grahame's parents' and the town of Guston in the Bernira earldom had set the two territories' power balance on a knife's edge.

Grahame's cloak did little to protect him from the deluge. His hands squelched when he pulled on the reins to bring his horse to a halt before the log wall that loomed over them. No handle graced the towering doors, though Grahame assumed a large iron bar lay on the other side to secure it. Clayton House's planked roof peeked over the fence like a curious child. At least the misery of the rain and the mud were enough to distract Grahame from mulling over the reasons why Adara summoned him.

As the rest of the men approached the fence, the mighty door inched open. Ridley's horse paced from side to side, as impatient as the man atop. Grahame released a breath through his teeth, eyes ahead. He'd learned the hard way on the journey that when he made eye contact with the others, their sympathetic grins and unsure shrugs made him feel like a lamb on its way to slaughter. Perhaps he was.

"Back up!" came a shout from behind the opening door.

The owner of the voice was tall and broad and laden with his own armor. He planted himself about ten feet from the fence, left hand on the pommel of a wicked blade glinting at his side. A handful of guards followed Adara on her towering black horse.

Grahame clenched his jaw so it would not drop open.

She wore a crimson cloak, the cloth fanned out against the rump of her steed. Her hood was up but Grahame could make out her regal features within its shadow; chin raised high, black hair swept back from her face, mouth slotted into an impassive line. Grahame forced himself to breathe. He would not let her beauty steal his breath as well.

Trailing behind her, hands bound, a sack covering

her head, was Yrsa. A rope was wrapped around her neck overtop the cloth covering. Adara held the end of it in one hand. Yrsa's blonde hair, singed with dirt, hung lank over one shoulder. She wore the same trousers and tunic as the day she was taken, and though she appeared unsteady on her feet—likely from not being able to see—she did not appear harmed.

Relief was a wave inside Grahame. Yrsa was alright. He did not know how tightly wound his body was at the prospect of her being hurt until he set eyes on her. It made him sit straighter, with purpose. His surrender would ensure her safety. It was a small price to pay.

As if unable to stop himself, Ridley dismounted, leaving his shield attached to the saddle like an idiot. He strode forward as if putting his hands on his wife was his only goal.

"Halt, Ridley Ward." Adara's voice cut through the rain and wind, clear as spun glass.

She tugged on the rope. The action nearly caused Yrsa to trip. Grahame's throat went dry. He swung himself down, ripping his bag off his horse. Mud squelched underfoot. Within moments he was abreast of Ridley, ready to jump forward to snatch Yrsa from Adara's hold.

"Ahhh, there he is," Adara said. Her hands moved on her horse's reins. Through the sheet of rain, Grahame could have sworn her nose wrinkled.

Rude.

"Grahame Shepherd is here of his own volition in accordance with your mandate that he take the place of my wife." Ridley's voice was strong amid the tension that Grahame knew lined his bones.

Somewhere behind them, one of the horses stirred. Grahame kept his eyes on Adara. She sat like a queen looking upon her subjects. Her spine remained straight and the line of her mouth unwavering.

"Indeed. I accept the exchange."

The words rang through Grahame's marrow. He was something to be bartered. Which made sense, though, in his mind, he'd always deemed himself worth very little. A lowly shepherd, then; when his father had become prosperous, a wild boy who would not tie himself to marriage or responsibility. Apparently, now he was a worthy enough exchange for the chieftain's wife. The thought of him being as valuable as Yrsa made the back of his neck itch with discomfort.

The tall guard said, "Grahame Shepherd, step forward."

Ridley had his arm out to halt Grahame's progress before Grahame could move.

"Before I allow my trade to pass into your clutches, I will see my wife."

Grahame forced himself not to flinch. His trade. That was all he was, then. Grahame forced himself to bury the hurt that surfaced.

The comment was enough, however, to garner a reaction from Adara. A smile wended its way up her lips, revealing teeth, eyes shrinking a little as they creased in delight.

"I do not believe you are in a position to make

demands, Ward." She spat the last name delineating Ridley's surname and station. "Though, I give you my word that your wife has gone unharmed. Send over Shepherd or turn 'round. Though I will not grant my captive safety a moment longer if you choose to abandon her."

The growl that sprang from Ridley's chest was more animal than man. He dropped his arm to draw his sword, his shoulders riding high on his neck. Grahame would not allow a drop of blood spilled because of pride.

He tossed his head to rid his forehead of the hair pasted there and sewed a grin into his mouth as he stepped around Ridley. His friend caught his arm. Before Grahame could stop Ridley's pull, he was being spun into a mighty hug.

"I will come for you," Ridley rasped into his ear. The metal of his armour was a strange, slippery thing to hold, but Grahame embraced his friend all the same.

"I'll be fine," he insisted, though he knew it to be a lie. Fear slithered through him. "Make sure you get Yrsa out. Ensure her safety. Afterwards, Lady Wolf can come save me herself."

A cross between a grunt and a laugh passed Ridley's lips. When he let go, Grahame was bereft. With quick strides, head high, Grahame placed himself beside Adara's horse. He ignored the way she watched him, as if she was a cat and he an injured mouse. Longing to pull the sack from Yrsa's head or give her a hug ate at him as he passed his friend, but she was handed off to the tall guard. Before he could see her shuffled to Ridley, one of the other guards pulled a short sword and pointed it at Grahame, the blade gleaming as if hungry.

"Move inside. Now." There was nothing but command in Adara's tone.

Grahame dared turn back for one last look at his friends. Everyone's eyes were locked on Yrsa as she was pushed forward by the guard, falling to her knees in the mud halfway to Ridley. Grahame turned to help her up, but before he could do so, Adara was rushing at him with her horse, the other men quickly herding him through the gate. Grahame twisted so he could see the reunion, to know that his sacrifice was for good. His vision was blocked by Adara's horse moving in the way.

"Move," she snarled. Then they were through the closing door.

A bellow of rage rose behind them. Adara's steed moved to the right just as the door shut. Grahame craned his neck, pushing against a man in a guard's uniform so he could see what was going on.

Through the rain, Ridley ran at the door. A blonde haired woman knelt on the ground behind him but her features were round, her nose slightly bulbous—nothing like Yrsa's sharp countenance. Ridley ran, arm outstretched, as the door closed. Barred shut. The last thing Grahame saw was the panic in the eyes of a man who realized, too late, they had been tricked.

Adara

Satisfaction curled in Adara's belly at the sound of Ridley's enraged yells from the other side of the gate's door. The pounding of his fists on the heavy logs must have hurt. She hoped he broke his skin on the rough wood. A wicked grin slid up her mouth as she dismounted from Ulrich.

"You tricked us," came Grahame's stony tone from beside her.

It appeared that her satisfaction was to be short-lived. Still, she savored one more moment of a world where Ridley Ward was at her mercy. For once, she was the victor, not the one to rage at God for the injustice of her grief. He could wallow in the misery she'd experienced since the Deircia earl had set him upon Bernira lands.

"Indeed."

Adara halted and turned to her new captive. She should have braced herself. Grahame Shepherd had grown. Her imagination paled in comparison to what he was. Even with his burnished hair stuck to his forehead, his cloak dripping wet, she could see the height, the thick set of rounded shoulders. His drenched tunic pressed itself to him like a mistress. Adara turned away. She was not one to gawk and would not give him the satisfaction of her blatant appraisal.

"Where is Yrsa?" Grahame demanded.

Lips that had no business being so tempting contorted into a snarl. Grahame took a menacing step toward her. Thorhild had a hand on his shoulder before he could invade her space. Grahame's eyes slid to the large, blond man, then to Hagan who had stationed himself on Grahame's right. And though Grahame had filled out nicely, Adara doubted he would try anything with two hulking bodies guarding her.

Triumphant, Adara stepped up to him, putting them toe to toe. She had to lift her chin in order to meet his gaze but was able to keep her features neutral despite the galloping of her heart. Cold rain trailed down his high cheekbones, practically caressing the straight bridge of his nose.

"You are not in the position to be demanding answers," she pointed out, her tone cool.

If contempt could heat someone from the inside out,

Grahame would have dried. As it was, he just glared down at her. Adara was surprised to find she'd remembered the exact color of his eyes. Like fresh clover. After all these years, she thought she had dreamt it up. If Grahame saw her shiver, she hoped he would think it because of the rain.

"Come. The answers you wish for are inside."

Needing to get out from beneath his heavy stare, Adara turned on her heel and made her way up the path that led up the small, grassy slope to the house. She tried to ignore the feel of Grahame's eyes digging into her back like daggers. Told herself she did not care if he thought her heartless.

At the house's threshold, Muretta waited.

"I do not think this will work," her friend said under her breath.

"It will," Adara dismissed.

Muretta turned with Adara who nodded at Bhlaine, her tight-lipped housemaster. Adara offered him a wide grin. The stoic man tipped his head, his long, lined face almost bored. As if Adara's schemes did not faze him in the least.

Muretta peeked over her shoulder at the men coming up the path behind them.

"He is staring at you as if to wring your neck. Do you truly think this will work?"

"Hush," Adara hissed. She did not intend for Grahame to catch wind of her scheme before she was ready. Muretta didn't seem deterred.

Adara thumbed open the silver clasp at her neck.

Within a moment, she was free of her sodden cloak, which she passed to Bhlaine without comment. Warm, dry air kissed her damp skin.

Proceeding through the short entryway and into the great room on her right, Adara came to stand before the crackling fire harboured in the room's huge hearth. Her hands held a chill she knew would be almost impossible to ward off. Thankfully, her burgundy wool dress, almost too heavy for the summer months, was a godsend on rainy days.

Turning her palms to the fire, Adara allowed herself one more moment of satisfaction. Ridley Ward's shouts were still echoing past the fence. She was in command. Her life was hers to wield. No matter the threats posed against her and those she cared for, in this moment, she'd done what she'd set out to do.

Muretta came to stand beside Adara, her frizzy blonde curls bobbing with movement. She opened her mouth, closed it, then pressed her hands beneath her breasts to smooth them down her yellow dress. The fabric was fine and likely did not provide much warmth. Adara had told her she need not join them, but Muretta insisted on seeing the man who had plagued Adara's memories for so many years.

"Ridley Ward seems a fine cut of a man, your Shepherd even more-so," Muretta murmured, keeping her tone light.

Hers was a voice that Elvin had loved, for it embraced a feminine tinkle when in the company of anyone other than Adara or Hagan. The comment made Adara feel as if silvery spiders were climbing up her flesh.

"Perhaps you will lend Ridley Ward to me before torturing him? He has an appealing ferocity I think I might enjoy." Muretta scratched her long nails up her sleeve, then down. "Although, if you wish to keep the Shepherd occupied whilst you plan your schemes, I would be happy to warm his bed. He looks like the golden gods the Romans prattled on about."

"I think not," Adara snapped.

Though forever grateful the woman had taken over her late husband's sexual appetites, she wanted Muretta nowhere near Grahame.

"Where is Yrsa?" Grahame's voice crashed into the room. For a sliver of a moment, Adara closed her eyes and allowed herself to bask in it. To remember when a lighter version of it called her name with mirth as she ran over fields to see him. He had always been jovial, other than the last, terrible time they saw one another. When she opened her eyes and turned, she was ready to face him.

Or so she thought.

Grahame stood between Hagan and Thor, shoulders stiff, head high. He'd pushed his hood off but kept his cloak tied about his throat. Adara tore her gaze from the strong, tanned column. There was no point in focusing on parts of him she used to adore. There would be time to evaluate him later.

"Welcome to Clayton House."

Adara spread her chilled hands in a gesture of greeting. Beside her, Muretta preened.

Grahame remained tight-lipped, a muscle working in his clean-shaven jaw. Adara tracked it like a starving cat. After all the time apart, all her tears over the way they'd left one another, here he stood before her, nostrils flaring like an angry bull. She'd take it. Any version of him, she'd devour.

"Spare me, Adara. What have you done with Yrsa?"

Hagan shifted his weight, as if assessing the need to put himself between her and the man almost vibrating with rage.

"So, you remember who I am," she murmured, more to herself than the rest of the room.

Grahame jerked back then stepped forward, hands out as if ready to plead for Yrsa's release. Hagan was right there with him, a strong hand wrapped around Grahame's upper arm.

"Of course. Do you think me simple? The girl I knew wouldn't—"

"The girl you knew is gone. Used up and taught how to behave at the hands of a husband who wanted her to heel. Only I stand before you, and I've learned well." Her words overtook the room. She pasted on the grin of a snake, calming her tone.

"But, to ease your mind, I will tell you I've done nothing to Yrsa other than take her clothes to trick your chieftain. She is safe in the dungeon. Almost bit off Hagan's hand when he was charged with changing her."

It was the wrong thing to say, or perhaps it was

perfect, for Grahame pulled against Hagan's grasp, his hands twisted into fists ready to maim. "You had a man undress her against her will? I hope she cut his hands off."

Hagan held up his hand, showcasing the crown of teeth marks on the fleshy side below his little finger.

"Got me good," Hagan grumbled.

Grahame's face became something ugly as it contorted, ready to spew more vitriol at the man he assumed harmed his chief's wife. Adara moved forward, cutting him off before the men came to blows.

"She was sensible enough to undress by herself. I oversaw it, holding the torch so Hagan could take her clothes from her and she could dress."

Grahame's eyes bore into hers while he panted, his anger a living thing. The petty, lonely, sad part of her wanted to gulp it down. During that fateful summer, despite her arguing for him not to, Grahame had left her to go fight raiders with his friends. *He had left her.* Adara was not ill-informed. She was the only daughter of Bernira's earl. There was no world in which she and Grahame could have been together. And yet, now, she delighted in the way his nostrils flared, how the muscles in his chest bunched as he strained against her guards' hold.

"He didn't look. She wasn't touched. You have my word."

"Forgive me if your word means less than nothing, Adara." Grahame drew out the last 'a' of her name as if it were a curse. She supposed it was. There was no reason for him to believe her.

It was then that his eyes flew around the room, taking in the hearth, the table, the small bouquets Muretta had placed around the surfaces. He stopped pulling against Hagan's grasp, mouth tipping up at the sides. His eyes were caverns of malice. The look was more haunting than his anger.

"I suppose I will be put in the dungeon as well." He held his wrists together. "Take me."

"Whew," Muretta fanned herself with her splayed palm. "This one certainly is bossy, considering his status."

Grahame's eyes flicked over Muretta's pretty face then landed back on Adara. He raised an eyebrow as if to ask, *why is she speaking?* Adara bit her bottom lip to stifle the laugh that threatened to jump out. Grahame's gaze tracked that movement too.

"You will not be placed in the dungeons. You'll occupy the room beside mine."

"And why do I deserve such treatment?" Grahame asked, wrists still together as if bound. "I am nothing more than a prisoner, like Yrsa."

Adara shrugged, the familiar way he said the other woman's name snagging something inside her. Yrsa was a beauty. Tall and angular, her white-blonde hair a cascade of moonlight down her back. Or, it used to be. Her features were the opposite of Adara's squared jaw and sturdier, shorter frame. Perhaps she garnered the attention of more than one Hyrstow man.

Not that Adara cared.

She smiled, her grin stretching because of the delicious way she knew her words would land. "You are not, in fact. You came here of your free will. And you have yet to hear my proposal. I will save it for supper. Come, you can settle yourself and clean up before the meal."

She sniffed, glancing in the direction of Grahame's dripping cloak. Water had pooled beneath him on the floorboards. He must have been freezing.

"I'd rather take my chances in the dungeons then be anywhere near you," he snarled.

Adara refused to be hooked by his barb. She knew he was not going to throw himself at her feet, joyous over their reunion. She knew it and hated that she was disappointed anyway.

Hagan's dark brows descended, along with his lips. He shook Grahame's arm as if he were a doll. "You'll do as Lady Clayton says. Lest you'd like a black eye or a boot to the belly."

The column of Grahame's throat worked as he swallowed, contemplating what to say. Adara found herself leaning forward to hear his retort. Would he be honorbound and take the beating to be thrown in the dungeon? Or would he acquiesce to a comfortable room while his friend remained in squalor?

Grahame smoothed his mouth into a neutral line, wiping his brow of any emotion. "Fine. Take me to my room."

Somewhat disappointed to have him so quickly out of her sight, Adara cut Hagan a quick nod. Hagan indicated with a gesture for Grahame to leave the room. Once they'd gone, she let out a long, slow breath.

"I thought he'd fight harder," Muretta said as she settled herself in one of the sturdy chairs near the fire. Thor nodded his agreement, murmuring his leave before turning from the room to see to other duties.

"So did I," Adara croaked.

She should not have been surprised. Grahame Shepherd was all posturing and no follow through. She'd heard his family had prospered in the years since their time together. Perhaps anything less than comfort was beneath him. Just like when they were younger, he cut out when he needed to.

CHAPTER

EIGHT

Grahame

Grahame yanked his arm free as the burly man beside him gave him a shove out of the huge room. He caught himself before he fell flat on his face, doing his best to breathe through his nose to calm the temper that raged. If it came to blows, he would likely be knocked to the ground with one meaty fist. Instead, he ground his teeth and kept his eyes ahead.

Lit sconces peeked between thick tapestries colored in patterns of reds, browns, and creams. The scent of cooked venison, rosemary, wool, and woodsmoke filled the place. It was a welcome reprieve from the wet that still drenched him. Grahame suppressed his shudder at the glowing warmth.

Yrsa was in a cold dungeon somewhere deeper in the

godawful house and here he was, choosing comfort because he could not stand Adara's vengeful presence. Shame rolled up his neck.

The guard pushed open the second door on the left. A bed twice the size of his own lined the left wall, a table for two sat along the north side of the space, while a wide chest he assumed was for clothing squatted along the right wall, a small shelf beside it. Grahame noted the tapestries in this room were grimmer. Tones of burnt vermillion and dark crimson made him wonder if the previous occupant enjoyed the color of slaughter. His bag had been rifled through, the damp clothes laid out to dry overtop the closed chest. The food his mother gave him had been neatly arranged on the table. So much for privacy.

"Since I am not a prisoner, I suppose I am allowed to come and go?"

The guard smirked and hooked his thumb over his shoulder, "Privy is through the back. Knock if you have to be let out."

"Leaving so soon? I hoped you'd be the one emptying my chamber pot," Grahame said, stepping into the room as if he owned it. Meekness would not do in the face of such a man.

The guard chuckled, scratching a dark eyebrow with the back of his thumb. Grahame briefly wondered how he received the scar that decorated the left side of his face. His frame swallowed the doorway. "This is the part where I'm supposed to threaten you behind my lady's back. But, now that I've seen you, I'm not worried. I'll come to collect you for supper."

He left, the door's wood smacking against the frame as it closed.

Grahame let his chin fall to his chest. He hooked his hands on his hips, despair a seed that had been planted as soon as the gates had closed on his friends. He blew out a long, unsteady breath. They had been lied to. Tricked. Adara's treachery knew no bounds.

How was he supposed to oppose her?

At the exchange, she sat like a queen atop her horse. In the great room, while the blonde woman had undressed him with her eyes, Adara remained so...cold. Had their bond that summer meant so little? Clear, grey eyes rimmed in dark lashes had skimmed over him as if he had been any other man. As if she and Grahame hadn't shared their first kiss in a flower-peppered meadow beneath a cloudless sky, or walked the fields with his sheep, fingers intertwined for hours.

Grahame placed a hand on his chest where it felt as if his heart would beat through his ribs. After all the years apart, Adara's dismissal sliced worse than he could have ever imagined. That summer, after her father had summoned her home—after his utter and complete heartbreak—Grahame had built up careful walls to ensure no woman got so close. Once he got a taste of Adara, no one else could compare. If that made him hopelessly soft, so be it. Yet, now, he was just a pawn. As if their young love had meant less than dirt.

Grahame shoved the heels of his hands into his watering eyes then took another look around the room. He sniffed as he removed his sopping cloak while searching for an escape. Of course, the room was a wooden box; not even a ring of firestones or roof vent graced the corner. Though the bed boasted a thick quilt, the room was certainly not made for comfort, considering the wealth of the house. A threadbare rug covered only half the planked floor. Of the plentiful sconces, only three were lit. It was apparent that whoever usually used the room was not a favorite of Adara.

Grahame paced as he mulled over how he could free Yrsa. Somehow, he had to convince Adara to let her go, to leave Hyrstow be. An impatient rage at Adara's trickery itched in his hands. He was tempted to throw the food from the table just because he wanted to break something. However, sense prevailed when he thought of the way Adara could starve him if she wanted. Fisting the back of his tunic, he shucked it off, then his trousers. The clothing laid out over the chest was mostly dry, the worst of the wet clinging to the left shoulder of his fresh tunic. As he redressed, he wished for a drink. Lacking, he settled for sitting on the mattress, stewing in his rage over Adara's cruelty. As time inched toward the supper hour, Grahame did something he never allowed himself to do: he dove head first into his hate and let it grow.

THE GUARD RETRIEVED him some hours later. Ridley's shouts intermittently echoed in the distance as Grahame was brought to the great room. The ragged sounds sank into Grahame's gut. This far past Guston, the men of Hyrstow were not in comfortable territory. If Ridley had planned an alternate form of attack, Grahame did not know of it. And why would he? He was the one to go into the lion's den. Plans were withheld in case he was broken by those who kept him.

"Here he is," the pretty blonde woman said upon his entry.

A large table laden with food stood on the left, the fireplace roaring with flame to the right. Grahame had not noticed before, but windows bracketed the fireplace. The Claytons were truly wealthy if they could afford such an extravagance.

The hulking guard tossed a glare over his shoulder.

"Oh, stop it, Hagan," the woman admonished. She stood on the other side of the table, a smirk curling her lips. Her hair was a mass of bushy curls that encircled her head like a halo of gold, not tamed in the coiled manner customary of a noblewoman. The scoop of her neckline gaped, allowing for an eyeful of cleavage.

Hagan ignored her, gesturing forward so Grahame could step fully into the room. He had discarded his armor though the light-brown tunic he wore did nothing to detract from the threat he imposed. The way the material stretched across his broad chest reminded Grahame he would not stand a chance against him in hand to hand combat.

Adara sat in a butter-colored cushioned chair before the fire. Her hands were still in her lap, her eyes locked on the flames. She had also changed her attire. The rich velvet of her amethyst dress brought out the rose shade of her lips, the sheen of her raven hair. It was unbound, coursing down the back of the chair in lush waves.

Something stirred in him to see her pensive. For all the days and months and years that had passed, she looked the same yet completely different. She still harboured dark, shapely brows though she wore her nose now, rather than it wearing her. Grahame felt utter madness at the melting together of the two versions of her he knew.

As he stepped forward, she turned, those eyes like liquid steel locking on him. There were no words for the lust that shot through him. It twisted his insides. She was beautiful. Not in the pretty way of the village women back home. Adara held a regal confidence, something that came from birth and conditioning. He had seen glimpses of it when they were younger, but she now exuded a quiet power that Grahame didn't know if he could fight. She was utterly, frustratingly breathtaking.

To cover his gawking, he smirked and let his eyes go dead. For a moment he thought she startled, but then she was up and moving to the table, gesturing for him to sit. Her dress, cinched at the waist, followed her about the room, lapping leisurely at the floor as she walked.

"Come, sit. Enjoy a warm meal."

The words were a command wrapped in pretty dressing. Grahame obeyed. He didn't know when he would eat next and knew he needed his strength if he was to make any sort of escape with Yrsa.

Except Adara did not sit at the head of the table. She shuffled into one of the chairs beside the blonde woman then gestured for the guard standing behind Grahame.

"Hagan, come. It will get cold."

The guard lumbered over to the chair beside where Grahame stood, the seat creaking as he settled. Stupidly, Grahame looked between the three of them as if their heads were put on upside down.

"Sit, Shepherd. It's just us. I trust you have questions, and I am prepared to answer them. However, I have much to do so this may be your only chance," Adara said.

She reached for a slice of meat with her table knife as she spoke. He sat, noting the weapons available to him. A table knife and spoon. A goblet, heavy brass pitcher, ceramic plate that he could break into shards. Not for the first time in his life, he wished he'd paid more attention to Ridley's incessant defense lessons.

"Don't even think about it," Hagan snarled beside him.

Grahame picked up his knife, then leaned back in his chair, twirled the end of the blade between his fingertips. He stuffed his emotions down deep, allowing them to simmer but not boil. Any hope of survival lay in his ability to remain unaffected.

"What?" he asked, innocently.

With a grin, he leaned forward to scoop a bun onto his plate then served himself a hefty portion of meat as Adara had done. They watched him as he pretended he was around a table with his friends, helping himself to every morsel. He grabbed the pitcher last, pouring himself whatever was in it, then held his drink aloft with a raised brow.

Hagan remained still for a heavy moment, then his lips inched upward, the skin beside his brown eyes crinkling. "He might well work, Adara."

"I know," was Adara's response.

She eyed Grahame with mirth overtop the rim of her brass goblet. Something eased in the set of her features and, like a tulip springing from coarse dirt, the edges of her lips curled upward.

"What are you not saying? Why will I work?" Grahame asked.

He cut himself a bite of meat. Let them think he was settling in for a long meal, that they'd tricked him into whatever they were planning. Acting happy and proper was what everyone expected of him. He'd been doing it for years.

"Well, I am the best player of the bunch and am not yet convinced. He had his heart on his sleeve earlier, all full of hate and anger for you," the blonde woman nodded at Adara, her curls bouncing, "and even now, I think it's fake. He's trying to gain our trust."

Grahame shoved a bite of meat into his mouth and chewed. It was well seasoned and had been cooked slow though he refused to acknowledge another mark of Adara's prowess. She had too much on him already.

Beside him, Hagan was nodding around a bite of bun. "It does not matter if he is fake. What matters is that we get more men on our side before Adara makes the journey."

Grahame looked back to Adara, trying to keep up. She didn't seem to notice Hagan's uncouthness or that the blonde kept leaning on her elbow, drink in one hand and food untouched. The three of them spoke as if they were some merry band of thieves. And Grahame hated the fact that he had somehow been brought into their schemes.

"Pardon me, but is someone going to tell me why I'm here?"

For once, Adara's eyes widened. It reminded him of the first time she'd seen his sheep flock towards her. As if she wanted to turn heel and run but doing so would make them chase her. In a blink the memory was erased as she straightened.

"I will tell you. But you must swear upon Yrsa's life your loyalty to my cause."

Grahame nodded his assent.

"You agreed to that rather quickly," she observed.

Grahame lifted a shoulder in a shrug as he spoke around another mouthful of meat. "You will continue to hold her safety over my head, and I will continue to do what is asked to ensure it. So get on with it, *Lady.*"

Hagan reached out with a broad hand and smacked the back of Grahame's head. He lurched forward, bracing his hands against the table in order to not face-plant into his plate.

"Hagan, please," Adara admonished.

Hagan appeared unperturbed.

"He disrespected you."

Grahame straightened, ignoring the blush that swamped his cheeks at being treated like a child. Rather than issuing a retort, he drained his goblet. Adara set down her knife, placed her hands on either side of her plate. She seemed to be pondering her words, as if reluctant to speak them aloud. Then her eyes snapped to him. Grahame's heartbeat quickened beneath her silver stare.

"I would like you to marry me."

CHAPTER

NINE

Adara

Mead sputtered from Grahame's mouth onto his plate. He reached for his napkin as Hagan patted him heartily on the back. Adara tried to hide her smirk.

"Christ, Adara, give a man a warning," Grahame wheezed. He sat back, running a hand over his front to ensure no droplets of liquid coursed down his tunic. In a strained voice that made her wonder what he sounded like in the dark, Grahame said, "I can't marry you."

Of course, she was expecting him to refuse. She was playing puppet master with his friend while she held him prisoner. Still, it felt like salt in a wound he'd caused long ago.

"Why not?"

"I am not of noble blood."

Adara blinked back her shock. Not because he hated her. Not because she manipulated him and harmed his friends. He couldn't marry her for the same reason they couldn't be together in the first place.

Adara leaned forward, lacing her fingers beneath her chin.

"My husband died of an illness a few months ago. Recently, my father has sent word advising he has arranged a new marriage for me to a northern prince. Currently, I hold power over my own estate. I need a husband, one that will give the illusion of influence over me yet will actually allow me to reign over my affairs and tenants."

"And I'm the one you can manipulate to get what you want?" he asked, sarcasm lacing his tone. The swell of his arms as he crossed them over his chest drew her eye. Adara notched her chin upward in an attempt to control her gaze.

"Yes. Your family has wealth. You do not care about the affairs of my territory so I would still make all the decisions concerning my estate. You would be a kept man, doing as you wish."

Grahame stretched his legs out beneath the table. One of his boots hit her foot. She moved away. A dimple popped in his right cheek as he smirked, the bastard.

"I doubt your father would accept such an arrangement. He is Bernira's earl. There is no way he would allow you to align with someone from Deircia."

"We will lie. Your parent's land is on the border of the

two territories. A neutral party. I will have men from Guston cite that you sell your family's wool at their market."

Adara didn't know if she should feel proud or vulnerable at the manner in which Grahame's tawny brows shot up.

"You have put a lot of thought into this."

"Of course."

"Why?" Grahame's lowered tone caused her heart to flutter.

The sensation went to war with the untimely lump that formed in her throat when she thought of her past marriage. She stilled the tremor in her hand by grabbing for her knife. Adara couldn't look Grahame in the eye any longer. The wrinkle of concern etched across his brow, as if he cared about what haunted her, was too much for her strained heart to bear.

Instead, she focused on spearing a slice of carrot as she explained, "I will not be married off again."

Hagan and Muretta's heads swivelled from side to side watching the exchange. Adara rolled her lips together. It was one thing to outline her plan to her friends, quite another to propose marriage to the man she used to fantasize about. She felt raw, scraped open in a way she hadn't felt in years. It was detestable.

Grahame sighed, pushing himself out of his chair. He ran a hand through the golden curls on his forehead. Uncaring when Hagan moved to get up to follow him, Grahame paced to the chairs before the fire, then back to the table, his pinched gaze locked on the floor.

Adara forced herself to remain still by threading her fingers together on her lap. Being a simpering fool hadn't gotten anyone far in life, and she wouldn't begin now, no matter how her heart thrashed against her ribs.

"When?" Grahame asked as he paced toward her. His voice was ragged, as if he'd just run from Hyrstow. Instead of halting on his side of the table, he stormed right up to her chair, hands on his hips. Adara craned her neck to stare up into his handsome face. He towered over her, green eyes locked on hers, swirling with something more than fury.

Then Hagan yanked him back.

"It's alright, Hagan." She murmured as she rose from her seat, not breaking eye contact with Grahame. They were two hand-widths apart, the space between them aching with time and loss. Adara willed the cage of fluttering birds in her chest to calm. "He won't hurt me."

Grahame's head tipped to the side. He crossed his arms across his broad chest. His tone was lethally gentle as he said, "Won't I?"

Adara scoffed, her words more of an afterthought than an answer. "I've been hurt in so many ways, Grahame. Once by you. Hundreds of times by others. Whatever you could do to me is nothing compared to what I've already gone through."

Some unnamable emotion flitted across Grahame's features. Perhaps confusion or concern. Adara couldn't allow herself to dwell on it. To do so would soften her to him. He opened his mouth, but a far off crash of wood on wood snagged their attention.

A commotion of shouting and a loud, rhythmic bashing began. Hagan strode to the window to listen.

"He won't stop," Grahame said.

He hadn't moved. Rather, he stood close enough that if Adara wanted to press her palm to his chest, she could have. Instead, Adara curled her hand into a fist at her side to alleviate the temptation.

She counted to ten in her mind, reminding herself that she had craved this. Dreams of Ridley Ward's frantic worry had kept her going in the days and months following her heartbreak. Though, now, facing Grahame after all these years, the timing felt off.

"Confounding man," she muttered to herself.

A small, mean grin wound up Grahame's mouth. It did nothing to detract from his beauty. "Ridley?"

Adara nodded.

"He loves her."

"I know," she snapped. "I planned for this."

Grahame's lip curled as his frustration boiled over.

"Why?" His shout echoed through the room.

Muretta startled while Hagan cut him a look that promised death.

Adara rubbed her temples. It was too much. Everything she worked for had come together yet her satisfaction was left wanting. Grahame, all tall and bronze, was full of hate for her. Ridley Ward was taking a tactic she did not expect. Plus, her father's demands she marry after she'd just escaped her last marriage...

Adara's clothing felt too tight. She could not draw a

proper breath. Not with the incessant pounding in the distance.

"Why do all of this?" Grahame pressed, stepping closer. She could feel the heat from his body, could only see the breadth of him before her. Rage shot up her spine.

"Because he killed my cousin!" she shouted back.

As if she had slapped him, Grahame fell back a step. The shock that painted his features only enraged her further. How dare he think she was doing all of this just to terrorize his pathetic village? That she had disappeared from his life and come back a monster? Monsters were created.

Adara stormed forward, a finger pointed at Grahame's chest.

"It was Cecilia." He had the grace to flinch at the name. "She and her husband oversaw her parent's land. Ridley's men stormed through to take back the disputed territory on behalf of Deircia, and he slew her as if she was nothing."

Adara forced her voice not to crack on the last word. Grahame's mouth flopped open then closed, his jaw working as he kept whatever words he wanted to say clamped inside. It wounded her that he had no response. He'd met Cecilia. Had known she was Adara's only true friend when they were younger.

A familiar mix of hate and sorrow coursed through her. For the loss of her cousin, the cruel way she died. She could not stand it. Adara shoved his chest, her hands conforming to the muscled flesh before pushing him away.

"How dare you look at me like that. How dare you come here and think *I* am the evil one. Your chieftain dealt death throughout the countryside on behalf of your earl. And you have the audacity to look at me as if *I* am the terrible one? *He* ran a sword through her back when she was only defending her home. *He* killed the only person in the world I cared for, and he is going to *suffer* for it."

Adara whirled, clenching her fists as she stalked back to the table. Muretta was staring at them, white-faced. She offered Adara her goblet, which Adara snatched, gulping down the biting drink.

"He is." Grahame's voice came low from behind her. "Suffering. You have accomplished what you've set out to do. We all suffered, Adara. Every person in Hyrstow has suffered at your hands."

The words were not the balm she wished them to be.

"Good." She downed the rest of the mead, then turned to Hagan who stared at her in that blank way of his when he needed to be calm for them both. As if he would carry out any order, even to the detriment of himself. A wave of affection hit her. He and Muretta were all she had.

"I am retiring. If Ridley Ward continues to be a problem, tell the men to kill him. I am tired."

"No." Grahame's voice cut through the room.

She turned to find him nearly on her. With the raise of her hand, Adara stopped Hagan from burying his knife in Grahame's side. And, damn it, a thrill spun through her at the way Grahame leaned into her space, his tall form arching over her. She caught a whiff of rain and wool, sweet straw and rugged male. It caught her by the throat and tugged. Suddenly she was a youth lying on the grass amid the sheep, Grahame at her side as they stared at the sky, watching the clouds move.

"I will not concede to more bloodshed. Please, Adara. I will agree to your demands if you leave my people alone."

Grahame's breath fanned over her cheeks as he spoke, his words carrying the same pleading tone it had when he'd left her that summer they spent together. Something hot and reckless spiked inside her. She pressed upward on her toes causing their noses to almost touch. His eyes widened as his nostrils flared.

"I will marry you," he said, his tone strained, "on the condition that you stay your grudge against Ridley and let Yrsa go. Forget about Hyrstow."

Adara pressed her lips into a line as she rocked back on her heels. The offer was tempting. She hated Ridley Ward, yet each moment she spent in Yrsa's stoic presence was one more that she did not want to kill the woman to make him suffer.

"What of my cousin? Should he not pay for the crime of her murder?" she asked, crossing her arms against the warm feel of him so close. She would have to keep her guard up around him if this was how quickly she wanted to melt in his proximity.

Grahame's features crashed. He rubbed a wide hand against the back of his neck. The motion pulled Adara's eyes to the bulge of his upper arm. She licked her lips. His green eyes tracked the movement.

"I...I don't know. I am sorry to hear of Cecelia's passing. She was lovely and kind, and I know the two of you shared a special bond."

Adara's throat was suddenly thick with emotion. The urge to be held—to have those words whispered into her hair with strong arms wrapped around her—was overwhelming. It was wishful thinking. She hadn't been embraced in years.

Grahame's features hardened as he straightened, as if realizing how close they stood. "Let go of your mission against Ridley. Release Yrsa."

Adara bit down on her lip to quell the urge to tell him to rot in hell. How dare he try to manipulate her? With his looming body and sharp tongue, Adara hated that Grahame wasn't the happy shepherd's son she once knew. He'd gained layers, a certain slippery veneer. She had to retreat to reorient herself.

"I must contemplate it. Alone."

Grahame nodded. "Of course." He stepped away, clasping his hands behind his back. "At least permit me to see Yrsa to confirm she is alright. I can then speak with Ridley to hold him off. He will not stop. You have taken the one person he would sacrifice everything for. Myself included."

His mouth twisted upward in a wry grin that reminded Adara of when he once confided in her that he felt like Ridley and his other friend—Brannon? Branton, was it?—shared a deeper bond than with him. It made her chest feel tight.

"Fine. I will take you to her. You will find her unharmed. Then you can tell Ridley Ward she is safe. He will have to stand down, or I will have him killed." Adara returned his smile with one of her own. "It matters little to me."

CHAPTER

TEN

Grahame

The swish of Adara's black hair against her backside had Grahame clenching his jaw. She'd grown curves in their years apart, her hips round and welcoming. That damn purple dress she wore pulled to taper her waist in a manner that made him forget how to breathe. Her limbs had been like sticks when she'd spent the days shepherding with him. How cruel was it that the shape of her now made him salivate?

Grahame wished he could retreat to his room and shut his eyes against the utter temptation that swamped him when he looked at Adara. There were decisions to make. He was no leader. The hasty acceptance of Adara's betrothal was due to his panic. He'd needed to stop her from killing Ridley. To find out about Yrsa's wellbeing. And the first thing he jumped to was to give in and marry the woman that tormented them?

Idiot.

Behind him, the brute called Hagan was practically breathing down Grahame's neck while the pleasant blonde had abandoned them, citing her hate for the cold dungeons.

Adara stopped at the end of the hall, took a torch from the wall, lit it on the nearby sconce and hauled on the iron bar across a thick wood door. Grahame tried to hide his surprise when Adara gestured into the gloom. He assumed the big man, Hagan, would take him down.

"Down here," she muttered as she proceeded into the blackness.

Hagan lit a second torch then Grahame was descending stairs so short they didn't even cradle the length of one of his feet. In the torch's glow, walls of wood gave way to stone and clay. They pressed in on Grahame. He had to bend his neck so as not to hit his head on the roof. Some small creature rustled below. He wanted to vomit at the thought of Yrsa down in this hole.

At the bottom, Adara moved to the left. Her shoulders rolled back as if slipping on a different version of herself. Two cells made of bars ran from the floor to the ceiling. There was no light, only clay and stone and iron. Stale air greeted him as he stepped off the last stair.

Yrsa's voice, gritty with surprise and terror, said, "Grahame?"

A figure hobbled to the bars, filthy hands encircling the thick metal keeping her in place.

"Let him go! He's done nothing! You cannot keep us here!"

Yrsa's voice broke on the last word. Grahame was at her side within a stride, wrapping his hands around hers on the bars. They were frozen.

"It's alright, Lady Wolf. It's alright."

Tears glinted in the corners of her eyes. A filthy, too-small dress covered her, and though she appeared to limp, Grahame quickly realized it was due to the low ceiling. Instantly, Yrsa flung her hands from beneath his and reached through the bars, pulling him to her. Grahame shoved his forearms through, embracing her as best he could.

"Keep me, if you need. Grahame has done nothing. This isn't what we discussed," Yrsa was saying, her mouth not stopping as she snuggled into him, as if trying to absorb any warmth he could offer.

Fiery indignation scored his middle. He looked over his shoulder to glare at Adara.

"The most she's spoken the entire time," Adara drawled, her gaze locked on the cell's wall, "other than when we made her change."

"It's a hideous dress," Yrsa said against his chest.

Grahame pulled back slightly to look her over.

She seemed to understand because she said, "I am alright. Cold. But they have kept me fed. She comes down every so often. Gods, I'm glad to see you, Golden Boy."

Tears pricked the backs of his eyes at the nickname. Even in the midst of terror and hopelessness, Yrsa remained herself.

"Good," he said, his voice hoarse.

Yrsa pulled back, her eyebrows tented with confusion.

Grahame bit out the words of explanation. "I am here as a prisoner as well. Adara—"

"Lady Clayton," Adara interjected from behind.

Grahame scoffed. She wanted to pull rank while she kept one of his best friends cold and dirty in the dungeons? He would not heed her command.

"*Adara* tricked us. We came for you, Yrsa, we did. It took everything in Ridley to turn back to Hyrstow and regroup after we tried to rescue you. I exchanged myself for you, but at the last moment, we were given some poor woman dressed in your clothes. She had your yellow hair and a hood on her head. We couldn't tell from far away, and by the time Ridley took the hood off, it was too late. He's still here, trying to bring down this godforsaken place to get you out." Grahame rubbed the sides of Yrsa's arms to warm her as he spoke.

Yrsa's face lit with hope and crumpled all at once. She tucked her chin to her chest. "He can't..."

Adara let out a long-suffering sigh behind them. The light in the small space moved from the left to right as she switched the hands that held the torch.

"You've seen her," she said flatly, "now let's get on with it."

The flames flickered again as Adara made to ascend

the stairs. Horror gripped Grahame by the throat. He couldn't leave Yrsa in the cold and dark. She couldn't remain in such a hellhole alone. He tightened his grip on her.

"You cannot leave her like this," he snarled, glancing back at Adara.

He was met with incredulity and shadows. Hagan turned toward him.

"Indeed, I can. In fact, I can do much worse. So if you would like to keep her in all the pieces you've found her, you will come with me."

Grahame pressed his nose into Yrsa's hair. Sweat, piss, and damp earth swamped him. She shivered in his grasp, and he had to force the bile down his throat at the thought of her being pulled apart underground.

"We will come back for you. I will come back. Ridley will never give up." He sewed the words into her filthy hair. This woman, so like the sister he'd lost, the sister he'd loved beyond measure.

"No, no, no—you can't. Get out of here, Grahame. Tell Ridley I love him, but please do not risk yourselves for me. He cannot die because of me. He *can't*—"

A sob wrenched from her just as Hagan caught Grahame's upper arm in a punishing grip, yanking him back. Grahame had to release Yrsa lest he bang her head against the bars by holding on.

"Come now," Hagan said, as if Grahame were a dog in need of scolding.

He felt like one. Leaving Yrsa in the dungeon to rot twisted something in his soul.

"No. I will stay down here. I will take her place." His words were frantic as he planted his feet to pull against Hagan's hold. "Let me stay. Keep her in my room. Please!"

Grahame didn't know if Adara heard or even cared that he was begging. That he was dragged up one stair before throwing his weight in the opposite direction causing Hagan to stumble, though not enough to break his grip.

"Do that again, and I'll knock you out. Can't help anyone if you're asleep," Hagan growled.

He had to help. Had to get Yrsa out of there.

"At least give her the torch," Grahame demanded, wishing he could straighten to his full height, however the low roof made it impossible. Even Hagan had to bend.

"She'll do something with it."

"She can barely stand!" Grahame hissed through his teeth. His breaths sawed from him as he shook with rage. "She will not burn down this place of dirt and iron. Allow her some warmth and light, *please.*"

Hagan glared at him for so long, Grahame thought he would follow through with his threat to knock him out and drag him up the stairs.

But then Adara called down, "For God's sake, Hagan, do it."

The man released him to stomp over to take Adara's offered torch and give it to Yrsa. He thrust the flame though the bars, keeping his eye on Grahame the entire time, as if knowing a back turned in a dungeon was a dangerous thing.

Yrsa grabbed the torch's end with both hands and scampered backward. The light revealed a moldy looking mattress and blanket at the back of her cell, along with a pail and a cup. She nestled onto the thin bed, holding the torch as if it were a precious gem. Grahame caught her nod of thanks before Hagan moved, obscuring Grahame's view.

"Happy?" he asked.

Grahame curled his hands into fists. Yrsa must have seen the murder in his gaze.

"Grahame, do what they say, so you can get me out of here."

The words held the quiet steel of command. It was enough to have him draw a breath of dank air to steady himself. He knew Hagan would throw him in the cell next to her, and they would be no further ahead. And, as much as the impulse screamed at him to be petty and remain with her, he knew the only hope Yrsa had was for him to be smart.

With a snort, he made his way up the treacherous stairs. Adara waited at the top, staring down at her nails, as if bored. Rage carried Grahame on swift feet. He pressed into Adara's space, knowing Hagan was behind to pull him back at any moment. Toe to toe with her, he crowded her against the tapestry-lined wall. Rather than shrink, however, she tipped her head back to stare up at him, grey eyes sparkling.

"You're a monster," he snarled into her face.

"And you've never figured out how to slay my kind, have you, Grahame Shepherd?" she clucked back.

Hands on her hips, she placed one foot on top of his and ground down. Pain began to ache in the thin bones of his foot, yet he did not throw her off. There was something heady about her touch, even if it was to maim.

"What did you think happened to me after you went about your happy life all those years ago? A monster I became, to deal with men more terrifying than you."

Grahame couldn't help but blink stupidly at the slap of her words. On its heels, the heat of anger. He ground his teeth against thoughts of what could have happened to her to mold her into the cold, lifeless woman before him.

Adara simply watched as he tried to keep his face impassive. The corner of her lip ticked upward.

"Ah, now you're starting to understand. I see the wheels in your head turning." She pressed a single finger to his chest. "Whatever you're thinking is much less than I've endured, I assure you. You can take comfort in the fact that Yrsa is safe in that dungeon."

"Let's get on with it," Hagan said. The clunk of a lock sounded in the hall.

Grahame pulled his foot from beneath hers. He had no response. No words to fling in her face. She'd effectively stalled his mind with her smug grin. Instead, Grahame turned, unable to face her any longer.

Hagan led him to the great hall where two other men were waiting.

"Thor. Grumb."

Hagan nodded to the men. The wide, blond one who Grahame had shot his arrow at while he fled on horseback stepped forward. He wore a sly grin. The other wiry man hung back, his hip against the table, arms crossed over his chest.

"We're to go out to those savages?" the thin man grumbled.

Anger flared in Grahame. Savages? They were calling his people savage after what they'd done?

Grahame stepped forward, his hands balled. The blond one must have seen the murder written on his face because he held his hands up.

"Woah, there," he said in a lighthearted voice, "step back, friend. We're here to escort you so you can tell your leader to stop the incessant noise. Will you be alright with that duty?"

Grahame tried to unhitch his shoulders from around his ears. He had to get his head on straight, for Yrsa. For Ridley.

Hagan stepped into his line of vision. The man's glower was truly something to behold.

"Thor is right. You tell them you saw her. That she is well. Tell them to stand down lest we bring our forces down on them."

Grahame nodded. He unclenched his fists at his side, trying on a smile. Hagan gave him a look that told him he didn't believe him. Suddenly, the others were at his side. Grahame forced down the urge to shove them away. He grinned wider and cast his mind back to Yrsa in the dungeons—the true reason why he was there.

"Let's go," he said.

They did not bother with cloaks. And, despite the hope that it would be only the three men leading him to the gate, a small force was gathered at the front door, ready to fight if Ridley chose not to back down. It made Grahame's head swim. His friends had to trust him. He didn't know how, but he had to make Ridley understand that he would get Yrsa out, despite Adara's treachery.

A memory of Adara's furious face came back to him. She was so sure of herself, so filled with hate for him and his kind. As they trudged through the mud, Grahame knew he would have to ignore that her touch, even to cause pain, was like bringing a stone to life. As much as he tried to tell himself otherwise, being in Adara's presence made him realize what a statue he'd become.

Adara

Adara's skin felt slimy. The worst of it was, there was no way to get it off. After she'd told Hagan, Thor, and Grumbheld to handle the Grahame and Ridley liaison, she'd had Bhlaine heat water for a bath. Vigorously scrubbing herself hadn't wiped off her self-loathing. Only when she was pink as a rose petal did she wash her hair, needing the wet scent of dungeon and Grahame to be washed away. Still, the sensation remained.

Dressed in her nightclothes, Adara sank into the wide, velvet-cushioned chair before the fireplace. The heat ate its way into her bones, easing them in a way the bath hadn't. A half-scoff, half-laugh cut from her. Her entire time living at Clayton House, she had hated this room, this too-hot fireplace. When Elvin had pinned her to the bed to satiate his lust, when he'd forced her to perform various acts she detested, the bloody fire was always roaring. The large room, with its huge tapestries and thick carpets, had always felt too warm in comparison to her smaller, colder chamber next door. Only after Elvin's death did she feel comfortable in the space, accepting its warmth for what it was: a luxury.

And her old room? Currently occupied by the one man she couldn't stop thinking about.

Impatient with herself, Adara took the woven blanket from the back of her chair and wrapped it around her shoulders. Just before her bath, Thor had come in, cut her a smile, his light hair darker from the damp, and told her Ridley had agreed to stop terrorizing the gate. He would remain, however. Adara practically grunted her response. Grahame had succeeded in placating Ward. She would take it as a win. A reprieve from her worries was welcome.

A knock caused her to sit up in the chair where she slouched. "Enter."

Muretta poked her head around the door, her golden halo of hair leading the way.

"Time for a night cap?" She held a bottle of liquor through the crack and shook it.

Adara chuckled. "Yes," she said, moving over in the chair so her friend could join her.

Muretta closed the door, swishing over in her nightgown. She took the offered space next to Adara, curling her legs under her so that her feet were tucked between their bottoms.

"Chilly?"

"Aye. This room always had the best heat in the house. Elvin would ensure the fire was kept day and night. It is just taking some getting used to, staying in a new room, is all."

Adara brushed a hand over the top of Muretta's curls in an attempt to tame those that tickled her cheek. Her friend gave an exaggerated shimmy of her shoulders to cover her shiver.

"You can have Bhlaine stoke the fire in your room all day; I don't mind," Adara said.

"Seems like a waste. And I'm not complaining. I'm grateful to have such a room at your house. I need to take advantage of it while it lasts."

The words were said with humour, though they landed heavy. If Adara's plan didn't work and she was married to her father's match, Muretta would be forced to leave. Unless they make the same arrangement she had with Elvin. Adara pinched her eyes shut.

Muretta had saved her from a lifetime of warming Elvin's bed by offering her own body. There was no way she would betray the woman by ousting her from Clayton House.

"It will last a long time, Muretta," Adara insisted.

Muretta took a swig from the bottle then passed it to Adara. Gold-white bubbles dribbled down her chin. She scraped them away with the back of her hand. Adara sighed then closed her eyes and tipped the bottle back.

Ale, strong and hoppy, bit the back of her throat. She hoped it would dull the ache that had taken up residence in her temples.

"It didn't take much for Shepherd to agree to marriage."

Adara rolled her eyes and took another drink before passing it back. "Only death threats to his friends. Gee, how easy that was."

"Spare your jokes, Adara. It will get you what you want."

Muretta drank from the bottle then settled it between their legs, available for either of them to pick up.

"And what do I want?" Adara asked. She pulled the thin material of her nightshift through her thumb and forefinger, her gaze unfocusing as she let the liquor drift through her.

"What any of us want. Freedom. Love. A life worth living."

Muretta plucked up the dark hair that spilled over Adara's shoulder. She began to twine her fingers though the strands, going from top to bottom, knowing Adara loved the gentle, pulling feeling.

Adara offered a bitter laugh at her friend's summation. Her gaze remained on the crackling flames as she spoke.

"I agree with freedom. I thought, after Elvin died, I could remain Lady of Clayton House, pay a widow's tax and live my life. A bout of stupidity on my part. I should have never underestimated my father's ambition to keep his earldom secure. Though, I will reject your assumption of love. I have no need for it. Let's replace it with revenge, cunning, and ownership."

Rather than incite laughter from Muretta like expected, her friend went quiet. Her fingers slowed in Adara's hair. Adara bumped her shoulder with her own.

"What? I was speaking in jest."

Muretta nodded, offering a bright smile that didn't reach her light brown eyes.

"I know. I just…I hope for love. One day. And I hope for a life where I am not worried about being thrown to the wolves. Elvin did that for me. I know you could never suffer his mistreatment, but I thrived within the safety of it. For less than the time it took to eat supper, I could secure my lodging, be clothed and fed and treated well enough most of the time. I never thought of love because the arrangement worked. Yet, now that he's gone…"

Adara waited, her headache throbbing in her skull. She took the ale from between them and swigged. It did not dampen the sense of responsibility she had for this woman who she felt indebted to. Elvin had required Adara to satisfy his physical needs in the marital way for years until Muretta became a servant. Wide-eyed and pretty, Elvin began to show interest in her. She and Adara were the same age, though of very different stations. Adara refused to allow their union, following Elvin around, getting in their way until Muretta was older and could enter into a sensible agreement with him for better lodging and care as his mistress. Until then, Adara kept his attention as his wife. Every time she bedded him, she thought of her shepherd boy. Every time, her heart broke a little bit more that she was nothing but a slave to the man she hated. The fact that Muretta found comfort in Elvin did not make her jealous, but the talk of safety did. She was never safe with anyone but Grahame.

Adara cleared her throat. "It is alright to miss him."

Muretta blinked several times and stared into the fire. She sniffed before replying. "I know you protected me when you could. I do not miss *him*, but I miss the surety of my role. I'm sorry. I did not intend on coming in here and becoming a simpering mess." Muretta swiped at her eyes with the backs of her fingers.

Adara only offered her the bottle, which she took and drank from greedily.

"What of your shepherd? He is obscenely handsome. And you didn't answer my questions. You haven't told me much about him other than he lives near Hyrstow and that you'd spent a summer with him in your youth."

Adara's heartbeat quickened at the thought of Grahame, as it would forever, apparently. She pressed her lips together, trying to parse out what details she could give to Muretta and what she would spare for herself.

"There is not much to tell. He lived near Cecilia. I was sent to stay with her family one summer when my father deemed me too pig-headed to remain in the keep. Of course, it wasn't really a punishment since Cecilia and I were thick as thieves. Though, while she had chores and lessons and responsibilities, as the earl's daughter, I did not. Or, rather, I did but the nurse there gave up when I put a snake in her shoe and she sent me outside, rain or shine."

Muretta grinned, turning to face Adara. She brushed her thumb across Adara's cheek, catching a tear. Adara looked at it in surprise that she was both crying and smiling at once.

"I became bored and started roaming the estate, then further. One morning, after a fall down a large slope, I came across Grahame shepherding. Actually, I believe I rolled down the hill and nearly fell atop him. He shoved me off and told me a joke to put an end to my mortification. We were inseparable after that."

The fire popped, sending a spark onto Muretta's nightdress. She screeched, her hands whipping the thing away before it burned through the light linen. Almost immediately, two knocks sounded, one at the door, another against the wall. Accompanied by both were Hagan and Grahame's voices through the wood.

"Lady, are you alright?" Hagan asked.

"Keep it down!" Grahame rumbled.

Muretta's brows shot up as she tried to settle back down, but a laugh caught in her throat at the two differing tones. Adara just shook her head, suddenly feeling very tired.

"We are fine, thank you," Adara called to the door as she shooed Muretta off the chair. Both women stood, Adara stretching her arms over her head in an effort to loosen the coiled sensation in her limbs.

"It appears that, after all your time together, he still is angry with you. One would think a little part of him would be happy to see you," Muretta said over her shoulder as she walked to the door.

Adara shrugged. "I did not leave on good terms at the end of that summer. We..."

She fell silent, the words bungling in her mouth. How could she tell Muretta of the tender way he kissed her for the first time, her heart so full it felt like her entire world was right at that moment? There wasn't a proper way she could convey the hurt and anger she harboured when he abandoned her to chase after raiders with his friends.

Oh yes, another slight against Ridley Ward, for taking Grahame from her. It was the last time they had seen one another. She had begged him not to go. Her heart had been torn asunder with fear for him. Her father's men came the next day with the news she was to be taken home. Two years later, she was married to Elvin, Lord Clayton of Guston, a pivotal landowner in her father's earldom.

Muretta seemed to sense Adara's growing unease. She smiled widely, as she opened the door. "Enough bedtime stories. Goodnight, Adara."

"Goodnight."

After the door closed, Adara stood before the fire, trying to embrace the stillness. Flames danced in the fireplace, but the room was otherwise dark. She closed her eyes and willed herself to stop thinking of the boy she loved. He was not the man next door.

Grahame had barely reacted to seeing her again. Other

than the tightening of his jaw and the casual use of her given name, it was as if she were a bother rather than someone he'd shared his soul with eight years ago. She was a means to an end in his eyes, someone who held power over his friends. If not for her order, their paths would likely have never crossed. For all she knew, he was already married.

The errant thought wormed its way through her causing her very bones to vibrate.

Could he have agreed just to appease her? To trick her as she had done him?

Shaking out her hands, Adara stomped her foot. The floor thumped and it sent a slight pain into her that was rather pleasing. She did it again, letting her frustration gather and expel through her sole. Again.

From her right, three sharp thumps met the wall. A muffled "stop your noise" found its way through.

Straightening, Adara bit her lower lip. How dare he tell her what to do in her own house? Before she could rethink it, she stalked to the door, pulling it open and slipping past Hagan.

"My lady, how can I be of service?"

He pushed himself off the wall, ready to do as she bid.

"Unlock his door," she ordered.

Hagan hesitated, then did as she said when he beheld the fire in her eyes. Springing the lock from the iron, he stepped back, allowing her to storm forward.

"I do not think you should go in there alone, lady," he said, crowding behind her.

"You may wait outside, at the ready. Do not follow me. I will be fine."

Hagan slunk back when he heard the ring of authority in her words. Harnessing her anger, she yanked the handle and stepped into Grahame's room.

CHAPTER
TWELVE

Grahame

"You dare tell me what to do in my own house?" Adara demanded as she stalked through the door, yanking it closed behind her, her straw-coloured nightdress swirling around her knees as she moved. Bearing down on him, her eyes widened for less than a heartbeat when she saw that he was without a tunic.

"How dare you come barging in here! What if I was pleasuring myself?" he shot back, aiming for humor to disarm her. He hooked his hands on his hips.

Adara halted mid-step, her face leaching of color. Hungry grey eyes climbed the length of his body once then settled on his waist, as if looking for proof of his claim. It was so unlike her detached demeanour, he didn't bother to hide the laugh that barrelled out of him.

"Same Adara, always so gullible." He smirked, tossing his head so his hair would stop curling over his eyes.

She tracked that movement, too, her full mouth opening and closing, tripping over a retort.

"You were *not…*" She trailed off, crossing her arms over her bountiful chest.

It was unfortunate because her forearms shelved her breasts in the most enticing manner, and the glide of her nightdress over her ample hip only made him think of how good she would feel in his grip. He couldn't stop staring, yet if he did not, his best part would, indeed, think it was time for the pleasure he alluded to.

Grahame rolled his eyes. "Perhaps I was plotting your demise, or chewing my toenails, or building my strength by trying to lift that chest over there." He pulled his arm up to flex his muscles, but Adara was onto him.

Her stormy gaze locked on his face and didn't waver. "Are you married?"

Confusion swept through him. "Pardon?"

She took a step forward, those distracting hips swinging. "Are you already married? To someone in Hyrstow? Did you promise marriage to me, knowing full well it would not be binding, just to free your friends?"

If smoke could have shot from her nostrils, it would have. Dark eyebrows drawn down, pouty mouth more-so, her words were nearly a growl. Grahame swallowed around the wave of affection that hit him. The stubbornness that peeked through was why he'd fallen in love with her in the first place. This was the version of Adara he knew: impulsive, gullible, strong, and demanding. He had never cared when she was that way with him. In fact, he found it delightful.

"Why, 'Dara? Jealous?" he taunted, invoking the name he used to call her for good measure.

She moved so quickly he could barely hold her off. Suddenly, her hands were pushing at his chest. Before she could kick her knee between his legs to ensure he couldn't father children, he took hold of her upper arms and shoved them behind her.

"All it takes is one scream from me for Hagan to come in here and run you through," she snarled.

Her breath tickled over his neck while her ample bust pressed his chest, her teeth close enough to bite through his throat if she tried hard enough. Restraint had never been Grahame's strength, and he begged for it right then. Adara molded to him was something he had dreamed of, though never like this. He squeezed her tighter, trailing one hand down her arm to snag both of her wrists. It forced her chin up. The look she gave him was feral.

"You wouldn't do that to your soon-to-be-husband, would you?"

A bitter laugh escaped her. "You have no idea what I would do to a husband."

"You're right. I do not. Did you kill the last one?" he asked in a singsong voice.

She struggled then, thrashing against his grip. He

couldn't resist tightening his hold on her wrists, just to incite her anger. Wild, she pushed at him with her chest. He laughed. This feeling of challenge, the verbal sparring —he'd missed it. Missed her. Too damn much.

"Let me go."

"Never," Grahame said darkly. She smelled too good. Clean and perfumed, as if she'd slicked herself with rose oil. His lower half thickened. "We are to be married. I will never let you go again."

Adara released a little shriek then leaned forward. Before he knew it, teeth sank into the flesh above his heart. Pain wrought through him, hard and fast. He released her in surprise, but she held on, clenching her jaw around his skin. Grahame smashed his lips together so as not to shout. It would not do to have Hagan come in and slay him. Right before she drew blood, Adara let go.

"Christ, what in the bloody hell?" he growled.

A crown of teeth marks etched his flesh.

"Do not," she panted, wiping spittle from her mouth with the back of her hand. The murder in her eyes did nothing to calm lustful outrage that swirled inside him at having her so close. "Speak ill of me in my house. I may need a husband, but you cannot use your pretty smiles and slick jests to risk all that I have built."

The pain of her bite ebbed then throbbed, sharp and stinging. It made him want to work her into a rage. "You think my smiles pretty?"

Adara clenched her hands into fists at her sides. "I think it is no secret your smiles are pretty. What I'm doing here *matters,* Grahame. To me, to those in my care, to the earldom."

"Your earldom. Not mine."

Grahame rubbed at his chest, turning from her so he could re-orient himself. In their meeting at the gates, Ridley had been clear: he would back off to ensure Yrsa's safety, but Grahame had to get her out. Ridley would remain camped outside Clayton house until she was freed.

Grahame closed his eyes. He could not let his friends down.

Tipping his head back, he sucked breaths through his nose to gain a sense of calm.

His chest throbbed, and his lower half didn't seem to understand that the nearly naked woman in his room wasn't for him. Ever. Calm was impossible. However, there was something about being in Adara's presence that made him feel more alive than he had in years. Despite the flame kindled in him, especially in such a state of undress, he had to win.

When he turned, he ensured his face was impassive. "Free Yrsa. That was the agreement."

Adara canted her head as she regarded him, her proper mask of regality back in place.

"Not until we are wed."

"When will that be?"

"Tomorrow, if it suits you."

He raised an eyebrow. "Not going to ensure dear Father is in attendance?"

Adara scoffed, shifting her weight to her other foot. It

caused his attention to snag on her legs, bare and shapely, her feet strong and lithe. He told himself he was examining how she'd grown and was resolutely not interested in the curve of her calves, or how they would feel in his hands. If they were chilled or warm.

"I care less for my father now than I ever did when you knew me. The sooner we marry, the better. That way, when we travel to his keep in a fortnight, I will already be wed. He won't be able to change that."

Grahame swallowed, dread trickling through him. "What if he does not care?"

Adara pursed her lips. She paced toward him, then back to the door. Her backside had no right looking so good as she strode away.

"He will," she threw over her shoulder. "He has to."

"'Dara," Grahame said, trying to keep up.

Her plan was full of folly. The Earl of Bernira was known for his cunning and cruelty. He could kill Grahame with ease and marry her off to whomever he wanted. Grahame would forfeit his life for Yrsa, but he did not want to die at the hands of these cold, terrible people. At one time, Adara had been his safe haven. He never would have guessed she would put him in such a precarious position.

Before she could make it to the door, he gripped her upper arm, whirling her around. Her eyes were lined with silver, her breaths short. As if the fight had melted from her, she let him hold her arm without protest. And while her lips trembled, Grahame couldn't help but stare at their fullness.

They stood there for long moments, gazes scouring one another, drawing and exhaling the same breaths. Her arm was strong yet soft beneath his fingers. Thick, dark eyelashes fluttered as she took the measure of his face. He wondered if she saw every age he had been, just as he could imagine hers. If she felt as lost and hopeless as he did that they had missed so much time together.

"Grahame," she breathed.

He couldn't stop himself. When he was younger, he had sworn a vow to himself that if he ever saw Adara again, he would profess the manner in which she'd snatched his heart and kept it with her. He had imagined saying something poetic. Something along the lines of "How does it feel to have two hearts rather than one, as you've kept mine all this time?"

Now, with her body so close and her lips parted in a manner he wanted to taste, Grahame couldn't force the words out. She had changed. As much as he craved her, he was simply a pawn. One she would risk the life of as if he were nothing.

Before his lips could skim over hers, he pulled himself away, dropping her arm as if it were a flame.

"Good night, Lady Clayton."

Her eyes shuttered as she bit that tasty-looking bottom lip of hers. Without a glance, she turned and exited. No further sounds came from her room. Grahame knew because he remained awake most of the night, trying to forget that the very grown-up version of Adara, clad in only in her nightshift, was just a wall away.

CHAPTER

THIRTEEN

Adara

"Almost finished," Muretta murmured, her fingers nimbly working the laces on Adara's bodice. Adara had donned her favorite dress for her second wedding, blood-red and brilliant. She'd been merely ten and six when she'd been married to Elvin and her body had blossomed since then. This time, she would have a choice. In everything.

A rightness settled in her as Muretta worked to cinch her up. Since Elvin's death, Adara had liberally exercised her choices. Raids, revenge, tricking those who had wronged her. It was as if she were making up all the choices she never had in her earlier life.

"Suck in," Muretta said.

Adara complied though her inhale did nothing to

assuage the barbed ball of tension that sat at the base of her ribcage. It had nestled within her since the day the Hyrstow raid had gone wrong. Every day since then, it had grown a little. Adara shook out her shoulders. She reclaimed her destiny with patience and sheer will. Even the marriage she was preparing for had been her decision.

Adara shifted, trying to ease the sense of selfishness looming like a dark cloak around her. Was it selfish to trap Grahame into a marriage? Perhaps. His heated gaze the night previous told her he desired her, though he abhorred her. If he didn't, he would not have kicked her out of his bedchamber so readily. Adara had returned to her room, her skin aching for the feel of calloused hands.

"There," Muretta said, satisfaction layered in her tone.

Adara smoothed her clammy hands over her skirts.

"Aren't you a sight," Muretta mused, her eyes flowing over Adara in appreciation.

The dress scooped low over her bust, sucked in tight at the waist, then rounded spectacularly over her ample hips and bottom. The skirts were a combination of wool layers and linen so fine it appeared as gossamer. It was the first dress Adara had the dressmaker create after Elvin passed. Freedom with her purse was a heady thing. Adara had dresses made for herself and Muretta, given a new tunic and pair of trousers to Thor, Hagan, and Bhlaine, and even commissioned a couple of pairs of trousers and tunics for herself. After seeing how well Yrsa Ward looked in her own tunic and pants, Adara was glad for the purchase.

"Too much?" she asked, arms wide.

"No, Lady," Hagan's voice boomed from the doorway.

He held the door with one hand, the other was hooked into his belt. Not for the first time, Adara wished she could have fallen in love with Hagan. His roughly hewn features were handsome. He was also as strong as an oak, and his gruff kindness was constant. He had even changed into his finely made tunic for the wedding.

"Well, look at you," she said, crossing to him, though not before catching the way Muretta's eyes slinked over his frame.

A small, pleased grin pressed Muretta's lips. Adara opened her arms, her own smile widening as Hagan scooped her into a hug that she felt in her bones. She held him for longer than necessary, hoping to impress upon him her gratitude for his steady friendship. When they parted, his cheeks were tinged pink.

"Am I interrupting something? Only a few moments left before it would be uncouth to do that out in the hall." Grahame's voice was jest and misery rolled into one.

Hagan set her down, stepping away as if he'd done something untoward. It burned Adara that Grahame dared to belittle them.

"I'll have you know—" The words dried on her tongue as soon as her eyes found him.

To say Grahame looked like a god would have done him a disservice. His shoulders stretched the near-black tunic that draped down his torso in such a marvellous manner, it was unwelcome. One would think the dark tone unsettling but it only emphasized the tan of his skin, the leather ties at the neckline drawing her eye to the hollow of his throat. A belt cast in violet and lavender accented the taper of his waist while tan-colored trousers wrapped legs she could only imagine were well lined with muscle. And why did his lips appear so smooth and full? As if he'd taken a bite of honey and some had stayed behind because it couldn't bear to leave the dastardly curve of his mouth.

"Cat got your tongue, missus?"

Two dimples buffered Grahame's flash of white teeth. Adara cleared her throat, suddenly humbled from hungrily devouring his appearance when he'd not so much as blinked at her dress.

"You'll treat Lady Clayton with the respect she deserves," Hagan stated.

Adara placed her hand on Hagan's forearm to stay him. Green eyes tracked the movement.

"Oh, I believe I've treated her with as much as she deserves, if not more-so. Though, our wedding night may tell a different tale; perhaps she'll like it when I disrespect her fully."

Grahame's eyes gleamed like heated jewels as his smile carved his face into something sinister. A shiver lit from the crown of Adara's head to the tips of her toes.

"You dare—" Hagan lunged, half drawing his short sword, when suddenly, Muretta placed a hand on his back. It was dwarfed by the wide expanse. He stilled.

"Come now, Hagan. Let us retire to the great room. I believe the priest will be here soon. I know he was ruffled by the prospect of not having the ceremony in a church. We can go greet him and the others."

As if the wind had gone from his sails, Hagan leaned down to listen to Muretta. Adara bit her bottom lip to hold in her chuckle. It appeared that with marriage in the air, they aligned like the moon and the stars.

"Yes, please meet the priest. We will be along shortly," Adara insisted, moving aside so her friends could make their way down the hall.

Hagan shot her an annoyed look, to which she clucked at him to get moving. Muretta helped by looping her arm around his, practically dragging him away. Grahame watched the exchange with increasing curiosity.

"Very strange house you run, 'Dara," he mused, his gaze narrowing at the way Hagan canted his head to listen to Muretta. "I cannot parse out if you are sleeping with him. Or if you're sleeping with her. Or all three of you enjoy your evenings together."

Embarrassment flooded Adara. She bit her bottom lip and glanced at her shoes to hide the flare of heat in her cheeks. The audacity of the man. Then she remembered the way they used to barb one another.

She couldn't resist hooking an eyebrow while offering a salacious smile. "Jealous?"

Mirth filled his features as he bent forward, his hands anchored to his hips. There was something artful about those hands; the long fingers, the bones beneath the tanned skin. "Not if I'm invited."

God, he had an answer for everything. A tired sigh worked its way from her as she tried to suppress an image of what the four of them together would look like, feel like. Warmth pooled in her cheeks. He was too clever. Her mind stalled over a retort so, for once, Adara decided upon the truth.

"You are confounding. I doubt you carry any desire to see through on your threats. You are all talk, Grahame, as you have always been."

A flame of something ominous ignited in his eyes. Excitement shot through her as he stepped closer, his foot going between hers. Grahame towered over her, his legs brushing her skirts. Adara stood her ground. His scent, clean from a bath she'd ordered for him that day, still found a way to torment her; fresh straw and clean wool and something bright she hadn't picked up on the day prior. Mint?

Grahame arched toward her, his breath like a feather on her cheeks as he spoke. "As man and wife there will not be anything left unsaid between us, Adara. And believe me, as much as I want to talk to you, to find out what in God's name happened all those years ago, I want to exercise my rights as a husband more. We were not wed when you came to me, barely dressed, last night. This evening? With eyes on us to relay to your father the truth of our coupling? I plan to take out my anger and confusion on my willing wife."

Adara should have shrunk from the confession. Her

first marriage still haunted her. Yet she was no longer a girl with an old man atop her, his men looking on to claim the marriage consummated. She was a grown woman who had chosen the rugged man before her. As much as she was surprised at his knowledge of noble weddings, the errant thought of his calloused hands on her caused her heart to quicken. A curious, hopeful part of her wished to see how far Grahame would go.

Adara wrinkled her nose, daring to skim her forefinger along his padded chest. It was more muscled than she imagined.

"You enjoy the idea of eyes on us?"

She couldn't help the breathiness of the words. For a single heartbeat, Grahame's eyes narrowed on her like a hawk to a mouse. Then his firm hands were secured about her waist and he was pushing her until her backside met the wall.

"Don't, 'Dara," he growled, his lips finding their way through her loose hair to brush along the shell of her ear. His thighs pressed her own as his hands roamed from her waist upward, his thumbs scoring lines of fire across her ribs, beneath her breasts. Adara thought she might faint at the pleasure of being utterly surrounded by him.

"Do not push me. I have agreed to marriage in all ways that count. I will stand before your father, as I should have long ago, and tell him of my vow to you. I will play the part of puppet husband. But do not underestimate all the ways I will take you. I have had years to think of your body beneath mine. If you insist on this marriage, I insist on my due."

Adara secured her hands to his chest, her fingers digging into that fathomless black garment to keep him at a distance. Or was it to pull him closer? She did not know. All she was aware of was the clench in her middle at his confession, of the absolute certainty that she'd never wanted anyone else. As if to prove his intention, his nose scored her cheekbone, his lips aligning with hers.

"You're mine, Adara. Forevermore." His words ghosted along her lips. Then his mouth was on hers, languidly moving as if they had all the time in the world.

Adara whimpered. She had not been kissed in *years*. Not since Grahame. He was the one and only man who had possessed her lips. And she wanted to melt into how perfect his kiss was.

A chuckle vibrated from Grahame into her while he played at her mouth, gently teasing then prying, sipping as if she were the richest wine. It was too much and not enough. Dizzy, Adara complied with his silent demands, opening her mouth to his tongue, scraping her own against his.

Pleasure was an arrow straight through resolve.

In the back of Adara's mind, she knew she should corral herself. Control was of the utmost importance. However, nothing else existed other than Grahame. Nothing but his strong hands trailing up her ribs, then scraping along her back, as if trying to relearn the feel of her. And damn it if she was not going to take something for herself after so many years of pain. She gave herself over to the kiss, to show him a glimpse of what he had left behind years ago.

The clearing of a throat behind them caused Grahame to pull back, though he remained in front of her, his eyes on hers. They were wary, searching. As if checking how she would react. Adara pressed her lips together as she smoothed her hands across the expanse of his chest one final time.

"Grahame Shepherd. What a coincidence," the priest's voice rang down the hall.

As if he were a bear caught in a trap, Grahame's entire being coiled tight. His hands flexed on her hips. Adara caught the way his eyes widened. The color drained from his face before he turned, fists clenched.

"Nice to see you again," The High Priest of Hyrstow, now of Clayton House, said.

Grahame

"What in all hell are you doing here?"

Oswald's grin was like a serpent's. The hall's flickering candlelight caught the haughtiness of his hooked eyebrow. It appeared the time away from Hyrstow had been kind to the priest: the roundness of his double chin was restored. Though, the fine linen of his bone colored robes did nothing to suggest humble servitude.

"Why, I am here to marry you and Lady Clayton," he tucked his hands within his oversized sleeves, his thin grin sliding higher. As if bidden by the devil himself, Grahame took a step forward, ready to put his fist in Oswald's smarmy face.

"You came here?" Grahame asked in disbelief. "Emma saw you the morning of the raid. You left before anything happened. You deserted your patrons, your priests. We thought you dead. And you've been *here*?"

Rage filled the space between his words. Oswald was Ridley's brother and Grahame had known him his entire life. Though, Grahame had no qualms over striking the man to the ground. He had a tendency to look out for the glory of his church over the people in it. Until he deserted both.

"Indeed, I have. Lady Clayton offered a deal too significant to ignore." There was a twinkle in the priest's muddy brown eyes, one that caused foreboding to dig around in Grahame's gut.

"How?" he ground out.

Vicious triumph lived in Oswald's countenance. The priest opened his mouth to respond before Adara's voice rose from behind Grahame.

"It is of little consequence."

Grahame would not have it. There were too many questions. Layers of treachery that went too deep. He whirled, finger aimed at her.

"He tried to have Yrsa killed when he found out about her. He caused a riot in our village. He ran away when we were raided by *your raiders* only for me to find out he's made a home for himself *here*?"

Adara's eyes narrowed, her kiss-swollen lips pinching together as she swatted his hand away. It shredded the bit of hope that had spouted in Grahame during their kiss. It wasn't enough that he'd wrestled with how torn he felt over having to wed her and wanting to bed her despite knowing she was the cause of all his problems. That she was no longer the person he thought her to be.

Grahame scraped a hand over his chin as he said, "Not to mention, he's a general piece of pig shit..."

"Enough," she hissed. "The Reverend is now a part of this household."

"He lives here?" Grahame demanded. He thrust both hands into his hair to pull at the ends. He wished for the pain to distract him from the madness surrounding him.

"Of course not," Oswald quipped from behind him.

Grahame turned again, stepping to the other side of the hall so he could observe them both. He needed his heart to still. He needed his mind to stop tripping over important facts. Strategist he was not. And Adara had outplayed him once again.

"I'm staying at the structure that will be my new church. Generously funded by Lady Clayton, I will oversee the souls of Guston and beyond."

"Why is that not surprising?" Grahame snarked.

He allowed his arms to drop only to find Adara had crossed hers. The move ensured her breasts were part of the conversation, a detail Oswald didn't miss either. Unfortunately, Adara was only pinning Grahame with a glare. Grahame gnashed his teeth so he wouldn't feel inclined to poke Oswald's eyes out.

It did not work.

"You poached him from Hyrstow?" Grahame demanded.

A little laugh escaped Adara. The sound was like the stroke of her hand against his lower half. Her mouth had tasted better than it had when they were younger, but there was a brittleness to it, a tentativeness that made him think she hadn't been kissed much in their time apart. Damn it if that thought wasn't satisfying. He wanted to be the only one to have kissed her, even after all these years. And now, Oswald of all people, had interrupted the first clash of their desire.

"I did." Her chin rose a fraction as she met his eyes, though there was something in her own that betrayed her confusion over his anger, "I needed a priest. He wanted a congregation that valued him. Hyrstow doesn't treat its own well if they are so willing to abandon it for a run down church. It was a blessing that he happened to be Ridley's brother as well."

"Of course, this is another ploy against Ridley," Grahame shot back.

All of her planning against his friend; if only she had gone about it—any of it—differently. She could have come to him first. It would have saved them so much agony. Anger mounted in his shoulders, in his arms, aching to be let out. He felt as if he could pummel something.

"Indeed! And?" Adara snapped.

"Can you not see? It is not about us or Ridley or even your church; it is about him serving himself, always."

"He and I have that in common then!" Adara thundered, her hands splaying as she took a step toward him.

Oswald merely stood there, watching Adara with pride in his eyes.

"You're self-righteous in your old age, Grahame. You speak as if everyone in Hyrstow is one large, happy family. Well, he was unhappy enough to settle for what I had to offer."

Disappointment licked his bones. In a breath, some of the fight left him. How could she have orchestrated all of this? He understood the ways; she was a single, powerful woman with a fortune at her disposal, bent on revenge. What he did not understand was how his noble lass had been twisted into this stunning creature filled with hate. She was wrath and vengeance, beauty and plans, and he already felt as if he was drowning against her current.

"So am I, it would seem."

He let the words hang in the air between them. Adara seethed, her eyes narrowing on him, while Oswald continued to stare with his bland shit-eating grin. Grahame's skin crawled with another betrayal. He scoffed, moving around them and into the great room.

Hagan stood near the fireplace, offering the flames another piece of wood while Muretta spoke to the house-master. The man with a wizened brow and hair the color of smoke nodded as she spoke, a ghost of a smile threatening. Everyone's eyes lifted to Grahame as he stormed into the room. Muretta seemed to understand his mood.

"Does it not look lovely here?" Muretta asked.

She strode to him, taking him by the wrist. Some of the fight in Grahame dissipated.

The great chairs before the fire had been pushed to the side while sprigs of greenery hung in small wreaths on the stone mantle. In fact, little bouquets of flowers adorned every surface. All down the table, clay jars held bursts of purple and white and green. The shades almost matched the colors of his belt.

Muretta moved him about, positioning him to where she deemed fit. He let her, his shock and despair growing with each passing moment.

How could he fathom Adara's next move when she had so many intricate plans? Was her father even threatening her with marriage or was it another ruse? Did it matter? He was to pledge himself to her, regardless. And though he hated the way she had gone about involving him, there was a part of Grahame that revelled in their reunion. It was something he had wrestled with all day: regardless of Adara's treachery, he still wanted her.

"It is wonderful," Grahame answered Muretta, running a hand through his hair.

He offered Hagan a brittle smile. The man did not return it.

Finally, Adara entered the room, Oswald at her heels. Adara's dress, a few shades darker than a poppy, clung to her in the most delicious manner. It was a wonder any of the men in the room kept their eyes off her, though he and Oswald weren't trying. The priest had a slick grin pasted on his round face. Grahame swallowed down the urge to grab Adara by the waist and pull her body behind his. He didn't want her anywhere near the traitor, even if she'd made him one.

"Shall we begin?" Oswald asked.

His hands were spread, fingers aglint with jeweled rings. His left hand neared Adara's rear, close enough that Grahame stepped forward and grabbed Adara's forearm, pulling her to him. The fabric of her sleeve did nothing to hide the strong, slender feel of her in his grasp. It elicited the sharp hunger he felt any time he touched her.

Adara's face twisted into a scowl. She yanked her arm away while she positioned herself across from him.

"Indeed," she said, looking behind her as if to check that Muretta and Hagan were there.

She wore no smile, offered no words as her gaze met his again. Grahame forced a wry grin. It did nothing. Adara had gone utterly still, her hands at her sides, a look of sharp determination on her breathtaking face. Oswald took up residence between, boxing them closer to the fire.

"Do not begin without me!" said a male voice from the hall. All gazes fell on the guard, Thorhild, as he ran into the room, a wide grin laying within his blond beard. "I don't want to miss the festivities."

A scoffing laugh fell from Adara's mouth. It eased the brittle tension in the room while Thor ran over to stand shoulder to shoulder with Hagan behind Adara.

"Now we can get on with it," Adara said with a roll of her eyes though there was mirth in her tone.

"I cannot allow my lady to be wed without proper witnesses," quipped Thor.

"Are you quite done?" Oswald asked, his tone thick with annoyance.

The three behind Adara cleared their throats to stifle their chuckles, shifting from foot to foot. Oswald gave them a sharp look before turning his focus to Adara. She remained unchanged other than the upward curl of her lips.

"We shall begin," Oswald pronounced.

All at once, Grahame was too hot. He slipped a finger beneath the collar of his tunic to loosen the laces at his throat. It was all wrong. In all the fantasies he'd had, all the wishes he'd held as a stupid boy, none of them had panned out like this.

"We did not walk together down the aisle," he blurted.

Adara's lips folded downward, her brow tenting. Behind her, Muretta put her hand to her bosom, her mouth dropping open. Oswald snorted.

"Does it matter?" Adara asked. "That is an old custom. One that is rarely done anymore. I have no kin here, no father to give me away. In a marriage such as ours, I do not think we need to keep to tradition."

Grahame searched for something, anything to say. It was all happening too fast, too formal.

He settled on, "Are we not to wed as a love match? Otherwise, why would your father believe the story we tell of our wedding?"

Something contemplative swirled in Adara's eyes as she chewed the inside of her cheek. Slowly, as if weighing his argument, she replied, "We shall walk from the entrance to the fireplace, then. Perhaps we should also commence with the hand fasting. Bhlaine, do you have a long piece of cloth we might use?"

The houseman bowed. Without a word, he disappeared into the room that Grahame assumed connected to the kitchens. Adara strode to the doorway. Her shoes clicked on the wooden floor, so loud without the customary straw lain overtop. Grahame supposed she was wealthy enough in the big, almost empty house that she didn't need the extra layer of warmth, though it didn't sit right that there wasn't even a rug laid out as a makeshift aisle. As if she believed that their marriage didn't matter.

None of it felt right.

"Coming?" Adara asked.

Mute, Grahame followed her to the door and offered her his arm. She looked at it as if it were a snake.

"What? You dislike chivalry?"

She blinked, those pretty lashes fanning across her cheekbones. "I am unused to such gestures. There is no need for you to be kind. I understand I've trapped you in this arrangement. You do not need to behave as if you are alright with it."

Grahame blew a breath through puffed cheeks. His arm remained in the air.

"My mother would hit me if she knew I wasn't giving the proper respect to my bride."

Adara's lips curved at the corners. "I can imagine that."

She had met his mother once, during lambing

season. Adara had travelled further afield to find him and came upon their hut. His mother had insisted Adara stay for a meal and fed her scones with currant jam while his father eyed Grahame with a stern look. When she finished eating, she watched a pair of lambs be born before they sent her on her way with Grahame to escort her so nothing bad befell her.

Adara seemed to recall the afternoon because she said in a low voice, "Best currant jam I've ever had."

Something in Grahame's heart squeezed at the acknowledgement. He found it easier to grin down at her. "Y'know my father tore a strip off me when I returned from walking you home? Said if I ever laid with you and got you with child, he would flay me himself so your father would be spared the joy of it."

"How did he know us so well?" she teased, her nose wrinkling with laughter. Affection was like a great wind through his chest.

"Probably because he had eyes in his head, 'Dara. Any fool could see how gone I was for you."

Silence dipped between them as they held each other's gazes, grins touching the corners of their mouths. A warmth settled in Grahame as they stared at one another for too long, until Adara slipped her hand through his arm, linking them. Her touch was a solid balm to his uncertainty. She tore her eyes from his first.

"Let's get on with it, then."

FIFTEEN

Adara

Adara swallowed her last bite of roasted pheasant. Worry slicked the savoury flavour from her tongue. Across from her, Grahame ate slowly, chewing with more diligence than she'd ever seen. His eyes lifted to hers then dove toward Hagan who had finished his plate long before. Knives clanked, the only sound other than the crackle of the fire.

"Shall we retire?" Muretta asked, her tone too innocent.

With a nod, Hagan stood. His gaze remained locked on the table, his cheeks tinged pink. As a man and her guard, he and Thorhild would be trusted with viewing the bedding. Oswald suggested the legitimacy of the union would be contested if there was not a priest present but Grahame had become something akin to a roaring beast at the suggestion. He'd stood in front of Adara, almost backing her into the fire, refusing to move until Oswald agreed to vouch for the union without viewing the coupling. Thorhild had offered to escort the priest back to the property's small church.

Adara pressed her shoulder blades back. She fought the impulse to bite her lip. Her false confidence didn't help the feeling of butterfly wings that scraped along her midsection. "I suppose so."

From across the table, Grahame's gaze sank into her as he drained his wine. She had called for a good bottle to be brought out. Unfortunately, the drink did not loosen her limbs or the knot in her belly like she wished it to.

Without speaking, Grahame stood, his chair scraping slowly against the floor. The hair on the back of Adara's neck stood. Her hands felt clammy.

"Hagan, please accompany us to the bedchamber."

She could not help the way her chin dipped with embarrassment as she rounded the table and heard the men follow. There was a slight murmuring between Muretta and Hagan before Muretta retreated to the kitchens.

Adara began to count backwards from one hundred. It was an old habit she employed when she had to lay beneath Elvin's sweating mass. Now, it seemed out of place. She had chosen her groom, and though Grahame seemed to hate her, they had cared for one another once. Perhaps he would go slow. Though his earlier threat rang in her ears. He promised to take his due. Whether out of lust or hate, she guessed it did not matter. She would not blame him for using her.

Adara's heart thrummed an unsteady beat as the reality of what she demanded of him hit her. She was no better than Elvin. The dream of bedding him had kept a spark alive within her for years. As she grew into an adult, imagining their coupling was one of her favorite past-times. Yet, with the deed looming before them, Adara was faltering.

"You may remain stationed at the door. No need to enter," she said, as the men halted at the door to her bedchamber. A shallow breath was not enough to calm the swirling that crawled from her middle up to her chest.

"Yes, My Lady," Thor murmured.

Adara stepped into the room. The bedclothes had been fluffed. Soft scents of woodsmoke and daisies hung in the air while the vermillion glow of candles brightened the tapestried walls. It was a beautiful marital chamber. Adara bit the inside of her cheek, hard, to halt the sting of tears that caused the bridge of her nose to prickle.

"How would you like to proceed, Lady?" Grahame asked, his tone too formal. He had not so much as moved from the doorway. For less than a heartbeat, Adara allowed regret to overwhelm her.

It was all wrong. Before they even knew what coupling was, she'd been Grahame's. The sun-drenched summer with her farm boy was the happiest she'd ever been. Once, they'd been free. Once, she thought she would be his wife. Not like this.

Never like this.

"Adara?" Grahame's voice was husky, closer than before.

It snapped her out of her trance. She brushed a finger beneath the eye that dared release moisture.

Like a gust of wind, Grahame was at her back.

"Adara, look at me," he said.

His fingers grasped her elbow. The pressure was delicious, warming her arm. He would be gentle, she knew it in her bones. Slowly, she allowed him to turn her. Her face was stone when she met his searching gaze.

Grahame's jaw worked over words he did not speak. Instead, he stared into her, his brow furrowed as if trying to learn her through a look. The hand that cupped her elbow inched up her arm, his fingers spread wide over her flesh. Unable to withstand the scrutiny, she dropped her gaze to the hollow of his throat.

She could do this. She had to do this.

Adara had done much worse in her life. Making the beast with two backs with Grahame wouldn't be a hardship. An attack of feeling wouldn't derail her.

"Let's get this over with," she grumbled.

Without preamble, she rucked up her skirts, diving a hand beneath to drag her undergarments down. They were small, chosen specifically for the purpose of not having to remove her dress. With Elvin, she'd found short, dainty undergarments easier than having him rip at her longer underthings.

Tears welled again, for all that she and all women before her had endured. Before she could pull the material down, however, Grahame's hands were on the front of her shoulders, pressing her upward.

"'Dara, wait," he said, his voice soft.

She didn't resist his touch, but could not bring herself to look at him. That was until he caught her chin with his finger to lift her face. Blinking away the tears that spiked her lashes, Adara glared up at him, her petulance an armor she was not ready to discard. A line appeared between his sandy brows. Adara had to stifle the urge to reach up and smooth it away.

When Grahame pulled her into his embrace, Adara stiffened.

"Shhh," he said, his arms resting on the tops of her shoulders.

They were heavy and solid and a comfort she didn't deserve. His grass-sweet scent wrapped around her, beckoning the tears she fought with gritted teeth. Still, wetness slid down her cheeks.

He should have been taking his due out of her skin, using her up in the way men did when they wanted to exert their anger. Then his lips were brushing the bridge of her nose, his hands wandering to her lower back to bring her body flush with his. He was all hard muscle and warm strength. His lips met with the blade of her cheek. Softer than she remembered. Grahame dragged those perfect lips across one cheekbone, then the other, quietly kissing away her tears.

"I..." she started. She could not finish. Her men were watching, likely impatient.

"There is no rush, 'Dara, no rush," Grahame murmured against her skin, shifting downward to place a gentle kiss at the corner of her mouth. His tenderness made her tremble. Her traitorous arms wrapped around his waist and clung.

"It was never supposed to happen this way," she said as she dipped her chin.

The movement pressed her forehead to his chest. Grahame buried his nose to her hair, inhaling.

"I know, 'Dara. I know. If I have wished for one thing —" he stopped.

What could he have wished for? They hadn't spoken in years. Curiosity gnawed at the words he left hanging. Instead, Grahame released her shoulders to cup her face. He had no reason to be so careful. It caused the stony wall she'd built within her to crumble a little.

"My husband was rough with me," she said. She had to make him aware in order to assert her dominance in a situation she was losing control of. Adara blew out a breath. "I didn't make it easy. Though, perhaps I should have. It may have been over quicker if I had simply laid there."

"This can be as quick or slow as you need," Grahame whispered.

His breath caressed her cheeks and lips. It stole along her neck causing her skin to heat from the inside out. There was a fervour in his green eyes, whether from the wine or her confession or satisfaction of her discomfort.

The latter seemed unlikely, however, as he carefully shifted his body so that she was entirely engulfed by him, blocked from the eyes at the door.

"I want this over with. I know you said you'll take what you believe I owe. I understand what a husband requires, but tonight, let us move this along, for the men's sake," she insisted, releasing his waist to grip his wrists.

His hands did not move from her face, though his thumbs scraped her jawline. The sensation was slow and rough and sent a shiver down Adara's spine.

"I don't think you know how a proper husband treats his wife. How I would have treated you, had we been able to marry."

Her scarred heart broke a little at that. She did not know when—or if—they would further discuss their past.

"'Dara, forget the men. It is just you and me in this room. After all these years, it's just you and me." His thumbs hadn't stopped stroking.

Adara wanted to look away but couldn't. Her heart was no match for the sweet way he held her as his mouth descended on hers.

Gone was the furious passion of their first kiss. Grahame's lips were soft, moving in slow, purposeful motions against hers. Adara's muscles unwound at the calm insistence of his mouth.

Steady, that was what Grahame had become. She hadn't realized it until her own lips answered his. He was jest and fire, loyalty and spirit. Somehow, instead of the reckless smiling youth she'd known, he had turned into a kind, humorous man. Despite every reason to be terrible, Grahame suddenly became a rock for her to cling to. And cling to him Adara did.

The rasp of her skirts against his trousers filled the room. Hesitant, Adara laid her palms on his chest. She did not think she would get used to the feel of the slabs of muscle there. A groan escaped him as she parted her lips. They moved in sync, Grahame angling his face when needed, his fingers wandering to her hair, tangling in the loose tresses. A nip at her bottom lip had her sighing, had her opening her mouth to his probing tongue. Adara felt as if she was heating from the inside out as it swept inside, tasting of pheasant and wine. He was melting her.

"However you wish, we will give them what they need," Grahame murmured against her mouth, his hand tightening in the hair of her nape. The other skimmed down her throat, settling on the swell of her breast. Her nipples pebbled.

"Tell me how you would like me to proceed," he said around the kiss. "Lead the way, Adara."

Never in her life had she been asked what she wanted by a man. The sentiment nearly knocked her to the ground.

Grahame's hand dipped lower, the tips of his fingers skimming the neckline of her dress. Her skin began to sparkle beneath his touch.

Before those fingers dipped beneath the material, however, Grahame broke their kiss to say, "Is this alright?"

His other hand untangled from her hair to glide down her back, pressing her closer, as if he did not want her to slip away. Adara allowed herself to be plastered to him, every hard line of his body pressed each soft curve of hers. An ache bloomed in her neither-region.

"That's good," she said, drawing in a ragged breath.

If there was triumph in his gaze, she did not see it, for she pulled him down for another kiss. Thorough and languid, Grahame's mouth met hers. As if she was water after he'd gone without for days. When Grahame's hard ridge rubbed her belly, greed struck her, hot and insistent. She wished to see him, to feel him move against her. It nearly sobered her, for her past physical requirements in the bedchamber had never elicited such an urge.

"God, your lips..." His words died as he broke away to kiss a trail down the side of her neck. Adara couldn't control the shiver that rolled through her. The sensations he evoked in her skin made her tip her head back for more. Grahame's hand at her back pulled her closer while his hips gave a little thrust upward. Need, perilous, reckless need pounded through her.

They deserved this. After the agony of their separation and the ensuing years of torment. Elation made Adara bold. Little breaths escaped her as her other hand travelled to his belt.

"How is this?" he asked as the backs of her knees met with the mattress.

She hadn't even noticed him backing her to the bed, so lost she was in his handling. Adara's searching hand brushed the bulge prodding her middle. A deep groan sprung from Grahame. The sound caused the juncture between her thighs to become a puddle. She would do almost anything to hear that sound again. Then fingers were plucking at the ties of her bodice, searching, loosening. Adara bit her lip against the feel of his mouth exploring the base of her neck. She couldn't help but sink her hand into his hair to hold him to her.

"'Dara, you're leading the way. You've got to tell me what's alright or not," he said into the skin at the base of her throat.

Adara was panting, nearly delirious when his hand worked its way past her neckline to score her nipple. "It's alright. You're fine," she murmured.

"Just fine?" Grahame asked, rearing back. He arched a sandy brow, his hair sticking out around his head where she'd run her fingers through. Dishevelled, he was the most delectable thing she'd ever seen.

He brushed his thumb over her nipple once, twice. A shiver coursed through her.

"Undo the belt. I can't get it off myself," she said. Her voice sounded like smoke.

Grahame thumbed her nipple again, as if resistant to let her go. He withdrew his hands only to grab a handful of both breasts before unbuckling the clasp at his waist. The sound of metal on the floor snapped through the otherwise quiet room. Remembering the others watching, she ducked her head again, her cheeks on fire.

Grahame would not abide by her shame. He grinned, dimples flashing, and dipped close to whisper in her ear,

"I bet they're hard as stone watching us. Hard for something they can never have. As I have been, most of my life."

She dared not look over at Hagan and Thor. All she could do was take in Grahame as he reached behind himself to drag his tunic overhead.

All moisture left her mouth as the material left his body. He was...too much. Lean and golden, with muscles that popped and rippled in the firelight. A dusting of light brown hair trailed from his navel into his trousers which did nothing to hide his reaction to her. He smirked as he threw the tunic to the floor and placed his hands on his hips.

"See something you like?"

Adara felt her mouth drop open. She stepped back, falling gracelessly to the bed. It did nothing to dampen the hungry gleam in Grahame's eye. He ran his tongue over his bottom lip. Adara felt as if her heart would wrestle its way through her ribs. This tousled, perfect man was too handsome to be bedding her. And yet, she was not one to waste an opportunity.

"Come here," she said, scooting back to give him room.

Grahame's eyes ate her up before he acquiesced to her demand. When he did kneel on the bed, he wedged one thigh between hers then slid along her body slowly, as if to memorize the feel of her. Adara lay back, welcoming the lithe weight.

Careful of her splayed hair, he braced his elbows on either side of her head as his nose scored along hers, though something in his gaze turned serious. With his hips pressing down on her, he dipped his mouth to her ear and said the words that made Adara's thawing heart freeze again.

"Let's give them the show they need."

SIXTEEN

Grahame

Adara's limbs became as stiff as tree branches as soon as he climbed on top of her. He was a bastard. She had been treated terribly by her late husband—something he didn't dare think about because the mere mention of her past experience in the bedchamber made his blood froth—and he didn't want to scare her. However, the only way for his plan to work was to make it appear as if they were christening the marriage bed.

Beneath him, Adara was splayed out, her arms around his neck, breasts straining against her dress. They made him salivate. He wanted those breasts in his mouth, wanted his cock between them.

He should have taken her quickly. It would have

been just as easy to shove into her, to stroke them both to completion. With the way her body cradled his, he knew he wouldn't be forcing her. But, at the wedding, her eyes had gone soft when he'd referenced his parents. The little smile that adorned her mouth caused affection to unfurl in his chest. And, as tempting as she was in that dress, when Adara wandered into the bedchamber alone, expectant and worried, something in him cracked. She needed someone to protect her for once. So, Grahame planned to honor her propriety. The men didn't need to know. He figured he could get Adara under the blanket and move in a way to make it look as if they'd completed the marital joining. Even if her kisses and wandering hands made him as hard as stone.

"Indeed, we shall," Adara said into his ear. Her tone was different. Back to being sharp, well-spoken. Not like a woman in the heat of making love, her voice husky with need.

Grahame pulled back.

Her kiss-swollen lips had firmed into a line, the cant of her head like that of a snake's preparing to strike.

It shook him.

But then Adara undulated her hips, pulling his mouth to hers, and Grahame was lost. He kissed her like he'd wanted to for years. With his entire body. Adara gave it back to him, opening her mouth, tonguing him until he was breathless.

"Can you move back?" he managed to ask as he grabbed a glorious handful of her backside and squeezed, all the while grinding himself against her. It was sincerely regretful that he was still wearing pants.

Adara emitted a strangled little sigh. Grahame wanted nothing more than to make her make those sounds for the rest of the evening. Hate for himself threatened to fester—he dared betray his friends by enjoying her too much. But then she raked her nails down his back, a gentle tease, and he damned himself to hell by resolving not to bring Hyrstow into their bed. Adara was his, even if just for a time. And he'd spent most of his life swearing to the Creator he would do anything for one more moment with her. He would live up to that promise.

Grahame dipped his lips to her ear to say, "God damn me, Adara. I promise I won't take you, but I cannot promise I won't spill all over you. I need that dress rucked up, my trousers down, and there will be no question from the men as to whether we consummated this."

Grahame rose off her enough for her to bury herself beneath the coverlet. Removing his hands from her body was every bit as torturous as having his hands burnt. Now that he'd touched her again...the need to keep doing so was overwhelming.

As if unable to help herself, Adara's eyes wandered to the men at the door. A small frown marred those perfect lips. He couldn't lose her, couldn't let her fall back into that cloud of despair.

"Do you like them staring?" Grahame asked, his cock throbbing.

He ran an impatient hand down his length,

squeezing on the upward stroke to ward off the pressure that itched along his lower spine. Grahame's pride puffed his chest as her gaze flared. Adara ran tongue over that full bottom lip of hers as he re-settled between her legs, bracing himself on one arm. He was too eager to settle his starving hand back on her ample hip.

"No. And yes. It is...different this time," she said, her voice low.

"It had better be," he growled, dipping to nip at the bare skin where her neck met her shoulder. Unable to help himself, he kissed her lower, then sucked the delicate skin. "Ruck those skirts up. I'm taking this off."

Adara's eyes widened with appreciation as he untangled the laces of his trousers. His cock's head popped out, thankful for the air.

"Impatient bugger, isn't he?" he asked with a raised brow.

Adara grinned, her eyes locked on his crown. Hunger simmered in their depths.

Shuffling started at the door. Grahame ignored it. Thankfully, Adara did not seem to hear. Instead she reached forward, her fingers curling around the material at his waist.

"Can I?" she asked. A flush stained her cheeks a rosy pink.

"Fuck, yes," Grahame replied, hoarsely.

"You have a dirty mouth," she said.

Some of the ice seemed to ease from her limbs as her knuckles met with the skin above his trousers. He bit back a curse at the contact.

"Oh, Adara, you have no idea how dirty my mouth can be. I yearn to dirty it up with you."

It was permission enough for her to tug his trousers down, revealing the length of him. Grahame grabbed the blanket at his side and flung it over his bare ass. Decently covered, he could hide their lack of joining beneath the blankets.

Safe within the confines of his arms, Adara's eyes were locked on his swollen cock, her hands bracketed on his hips. Almost absently, her thumbs stroked the V-like indentations near his waistline. The rasp of her skin against his was delectable torture.

"Grahame," she murmured before her hand wove 'round the root of his cock, "you're...so well endowed. How...how am I to take all of this?"

He grunted as she stroked upward, fingers loose. She circled the head, her hand a tantalizing mixture of soft firmness before it slid back down. Grahame had to lock his limbs in place to stop himself from thrusting into her grasp.

"I know you can take it, 'Dara," he whispered, his mind going blank as she ran her hand up his length a second time.

Grahame closed his eyes and forced himself still. If Adara wanted to explore his body, so be it. If he had to sit there and think of Joseph Builder's gnarled toes so he wouldn't come too quickly, he would.

Two leisurely strokes later, Grahame gave up.

"'Dara," he moaned, flexing his hips to try to alleviate

the urge to blow all over that goddamn red dress, "focus on me. I'm going to enter you."

Adara nodded, eyes turning glassy as he lowered himself to her, nearly covering her with his body entirely. He'd said it for the benefit of the men watching, to get her onboard. To remind himself that he would not take her even though his body was screaming at him to.

With one arm braced to hold most of his weight off her, he grabbed her skirts and pulled upward with the other. Adara's undergarments were of fine, light, linen almost matching the color of a pearl. Beneath, he could see the outline of her lips, the dampness of the material betraying how she hungered for him. It wasn't a surprise with the way she kissed him, but pride was an unpredictable thing. The sight of her want turned him into a salivating fool. He was so close to heaven. How could he not capture a slice of it while visiting?

As if under a spell, he ran a knuckle over the wet material. Adara shuddered once, then her entire body went still. It snapped him out of his trance, reminding him of his pledge to *act* as if it were all real when none of it was.

Dipping close, he nosed through her luscious black hair to whisper, "Act however you like to make the men think we've joined."

She stiffened again and regret hit Grahame squarely between the shoulder blades. No part of him wanted to fake it with her. Despite all she'd done, she was still his Adara when they were like this.

With resolve, he yanked her underthings down. She

wiggled her hips so the garment hung off one leg. Then he was on her, gliding against her, his flesh on hers, seeking release.

"Ahhh," Adara shouted, the sound ringing through him as his cock met with the skin of her mound. Her hair was slick, her body hot. There was no getting out of the situation with his pride intact. Merely pretending to reach completion wasn't an option when his cock slavered with pent up desire.

"God, Adara, there is no way you feel like this," he rasped, rearing back slightly so he could thrust against her. Any dream he had of her had been nothing compared to the real thing. Her heat, her quivering body beneath his, the small sounds she made as he nudged the bud at her apex were going to drive him mad. And he wasn't even inside her.

Gone with want, Grahame plucked a quick, harsh kiss from her mouth. Without his prompting, her hand snuck between their bodies, fingers dipping into her center to slick them then brought them up to wrap around his length.

If Grahame thought he was mad before, Adara's understanding of the situation was the last straw. There was no way for him to last any amount of time with her determined, lust-filled gaze taking him apart from the inside out. Perhaps that was for the best, because there was something dangerous about this act, this service that they were doing for one another. She was all of his fantasies combined, yet still out of reach. He was her means to an end, and like so many other women before her, his body was a tool. It broke him as a tide of desire burned down his thighs.

Grahame shut his eyes against Adara's beauty, against the hopelessness that overtook him in the knowledge he was protecting a woman he no longer knew. As if in answer, she tightened her fist around him as he thrust again. The sweet, hot glide of her hand was too good.

Adara. His Adara. Her scent cloaked him. He wanted to bathe in it.

"Grahame," she said, her tone pleading. Instead of reply, he moved back and forth, fighting the urge to come all over her. He couldn't look at her.

"Grahame," she said again, her tone strong, grip twisting. It caused him to thicken, to surrender to the inevitability of his marking her. "Grahame, look at me."

Adara. Adara. *His* 'Dara.

He'd dreamt of this moment thousands of times. The fire for her threatened to swallow him whole. She pumped her hand with his rhythm, bringing him to the point of no return.

"Please."

Grahame's eyes flew open as he jerked, spilling onto her creamy skin as wave after wave of release shredded through him. It was pain and pleasure like he'd never experienced. A wringing of his worthless soul.

When he'd finished, he collapsed on top of her, burying his nose in her hair so he wouldn't have to look at her beautiful, tortured face any longer.

After a few heartbeats, he turned his face to the side to see Hagan and Thor adjusting their lower halves.

"Get out," Grahame growled, hating that they witnessed her in a state of undress. That they were a part of the lies he told himself about his feelings for her. "You've seen what you need. Be gone."

The men turned and fled as if their tunics were on fire.

Exhaustion climbed into Grahame's bones and nested. He wanted to sink into sleep, to avoid everything that he knew would come. The urge to throw his arms over Adara and lay with her all night was unacceptable. It made him want to run from the room like the others.

Slowly, he peeled himself off his wife. His spend slicked their skin. Adara would not look at him. He tossed off the blanked and picked up his clothing. Humiliation at her shame snaked through him as he wiped himself off with his underthings. Once finished, he offered the material to Adara. She snatched it, wiping herself down without a word. Hastily, he threw on his tunic, thrust his wobbly legs into his trousers.

"I've done what you required of me. I expect Yrsa to be freed from the dungeon immediately."

No words were spoken as Grahame accepted his balled up underclothes and left.

SEVENTEEN

Adara

Yrsa was released from the dungeon before dawn. She was given a small room in the servant's quarters, stripped bare of anything that could be construed as a weapon.

"One night with the farm boy and you've abandoned your mission?"

Muretta paced the great room before the fire. She wore a navy shawl about her shoulders despite the high fire warding off the cold that clung to the walls. Adara absently wondered how her farmers would do after the deluge. Rain was always welcome. Too much, however, was disaster.

"I'm not abandoning anything. Yrsa Ward is still my

prisoner. I have simply reconsidered her place in the dungeons. She can be a prisoner upstairs."

Annoyance prickled the back of her neck as she reviewed the tax amounts she would have to collect come harvest. The sums had been sent by her father last month though the increases were out of reach for nearly all tenants in the area. She placed the parchment on the table before her and rubbed her eyes. A visit to her tenants was needed. It would get her out of her head, out of this oppressive house she was working so hard to keep. Though she couldn't very well leave when Ward threatened her doorstep.

"She could kill us with *anything* up here. Hagan and Thor both said she was lethal." Muretta's hands moved at her sides with the flurry of a bird's wings as she paced.

Adara felt a stab of affection for her; Muretta could be utterly brave in the face of a man yet worried over a Viking woman.

Adara let her shoulders drop. Exhaustion wound tight along her limbs. There had been little sleep after Grahame left the room the night previous. Instead, she'd removed her dress then sat by the fire in her nightclothes, reliving every moment she'd spent with Grahame. Her mind loved to remind her of the tiny creases in the corners of his eyes when he smirked and the mountain range of muscle that was his lean stomach. Of the way it flexed when he came all over her, his face awash with guilt and loathing.

"She should be fine if one of the men is with us."

"How? She could kill them, too!" Muretta's hands spread with her words. "Adara, why? Her husband has agreed to wait until she is released. We have her where we want her, and you need to focus on your new groom. You travel to your father's in less than a fortnight. The two of you should be preparing."

Adara pinched the bridge of her nose. She wished for some tea but Bhlaine had disappeared into the kitchens a while ago.

"I know, Muretta, I do. But I also hate the thought of a woman down there in the cold and dark for no other reason than I want to punish her husband."

Muretta's mouth dropped open. She pressed her hands to her fine, yellow skirts.

"Adara, I must be so bold as to say your new husband has screwed the sense from your head. Why should you care about the woman down there? From what you have shared about the villains in Hyrstow, the whole lot of them can rot."

Adara shook her head as she glanced back down at the parchment. Her tone was wry when she said, "Believe me, no amount of bedding from Grahame would strike sense from me."

Muretta wrinkled her nose. "Ah. No good then? I thought with his jokes and that smile he'd have a way with women. But, I guess you never know until you take them for a ride..."

"That's quite enough, Muretta."

Adara did not want to talk about Grahame. Not about the way he kissed her like he wanted to steal her breath.

Not about the manner in which his hands traced her outline like she was something he craved. Certainly not about the women of his past while he left her panting and alone in her bedchamber.

She also didn't want to discuss the growing, messy sense that her exhaustion was not simply from brooding over Grahame. It was due to the heaping pile of second-guessing that occurred along with it. Thoughts of Grahame made her question how much he cared for his friends if he was willing to sacrifice himself in service to them. She wondered how the dreadful people of Hyrstow had inspired such loyalty.

Adara blew out a breath. She leaned back in her chair, her back thanking her for the stretch.

"I am getting my revenge. Stealing the priest from Hyrstow was another part of it. And yet, Ridley's wife has a will of steel. I do not think she will bend further to me, even if I decide to torture her. It will be punishment enough to keep them apart until I decide what else needs to be done."

"Do you hear her?" Muretta gestured with one hand to Hagan as he and Grumb entered, Yrsa between them.

The woman's skin was sallow, her hair filthy, yet she stood with an intangible grace that Adara envied.

"I do. I also know my place when it comes to our lady," Hagan said.

Adara tensed when she looked upon her guard. She knew there was no point in dwelling in her embarrassment over the night previous. Though, she couldn't help notice the way Hagan avoided her gaze as he brought Yrsa forward.

"That is why I am here. I will ensure no one acts untoward."

Muretta gripped her top lip with her bottom teeth. She nodded once then wiped any emotion from her features. It was a skill Adara admired.

Thor and Grahame entered a moment later.

"Yrsa." Grahame moved forward as soon as he spotted her. He halted when Grumbheld put his palm up before Grahame could get close.

"Wait there," the guard said.

Grahame turned his gaze, burning with anger, on Adara. There was no softness in his countenance, no flicker of acknowledgement over what they had done the night previous. Adara told herself she did not care about his ire.

"He is permitted to touch her," Adara ordered Grumb.

He nodded, stepping back toward the door. Gratitude for him warmed Adara. Grumbheld always listened. She stood, rolling the parchment, trying to avoid looking at her husband. Thor caught her eye, offering her a friendly wink as if to say anything he'd witnessed the night before had been forgotten. Adara nodded her thanks, not missing the affronted look Grahame issued them before he dragged Yrsa into his embrace. Hagan did not release Yrsa's arm as she hugged Grahame around the waist.

"For the love of God, man. Look at her, she can't do anything," Grahame seethed.

Adara rolled her eyes. "Show them how well you are, Yrsa. I have not starved you. Other than a little darkness and chill, you should be at full strength."

Yrsa's navy eyes narrowed on Adara. She released Grahame, fisting her hands at her sides as she straightened. Adara gave a self-satisfied smirk at the shock that coated Grahame's handsome face.

"What is the meaning of this?" Grahame demanded as he reached for Yrsa again.

Her arm entwined with his just as Adara's had during their wedding ceremony. Something ugly turned over in Adara's gut.

Rather than answer, she poured herself a cup of watered ale from the jug on the table and took a drink. The hoppy flavor did nothing to calm her, yet allowed for a pause to show Grahame who was in charge.

"I have followed through on my bargain. Yrsa may stay in the upper house. You are welcome. Or would you rather your friend remain in the cold dungeon?"

Hagan stood by the door while Thorhild settled himself at Adara's side, ready to defend if the need arose. Grahame put a wide hand over Yrsa's where she clutched his upper arm, anger radiating from him.

"The agreement was that you set her free."

Heat rose to Adara's cheeks. He dare defy her in front of her men?

"I will keep my word as needed, Husband."

The use of Grahame's new title gave the desired effect. Yrsa's mouth dropped open, her eyes going round as she clung to his side.

"Husband?" she breathed.

Adara couldn't help the sense of pleasure she derived at the sliver of distance Yrsa placed between herself and Grahame as she searched his face. The sorrow in her pretty features begged for it not to be true.

Grahame set his jaw, his entire body going rigid as he issued a curt nod. "Aye, Yrsa. We were married yesterday. I am a prisoner for life, it seems."

Adara froze her features in place. She would not reveal how his simple words sliced into her like daggers, each finding a mark close to her heart. It was her own folly to think he'd imagine her as anything other than a gaoler.

Adara bared her teeth in a feral smile. "You did not complain about the jail between my thighs last evening."

Yrsa watched them volley words.

Adara's must have hit their mark because Grahame's cheeks turned from tanned to ruddy. "A prison is still a prison, no matter its beauty."

"Ah, you think I'm beautiful?" Adara pretended to preen, yanking her fingers through her long, dark locks.

Grahame's grip around Yrsa loosened as he stepped forward, ready to argue. Adara refused to admit the way it thrilled her. That she could still encourage a response from him, even an angry one.

"Enough."

The word rang through the room with the authority of someone listened to. Everyone turned their gazes to Yrsa.

"You argue like children, both of you." The sharp-tongued woman inclined her head at Adara. "My Lady, I will not insult you by saying I will be a good captive. I never have been. However, I will remain docile enough to receive a bath and a meal, if you would be so generous."

Adara fought the grin that threatened her mouth. As much as she wished to impart sorrow upon Ridley Ward, his wife was entirely fascinating. A woman of strength and determination; Adara admired both attributes.

"I will allow it. Men will guard your room. No one will assist you as I do not trust you not to kill them."

Yrsa grinned. It was beautiful and terrifying. "Smart choice."

Adara snatched an apple from the plate on the table.

"Grahame, you will accompany me. I'd like to have a word with you."

With a forced air of indifference, Adara walked around them. She ignored the way Grahame pulled Yrsa back into a hug and whispered comforting things into her hair. Ignored the twinge of guilt she felt. She also squashed the feeling of betrayal at Grahame's proclamation of imprisonment. It was true. Even if it felt ugly.

By the time she reached the front door, she'd almost convinced herself she did not care about any of it.

EIGHTEEN

Grahame

Grahame drew a deep breath for patience as he followed his wife through the door. The hinges creaked, the great wood slab thudding closed after him. Mud slicked the paths that wove around the house, one leading to a flourishing garden on the left, the other to the stable on the right. Grass speckled with tiny white wildflowers climbed the short hill the house resided upon. Grahame was glad the rain had turned to mist.

God, had it been mere days that he had resided there? Adara had taken hold of his senses, wrapping him in a hold he could not escape.

After the night previous, he wasn't sure he wanted to.

Adara's heel ground into the stone pathway as she

halted next to an ancient oak tree that grew unnaturally close to the house. The twitching of her right hand caused something in Grahame's chest to tighten. The desire to take her in his arms, to lift her chin so he could taste her lips was overpowering. It grated.

All night Grahame had wrestled with the fact he did not want to leave his wife in bed alone. She held terrible power over his friends, yet he wanted to *learn* her. To bed her, yes, but also find out about her likes and annoyances. To dig deeper beneath her tough outer shell. They had not had the time in their youth. Yet time was presenting itself now.

Grahame decided to fend off his traitorous thoughts with questions that he needed answered.

"What is your game with Yrsa? Are you going to free her?"

Adara held up a hand for silence. Two small lines appeared between her brows. Faint shadows lived beneath her eyes. Had she barely slept after their marital joining, just as he had? Seeing Yrsa in the great room was an intense relief. One that gave him hope. He decided to push.

"Adara. Please, tell me what you plan to do. I've upheld the terms of my bargain. Yrsa should be freed."

"Would you give me a moment to think?" Adara exclaimed, stomping her foot. "All you have are questions. Like everyone else. 'Lady Clayton, do we need to worry over Hyrstow encroaching like they did near Guston?'; 'Lady Clayton, how will we be able to afford our taxes?'. Not to mention the demands of my father and Hyrstow breathing down my neck."

She rubbed her temples as she spoke, one hip popping out as she settled her weight. Despite his frustration with Adara's schemes, the movement carved out a small crescent of affection in Grahame's heart. He had learned to expect the worst from her. Such concerns were a surprise.

"You...have such worries?" he ventured, stepping forward as if he were on the end of a string she wound toward her.

Adara shoved out an impatient breath. "Are you daft?"

"I try not to be, yet I am but a humble shepherd. I have no knowledge of how you run your household. Or that you oversee tenants. How would I know they are worried over Hyrstow's encroachment? Though, as your husband, I assume I must learn."

Grahame crossed his arms over his chest as he spoke. To guard himself against her. Adara's worries were a distraction. She had promised to free Yrsa. Bringing her out of the dungeon was a start; however, Grahame did not yet trust his wife's word.

Adara's hands flared as she slapped the sides of her thighs in frustration at his impudence.

"Of course they are worried about Hyrstow overtaking them! Not that you care, but two years ago Ridley Ward came through with his men and snatched up prime farmland. Who knows if he will do it again? I make no secret of wanting revenge on him for harming my family, but my father also ordered for Elvin to keep him in check. I've...taken the liberty to continue. The only thing stopping me from sending men to finish him off is that I do not want war from the Earl of Deircia. However, I will admit to being...ambitious with my vengeance after Elvin died. I had his funds and his power. Yrsa was supposed to be captured during that raid. The market upset was a distraction that got out of hand."

Grahame could barely hear Adara's final words over the thudding of his heart. The raid hadn't gone to plan? Not that he condoned any raid on his people, however, he could not deny how Hyrstow had prospered with the additional farmland. His village was a place where people congregated, where they sought comfort. It was natural to assume the Earl of Deircia's ambitions could extend further into Adara's territory. Ridley would follow orders, as he always had.

Adara rubbed at her pinched brow with her thumb and forefinger. She stared at the ground as she spoke. As if the fight had left her, she sighed. "Never mind, Grahame. I will be the villain to you and your friends. I do not know why I bothered to tell you any of this."

Adara moved to turn down the path away from him, but Grahame's hand shot out to stop her. He could not let her wander. Not when Ridley was just beyond the gate, waiting for any sign of Adara's vulnerability.

"No disappearing on me. You called me out here, Wife. Or should we let everyone think we are coupling like blissful newlyweds? Hmm?"

Adara scoffed, "You always jest. It is infuriating."

Grahame tightened his grip on her arm as his patience with the conversation slipped. He infuriated her? Adara did not realize the breadth of his frustration. She did not understand how horrific it was to be summoned and married to the one woman he'd always wanted only after she had changed so deeply. The truth spilled out of him, unbidden.

"I jest because the more I learn, the more it tears me apart to hear of the horrors of your life. It angers me to witness what you've become as a result. All I've had to suffer is your absence."

"Do not tell me you suffered in my absence," she spat. Like a change of wind, Adara pushed at his chest, her words slapping him with their force. "Do not tell me *I* was the cause of any discomfort. Not when you so readily chose your friends over me that summer. Not when you said goodbye and I worried over you. For months, Grahame! I had no idea if you lived or died until Cecilia told me at the Yuletide feast. I agonized over you."

Grahame flinched against the truth. Her hands pressed into his chest, turning into brands as he remained still, praying she wouldn't remove them.

"You may not want to hear it, but I pined for you for years, 'Dara. Each day I regretted my choice to follow Ridley, to find those who killed his parents. If I had known you would have been summoned home while I was gone, I would not have left. I was so in love with you, 'Dara, so young and daft. We knew we could not be together yet I would have likely risked the noose for your hand."

A tear spilled down her cheek. It cut straight through him, striking his well-guarded heart.

"That would have been worse," she whispered.

Grahame shook his head. "I carried that wound inside me, that you were never to be mine. I let it fester until I heard you were the one to orchestrate the most recent raid on my people. My thoughts of you changed, then. I couldn't reconcile *my* Adara as someone who would do such a thing."

"I..." she trailed off as if she was going to protest her actions then decided against it.

Her mouth set in a wobbly line, her hands dropping from him. And, as much as she was the villain in his life, the tenderness he felt for her was raw. It would have been so much easier to hate her.

Grahame drummed his fingers on his leg. Their arguments carried too much hurt. He needed to get back to what mattered now.

"I am sorry that you have these worries. I had not thought of Ridley in this way. I...he's my friend. I do not agree with your actions, Adara, but thank you for telling me. I can see the grief you carry and the pressure from your tenants."

Her face jerked upward, confusion and anger warring on her perfect features. Grahame stopped fighting his urges. She was his wife, no matter how the arrangement came to be. He tugged her to him then dipped a kiss to the tip of her nose, his heart hammering.

As if to break him further, Adara stepped away. Tears

lined her lower lashes, though a challenge lay in her words.

"I made you my prisoner."

A scoffing laugh cut through him. He scratched the back of his head, noting the way Adara's gaze followed the curve of his upper arm. "Chain me up, then. You are mine and I am yours. The decision has been made. Now what are we to do with it?"

Adara paled. Her mouth popped open, then closed, her palms lifting in a gesture of uncertainty. Grahame held his breath.

She could have chosen any man to be her puppet. He yearned to know why she had picked him. It cut him to the quick to think it was simply because he had land between Hyrstow and Guston. And, damn his heart, he held out a sliver of hope it was because she cared for him the way he still cared for her.

It was at that moment that the thunder of hooves rattled the air. Adara turned to face the sound. Issuing a grunt of annoyance, Grahame strode to the gate, wrenching open the viewing panel to see the commotion. Adara was on his heels, pulling at his arm so she could see. Past the fence, amid the well-worn field beyond, an army sat at Adara's doorstep.

CHAPTER

NINETEEN

Adara

Grahame braced an arm around Adara's waist and shoved her behind him so fast her head whirled. Her face met with the cloth of his tunic as he anchored her behind the wall of his body. Adara's hands molded to his arms in an attempt to right herself against the sheer magnitude of his protection.

"Get inside. Ridley's called in more men," he snarled.

With a grunt, Adara was able to stand on tiptoe to see around him. She wished she hadn't. About three hundred yards past her gate was a collection of soldiers. Each held an implement of death, whether it be a sword, shield, knife, club, or ax. They'd come on horse, with armour and without, their solemn faces painted a dark green. Ridley Ward was shaking the hand of one of the armored men while the small band of men he'd brought from Hyrstow remained by his side, ready to help their leader in this battle Adara had waged.

"Get inside, Adara," Grahame seethed through his teeth. His muscles bunched beneath her hands.

Adara shoved down the panic that greased her insides. She couldn't let it take hold of her. If she did, her command was over.

"Come with me," she ordered, pulling his tunic. There was no way she would leave him to fend off an army, even if it was made up of his own people. They wouldn't know it was their friend behind the gate if they chose to plow it down.

As if unable to let his guard down wholly, Grahame turned to the side allowing him to keep an eye on the figures in the distance. His mouth was a grim line.

"No, Adara. I need to speak with them. I need you inside. I need...Christ." Grahame shoved a hand through his unruly curls, his straight nose wrinkling with a grimace. "I need to talk to Ridley. I need you to go somewhere where you'll be safe."

"I will not run away," Adara began. Her words were cut short by Grahame picking her up and throwing her over his shoulder. With purposeful strides he went back to the house, his arm like a steel band over her legs. She shrieked with frustration, but Grahame ignored her as he worked through what to do.

"Those must be Lachlan's men. I'll try to reason with him. We can give Yrsa back, they can see she's unharmed, and..."

The warm light of the entryway greeted them as they moved over the threshold. Thorhild's steps thudded down the hall, his protest as to what Grahame was doing to Adara overshadowed by Grahame's booming orders for men to assemble in the great room immediately. With little ceremony, he leaned down and righted Adara. His hand didn't leave her hip until he knew she had her balance, though his gaze cut past her to Thor and Hagan, who were crowded in the hall behind her.

"Ridley has reinforcements. Likely men from Lachlan's keep. It's not a whole army but enough to overturn the house."

Thor moved around them to the door, poking his blonde head out to see for himself. Hagan simply stared at her in shock as if Grahame taking charge of the matter was the most distressing part of the situation.

"The men do not appear to be approaching. Hagan, gather everyone in the house, take them out through the rear. Perhaps we can ready the horses and leave before they catch wind that we're gone." As Grahame spoke, Thor's hand shifted to the wicked dagger on his belt.

"We will not leave," Adara sputtered. She had never seen this decisive side of Grahame. A tiny, selfish part of her rejoiced at the thought of his dominance. However, there would be no escape. She still held Yrsa. They would not desert her home.

As if she was not there, the three men all began speaking at once.

"There are too many..."

"We don't have the men for battle..."

"Time is of the essence..."

Adara held up her hands in a gesture for silence, her tone slipping into one of command rather than consternation. She had to wrangle a plan. One that would keep the people of her house safe. The familiar clutch of panic wove up her shoulders.

Rather than cave to it, she ground her teeth and shouted, "Listen! We shall not leave. This is my home. I still hold the upper hand."

Her words were met with open mouths and straightened shoulders. The men blinked down at her as if she had set fire to the tapestries. They thought her a woman not thinking clearly. Little did it matter, for her mind was racing over the things she could offer and what she would have to sacrifice. She could free Yrsa, which meant giving up her revenge. She could fight or be locked in siege. Both would call her father down from his keep to defend his daughter, something she absolutely did not want. Adara fisted her clammy hands. Her ambition had landed her in the situation and it would damn well pull her out of it.

"'Dara," Grahame started, reaching for her wrist, as if their fresh argument gave him any right to overrule her. She pulled her arm away.

"Hagan, take me to Yrsa Ward. I will speak with her and stop this madness before it even starts."

Adara stretched a hand between Hagan and Thor so as to move between them. They yielded to her immediately.

"Lady, we must do away with the chieftain's bride, " Hagan said as he fell into step beside her.

She sensed the alertness he wore like a second skin. It was a comfort and a curse. Hagan would die to protect her, she knew. Many of them would. Yet she did not want them to. She loved those in her care: each tenant, every homestead leading up to Guston, even those inside the turbulent village. Those who served in her home would not live in fear. Which was why she had to protect them from her father's rule.

Hagan unlocked the door to Yrsa's room. He braced his hand on the handle, his large body taking up the doorway.

"Step aside, please. I would like to speak with her alone," Adara said. She puffed out her chest with resolve.

"I will accompany you," Hagan retorted.

Adara felt both Thor and Grahame at her back. Murmuring from the kitchens grew louder. Somewhere from the yard came shouts and the sounds of clanking weaponry. Worry was a finger along her throat. The property was a handful of cooks and washing maids and stable hands. Muretta and a small force of men. They could not hope to take on the soldiers Ridley threatened. She widened her stance, locking her legs in place.

"You were not with me when I visited Yrsa Ward in the dungeons at night."

Hagan stiffened. Adara continued. She ignored the stab of guilt she felt at the disregard she had shown her guards by lying to them.

"You know I'm a poor sleeper, Hagan. I grew lonely. I

yearned to speak to someone who had an inkling of power such as mine. She and I got along when we were not under the threat of male presence."

Warm fingers locked around her wrist. She didn't have to look up to know Grahame's touch. His thumb brushed the tender skin of her pulse; a thank you, a show of protection, she wasn't sure. Whatever it was, it bolstered her.

"Move, Hagan. I will settle this feud with Yrsa."

"You are to let her go?" Thor interjected. His hand twitched at his side, his gaze locked on Grahame. He wore his mistrust like a heavy cloak.

"Not quite," Adara muttered. She swallowed the fear that snaked up her throat. The only play she had was her strength, her integrity. All she could do was hope Yrsa Ward would accept her proposal.

"Leave us."

Hagan's jaw rippled, his face stricken as he slowly coaxed the door open. Grahame threaded his fingers through hers. He walked with her into the room, sticking to her side like a burr.

Pleasure and uncertainty warred within her. Despite Grahame's words that he suffered her absence, his loyalty was to Hyrstow. Hyrstow wanted her dead. Adara stuffed her doubt to the back of her mind as Yrsa stood from the mattress and faced them both with a smile on her perfect lips.

Grahame

"What have you done to your hair?"

Yrsa stood before them in borrowed tunic and trousers, her hair no longer uneven. The light strands had been cut to her jawline, framing her face in a fetching manner. With her blade of a nose, the haircut made Yrsa appear sharper, like a sword whetted on a stone.

"I improved it," Yrsa said, twirling a short handled blade between her fingers.

Grahame had no idea where she procured the blade from. He assumed none of Adara's men were careless enough to allow it. Yet there she was, with a knife, running a hand through the freshly washed hair.

"I helped."

Muretta stood near the washing basin that had been brought in. She was no worse for wear and did not cower before the towering woman. Grahame tensed. He offered a hooked brow of suspicion.

Yrsa shrugged. "She helped."

"You gave her a *knife*?" Adara demanded of Muretta.

Muretta shrugged as she moved around Yrsa, a grin pasted on her heart-shaped mouth. Her skirts swam with her quick, bird-like movements. Grahame doubted Hagan was aware Muretta had snuck in. He had half a mind to tell the man.

"You assured me she was not a danger." Her shrug made Adara seem silly for asking. "She didn't stab me."

"Not something I want you to find out the hard way," Adara snapped, stepping forward with a hand stretched toward Muretta's.

Muretta offered Yrsa a beatific smile before stepping around her.

"Muretta, please retreat to your rooms. I would like you to be as safe as possible."

Muretta nodded, offering a small curtsy, then left the room, though not before her curious eyes scoured the inches between Grahame and Adara.

Yrsa stepped forward, a hand on her hip, knife gripped loosely in the other.

"Interesting company you keep, Lady," Yrsa said, nearing.

As if pulled by a rope, Grahame angled his body in front of Adara's.

Yrsa's eyebrows shot up. "Well, well." She wrinkled her nose. "What a development, Golden Boy! I wondered earlier who you would defend if the time came, and it seems I have my answer."

Grahame shot a deep breath out his nose to stop the reeling sensation that overtook him. He clenched his jaw over the protest that he would not choose between them. Yrsa was no fool.

"Are you here to inflict pain? Or is my husband here to collect me?" Yrsa asked. She blinked innocently as she spoke.

Adara released a breathy chuckle beside him. It struck Grahame to his marrow. Desire and hope and worry fought for dominance within him. There was no way out of this. Adara had done horrible things to his people. Yet he wished he had the words to stay Ridley. His own uselessness in the whole endeavour struck him dumb, even as his entire body felt like an iron rod as he readied to throw himself between the women should they try to gut one another.

"Indeed. Your husband has garnered much loyalty in his earldom. More men have come to set you free."

Yrsa's grin widened as she gestured to the room around her. Her eyes sparkled in a manner that had Grahame pressing himself into Adara's side.

"Shall I take any requests before I am granted my freedom? Or is your intent to kill me and have my husband raze your home to the ground?"

"Now Yrsa, you know I would not assume either outcome so quickly." Adara's own grin widened to match

Yrsa's. She tried to shake off Grahame, something Yrsa tracked.

"You seem to have garnered some loyalty of your own, Lady Clayton." She raised a light eyebrow in the direction of Grahame's hand locked around Adara's wrist, her stormy eyes straying to his for a moment.

Grahame tried to ignore the flash of hurt he saw in them. He was stuck. Surely, Yrsa would understand. She once was torn between her people and her love of Ridley.

She chose Ridley, he thought. Yet would he choose Adara? If there was no bargain, if she'd not attacked his village, if she'd not taken Yrsa? Yes. A thousand times yes.

But after all her misdeeds?

You still would.

Grahame cleared his throat in order to usurp the dark whisper of his thoughts. He tipped up the corner of his mouth in a grin to let Yrsa know he was on her side as well, to insist to himself he was, but she wasn't paying attention.

Adara flicked the wrist of her free hand as if Yrsa's words meant nothing. She took another step forward, her shoes clapping against the floorboards.

"Grahame and I have history. Long before you knew him and long before your husband murdered my cousin, we cut our teeth on one another. Thankfully, your cooperation will also determine how he makes it out of this situation."

Grahame flinched at the callousness with which Adara spoke. As if he were a piece of chattel.

"And what cooperation do you propose?" Yrsa asked, her hands going to her slender hips.

"Your freedom will be guaranteed as long as your husband is willing to dine with us tonight. No siege, no battle, just a reasoning between two opposing parties."

"He'll never concede."

"I have two of his most prized possessions. One of which he gathered an army for. That tells me he is willing to listen, if only to get inside my home to destroy me."

Something red and hot coated Grahame's muscles. It was the same instinct he had when he caught sight of the army and had Adara over his shoulder within moments. The urge to throw himself in front of whatever dared harm her. He was going mad.

"Firstly, we are not possessions. Next, why would I bring my husband into your clutches? You'll kill us both, given the chance." Yrsa examined her torn nails as she spoke, as if she dealt with the likes of Adara every day.

Adara's smile was positively feline.

"I guarantee your safety. You have my word. And," Adara held up her hand, palm out, forcing Grahame to release her, "before you say my word is not worth anything, consider that I've kept it the entire time you've been here. No harm came to you, or your husband, as agreed upon in the forest. I've simply parted you both for a time."

Yrsa's eyes narrowed, but she did not dispute Adara's claim.

"I wish to use this opportunity to strike a bargain with your husband," Adara said, her tone even.

"I thought you wanted him to suffer?" Grahame's interjection was out before he could close his lips over it.

The women turned to him, as if surprised he was still there. However, Adara's steely gaze closed off. Irritation with them both itched along the back of his neck. He rubbed at it to halt the sensation.

"Oh, how I *wish* I could pick him apart. Yet I understand we've reached an impasse. Yrsa will be given back, unharmed, under the condition that Ridley Ward does not step foot within Bernira's border ever again. Too many have suffered under the threat of his proximity."

Yrsa made a sound of disbelief. Adara spoke louder to override the other woman.

"If he crosses into my territory again, he will be killed. Then I will come after Hyrstow in earnest. As one ruler to another, would you risk your people? Ridley is nothing but a conqueror. One who will not win a fight against Bernira."

"Why should I believe that you will allow us to leave? You hold Grahame here against his will."

Adara waved another dismissive hand in his direction. To his horror, the gesture cut. After he'd told her of his suffering without her, he was just another thing to be brokered.

"Yes, yes, he is required for a scheme to guarantee I do not marry whom my father has chosen. He will be freed when it works."

Grahame felt as if he'd been struck in the center of

his chest. All the air whooshed out of him as Yrsa nodded, stepping forward with her hand outstretched. As the women shook, hands to the inside of forearms, Grahame simply watched, stunned.

He wanted freedom. He'd been swindled into a marriage he could easily be killed in. And yet the careless manner in which Adara could cast him aside...he wished it didn't feel like a knife of fire had been buried in his chest. Was he so worthless?

The creaking of the door sliced into the room. Hagan entered, a look of gravity about his face.

"Ridley Ward approaches."

Adara cleared her throat. "Thank you, Hagan."

"Come, Golden Boy, let us greet my husband." Yrsa stepped up to him, patting him on the shoulder as she made to leave. Grahame only stood there, his gaze locked on the back of Adara's head as she gave direction to Hagan and Thor.

"Yes, Lady Wolf," he responded.

His heart beat too quick for him to gather his wits, but he kept his smile pasted on as they made their preparations. It was easier than he expected, as he'd worn the mask of joviality all his life. Resolute, Grahame ignored the stab of betrayal he felt every time he looked at his wife.

She didn't look at him, either.

TWENTY-ONE

Grahame

"You will not give details other than that of your well being. You will not tell of my plans until I reveal them," Adara said out of the side of her mouth as she stalked to the great room.

There had been some maneuvering in the hall, a demand for Yrsa to proceed first, while Adara and Grahame brought up the rear. Adara's hair swished at her back with her stride, a distracting reminder of how it felt threaded in his grip.

Grahame shook his head to remove the thoughts that arose of all the other things he could do with that hair and said, "Of course."

Adara glanced at him sidelong, arching a raven eyebrow of suspicion. He gave a snort in an attempt to dismiss her mistrust. Adara simply continued forward, though Grahame didn't miss the way she tilted her chin up in the same manner she did when they were younger. As if readying to shoulder the weight of the world herself.

Adara's back was so straight, Grahame could imagine the wings of her shoulder blades kissing beneath the sage green dress she wore. He wasn't much better, his throat thick with worry. As daring as Adara was, Grahame could only see the manner in which everything could go wrong. Despite Hagan and Thor taking away weapons, Ridley was feral when it came to Yrsa. It was all Grahame could do to let Adara walk beside him and not shield her behind his back.

"You can do this," he whispered, leaning into her space as they paused on the entryway to the great room. 'Dara's mouth quirked upward, the only indication she had heard him. If it meant peace between her and Hyrstow, he'd take it.

"Yrsa." The reverence in Ridley's hoarse voice tore Grahame's attention from his wife.

Ridley's hands hung at his sides ready to grab for weapons Grahame knew had been taken away. Dark circles had soured the skin beneath his eyes while shadows lived under the cut of his cheekbones. His haggard appearance did nothing to hinder the flame that lit his gaze as Yrsa walked into the room.

A pained gasp broke from Yrsa who ran at Ridley, arms outstretched. He met her half way, catching her in his arms, pulling her into him as if to meld her body with his. Grahame caught sight of tears glinting on Yrsa's cheeks until she pushed her face into Ridley's neck. All the while Ridley sowed words of love into her hair. Watching them was like staring into the sun.

Beside Ridley, Branton glowered, his entire beastly body as tense as the ridge of his clenched jaw. Surprise grabbed Grahame around the collar. He thought it impossible for Bran to leave Emma's side. Grahame's hackles rose. If Branton was present, they were in deep shit.

Grahame stifled his grimace, shifting his gaze to Adara. She did not turn away from Yrsa and Ridley's embrace, the pain she'd caused. Rather, a feline smile spread across her mouth, as if readying for battle.

"Welcome, Ridley Ward."

Both Ridley and Branton's gazes locked on Adara and Grahame, side by side at the entrance of the room. Bran scoured the space between their arms, his frown falling lower, if it was possible.

"Please, be seated," Adara commanded, striding forward as she gestured to the table laden with food and ale.

Branton's grim features did not change while Ridley's arms remained wrapped around Yrsa, his eyes narrowed on the woman responsible for their misery.

Behind Ridley and Branton, another man emerged, one Grahame had never seen before. Straw-colored hair, a stony face that had seen many more years than they had, a body covered in chain mail. It had to have been one of Lachlan's men.

Hagan watched coolly from near the fire, his hand on his swordbelt, while Thor stood near the kitchen door idly flipping a knife and catching its handle, the threat clear. Other men lined the wall, silent, watching.

No one moved as Adara came to stand at the head of the table. She did not sit. The impasse was enough that Grahame pasted on an easy smile, moving around Adara to break the tension laid thick in the room. Despite his friend's look of death, Grahame pulled Branton into a rough embrace. Bran accepted the hug, smacking him on the back loudly then running his hands over his arms as if checking for injury.

"Are you both well?" Ridley asked, his own gaze searching Grahame.

Grahame nodded, heartily punching Ridley's shoulder with affection. "Indeed, brother. We've been well kept."

"Some more than others," Yrsa grumbled, her face buried in Ridley's neck.

He relaxed his hold just enough for her to turn to face the others but kept his arms anchored around her torso. Bran's countenance softened as his gaze searched Yrsa.

"What—" Ridley began, murder in his features.

Yrsa's hand trailed over his face, while the other remained looped around the back of his neck, the knife still in her hand. Grahame caught the way Hagan glowered at the sight of the weapon. Grahame shook his head, holding up his hand in a gesture to remain calm. To his surprise, Hagan relaxed against the wall once more.

"I was kept in the dungeon, while Grahame was allowed to remain up above."

Furious faces looked to Grahame, then Yrsa. Grahame stepped back to gain some space from the sense of injustice between them.

"The dungeon?" Branton's quiet words promised torture.

"Indeed," Adara said from behind them, ready and waiting for their reunion to be over. "I couldn't very well have a skilled warrior in my midst. Now, shall we meet to parse out the terms of this agreement?"

"Agreement?" Ridley moved aside to push Yrsa behind him. Suddenly, he held her knife, clutched in one hand as if he would bring down the entire house with it.

The man in chainmail stepped forward while Branton thumbed his belt where his small ax usually sat. Grahame sidestepped to Adara. The movement didn't go unnoticed.

"You took my *wife*. Tricked us. Stormed our village, causing death. Now we have a host at your door. It does not seem to me like we are much inclined to agree to anything."

Ridley's words were hissed through clenched teeth, his entire body shoring up for violence. Grahame's heart beat faster. His muscles primed, limbs locking in place, readying to fight. A weapon would have been useful. He knew how deadly both his friends were, and though he didn't know the man in chainmail, he appeared battle-worn. A metallic taste sat at the back of his mouth.

Grahame glanced at Adara who stared at the

Hyrstow men as if she wasn't fazed in the least. Her perfect mouth slid into a knowing line, her jaw relaxed as if she'd been waiting years for such a meet. Perhaps she had.

"I had my reasons, Ridley Ward, and if you are inclined to listen, I have a further proposition for your earl."

Ridley's tawny gaze slid from Adara to Hagan to Thor, then scoured the room for further threat. Yrsa had no such qualms. She stepped around her husband, her hand twined in his, pulling him toward the table. Ridley's entire body puffed out for a heartbeat, as if readying to shove her behind him and slay them all, before he acquiesced to her and followed. Branton was next, his bright blue eyes narrowed on Grahame. Finally, the stranger in chain mail shuffled to the table.

"Who are you?" Grahame blurted.

The man's grimace could have been a grin but it folded as quickly as it appeared in his lined face. Brown eyes with an inkling of wisdom returned Grahame's stare.

"I am Sir Langley, cousin to the Earl of Deircia. I act as his steward and head commander in this matter."

If Ridley bristled at not being the head commander as he settled next to Yrsa on the table's left side, he hid it well. Branton plunked down on the edge of the bench, bracketing Yrsa, while Sir Langley settled on Ridley's left.

Grahame wished to join them. To have Adara across from him so he may hear her proposal with clarity rather than being so near that the scent and warmth of her clouded his judgement. As it was, he settled himself next to her, the only two on their side of the table. Grahame wished the act wasn't so symbolic.

"What could you have to barter with?" Ridley asked, words spewing from his mouth like shards of metal. "You've done despicable things. What could have prompted such a dispute? You wish to lay claim to Hyrstow?"

Grahame tensed. Hagan crept forward with lethal grace, menace decorating his features while Thorhild continued to flip the knife, his gaze locked on Branton. He offered a lazy grin that only promised pain. And while Grahame thought Adara calm, she surprised them all by leaning forward on her elbows to spit her own words.

"I have no issue with your little nothing village. I take issue with *you*, Ridley Ward. Your bride was a convenient way to secure revenge."

"Revenge for what?" Ridley shouted, lips curling over teeth.

Yrsa placed a hand on his upper arm, her eyes tracking the men looming behind them. Grahame tried to catch her gaze to communicate with a look that they needed to stand down, to listen.

"You killed my cousin," Adara said, her tone like frost upon the ground. She straightened, a haughty knowing infusing her next words. "I have no dispute with anyone but you. When you overtook the lands outside Guston, you came upon a homestead. A woman tried to defend her land, and you ended her."

Everyone stilled at the pain entrenched in each word.

Grahame wished he could pull Adara to him, to let her cry that pain into him while he held her. Instead, he watched his friends, saw confusion mar Ridley's face, followed by recollection.

"Your cousin..."

"Owned the land butting up against the Shepherds'. She had yellow hair. A smile like sunshine. I received word she tried to stop your men, and you drove a sword through her without remorse. She was the only person I cared for in this world, and you cut her down. Since then, every act of violence I've enacted on your people was to get to *you*. I'd heard rumour of a love so great, you would cast off your own brother, your own people for her."

Ridley paled, his arm tightening around Yrsa's waist.

A sickly feeling swam in Grahame's gut, the fire in the room suddenly too hot. The implication hung heavy between them: Yrsa was the way to harm Ridley. Yet Grahame remembered the day of the raid. How Merthe found him at his home, out of breath, tears streaming down her face, begging for help. That her mother, Emma, had sent her to him for safety. He rode as fast as he could to the village only to find the raiders gone, Yrsa and Emma doused in blood, his nieces cowering in the hall. Murder sang in his blood for the one responsible. Yet he'd tied himself to her all the same.

Grahame drummed his fingers on the table top to lessen the tension coating his limbs. He needed to stand, to run, to break free of the madness of the conversation. But he was trapped. They were all trapped in a prison of their own making.

"I know of whom you speak." Ridley's voice was hollow. "She stabbed one of my men, barely older than a boy, a good man, right through the heart. I didn't hesitate. She met the end of my blade."

A sheen limned Adara's eyes, her lip trembling as he spoke. And though he hated every terrible thing she'd done in the name of her revenge, he couldn't let her soldier on alone. So Grahame covered her hand on the table with his. And, while Ridley's eyes widened at the gesture, Branton's narrowed in a way that promised suffering.

Ridley continued, though the words came slowly, as if he was unearthing a grave.

"I will have you know that your cousin's death changed my path. She was so resolute against our overtaking the land—land which has been in dispute for years and on which she could have likely remained—that she did not yield one inch to me, even in death. I resigned as a knight after that. Took up as Hyrstow's chieftain."

Ridley swallowed, the knot in his throat bobbing over the pain of the memory. Yrsa molded herself to him, her head coming to rest on his shoulder.

"For all that you've done to us, Lady Clayton, I will have you know I regret taking her life. I always have."

A shudder wracked Adara. Slowly, her head turned to Grahame, those grey eyes of hers pinning him to his seat. Anger lived in the slight jut of her chin, the flaring of her nostrils.

"Be that as it may, you slaughtered her at the behest

of your earl. Well, I have been tasked with keeping you in check at the behest of mine."

Branton inched forward in his seat, his mighty shoulders bunching as he leaned forward. "Your men killed a woman in our village. You stole our chieftain's wife. Our friend. That will not pass without consequence."

Grahame felt himself wind tighter. Something about the glint in Branton's eye told him his friend would have no qualms ending Adara. Panic arched through him.

"We are married," Grahame blurted. His voice rang clear and strong through the room. Every set of eyes moved to him.

Branton swore an oath, recognition splaying across the hard lines of his face. "You paid for word on her all this time, eh? Just couldn't let her go, and now look at you."

Beside him, Adara flinched. As if she wanted to question him but knew it was not the time.

"You're married?" Ridley asked.

Grahame told himself the disbelief didn't hurt. That he was more than the scoundrel everyone thought he was. Grahame waved a dismissive hand as Adara had done with Yrsa earlier.

"It's merely a ruse for her father. The Earl of Bernira."

Sir Langley leaned forward at that, scraping a hand over his scruffy chin. He had a straightforward countenance, one that Grahame would have trusted under other circumstances. "Aye, and how is that?"

Adara was steel and polish, ready with an answer. Grahame was surprised when she spoke the truth. "My husband died. My father wishes to marry me off in a northern alliance. The arrangement will give him more land, more men. I wish for no other husband to come and cause turmoil in my life here."

"So you've taken a husband in the hope it will usurp your father's bargain? Daring. And dangerous," Sir Langley mused, thrumming his knuckles on the tabletop as he leaned back in his chair.

Adara's answering grin did not meet her eyes. "Indeed."

Ridley shook his head, his gaze moving to his empty place setting as if it held the answer he sought.

"Why, Grahame? Are you to walk into the bear's cave with your new wife? To what end? Whatever she's made you do, you shall come home with us. We have a host of men. You will be freed. The marriage isn't even legal without a priest or bedding."

Grahame's gaze slipped to Adara's. She was already staring at him, though he couldn't quite read her stoic expression. His heart stuttered with the realization that the time had come. If he was to be her husband, to impress upon Adara's father that their union was real, the test of its truth was now. Grahame leaned forward on one arm, offering a crooked, conspiratorial grin.

"There was a priest. And a bedding."

He turned to Adara as he pulled her hand to his lips. Her silver gaze flared as he pressed a kiss to the delicate skin on the back of her hand before he continued. "The men behind us witnessed the bedding to testify to her father. Oh, and, Rid: Oswald performed the ceremony."

TWENTY-TWO

Adara

"I am exhausted," Adara said, stretching her hands overhead to loosen her tight shoulders. It felt as if they'd been rucked up around her ears for weeks. Heat from the fire blazed, sinking into her muscles, loosening her joints.

"Striking bargains with your enemy will do that to a person," Grahame said as he leaned against the wall, leanly muscled arms crossed.

A shiver worked through Adara at the deep timbre of Grahame's voice. He had followed her into her room after watching his friends travel through the gate, his hand raised in farewell. Sorrow had sown itself into Adara's heart as she'd watched them part, knowing it may be the last time they do so. If she couldn't correctly out-maneuver her father...she suddenly didn't want to think that far ahead.

Adara swallowed around the boulder that lodged in her throat. She had to beat back the slivers of panic that sank into her skin as soon as she'd struck the arrangement with Langley. After Grahame dropped the details of the High Priest of Hyrstow's desertion and an incensed Ridley had calmed, they'd forged a delicate alliance. Hyrstow would not storm Clayton House, and Adara would immediately halt any action of revenge she had for Ridley. The Hyrstow chieftain swore not to encroach on her lands. Begrudgingly, Adara had relayed her plan for Grahame to stand in as a husband. Though the beastly man, Branton, had muttered about it being a death sentence, everyone agreed that they did not want a northern army on their doorstep. Sir Langley had even sworn support from Deircia to fend off the expansion of Bernira if Adara and Grahame's marriage ruse failed.

Adara did not miss the way Ridley, Yrsa, and Branton had all paled when they realized Grahame's life would be forfeit if the plan went awry. She also noticed the jovial manner in which Grahame scoffed at the danger, offering easy, charming platitudes that allowed his friends to move on from their concern. He was a skilled talker, yet Adara couldn't help but wonder if the others noticed the drum of his fingers on the tabletop. Surely, his friends could tell he was putting on a show for their sakes?

The birch in the fire popped and fizzled.

"As if you would know," she said with a scoff, her eyes crossing and uncrossing as they followed the flames. "Have you any enemies?"

She felt rather than saw Grahame come to stand beside her, his arm brushing hers as he shrugged. It would have been better for her to step away, but it was becoming increasingly difficult not to fall into the old patterns of casual touch she and Grahame had once shared. They'd been so thirsty for one another once. As hard as she tried to resist, the habit was dangerously close to solidifying again.

"None that I know of," he said, mirth in his tone. She wondered if there was any truth in it.

For long moments neither spoke, worn out after a long day.

"Though, I am sure I will earn some," Grahame said softly.

He turned to her, his chest brushing her arm before he inched back as if too aware of their proximity. Adara had the urge to grab hold of his wrists and force his arms around her. Any comfort in the face of abandoning her revenge would have been appreciated. She knew it was evil, but her vengeance against Ridley Ward had been one of the things that she'd clung to when life seemed unbearable. Between Elvin's illness and her father's demands, she'd plotted, her mind sharpening with the promise of power.

"You do not gain in this life without conflict," Adara

murmured. It had been an old sentiment of her father's. One she had been told throughout her childhood.

"Gain what, 'Dara?" Grahame asked.

Adara flicked her gaze to his, a question forming between her eyebrows. Grahame's eyes, bright as polished emeralds, scoured her face as if starving. For her. After everything with his friends, he still looked at her as if she were something to covet. A blush worked its way up her neck and bled into her cheeks. She didn't think anyone had looked at her like that, other than him.

"Why, power and influence, of course," she answered, though the words tasted like ash.

Grahame dared to reach out, his finger looping around her ear as if brushing away a strand of hair. His brow furrowed.

"And is that all that matters?" he asked, his tone as entrancing as the midnight sky.

"I...I have been playing games of survival my entire life, Grahame. Yes, when it comes down to it, power and influence are most important. I can only hope giving up my revenge and looking onward will not end in the deaths of everyone I care for." Exasperation curdled her tone.

"What of yourself? You never seem to have concern for yourself."

Adara paired a weak shrug with a little laugh. Unable to look at him any longer, she shifted her gaze to the corner of the room. It was a poor attempt to cover up her newly developed self-loathing. The feeling was like a dress she'd suddenly outgrown, too tight and scratchy. And, despite her resistance to share her thoughts with her husband, Grahame's presence meant he would rather spend his time with her than alone in his quarters. It wore down her resistance.

Resigned, she said, "I am a pawn in the realms of powerful men. Always have been. Since Elvin died, I thought I could grasp a life for myself, yet in doing so, have brought worse down on those I care for. I wished to prove to my father that I could hold the line of our territory. That I did not need another marriage. Yet here I am, scrambling to find solutions to problems I created. I am so, so stupid."

Grahame's head was shaking as she spoke, his fingers grasping her upper arms gently. They were too damn comforting to be real. She took a breath, held it, let it go as she dared look at him again. The devastation written in his features nearly made her collapse.

"'Dara, don't," he whispered, leaning in. "Don't say things like that. I cannot stand to hear you speak so poorly of yourself. Not when I've come to admire you so ardently."

His thumbs worked the muscles in her arms as he spoke. She quirked her head, her gaze catching on his lips, the scruff along his jaw. He carried a slight scar along the underside of his chin, one he'd told her his sister had given him in childhood. There were likely other scars unseen, scars she'd been responsible for. Her middle churned.

"Grahame, you do not have to say such things. You cannot go home with your friends because of me."

She brought her hands up to twist herself out of his grip, but Grahame held fast. His fingers dug into her flesh just enough to let her know he wasn't letting go. Her pulse ratcheted higher.

"I am where I wish to be."

His tone held a severity she'd rarely heard from him. And when he leaned toward her, so close their noses would graze if she closed the hairsbreadth of distance, her senses came alive with the heat and strength and sweetgrass scent of him.

Want, untamed and urgent, was a bolt through her. Adara knew she should resist it. Knew that caving to her desire for him would only break her anew when she set him free.

The thought slammed into her with a fierceness that almost made her recoil.

She *would* set him free. If she could, if he wasn't struck down by her father, Adara would allow Grahame to return to his people. He could come back when needed if her father visited, a continued ruse to benefit them both. As selfish as she was for using him to her advantage, the part of her that would always care for him knew he deserved better. Though it would nearly kill her, she would do right by him.

"Your friend that was here...not Ridley..." She wanted to kiss, wanted to lick that strong column of throat.

"Branton?" Grahame's breath skittered over her mouth.

Adara softened. His friend had told them something Adara had been shocked to hear. Something that fanned the flames of her hope.

"He said you paid for word about me. What did that mean?"

She expected him to recoil. To become sheepish. But Grahame surprised her yet again. He slid his hand to her bottom, gave the flesh a good squeeze as he smiled broadly.

"Aye, I paid for word about you. Even if we were no longer in one another's lives, I had a compulsion to know how you fared. Do not begrudge the person in your household that sent it, for I paid handsomely."

Adara knew she should have been concerned but could not bring herself to care. Her heart beat the excited rhythm of a bird's wings at the thought of Grahame keeping tabs on her.

"I...I do not know what to say," she replied, breathily.

"Say that you will forgive me for leaving you that summer. Say that you have yearned for me as I have for you."

Grahame's other hand skimmed her jawline then dipped into her nape. He lightly tugged the hair at the base of her neck. It felt delicious. She was dangerously close to telling him anything he wanted to hear. A part of her wanted to rejoice, to have no secrets between them. However, her need for survival, for safety, overrode the impulse to give him what he asked for.

"It is late," she stated, though the words felt wooden.

Undeterred, Grahame murmured, "Mmhmm."

Grahame's eyes searched hers, gauging her reaction. There was a moment between held breaths where Adara wished to live forever. Where, in spite of everything, he wanted her for her. And, try as she might, there was no fighting the flame of desire that raged for him. Against Adara's better judgement, her hands fit to the peaks of his shoulders, tugging him down to her mouth.

Grahame's lips ghosted over hers. A whisper. A promise. Adara whimpered. She knew he could pull away at any moment, could take the lust that coated her insides and use it against her. However, the sound seemed to break whatever tether he had on himself.

Grahame's mouth crashed to hers, fast and hard. Adara stalled as his lips molded to hers, stroking, nipping, and, heaven help her, she was hopeless to resist. She kissed him back with every emotion she'd felt since they parted. His hands tightened around her waist, dragging her to him. She could feel every line, every muscle, and she wanted *more*. Damning the consequences, Adara skimmed her hands over his shoulders, up his neck, and buried them in his hair. Without hesitation, he canted his head, slanting his mouth as he ran his tongue over her eager lips. Adara was already opening for him, drinking his breaths like they were an elixir of life. He tasted like the ale from dinner and a slice of the sun, strong and hoppy and hot.

"Grahame," she sighed as he angled his head again.

A groan worked its way through his chest, rumbling into her. "I love when you say my name," he growled, one hand rising to capture her cheek. He slid his tongue into her mouth and made slow love to it before drawing back to speak against her lips. "For years, I thought I'd never hear you say it again. All this time, all the distance between us, what I needed was for you to sigh my name just like that, and I am a new man."

If she'd been of sound mind, she would have truly contemplated his sentiment, but Grahame's hard chest was against hers, and the sheer size of him had her grabbing hold of his face. Beneath her palms, his stubble scratched. She longed to know how it would feel on other parts of her but didn't want to give up kissing him, not yet. Grahame seemed to understand, for he slid a hand to her breast, his palm conforming to the soft mound. When he squeezed, something low in Adara liquified.

Then they were moving, Grahame crowding her toward the bed. His lips scored the corner of her mouth, then her jawbone. He sucked, eliciting a gasp from her at the wicked sensation. Never had she been kissed like that. Never had she wanted a man's hands on her in such a way. A moan slunk from her when he ran his tongue over the spot. All the while, his hand worked her breast, gently squeezing, then finding the pebble of her nipple only to nip at it with the tips of his deft fingers.

"I want to devour you, 'Dara. I want to lick every inch of your sweet skin. I want—no, need—to be inside you, to make you scream my name as you come."

Adara was nodding as he spoke, her hands trailing from his cheeks to his neck to the sinewed muscle of his chest. Madness had surely overtaken her because she tugged at the threads closing the top of his tunic. The need to see him, to feel him without it had overridden all thought.

"This has to...come off," she said, her words a breathy whisper as she tugged at the collar.

Somehow, Grahame's thigh had propped between hers, though the thick, hard muscle did nothing to satisfy the terrible ache that had blossomed in her nether-region.

His hands fell to her hips, practically lifting her onto him while he propped his foot on the bed. When he shoved his leg forward, grinding it between her thighs, a hiss spilled from her mouth.

Adara felt a smile curve his lips before he broke away to say, "I did not lie before. I will not stop until we've both slaked our thirst for one another. So help me, 'Dara, I am all but an animal in your thrall. Tell me now if you do not want this. If you merely want to be married in name only. I will leave. You do not have to bother yourself with me again. For, once I have you, I fear the craving I've always felt will never abate."

Grahame's thumbs dug into her hips as the feel of his thigh beneath hers started a slow madness in her core. Breaths sawed from them both, weaving between the space of his declarations. Leave it to Grahame to say things that twisted her heart. Despite knowing she couldn't keep him, that the game they played could end in disaster, she still wanted him. All of him. For as long as he would have her.

"We are married," she said, her voice not sounding

like her own. High and breathless, as if she were years younger. Yet she fought to keep control. "We might as well enjoy one another while the arrangement lasts. I want your pleasure, Grahame. I want you to make me see stars."

TWENTY-THREE

Adara

Grahame dug his fingers into Adara's sides as if ready to shake her. A ripple in the muscle along Grahame's jaw was all the warning she had before his mouth claimed hers again. Was the declaration of her want not enough? Did men not enjoy when women expressed their desire?

She was not well versed in the language of mutual satisfaction. Nimble fingers rounded the back of her dress to fight with the ties between her shoulders.

Yes, she thought, her entire body sparking with a riot of sensation.

Grahame was everywhere, and yet she wanted more. His mouth took and gave as his tongue slipped through her defenses, swirling, then coaxing. All the while his leg rocked beneath her, the grinding of it a sweet torture against her core.

This. This was what she'd always craved. The connection, the anticipation of Grahame's next move. Hands to his upper arms, she followed a path of sinewy muscle to his rounded shoulders and up over the smooth cords of his neck, as if she could hold him in place forever while he kissed her senseless. His tongue, the use of his teeth against her bottom lip and the way he dove back for more, made her dizzy. Yet she gave back everything she could. Each tangle of his tongue with hers, every push of his thigh, Adara was with him, sliding, rocking herself into him, chasing the teasing sensation that built low within her.

"'Dara, Christ," he muttered as he tipped his head.

Her fingers entrenched themselves into the hair at the base of his neck. There was nothing but Grahame's mouth and teeth and hands.

As if by magic, the material of her dress sagged open. Air caressed her back, the tops of her breasts. Adara's hands flew up to halt the flow of cloth to the floor. She never liked being fully exposed. It made her vulnerable, left her cold. Grahame's lips did not stop moving. Rather, he released her mouth only to score his own down the arch of her throat.

"We shall go slow." He sewed the words into her skin as he pressed a kiss to the upper part of her breastbone.

Adara shook her head. Embarrassment had her turning her face from his. It was coupled with the sharp lance of fear. Though Muretta spoke of mutual enjoyment, Adara's body had only been used. And, teetering on the edge of the contact she so craved, Adara was afraid.

"Give me your eyes, Adara," Grahame commanded, catching her chin between his thumb and forefinger and gently turning her face to his.

A gritty resolve stood in his gaze. His insatiable lips were swollen from kissing, which only made Adara want them on her. Excuses and worries filled her to the brim but did not spill out.

Grahame arched a sandy brow, completely at odds with the smooth caress of his tone as he said, "Where did you go, 'Dara? Tell me whatever it is you are thinking."

She swallowed, her mind a mess while her lower half screamed for his attention. Grahame did not falter. His thumb began drawing slow circles on her hip. The material of her dress, usually soft, began to feel like the scratch of sand, insistent and eager to be removed. She blew out a breath.

"I...I have never wanted to be with a man. I hate to speak of him now, but I never wanted to lay with my husband. Even the times where I acquiesced to his demands, it was only to get the situation over with."

Grahame studied her, tipping his head to the side. A full-blown grin widened his mouth.

"What about that could possibly make you smile?" she demanded, tearing her chin from his grip.

Grahame slid his fingers along her jaw, holding her still. The fact that he kept his grasp loose only bolstered her need for him. He wouldn't trap her, wouldn't force her into anything she did not want.

"It is a good thing I am not he," Grahame said as he bent to skim his lips over hers. The feather-light touch on her swollen skin caused a pulse of need to slam through her. He lifted his head to continue. "I've got you, 'Dara. I won't push, but I won't let up, either. Too much of your desire has been squandered. Today, you learn that you are in command."

Adara's mouth dropped open. Grahame gripped her by her backside and brought her flush with his body. The thick ridge of his desire prodded her, insistent. He still wanted her. In the face of her...lack, he was right there with her. She forced out the words that somehow colored her cheeks red.

"I know what is required of me, yet I may freeze. I may not feel good for you. I...I may be broken. Or unteachable. Or..."

"Nothing about you is broken, 'Dara. Even like this, you please me more than any other woman I have been with. It breaks my heart that you had to endure your first husband. But, enduring isn't something you will do ever again. Anyone else we've lain with is in the past and does not deserve our attention."

The words loosened something inside Adara's chest.

Grahame's white teeth flashed as he said, "I would love nothing more than to teach you, if you wish."

Something dormant inside her blinked awake. His words soothed. A laugh clapped from her. She let the dress slip a little. Grahame's eyes wandered, as if unable to resist a peek.

"Your breasts were smaller when I knew you before. And, indeed, I was trying my best not to be a lecherous bastard last night, though I believe I failed. May I see how they've changed?" he asked.

His finger hooked over the neckline of her dress and brought it to her waist. Her breasts popped free, nipples puckering as the room's warm air skimmed them. The black centers of Grahame's eyes grew.

"They have changed, have they not?" she jested.

Mute, Grahame nodded. As if unable to stop himself, hands moved to cup both breasts. Callouses, rough and delicious, scored her skin as they weighed her flesh. A low moan broke from Grahame.

"I must taste them," he murmured before doing the opposite. Straightening, he withdrew his leg from beneath her, supporting her with a hand around her arm so she'd find balance. With a nod to the bed, he reached for his tunic and ripped it over his head.

Adara claimed her own eyeful of Grahame's naked torso before she obeyed. It was as if he spent his entire life in the sun without a tunic. Shadows settled in the dents between the roped muscles of his middle. It was obscene. And she drank it in.

"I am happy to remain here for you to ogle at," Grahame said, flexing his chest muscles in a one, two motion, "but if you're going to do that, I want your hands on me. Or mine on you. I'm not picky."

Biting her lip against the fluttering in her belly, Adara

released the dress. Grahame watched, rapt, as the cloth slipped down her middle, over her hips and thighs. White teeth dented his bottom lip as a hungry grin spread along his mouth. A shiver coursed through her at the wicked glint in his eye. With a raised brow he toyed with the lip of his trousers, running a hand over his front while stretching the waist wide with the other. Adara practically salivated at the sight.

"Lay down on the bed."

The gravel in his voice made her slick.

With a coy smile she said, "You have watched me unwrap myself. It is only fair that you offer me the same courtesy."

A low chuckle escaped him. "I'd never deny you, Lady."

With a flourish, he shoved his pants and underthings to his ankles. Adara watched with rapt fascination as his manhood bobbed at her. She stared, memorizing the map of veins and ridges presented to her. The crown was nearly purple with need, the tip weeping. Adara gulped. She had seen him in his entirety on their wedding night, however, there hadn't been opportunity to drink him in. Grahame was magnificent. A sculpted piece of art. And yet, the piece of him that protruded at her was...large. She frowned. Elvin had been nowhere near Grahame's girth and length.

"'Dara," he said, his voice full of gravel, "if you look at me like that one moment longer, I will not be responsible for succumbing to my baser instincts."

For less than a heartbeat, she considered daring him

to show her what he meant. But a wariness had bled into his features, as if he were straining hard against himself to remain still. He wanted to treat her right. It made her move to the bed, as requested.

The mattress dented against her weight as Adara threw back the comforter then settled herself among the bountiful pillows. Like an animal after prey, Grahame prowled on all fours toward her. Catching her foot, he kissed her ankle before placing it against the outside of his hip, patting it once as if to tell her not to move it. Then he was sliding between her thighs, layering himself over her so that his arms supported his weight. Eye level with her breasts, he allowed himself a satisfied sigh before dipping his head and clamping his lips over her left nipple. Adara arched off the bed at the wet, hungry sensation of his mouth on her. She gripped his head in both hands, fingers threading themselves into his brassy curls. A deep hum from his mouth vibrated into her chest as he sucked then nipped then swirled his tongue around the bud. A spinning warmth ratcheted inside her.

"Grahame, yes. Teach me how to feel good," she moaned, trying to rub herself against him.

Teeth flashed and pulled, then Adara was bereft as he moved to her other breast, her nipple seared with delectable pain. His hips began to move as if by their own accord, pressing her into the bed. Slick with want, Adara mumbled something incoherent about needing him. Grahame chuckled darkly, glancing up at her with his mouth still on her breast.

"Greedy thing. First lesson: though you are wet for

me, I need you wetter. Trust me," he murmured as he lifted himself to slide a hand between them.

Adara's mouth formed an O of surprise as a finger slid over her slit. It swirled the moisture from her entrance around once, twice, then roved upward, circling the bud at her center. All the while, his mouth didn't stop sucking and pulling and laving at her nipple, causing a riot of pleasure. The warmth climbing within her spread through her middle, her arms and legs, tightening in the way she'd only experienced with her own hand. When Grahame placed the heel of his hand against her bud and rubbed, a gasp of pleasure wrought from her.

"There, now, My Lady. Come for me," he said. He licked from one breast to the other, leaning back slightly to allow for the movement of his hand. The loss of him chilled Adara for just a moment—until the heel of his hand rubbed a second time then was coupled with the insertion of a finger.

"Yes, yes, Grahame. Don't stop," Adara moaned, gripping the bedsheets. Eyes clenched shut, she had to hang on, lest her soul wander away with the pleasure that poured through her.

"That's it, 'Dara. You're doing so well," Grahame coaxed in a tone she'd never heard before. It was wine and smoke and stinging hot. His finger thrust in, then out; his hand's heel grinding propelled her higher into a sensation that nearly made her buckle.

"Grahame, I..." Adara bit her lip against the dive of his hooked finger into a spot that made her see stars. It was sublime and too much all at once. Never had she tasted the riot of this pleasure, and she was suddenly worried she'd only scrape the edge of it, unable to fully enjoy.

"Don't fight it, 'Dara. No matter the time it takes, this is for you," Grahame murmured around her nipple.

Another finger joined the first, stretching her in such a delicious way. And when he curled them? Her doubts shredded, her entire being a vessel. With a final rub to her apex, pleasure howled through her, relentless. It was sharper than she'd ever experienced, unbridled in a way that made her limbs quake.

Kisses dotted her hair, her forehead, her cheekbones as Grahame continued the movements of his fingers until the wash of her trembling subsided.

Slowly, Adara opened her eyes. Grahame was staring. Hunger had stripped his features raw. Though, rather than draw his hand away and thrust into her like she expected, he kept his fingers inside her. Languidly, as if they owned every moment in the world, he twisted, allowing his thumb to circle around the outside of her opening, just above the tender parts. Small waves of comforting pleasure lapped at Adara. All the while, he looked into her eyes as if her coming all over his hand was the answer his soul had been seeking.

She cleared her throat. "Well. Thank you for that."

Grahame's answering smirk made her swoon.

"You're welcome. Now, if you would be so kind, *Lady*, as to kiss me again. Lesson two is about to begin."

TWENTY-FOUR

Adara

The kiss was not simply a kiss. It was sweeps of tongues and nibbles on bottom lips and moans swallowed by one another. Though he'd covered her body with his, Grahame seemed in no hurry to have it over with. Her hands molded to the hard muscle of his back while his fingers flitted from her core to her thighs to her stomach as if he couldn't get enough of touching her. When he dipped his hips closer, the crown of his cock prodding her entrance, Adara was nearly out of her mind with want.

"'Dara," he said against her lips. He ran a finger through the tangled strands of her hair as he moved back enough to look into her eyes. "I don't want to stop. Kissing you...it's everything I've dreamed of."

Her hands came to his face, cradling his cheeks, the scruff that had grown with the day scraping her palms. His arms bracketing her head narrowed her focus to him. Only him.

"I want you inside me, Grahame."

Something flared in his gaze.

"You're sure?" he asked. Gone was his knowing smirk. Even seated at her entrance, he would not push her.

"Please," Adara panted as she slid her hand down the hills and valleys of his middle to where his cock strained for her. A stab of apprehension caught her by the throat as she wrapped a hand around his length. He was endowed. She felt it last night as she stroked him to completion, but having him enter her was something completely different.

Grahame closed his eyes, his face descending into a mask of near-pain. When they opened, gone was any shred of doubt. Adara gulped.

"God, I love to hear you begging for me."

"I..." Adara pursed her lips, unsure. "You're big."

"Why, thank you."

He laughed when she rolled her eyes.

"You're *very* big. And I fear I am not..." she protested, though a grin threatened her mouth.

Grahame bit his lip as he flexed his hips, causing the tip of his cock to prod her entrance.

"Second lesson: you have to be honest with me, 'Dara. Promise."

Adara was nodding before he finished speaking. He'd begun to rotate his hips in a very distracting manner.

"I mean it," he said, pulling his hips away.

Adara slammed her hands to his backside in an attempt to hold him to her.

"I know I am large. And I know it could hurt. So, you have to promise to let me know if it is too painful. I will stop. I swear, if you need me to, I will stop."

Adara's pulse beat inside her temples. There was no way she would stop him. Years had led to this moment. She would be damned if she halted him.

"I will," she lied.

Grahame's smirk grew, as if he smelled the lie in the air. Still, he nodded.

He brought up his hand, spit into his palm then coated his length. Inside a breath, Grahame nudged forward, his thick crown breaching her. A slight burn nagged her entrance but Adara ignored it. A deeper part of her needed to be full.

"More, Grahame. I want all of you," Adara demanded, cupping his face so she could bring her lips to his.

A shudder wracked him as he pulled back slightly then fed more of himself into her. Adara tried to stifle her gasp. The burn of the stretch, the slowness of it... Only a man who was ready to gentle himself for a woman should have had a cock so deliciously thick.

Grahame's lips moved over hers, one hand going to her breast to tweak her nipple as he withdrew then gave another shallow thrust.

"You're so good at this, 'Dara. Try to relax for me," he said against her lips. Then his mouth was moving with hers, his tongue sparring in a way that distracted her enough to have him feed in another inch. Still not fully sheathed, he halted, rearing back on his haunches, his eyes closed. The angle shifted the way he sat inside her, causing her to clench around the solid mast.

"Grahame, you're not all the way—"

"Give me a moment, Adara, please. You are so tight, and I feel as if I am ready to spill inside you already."

His shredded words were wrought with near agony. Messy curls fell over his forehead. His jaw rippled, muscles tight with restraint. Adara had never seen a more beautiful sight. She couldn't help but reach out and trace her fingertips over the V-like indentations that pointed to his manhood. His eyes flew open, flaring with steely determination.

"Bring your hips up," he commanded.

Adara did as told, tilting her hips to offer herself fully. Grahame placed his hands on her knees and spread her thighs. His rough palms on her hot skin made her tremble. She moaned at the change in angle.

"You look divine with my cock in you," he panted, his gaze darkening.

With a roll of his hips he pushed further. The movement hit something inside Adara, bringing forth a shout of pleasure. It seemed to light the fire in Grahame.

"You're mine, Adara," he snarled. Something broke in her at the feral quality in his tone. "Say it," he demanded, entire body taut, "say you're mine."

Adara didn't bother lying. She was ready to be consumed by Grahame. "I am yours, Grahame. I always have been."

A tear slid from her eye as he gave one final thrust, burying himself to the hilt. Fully seated, he fell on top of her, nearly crushing her with his weight. Adara could only clutch his shoulders as his hips undulated, her moans rattling along the room's walls.

He was so *big* and it was so *good*, Adara lost any sense as his thrusts came quicker, the sting of his stretch sharper. The edge between pleasure and pain was a cliff she rode, though Grahame ensured she remained on the right side of it. His mouth scored her neck, kissing and sucking, while her nails dug into the flesh of his back. It was more than she had ever dreamed of.

"Holy Mother, Grahame," she squealed as he bit down on the space where her neck connected with her shoulder. It was too much. The feel of his tongue against her skin, the pressure of him moving inside her, his hands roaming her body as if he couldn't get enough—pleasure came at her from every angle. She was a slave to it.

"Apologies, Lady, but I do not see the Holy Mother in this room." Grahame's smirk pressed along the column of her throat.

Adara buried her hands in his luscious hair, dipping her chin in search of his mouth. She felt his grin first, the shape of triumph along his lips. Then his calloused hand was wandering from her hip to her thigh, wrapping around to bring her leg up, closer to her chest. His tongue moved against hers, rolling and coaxing, the pleasure that was building in Adara threatened to swallow her whole.

"Grahame," she panted, desperate. She didn't recognize her voice. Perhaps Grahame didn't either, or perhaps he was pleased to see her at his mercy because he snapped his hips, shooting him deeper into her.

"*Christ*, 'Dara. You were made for me."

Through slitted eyes, Adara saw his grin fall, concentration etching itself into his brow. With gritted teeth he reared back then buried himself. Her inner walls trembled around him and, as if he knew she felt like a dammed up river, Grahame swirled his thumb around the bud at the apex of her thighs. Adara's entire body convulsed, back bowing, feet bracing on the bed as pleasure rioted through her, and with it, the knowledge that she would never, ever be the same.

"Yes, 'Dara. My 'Dara," he chanted, his movements becoming jerky.

A breath sawed from her as he buried his face in her neck, his release coupled with a desperate groan as he beat her into the mattress. Adara was grateful for it. All of it. Grahame's heavy body on hers, his hot breath against her throat, the sticky feeling that leaked between them. She held his head to her, trailing her fingers through his hair while he came back to himself. They lay entangled with one another for a long while, neither willing to move.

Eventually, Grahame began to twitch. A smile touched her mouth as a memory of him falling asleep next to her in the grass beneath a tree surfaced. He'd twitched then, nearly knocking her in the face with a stray hand.

"Grahame," she said into his hair.

He roused, slipping from her as he brought himself up on all fours and shook his head like a great dog.

"I am sorry. I must have crushed you."

He was dazed and naked and adorable. Adara smiled.

"I enjoyed it. Now, get me the cloth on the table near the water jug. Then come back to bed."

Grahame nodded mutely, as if their lovemaking had struck all the jovial words from his head. Lumbering to the side table, he grabbed the cloth as instructed and shuffled back to the bed. A laugh broke from Adara.

"What?" he asked, his voice gravelly.

"You're like a great, stupefied animal," she chided, rising on her elbow, the other hand out to accept the cloth. Within a moment she cleaned herself. Grahame watched, some of the fire in his gaze returning.

"I should like to see you with your hands on yourself sometime."

Adara sputtered a laugh.

"Grahame," she started as he knelt on the bed, aligning his body beside hers. He propped his head on his hand, chest to her side.

"What? I want all of it with you, 'Dara. That shouldn't be a surprise. I haven't been silent about my intentions." He shrugged a great shoulder as if their future had been predestined. "I want you in every way, Adara. As intimate as a man and woman can be."

The words tugged at something she didn't want to examine. He wanted her. That was all. That was fine. She was happy to take what he gave, for as long as he gave it. So, despite the hurt that stabbed through her at the thought of setting him free after everything was over, Adara cupped his face, bringing him down for one more kiss.

"And you shall have me in any way you desire, Husband. As long as we are together, we can delight in everything we've missed."

Grahame's tongue met with hers, and he covered her body with his once again.

TWENTY-FIVE

Grahame

The bed was empty when he awoke. Grahame tried to ignore the hurt that rubbed at him like a wet garment. Adara was her own woman. Had been for years. And he wasn't her keeper. It's what he told himself as he dressed in his discarded clothes, as he relieved himself in the chamber pot. The fire had burnt down to ash. He hurried out of the room, wondering after the time.

"Oy!" Thorhild exclaimed as Grahame nearly knocked him over as he strode into the hall. "Watch your feet!"

Grahame glowered, annoyed. "Why don't you?"

Thor scowled, but his attention was on the leather

strap connected to the shoulder piece of the breastplate he wore. A sword lay in wait in his belt. Grahame tensed.

"Are we under attack?"

Thor issued him a flat look then continued onward, albeit slowly, as he fiddled with threading the strap through its clasp. "Just from the lady of the house."

"What does that mean?" Grahame demanded. He ran a hand through the mess of his hair. Hunger gnawed at his insides and with it, an impatience that could rival a bear's.

Thor halted at the entry to the great room, his chin twisted to his shoulder as he tried to eye where the leather connected. Grahame rolled his eyes and took hold of the material, threading it and tightening so the armor fit around the man's bulky muscle.

"My thanks," Thor said, his countenance lightening. "She's out by the stable. Wanted a few opponents to skewer. Grab a bun from the table and follow me. I can take you to her."

"Opponents?" Grahame asked, after obeying the recommendation of food.

Thor grinned, his teeth flashing as he opened the front door and walked out. Sun poured down from the east; it appeared to be nearly mid-morn. Grahame stuffed the bun in his mouth, savoring the buttery glaze on top.

"Aye, she means to ravage us today," Thor said, then, as if realizing Grahame wasn't a friend, amended, "I mean, my lady wished to shape up her combat skills in the wake of our unwanted visitors. Hagan is putting her through it right now. I thought I'd don my armor so she doesn't stab me."

Grahame's hackles rose. Hagan putting Adara "through" anything had him clenching his fists. Though, as they rounded the right side of the house to the rear of the yard, Grahame saw Thor's meaning. In loose pants and a fitted tunic, Adara whirled, a short sword in hand. Hagan bared down on her with his shield, a grimace etched across his mouth. In a terrifying heartbeat, he slammed the thick wood against her weapon and brought his own short sword beneath her guard.

"No!" The shout left Grahame's lips before he thought to utter it.

Hagan paused mid-strike, his head jerking in Grahame's direction. The distraction cost him. Her features twisted in a scowl, Adara kicked his arm, sending his sword flying. He yelped, his focus finding her too late. She swung low, bringing the flat of her sword against his thigh. If the blade had been turned, he would have bled out.

"Nicely done, My Lady!" Thor shouted, hurrying forward.

Adara's furious gaze whipped to them. She stabbed her weapon into the soft ground.

"You dare protest when I am training? Is danger of no consequence to you?"

Adara's hair had been woven into a crown around her head. The style showcased the ripeness of her cheekbones, the austere set of her mouth. Grahame couldn't take his eyes off her if he tried. In the stable to their right, the horses snorted, Adara's raised voice causing them to paw at the ground. Hagan recovered quickly, stalking up to flank his lady.

"He was going to..." Grahame began to protest.

"Hurt me? Are you so simple as to think my trusted man would harm me?"

Grahame raised both hands in front of him. "I...I apologize, Lady, for I do not know what I thought. I reacted when I saw you in the path of a weapon. Forgive me."

Thor laughed, long and loud, a hand to his metal covered middle. The infuriating man strolled over to the others, covering Adara's other side.

"You thought Hagan was fighting her?"

The scoff broke up the look of murder on Hagan's features. He pushed Thor by the shoulder, a crooked grin winding up one side of his mouth. "Aye, she's safe with me, My Lord," the gruff man said.

Grahame blinked. He had the urge to glance behind himself to see to whom Hagan spoke but forced himself to refrain.

"Ah, yes! My Lord wished to seek his wife this morn and ran into me in the hall," Thor crowed.

Grahame ran a hand over the back of his neck to relieve the heat that climbed from his chest to his cheeks. The new marriage made him their lord, despite their mocking tone. A glance back to Adara had the tightness in his chest loosening. Her gaze had softened, her mouth curving with the slightest smile.

"You are forgiven, *My Lord*," she said, joining in on the teasing.

Grahame wasn't bothered when she did it.

"Would you care to watch? I train with Hagan five days a week to keep up my combat skills."

"Combat skills?" Grahame echoed. He shifted to his heels, crossing his arms over his chest. Would this woman ever stop surprising him?

"Why, of course. I need to be able to defend myself. I am no weak thing ready to wilt."

Grahame swallowed around the dryness in his throat. Adara was many things, but weak wasn't one.

"I would like to watch," he said.

Adara's gaze dipped to where the material of his tunic stretched beneath his forearms. He made his chest muscles dance, just to get a rise out of her. It worked. Adara's eyes widened then shot to his. Grahame smirked. As if annoyed by his antics, she shook her head and turned back to where she and Hagan had been sparring.

The big man shot him a glare before stating, "No interruptions."

Grahame nodded, crossing to the straw overhang of the stable. He veered away from the giant black horse that whinnied at him as if he were a meal, and leaned against the door of a stall that held a grey mare. It sniffed at his back but didn't try to nibble his clothing. The pungent, sweet sweat smell of the building reminded him of his sheep.

Over the course of the morning, Grahame watched Adara take her turns with Hagan, then Thor, then both at once. He had to fist his hands beneath his armpits when the swords slid too close to Adara than was comfortable, but he was able to stop from shouting at the men. Mostly, though, watching them spar was akin to a dance. Steel clashed on wood, bodies were shoved, Adara whirled as if she'd been born with a blade in hand. It heartened Grahame to see her prowess. She'd be no lamb to slaughter if the need arose.

Finally, they leaned their swords against the stable. Adara retrieved a set of small daggers from a cloth roll. A nearby stump had target rings etched into its side along with a multitude of scars. She proceeded to throw them at various targets, each finding their mark with deadly accuracy.

"When did you learn that?" Grahame asked, astounded.

Adara's answering grin was smug. She pinched a dagger between her thumb and forefinger then let it fly at the stump. It embedded a hairsbreadth from another dagger that claimed the centermost spot in the ring.

"After I was married. Hagan taught me."

When the sun was at its highest, Adara declared it time for a meal, to which Thor heartily agreed. Sweat coated his brow as he stomped up to the main door. Hagan, on the other hand, continued to lecture Adara over the position of her wrist during her last throw. Adara listened, her features schooled in concentration. When she snuck a look at Grahame, his heart beat faster.

"Aye, I can tell it's time to finish," Hagan muttered loud enough for Grahame to hear. "He is a distraction you cannot afford, my lady."

Grahame offered a mocking salute as Hagan left. The gesture caused Adara's mouth to tilt upward.

"You'll have to forgive him. He is always like this," she said as she walked to him.

There was a feline grace in the way she moved, even after a morning of slinging weapons around.

Grahame straightened from where he leaned, rolling his shoulders. "Aye, I've gathered he's miserable. Though I am pleased he takes the time to do this with you."

Raven-colored eyebrows rose. "Why, did you think I was a helpless damsel? Of course he takes the time. It is his job to ensure my safety."

Adara's teasing tone did nothing to temper the curiosity that Grahame wrestled with.

She must have seen it in him because she placed her hands on her hips and said, "Out with it."

Grahame scraped a hand through his hair then scratched the back of his neck. "Does he ensure your safety? Or is his loyalty to your father?"

Adara had the gall to tip her head back and laugh. It rang beneath the overhang, grabbing the attention of the horses. The sound did something to Grahame's lower half as well.

"I was wondering when this would happen."

"This?" Grahame couldn't help himself any longer. He placed a proprietary hand on the curve of her waist.

Adara smirked, the sly fox. "Your jealousy over Hagan."

"I am not jealous."

She placed a finger in the center of his chest then drew a circle, all the while batting her long, dark lashes at him.

"Hagan and I have a relationship that has nothing to do with you—"

"Relationship?" Grahame cut in.

He tightened his grip on her waist, the thick fabric of her tunic blocking his hand from the silk of her skin. His vision went hazy for a moment as he pictured his 'Dara splayed out under the brawny man. How they could have kept one another company for years while she was married. His mind hooked on the last thought.

Married.

Christ.

From what he knew of her, Adara wouldn't have bothered to entertain relations with other men. Hagan was her guard. Someone close to her age. A confidant. For all his care, Hagan looked at Adara with affection, though not in the same manner he looked at Muretta. As if he hungered for her.

Grahame flushed with embarrassment.

"Indeed, Husband. My relationship with my *guard* has grown over time. And though he was assigned by my father, I trust him implicitly."

Grahame was already nodding, his features collapsing into chagrin. "Forgive me, lady. I appear to be so besotted by our time together last night that I am a little tender about who you give your attention to."

Surprise colored Adara's cheeks at the admission. Her teasing veneer slipped away as her finger stilled from tracing patterns on his chest. A vulnerability lay in her eyes that Grahame hadn't seen before.

"Do you remember when your aunt found out you were slipping away from Cecilia? She made you clean the chamber pot and wash clothes and sweep and scrub the floor?" he asked.

Adara nodded, her fingers tightening slightly in Grahame's tunic. He relished the feel of her nails against him.

"Yes, but I managed it all and still snuck away. I couldn't be kept from you."

A smile split Grahame's mouth. The admission, years later, was like a precious gem he wanted to hoard inside his heart. He leaned to her, cupping her cheek. Her skin was too smooth, too tempting. He'd never met anyone with skin like hers.

"Aye, I no longer wish to be kept from you. Please wake me next time you go to train. We have lost too much time already. You invade my thoughts, Wife."

Grahame dipped his lips to Adara's. He did not bother with chaste or sweet. They were past the point of decorum. He plied her mouth with his thoroughly, daring her to rebuke his spike of jealousy.

True to form, Adara did not back down. She took his mouth and tongue and teeth. Her hands wound their way around his shoulders, twin snakes that he wished could anchor them together. When he dipped to rub his hardness between her legs, they parted. Gasps lived upon their lips like sullied prayers. And, though gruff, Grahame's last word felt like a heady promise. One that burned brightly in the wake of a storm.

TWENTY-SIX

Adara

"You must come across as strong, yet defer to me in areas of rule. He will notice, of course, but I have hope that he will recognize my input as simply helping to guide you in your new role."

Adara paced at the end of the dining table, her hands splaying as she spoke more to herself than the rest of them. Muretta was throwing small, rolled bits of bread into Thor's awaiting mouth across the table. She mostly missed her target, though Thor did his best to slide across the bench, angling his head to catch her offerings. Hagan stood against the hearth, arms crossed, staring at them, barely paying attention to Adara's instruction. She told herself it didn't matter. It was Grahame she aimed her words at. Grahame, who straddled the bench, his well built thighs cradling the wood, his left arm propped on the table. His upper arm bulged an obscene amount as he cradled his chin in his hand, his gaze fixed on her. It was the same arm she'd used as a pillow the night previous, after they'd sated themselves. Twice. As if he knew where her thoughts had gone, Grahame flexed that arm muscle, a devilish grin smearing his lips.

"You were saying, My Lady?" he prodded, stretching his arms overhead then scratching the back of his neck, ensuring his muscles popped in a comely manner.

Damn him. He knew exactly what he was doing.

"Will you stop it?"

"Stop what?"

He winked. The bastard.

"All of it! The flexing! Muretta! Thor!" Adara snapped, turning her irritation to the others.

Thor sat up straight while Muretta was mid-throw. The piece of bread bounced off Thor's nose. Muretta slapped a hand over her mouth to cover a giggle. Adara sighed, her shoulders deflating. It had been five days since the Hyrstow people had left. Five days of her practicing with Hagan in the yard, five days of preparing for travel, five days of Grahame wringing pleasure from her whenever he could. If he worried over staying with her rather than returning home, he did not show it.

Only Hagan knew of her father's shrewd gaze, his willingness to pick apart a person with words to back them into a corner. No one else had seen how ruthless Earl Eadric of Bernira could be. Adara turned to Hagan, lifting her hands in a helpless gesture. With a hefty breath, Hagan pushed himself from the wall.

"We leave in six days. None of this will be tolerated where we're going. My Lord, you will do well to listen."

Grahame snorted at the implication that he wasn't listening while Muretta slapped her hands on the table, shoving herself to standing.

She offered a bright smile as she announced, "I shall come with you!"

"No you shall not," Hagan snapped, going utterly still. The fire blazed behind him, giving him an eerie, beastly presence.

"I will be an asset!" Muretta insisted. She crossed to the opposite end of the table from Adara, her steps light.

Hagan's jaw clenched so hard Adara thought he might crack a tooth. Adara pinched the bridge of her nose between her forefinger and thumb.

"You are not coming,"Adara stated, her tone flat, "I have told you how dangerous my father and his men are."

Muretta just pressed her hands to her dress. "I am excellent at reading a room. At sneaking about."

"Sneaking around will only put you in danger with Eadric's men," Hagan snarled.

Adara's shoulders sagged. Dragging a hand over her face, she said, "I thank both of you for your willingness to help. Muretta, though I appreciate your offer, I do not want to risk you. My father may...enjoy your presence and wish to keep you. And I would have no authority to demand he release you."

Hagan's face paled, while Muretta gave a shimmy of her shoulders as if to shake off Adara's words.

"I was saying—" Adara was silenced by something bouncing off her nose. She shook her head, shock dropping her jaw.

The softness, the scent; someone had tossed a piece of bread at her. That someone straddled a bench to her left, his lips pressed together in an attempt to cage the laugh that clearly wanted to escape.

"Grahame," she said, piercing him with a glare as her hands found her hips.

"Adara," he retorted, that damned handsome smile climbing his mouth.

A small screech left her as she rolled to the balls of her feet and dropped back down. "This is important."

He swung a leg over the bench, bringing himself to his full height. Green eyes were pinned on hers but his wide smile didn't falter. There was an ease to the manner of his movements that Adara envied. She felt as if her insides were a coiled rope pulling tighter and tighter. How could he be so relaxed in the face of their treacherous plans?

"I know," he answered. The toes of his boots touched hers first. Then his hands came up to cup her face. "I know it is, 'Dara," he soothed, his voice deepening in a way that made her want to stretch like a cat. "There is only so much we can prepare. And while I appreciate your warnings, there is not much to be done until we are face to face with the earl. By his temper and mercy will our plans work."

Adara didn't miss the use of the word "our" rather than "your." A small part of her softened. She opened her mouth to respond but Grahame brushed a thumb across her lips, silencing her.

"Allow us to have these nights without worry. Let us act like fools to entertain ourselves. After all, what are we fighting for if not the hope of more nights like these?"

"Here, here!" Thor thundered behind them. The sound of a long drink was followed by a smack of a mug of ale on the table.

Muretta murmured something to Hagan that Adara didn't quite catch. All of it was lost to Adara as Grahame's gaze fell to her mouth. The tips of his fingers flexed against the nape of her neck then relaxed, as if he could absorb the tension that rested there. As much as visiting her father pulled at her mind, the way Grahame surrounded her was entirely too distracting. She let her head fall back into his hands, her eyes becoming slits as her mouth parted. Her hands were vines climbing the wall of his chest, smoothing over the dips and swells of hard muscle. She arched her brow.

Grahame didn't need to be told. His smile widened, eyes twinkling with satisfaction. He dropped his mouth to hers, dashing her worry with a kiss that wound its way into her soul.

Grahame

THE GRITTY FEELING of sleep lived in the corners of Grahame's eyes. He clenched them against Adara's shifting body. Her skin was soft against the proprietary arm he'd thrown around her waist during the night.

"It is morning. I must rise," she whispered.

Grahame cracked an eye open. He loosened his grip on her enough for her to roll to her front, stacking her hands on one another, her chin crowning them. Raven strands coated her shoulders, his chest, the pillows. Hair tickled his chin. With his free hand he tucked it away so he could move without pulling it.

"No," he chastised, leaning forward to kiss her shoulder.

A rooster interrupted from somewhere outside. Adara scoffed, her eyes dancing.

He couldn't help but draw her side closer to his front as he spoke, "We should do nothing today but indulge in one another."

He'd awoken hard and took the opportunity to press his length into her hip. They'd had years apart. It was time to learn one another, to bask in their marriage. Grahame knew it made him a sap, but he didn't care.

A black eyebrow rose as she rolled to her side so they faced one another. Still, he kept an arm locked about her waist like a manacle.

"Narrowly escaping a battle with Hyrstow is the very reason I am needed. Tenants will have questions. I should have done it as soon as your people left. Travel into Guston is needed to mollify those who will take issue with Hyrstow men tromping back and forth."

Grahame ground his cock against her mound, dropping a kiss on her nose as she spoke. Adara ignored him, though her hand travelled up his arm causing his skin to light up. He was thirsty for her.

"Can that not wait another day?" he asked, capturing her lips with his.

Adara didn't respond. Instead, her mouth answered his in kind, her hand rounding his shoulder to secure itself around his neck. He took the opportunity to skim his fingers over the swell of her ample hip then roamed to the juncture of her thighs, to the heaven he knew was waiting there.

"Grahame," she breathed, though her tone was pleased. Her eyes fluttered closed as he slid a finger through her soft folds and dipped it into her slick center.

"Yes, Wife?" He infused innocence into his tone.

Those grey eyes flashed open again, pinning him to the bed. Something uncertain lived in them. Her hand left his neck to tuck up against his chest. To enjoy the feeling of him or push him away, he wasn't sure.

"You keep doing that," she said.

He held her gaze as his finger circled her tight bud, then dipped to her entrance, plunging in agonizingly slow. Adara's hips jerked in response, wetness slicking his finger.

"My Lady, I have many ideas on how you and I should spend our morning." The grin that split Grahame's mouth nearly hurt. His thumb joined his finger, lazily drawing over her as he withdrew then pushed into her again. Adara's gasp was music to his ears. "However, afterward I suggest we exchange discourse."

Adara smacked his shoulder on a moan, a smile gracing her face at his lofty tone.

"I simply mean that I would like to know you, 'Dara. It's been ages since we just talked. I used to know you loved to watch the clouds form in the sky. I knew you hated goat cheese and loved the color brown, for some reason."

"It is an underrated color," she protested, though her eyes rolled back in her head as his finger curved inside her.

He dropped a kiss to her slanting jaw, the hollow skin beneath the bone. He spoke against her throat, unwilling to part from that tantalizing stretch of flesh.

"Tell me, if I weren't here and there was no battle to deflect or revenge to plan, what would you do with your days?"

Adara's hips arched off the bed. Her hand found his shoulder and squeezed. He relished it. Short, breathy pants escaped her as he curled his fingers in a come hither motion over and over, gliding his thumb along the hard point at her juncture. The rosy flush of her cheeks, the twitch of her thighs together as if she meant to protect herself and couldn't—Grahame was awestruck. Greedily, he watched as he brought her to the brink then smothered her mouth with a kiss as she tipped over. Her moan raked through him, stroking the flame of his own need. His cock was weeping by the time he pulled back.

"If I weren't otherwise occupied, what would I do?"

Adara asked as he flipped to his back then gripped her about the hips, hauling her overtop of him.

With one hand she gripped his cock, arching a delicate brow as she ran the tip of him across her center. Grahame's mind went blank.

Heat. Silky, wet, heat caused him to jolt upward, his body raging for release. Adara lifted herself just out of reach, hovering over him. A wicked grin sliced her mouth.

"I suppose I would have a leisurely breakfast with Muretta, read through some correspondence, go for a walk to the copse of trees and sit for a while. I like to look at more than clouds, you know. Flowers and animals are just as fascinating."

The heartbreaking simplicity of the enjoyment only half registered with Grahame as she slid him though her folds again, this time pausing a moment to glide over the crown of him. Just when he thought she would slide all the way, she popped back off. A loud curse sprang from his lips. But then she was running her core up and down the length of him, her little pants starting back up. He wasn't ready to surrender to the instinct that screamed at him to shove inside her like a madman. Adara was *talking* to him.

"Then what?" he ground out, fixing his hands on her thighs.

His fingertips dented her flesh in such a satisfactory manner, Grahame was tempted to grab her roughly everywhere to see how her soft skin looked with his claim on it.

"I would take Ulrich for a ride, with Hagan, since he would follow me anyway, and we would start slow at first, then I'd spur ahead. And since he's pigheaded, he would race me, nearly making me lose but then pull back at the end since I'm his lady, and he always lets me win."

Adara dragged herself off the tip of his cock, her legs shaking. Grahame was entranced by the pink spread of her being split by him. Jolts of pleasure wracked him, holding him hostage against the urge to dominate her. He reminded himself she needed this; needed to know she was in control.

Perhaps he did, too. With his other lovers, he'd taken the required time to please them, then raced to the finish. It made him a rogue, but he had no desire to mislead them with the promise of intimacy. Fortunately, they knew what he was about.

"Of course he does," Grahame huffed, grabbing the hand she braced on one of her legs and entwining their fingers. The way her lips parted in surprise made something in his chest cave a little.

"Would you seek out a lover later? Someone to have fun with?"

Adara shook her head, sliding along the ridge of him once. Grahame had to bite an oath in half at the way his cock strained for her. She must have seen it in the tendons that jumped from his neck, the tension in his shoulders as he held himself back. Blessedly, she brought him to her entrance again, her gaze unfocused as she looked between them, eyes wide. Pride roared in Grahame's chest. Not one to back down from a challenge, Adara sank herself onto him, inch by agonizing inch as she continued, albeit voice higher.

"No lovers. I enjoy the company of those at my table and have found no need for a man to satisfy me."

Grahame bucked his hips up at that. Adara lost her hold, her hands going to his chest as she sank all the way onto him. She was like a goddamn vice. Grahame began to think of his sheep. The sweet, shitty scent of them to stave off the pleasure that threatened to crush him.

"However," Adara amended, voice reedy, as she slid upward then down, "I am answering this as if you and I were not married, if I were living a day to myself without obligation."

Grahame's hands flexed on the fleshy part of her hips that he so desperately enjoyed grabbing handfuls of.

"Am I merely an obligation?" he rasped. A curl had fallen over his forehead as he arched his neck back trying to remain still. It hung in his eye but he wasn't letting her go to move it.

Adara's breasts hung heavy, her nipples pointed.

"No," she whispered, meeting his gaze.

Then she began to move, leaning back and rolling her hips to reach the spot he'd hit in her earlier. Grahame was lost to her movement, her scent, her hair falling around them. Adara's fingers squeezed and pulled while her legs pumped. They chased their release the same way she'd spoken of racing horses, each outpacing the other than drawing back, hearts hammering.

"'Dara," he groaned, pulling her toward him.

She fell onto him, forking her hands into his hair as

her mouth met with his. Their tongues crashed together, sighs and moans meshing. When Adara's rhythm became erratic, Grahame snaked a hand between them, swiping her center. Then...there wasn't a word for the sensation of her muscles clenching around his cock other than rapture. Her moan was loud as it rolled into his mouth. Unable to stop himself, Grahame thrust up into her, not breaking the kiss, until he was spilling inside her, his body jerking helplessly.

As she sagged on top of him, Grahame allowed himself a small smile. Adara must have felt it against the crown of her head for she nuzzled into his chest and asked why he was grinning like an idiot.

"I've spent my life waiting, 'Dara. I used to retrace the trails we wandered. I would wonder if you were happy or had children. Sometimes, when I was a little drunk or especially melancholy, I would look to the sky and wonder if you were looking at those very same stars, thinking of me."

Adara's lips pressed against the muscle of his chest, overtop his heart.

"I was, Grahame."

Any further words were caught in the swell of Grahame's throat. He pressed a kiss to Adara's head, his hand drawing through her hair.

They lay entwined for the rest of the morning, sharing small hopes and rediscovering old memories. And, for the first time since he was a youth, Grahame felt a sense of contentment grow in him. He resolved to never let it go.

CHAPTER
TWENTY-SEVEN

Grahame

The rat in the cellar should have been a sign. Cook, stalwart and sure, smacked the little beast over the head with a pot and continued as if Adara's face hadn't gone white upon seeing it. She handed the thing up to Adara, offering the warm little body rather than the dried meat she'd gone into the cellar for. At the sight of blood dripping from the creature's mouth, the tinge of Adara's cheeks went slightly green. Grahame swooped an arm over her shoulder, grabbing the thing by the tail to take it outside.

Adara could handle anything life threw at her except, perhaps, dead vermin. When Grahame returned through the back door from pitching it in the refuse hole, Cook was bundling the food she was to send with them on their trip to Guston. By then, Adara's pallor seemed better.

"I wish you a good journey," the sturdy woman said.

She passed the food to Grahame, who gave a wink in return. The older woman's cheeks turned the color of roses. Adara, ready to leave, bid Cook thanks and good-bye. They were to travel to Guston, spend the night, then be back in time to pack the horses and wagons for the long journey to her father's keep in three days. Thor and Hagan were already by the stable, waiting.

Grahame didn't bother wiping the self-satisfied smirk from his face when he and his wife approached the other men. He'd taken his time with Adara that morning, wringing breathless moans from her as precious as gold. Indeed, their joining might have held up the procession but Grahame didn't care. If he was to be threatened by her father and possibly dead within hours of meeting the man, Grahame was going to drink life in by the gallon while he still had the chance.

"What took so long?" Thor had the audacity to whine. He leaned against his horse's shoulder, picking at his nails with a small knife.

Hagan reached over the saddle and cuffed the man up the back of his head.

His horse nickered but didn't move as Thor said, "Ow."

"Mind your business," Hagan stated. He crossed in front of the great black horse Grahame now knew was Adara's mount, Ulrich, ready to assist Adara into the saddle. Grahame made sure to grab her about the waist and plant his lips on hers before she swung up without assistance. Grahame tied the bundle of food to his own steed before mounting. The sun dipped out from behind a cloud but another scurried in front of it. Though the air was cool, Grahame was excited to exit the gates of Clayton House for the first time since he'd entered.

Apprehension did not climb his spine until they were closer to Guston. Nestled between a stretch of grassland and a sprawling farm that boasted goats, horses and cows, the village was planted before a slim forest to the east. Sheep bleated in the distance, a mockery of Grahame's previous calling. Briefly, he wondered how his father was doing with the sheep, if Neil was helping, if they had gone to market in Eoforwic like the time of year demanded.

"You appear pensive,"Adara said, from his right.

On the journey, she'd pointed out places of note, sections of forest she liked to explore, and held an attentive ear for any of his questions. He did not have many. Grahame was struck by his luck to be riding with the woman who had commanded his thoughts for years.

"I only wish to absorb as much information as I can regarding your lands," he replied. His formal tone was something he worked on all the way to Guston. Grahame had never needed formality. He'd been bred into hard work and later, some comfort, but nothing more than shepherding had ever been expected of him.

Adara seemed to notice the stiffness with which he spoke.

"Are you displeased with our journey?"

"No."

She nodded, though she did not press. There was no time, anyway. Hagan plodded past the first wood-planked hut, its thatched roof so like those in Hyrstow. Something in Grahame's chest tightened. They travelled through and around a tangle of huts and animal pens. Mens' heads tilted up from their labor while women with children around their ankles halted to observe their procession. Adara wore a permanent smile as she lifted a hand in greeting which was heartily reciprocated.

Eventually, the latticework of huts gave way to several larger buildings that butted against the village square. A wisp of smoke curled from the great hall's chimney. As their party came to a halt, a man exited a well-built structure to the south. He lifted his hand in greeting, a smile on his broad face. Grahame's grip tightened on the reins. Any of the men in the village could have been related to the ones that attacked Emma and Yrsa.

Her pretty smile intact, Adara swung down from her horse and crossed to the stout, bulky man that held his arms out at his sides. Without hesitation she entered his embrace. Grahame, Hagan, and Thor dismounted, though Grahame was the only one to step closer to his wife.

"I was not expecting to see you until the leaves turned," the man said with a chuckle.

The sound churned Grahame's middle. Was he one of those who had stormed through Hyrstow's market? Adara stepped away from the man, her gaze finding him.

"I have someone I'd like you to meet," she said in a loud, clear voice. Several people had trickled into the square, their eyes on the greeting. "My new husband and now Lord of Clayton House, Grahame Shepherd of Hyrstow."

The announcement rippled through those assembled, their murmurs like wildfire catching on a breeze. Grahame didn't miss the turning heads, the eyes skewering him to the ground. Heat rose up his neck.

Adara simply canted her head as if she hadn't just announced the presence of an enemy. Her smooth smile in place, she reached for Grahame's hand, pulling him to her side. He threaded his fingers through hers as he notched his chin higher.

"Hyrstow?" the sturdy man asked. He wore a leather patch over one eye but his other, a muddy brown, narrowed in Grahame's direction. "It sounds as if you come with a story, My Lady. Please, come inside. Sup with us and tell the tale of this new partnership."

Grahame blew out a steady breath from his nose as they went into what was the village tavern. It was like rot in his belly to eat at an establishment where any of the patrons could have sacked Hyrstow. Yet he was surprised that those in the tavern greeted Adara with smiles and hand shakes.

The man with the eye patch was introduced as Uhtread, the owner. He settled them at the centermost table where Adara told the glorified version of her marriage to Grahame: that they met years ago, how he'd grown in prosperity well enough to court her, and how, despite their opposing earldoms, an allegiance would be beneficial to all. Uhtread listened intently, rubbing his scruffy chin, then disappeared down the short hall past the bar top to prepare their meal.

A stream of men and women came through the tavern. Adara nodded along with the men who complained of their crops, their families, and their taxes. Grahame tried his best to hold a smile while Adara remained focused on whomever she spoke to, however he was faintly aware that he was failing. Regardless, Adara soothed those who expressed hardship whether due to a poor crop, the loss of a family member, or the implementation of her father's new tax. It was a surprise they revealed so much to the earl's daughter, yet Grahame appreciated the loyalty these men seemed to have for her.

Food came, a hearty slab of meat and bread, along with a side of buttered carrots. As they ate, people continued to see her; one thanked her for sending a healer to their child, another praised her reduction of their tax rate when their crop did poorly the previous fall. How much she actually collected was not discussed; however, Grahame wondered what amount Adara paid to cover what her tenants could not. Surely, she would dwindle her coffers if she did so for any length of time. Only as darkness crept around the door did Grahame realize how late it had gotten.

"There is a room available at the back," Hagan advised, arriving at the table after paying.

Adara nodded, catching Uhtread's eye on the other

side of the room. The man inclined his head as he cleaned a mug.

"Finally," Grahame murmured, leaning close so only Adara would hear. He was starved for a morsel of her attention, which she had so freely given to everyone else.

Adara grinned before hollering a thank you to the barkeep and striding to the rear of the tavern, which served as an inn. Grahame followed her, his head churning. The day had been a reminder of his wife's schemes. He did not have the mind for politics, though that did not mean Adara wasn't making plans.

Behind a heavy brown curtain was a short hall that branched off into four rooms. Two doors lay open, one of which Adara claimed. Grahame noted the two small cots on either side and the wash basin on a stool in between. Three candles flickered beside the basin, the only light in the cramped room. The faint scent of onions and ale clogged the space, but Grahame wasn't one to complain. A roof overhead was more than welcome.

"Rest," Adara said, absently gesturing with a slender hand toward one of the beds. She worried her thumb nail as she stared at the closed wooden door of their room. Grahame slid his arms around Adara's middle. He drew the first loose breath of the day, his nose full of Adara's rose petal scent.

"I did not expect you to hold such a court here," he murmured, tightening his hold.

Her breasts were shelved by his forearms, soft and full. A snicker drifted from her lips as she curled her hands over his.

"It surprised you that I listen and speak to my people."

A statement but not a reprimand.

Grahame placed a kiss on the top of her head before pulling away to say, "The Adara I now know is a Lady. The ruler of Clayton House, where everyone is at her beck and call."

He hesitated, his tongue tasting words he was not sure how to say. The visit had shown him another side of her. A tender, kind side. Yet it reminded him that he had no knowledge of anything other than what she deemed to tell him. That, despite the deep affection and desire he felt for her, he still could not fully trust her.

"And? What else?" Adara asked, turning her face to the side so she could look up at him with one eye.

She was softer in the dim light, her features cloaked in shadow. It felt as if they were in a bubble, no one alive but them. Grahame swallowed around the knot in his throat.

"She's a raider, a fierce fighter, a strategic planner."

Adara's fingers on his arm twitched. She did not smile.

"Say what you wish, Husband. Though you've chosen flattering words, the tone in which you wield them suggests you do not think those traits admirable."

CHAPTER

TWENTY-EIGHT

Grahame

Grahame clenched his eyes shut before opening them. He was a traitor to his own people, having sat and ate among those who had terrorized his village. His affection for Adara compelled him to do things he'd never imagined. He was like a piece of cloth being torn in two.

"You've harmed my people. Those I love. It is difficult for me to reconcile your actions with your care for your tenants. It has shown me, again, that there is another side to you I do not know. One who will make decisions independently."

Adara shrugged out of his grasp. Though Grahame was loath to let her go, he did, fisting his hands beneath his arms as he crossed them.

"Indeed, I do. I have and I will continue to make plans and rule as I see fit."

She crossed the room to stand by the candle. Her hand moved a few inches over the flame. Frustration or annoyance crossed her features, Grahame was not sure which.

"You are upset that I do not share my plans with you? Is that it?"

Grahame blew out a breath. He turned to the door to gain his bearings. Were her plans the problem? Admittedly, he was not one for grand schemes. Yet Adara, the woman who made him whole, was still unknowable. He felt as if he would never know her.

He rubbed his palms together as he turned. She remained still, her hands on her hips. Gorgeous in the flickering glow.

"Yes. I know you have no reason to tell me as I am simply following your orders, but I would like to know what is coming, Adara."

His wife crossed her arms. The steely glint returned to her eye. "What is it, Grahame? You must be explicit. Are you angry because you wish to know my plans or are you angry because you must abide by a woman's rule?"

Agitation ignited in him at her tone.

"Both. Neither."

"Both?"

"Yes, Adara, both. But also neither." Grahane raked a hand through his hair. He slung his hands on his hips as he tried to articulate the duelling feeling of unease and hurt. "I cannot trust you for you do not share what is going on until it is in my lap. You do not trust me enough to tell me. I couldn't care less about your rule, yet I would like an equal part in decisions if they affect your life—our lives."

It was the wrong thing to say.

Adara's lip curled. "You claim to want trust, though you will not give me the same courtesy. Why would I trust you when you did not find me important enough to track down when you'd received word that Elvin was dead? You paid for information about me, yet you remained in happy Hyrstow, unwilling to bring us together. I had to do so through one of the schemes you hate so much."

"Do not act as if you are some savior to our bond because you forced us together. I had no idea I could come for you! Our differing status—"

Adara raised her hand for quiet. Grahame heeded her, biting off his words so that Hagan or Thor did not break down the door.

Adara hissed, "How can I trust a man who did not come for me? Why would I tell you all of my secrets when I have no idea if my plan will work?"

The words struck Grahame like a backhand.

"The plan with your father? Have you no inkling? Or do you care so little for me that you are willing to have me killed?"

Adara's face crumpled. Her hands covered it but not before Grahame saw the tears glistening in her eyes. He strode to her, pulling her hands away. Her next words were raw.

"I care too much for you, Grahame. I was selfish and so full of spite that I told myself what I wanted was all that mattered. I could not stand to be married off again. You were what I wanted most, so I claimed you. Now, I am sorry. So, so sorry. I panic thinking of the harm that might befall you because of me."

Tears slipped down her cheeks. Grahame brushed them away with his thumbs while his heart wrestled with his head. Fear for himself was a living thing inside him, yet would he rather she not have brought them together?

No. His life had been good, filled with friends and family. Yet, since meeting Adara, it has been flavorless. The same thing over and over. He'd dulled himself so expertly, even he did not realize until he saw her again how faded he'd become.

He placed a tender kiss on her forehead as a deep knowing settled within him.

"I hate that we lost so much time. I should have sought you out, regardless of your marriage. I loathe that I was not there for you in the ways that mattered, Adara. I accept the risks of being with you."

Adara shook her head. "No. You want to know my plans? Fine. They have all gone awry, anyway. I release you instead. You can go back home; I will marry who my father says, and you will be safe."

Every muscle in Grahame tightened like a string

pulled taut. He would *never* allow her to marry someone else.

"Never," he growled, running his palms down her arms. He knelt, keeping her hands in his as he looked up into her worried face. "You will never marry again. You are *mine*. I am glad you did what you did. Not the way you harmed my people but that you forced us together. I am glad for your sharp mind and steel spine. I simply ask to know more of you, 'Dara. Your plans and ambitions. I am but a humble man not bred for this life. I do not want to lead, I leave that to you. You can keep your sorrys because I choose you."

Adara sniffed as a small, crooked smile spread across her lips. Grahame squeezed her hands.

Despite the floor digging into his knees, he continued. "You tow a dangerous line with these people, 'Dara. How long until you have no funds with which to help?"

Adara let out a long breath. "I admit that my coffers are large, yet I wish to convince my father to lessen his tax. If I prove I can keep Hyrstow in check, that I can handle my own affairs with our marriage, he will see that I can set tax rules as I see fit. These people do not have much, and Elvin did not advocate for them in the manner which I want to."

Grahame kissed the backs of Adara's hands, love for her overwhelming his senses. He stood. Adara's arms wrapped around his middle, crushing him to her as tears soaked his tunic.

"I wish I had done it all differently," she sobbed.

Grahame held her to him, breathing with her until she calmed.

"Thank you for your truth," he murmured.

Her hands wove about his waist, but she did not speak further. Grahame did not tell her of the manner in which he loved her, nor the too large feelings of elation and fear that thrashed inside him. Instead, they stood like that a long while, just breathing the other in. When he skimmed his lips across the bridge of her nose, she sighed. And when his hands wandered to her hips, her mouth sought his.

They left in the watery grey light of the morning, dew wetting their boots. Across hills and valleys then further, Grahame was able to get a glimpse of the place he now called home. Clayton House's steepled roof peeked out from the log wall, its thatch bright in the timid sunlight. Closer, the fence's gate was open.

"There appears to be a band of riders at the gate," Hagan said, though such words were unnecessary. In the distance, riders bearing flags of dark grey sat atop horses.

Adara halted, her hands going white on the reins. Grahame snapped his gaze to her in time to see her mouth drop open, horror filling her eyes.

"'Dara?" Grahame stopped, reaching out for her despite not being able to touch her while horsed.

She tried to speak, her mouth moving over words that would not obey. Grahame yanked his horse in front of his wife so she would see something other than what terrified her.

Pain, raw and hot, lived in her eyes as she shifted her gaze to Grahame.

"My father," she said, the words like stones. "My father has come to Clayton House."

Grahame felt a chill burrow through his skin. As he tore his gaze to the house, his mind offered the memory of the rat in the cellar.

TWENTY-NINE

Adara

"You must bow when you enter but divert your eyes only for a moment. He does not respect weakness. Though, if you hold his gaze, it will show insolence. Stand beside me but do not reach for my hand. He may address you, he may not. Do not interject when I speak, do not—"

"I know how to behave, Adara," Grahame said. They rode together, albeit slowly, toward the house.

"Yes, of course you do," she said, softening her tone.

Her breaths caught in her chest; she had to focus on forcing them in and out. He had simply nodded and trudged ahead when she announced her father's presence in their house. Ready. Resigned.

"Had you reason to believe he would come?"

Adara was faintly aware of Hagan and Thor straining to hear her answer.

"I did not. I've avoided his summons yet advised I would travel to him as planned. He likely wants to order my marriage to the new suitor. At least our arrangement will provide a distraction. Perhaps he will see that you are capable—though, I should have given you more access to the accounts. He'll think you more worthy if you have knowledge of the last round of tax. I can show them to you tonight after we've greeted him. I thought we had more time..."

It was as if Adara's jaw had unhinged and words spewed out. She couldn't stop them.

"Good idea," Grahame murmured. He steered his horse around a pile of shit, his mouth a line. Gone was her jovial husband, in his place was the stoic man she first met at her gate.

"I don't know how long he intends to stay but I will be—"

"Adara," Grahame said, halting his horse. He stared at her as she reined in Ulrich, turning in her seat. Ulrich twisted his neck to look at her, his ears flickering. She gave him a good scratch.

For a scant moment, the sun peeked from behind a cloud and backlit Grahame's head and shoulders. Her throat went as dry as tinder. She was about to put the man she'd dreamed of for years, the man she dared to have deeper affection for than she could ever name, directly in the path of a man that could so easily cut him down. How could she have been so selfish? So enraged with losing her cousin and power-drunk after Elvin's death? She'd claimed the boy she had desired for years, yes, but Grahame had become so much more. He listened to her, tried to learn her. Despite her attack on his people, he stood by her, and had given her a taste of how a man could treat a woman. It felt as if someone was pressing a boot to her chest.

"'Dara?" Grahame asked, though his voice sounded muffled.

Her head began to feel like a cloud that might float away. She was about to sentence him to death. The fear in her chest wound tight. She tried to take a deep breath, only to find she couldn't. Her vision greyed.

"Adara!" Grahame shouted as he moved, flinging his leg over his horse. Her hands tightened on the reins but she tipped to the side, her chest burning. Thor yelled something while she slid.

Her legs felt like jelly as she tipped to the left. The ground rushed at her before darkness stole her away.

Wakefulness came in pieces. She was astride a horse, both legs folded over one side, her rump in the center. Strong arms and the scent of sunshine and clover held her. The skin of Grahame's throat cradled her face, and she breathed him in as if he were life.

"Welcome back," he said, the deep sound reverberating into her bones.

Adara shivered. "Hello," she barked out, her voice gritty. She opened her eyes to find them nearly through Clayton House's front gate. She had not blacked out for long then, though not short enough that Grahame waited.

"Are you feeling better? We waited for you to wake but the men at the gate started toward us so I thought it best to meet them rather than catching us unhorsed," Grahame said into her ear.

Adara licked parched lips and sat straighter, pushing away from Grahame as much as she could. His arms tightened around her middle.

"Relax," he said into her hair. "Rest a little. We'll tell them we're newlyweds and did not want to ride apart."

Adara tilted her head to look up at Grahame. His mint-colored eyes were lined with worry. Guilt gutted her.

"I should like to dismount as soon as we are past the gate," she said, pasting on a brittle smile for the guards.

Two men, each on a dark horse, watched them approach. Both held spears and wore the red-stitched sigil of a badger over a grey doublet.

Grahame's thumb scraped along her ribcage. Adara swallowed around the dryness in her throat.

"Good day, men," Hagan shouted as he approached. "I have Lady Clayton, returning home. Stand aside."

Adara straightened again, nodding with all the regality she possessed.

Without a word, the stoic men moved aside. Adara's heart lurched as they passed through the gate. Her father's men were everywhere. Some lay in the grass eating huge plates, some brushed and watered horses at the stable, others came and went from the house, the door hanging open like a lost tooth.

Grumb had been left in charge, but where was he? It was a testament to what her father really thought of her. Someone to be trodden upon. Fear slammed into her. If she was worthy of such indignity, Grahame would be thought of as even less.

"Grahame," she hissed, "we must appear as if we dislike one another's company. Act toward me as you did at the beginning of all this."

"Like I hate you? No," was his gruff reply.

He guided them to the stables, the men moving out of the way as he reined in Ulrich. Panic sluiced along her bones.

"Act as if you benefit from the marriage. You wanted land, title, all of that. You had your eye set high and settled for me as a wife in the process. *Please*. My father will respect that more than if you show affection to me or I to you. He will understand striving. He does not understand hearts and wishes. If this is to work, you must appear pleased with the status of the marriage but not me."

Grahame pulled away to properly look at her, a refusal written in his features. However, something in her pleading, or perhaps it was the desperation in her eyes, made him pause. His lips became a line as he nodded. Adara loosed a breath of relief.

They dismounted without further exchange. Adara marched across the threshold of her home, spine straight, hands clammy. A couple of men crowded the entrance of the great room with mugs in hand. The fire crackled and the scent of wet grass, mud, and ale wafted. Worry for her stores and the demand on Cook fought for dominance over her worry for Muretta.

A voice like a frozen hand grasping her throat said, "Hello, Daughter."

She could not halt the cringe that hunched her shoulders, nor the spiral of fear that wound along her spine. In her childhood, she could never escape that quiet, purposeful voice. Even wrapped in years of marriage and miles away, her father's tone came back to her in every letter, every bit of information passed down to her by Elvin.

Behind her, Thor grumbled about the earl's men being layabouts. Hagan's grunt was accompanied by a scuffle as if he pushed someone away. Directly behind her, Grahame hovered, his chest at her back.

Adara swallowed past the sensation of sand in her throat and pushed through men at the great room's mouth. They looked her up and down with half-lidded, greedy stares but let her pass.

"Father," Adara said, ignoring the use of his title.

Earl Eadric of Bernira sat in a chair at the table's head. Grey eyes the color of her own pinned her to the spot while a permanent scowl marred his thin mouth. Sallow skin accompanied stringy, chin length hair. There was a stoop to his shoulders as he sat with his arms draped over the chair's wooden armrests, hands dangling, open. Adara was not deceived by it. His posture in no way indicated poor health. Rather, it served as a representation of his spirit; downtrodden, bruised, yet vicious like a cornered animal.

"My daughter," he said, bestowing the same courtesy on her. "I trust you had a prosperous trip. It must have been pressing if you did not find the time to write to me regarding your marriage prospects."

He took a sip from his mug, the ale glistening on his lips as he brought the mug down. Adara strode forward, halting a few generous steps away. Muretta and Bhlaine were nowhere she could see. Hope that they were holed up in their rooms, unharmed, was a desperate shadow in her mind.

The men at the table shifted, one of them standing as Grahame followed. Eadric did not even look his way, his eyes boring into her. Adara steeled her spine. She could not falter.

"We did. Thank you for the concern, Father. Of course, I am delighted to see that you've made the journey in spite of my lack of word."

Eadric's eyes narrowed ever so slightly. "I am. There is no need for my daughter to be without a husband. Especially since you were unable to bear a child with the previous one. You are old enough that a child may be hard to come by, but there is still a chance. A marriage in which a suitable heir is created is your birthright. You've let this earldom down by not producing such."

Grahame's grunt from behind was like the burying of a knife in a back. As if he had to will himself not to retort. Eadric's gaze flashed to him, a shrewd question crossing his face, before continuing.

"It is the tenderness I carry for you that has moved me to configure a match. He is here. Galan, prince of the Britons."

Eadric gestured, palm-up, to the table. On the left, in Grahame's usual spot, rose a burly man with an unkind face. His hair was wild, the colors of the forest floor in autumn, his thick tunic the dull grey of dead fish scales. His nose had been broken and healed, leaving it thick and bumpy in the center of his scruffy face. Hands fisted at his sides as he came to his full height, about Adara's own, as if he'd like nothing other than to crush her within his thick fingers. His voice was high and smooth, completely at odds with his savage frame.

"Greetings, Bride."

CHAPTER
THIRTY

Adara

Adara didn't bother holding back her sneer. She could barely control the impulse to strike the man down, to haul Grahame from the room and ride with him to Hyrstow, where he would be safe. She wove her fingers together to halt herself from reaching for Grahame's hand.

"Thank you for your generosity, Father. I appreciate the care you've taken to find a marriage prospect. It is rather unfortunate that I have already wed. I took it upon myself to find a match."

Eadric did not allow one ounce of surprise to cross his face. Her intended groom, however, scowled, his wide face tipping into something murderous as he looked from the earl to his daughter.

"Have you, now?" Eadric mused. His voice was like the gnarled branches of a dead willow tree. He tapped his index finger on the armrest. "Can I hope it was for strategy? Or did you marry someone like Hagan?"

Adara wished she could spit in his face. Once, a few years into her marriage to Elvin, her father had pulled her aside at a Yuletide feast and asked after her ability to bear children. She'd been flustered by the question, but he'd told her she needed a little beast inside her whether she got it from her husband or her guard so long as the thing could pass as legitimate. Eadric assumed she was at least trying to fulfill her responsibility with Hagan.

"No, Father. I have not married Hagan. He is my trusted guard. He has my esteem and respect. I have married Grahame Shepherd, wealthy merchant of Hyrstow, and new Lord Clayton." The words were quick, hard-edged.

Grahame stepped forward, putting himself in line with Adara. She did not dare glance up at him, did not dare breathe as his sleeve brushed hers.

The grin that spread on her father's face made Adara's middle pitch forward. It wound up his cheeks until it collapsed his eyes as he let out a stunted clap of a laugh.

"So, the new priest told the truth. You cannot be serious, Daughter," he said as laughter creaked from him again. He pounded a hand on his armrest.

Around them, the murmuring of his men descended into scoffing chuckles. Adara tried to calm her trembling hands by holding them stiff at her sides. Oswald had relayed news of the marriage?

"Indeed, I am. I intended to travel to your keep in the coming days to announce the news but you have spared me the journey, and for that, I thank you."

From the corner of her eye she could see Grahame's passive grin. The one he wore when he acted a jester, or drifted off into his own mind to duck his feelings. It enraged her more than it should have. He was playing his part but that dismissive smile, the one she'd first seen when she called him to Clayton House, nearly carved her in two.

"Am I to suppose this lumbering fool is the man in question? He is pretty, Adara, but I thought you had more sense than to marry just to have a shiny toy in your bed. Not when I've been benevolent enough to bring a proper match."

Every one of Adara's muscles locked around her bones. She fought it, loosened her shoulders as she took a step forward, hands spread in supplication.

"I'll admit, his appearance was a happy accident. As you know, Elvin was sick prior to his death. I'd begun planning my next match as soon as my dear husband left this earth. You had chosen such a fine husband for me the first time, I wanted to make you proud with my next. It is all I've ever wanted: for you to be proud."

Eadric waved his hand dismissively. His hawkish eyes locked on Grahame.

"Flattery does not become you, Daughter. There is no need for it. If you would like to discuss the events preceding Elvin's death, how about you explain to me your Hyrstow raid? I heard you got Guston men involved in a squabble that landed you in Deircia territory."

Adara's face heated. A bead of sweat trailed down her spine. Was he really going to air her deeds in front of the whole room?

"You heard correct, Father. I wished to keep Ridley Ward of Hyrstow in check. As a gift to you, since he had stolen the disputed territory from us. It has since been settled with the marriage to Shepherd. He is the bridge to peace between the earldoms."

Eadric arched a brow as he scratched his grizzled cheek with his thumbnail. Grey dotted the scruff along his pointed jaw, matching the silver that streaked through his black hair.

"In check? A gift to me? You've only proven your weakness. Just like your mother. She's gone. Did you know that? Died last month. Succumbed to what ailed her, finally. If you had answered my summons, you might have known. Might have been a good daughter and shown the proper respects at her burial."

The news slammed into Adara as the blow it was intended to be. Her mouth moved, flapping open and closed as she harnessed words. A picture of her mother shoved to mind, though after not having seen her for years, it was a blurry imagining. Annallee of Bernira had been a waif, haunted and child-like, even in Adara's memories.

"Imagine my trouble when one of my lords died, my daughter enacted unprovoked raids against a neighbouring earldom, my wife dies, and my daughter took a new husband without my approval. This is why women aren't fit for anything. I can respect the jump your supposed husband has taken from shepherd to lord. At least he has enough of a mind to climb the ladder of nobility."

Adara barely heard the words as her father's attention landed fully on Grahame. Her mind raced, trying to keep up with the change in subject while her heart shouted with grief for her mother. Her mother, to whom her father had always been cruel.

Grahame played his part well. He did not reach for her nor did he offer a kind word for her loss.

"Have you bedded her under witness?" Eadric asked Grahame.

Adara shook her head to clear it. It was her task to confirm the details—to show she was the head of her house.

"Yes, My Earl. We were wed under the supervision of the church, and I bedded her with proper witness." Grahame's voice was full and strong next to her, suffused with something akin to triumph.

It made Adara's skin crawl. He sounded like any other man, satisfied in his conquering.

Eadric fisted a hand then released it. His bony shoulders shifted as he scooped up his mug and took a long pull. The Briton he had brought to wed her settled back down, but her father snarled, "I didn't give you leave to sit," and the man hopped back to standing.

"See?" the earl said. "See how Galan listens? Do you listen, Grahame of Hyrstow?"

"I've been listening this entire time, Earl. You want a man for your daughter who will lead, yet one who will be ruled. You want a match offering resources or power or both. I will admit, resources I have, and alliances I can broker. She raided my homeland, yet I was able to convince her to the marriage. Would that not indicate power of persuasion? Your daughter needs a strong hand to wield her. I am yours, Earl. Even if you are displeased, I claim her as my wife. We have completed vows, she's been bedded under witness. She is mine."

Grahame locked eyes with her father as he spoke. The words rang through the room with the easy confidence befitting a lord. The others were silent for long moments. A sly grin twitched at the corners of Eadric's beard.

"Come, Grahame Shepherd of Hyrstow. Adara. Eat with us after your long journey. I would like to hear further how this surprise alliance will benefit Bernira."

Grahame accepted a chair at the end of the table without waiting for Adara. Numb, she settled into the space next to him. Travel stories were exchanged, news of Bernira filtered through, though not one more word was exchanged regarding her mother.

Adara nursed her grief behind her ribs while she ate. The deliciously prepared food was like dirt in her mouth. Grahame played the part too well. Easy grins and hearty laughs were exchanged over tales of raids and travel and alliances. Adara knew Eadric was not fooled, yet he let

Grahame play the part of high-reaching husband. The Briton, Galan, glared his way through mug after mug of ale. Only toward the end of the meal, when the drinks had been drained, did her father give her a peculiar look that stuck her to her chair. One that said she hadn't fooled him, that her choice wouldn't stand.

CHAPTER

THIRTY-ONE

Grahame

Adara was silent as they walked the hall to Grahame's room. She did not say a word as they entered. Had barely looked at him at dinner. He'd sat through that miserable meal with Adara's father and intended groom, laughing on cue, disregarding her at every turn, and keeping his hands to himself when all he wanted was to touch her. To protect her against the words of a man who so obviously wanted to hurt her.

It was as if she was used to walking on knives. The only time Adara had faltered was when Eadric had used the news of her mother's death to shock her. Still, she played the part of cunning lady well.

Grahame hated it. Hated that she had grown up with

such a man teaching her that her survival meant parrying men like him. Hated she'd been twisted into the woman who understood only vengeance when her cousin was killed. Hated the only escape she could fathom was strong-arming Grahame into marriage, as if he wouldn't have come willingly if she had sought him out.

"I am sorry about your mother," he said, crossing the bedroom to where she stood before the bed.

The Earl of Bernira had taken Adara's room with the fireplace, of course. It was a miracle they'd been allowed into Grahame's room. She did not look his way as he approached. Absently, he wondered where the others ended up. If Muretta was safe with Hagan and Thor since they were removed from their rooms to make way for Eadric's men. Most of Eadric's entourage was to bed down in the great hall as there were not enough beds in the house.

"Thank you," Adara demurred.

Her shoulders slumped, her chin falling to her chest for a heartbeat. As if conditioned to not let herself feel grief, she shoved out a breath then straightened. She began to pull at the ties of her travelling clothes. Grahame's heart ached at the sight.

"'Dara." The nickname was nearly a gasp, so desperate was he for her to turn back into his Adara, not this person made from ice and stone.

"You played your part well," she said.

Grahame inclined his head, moving so he was in front of her. She kept staring ahead, as if he wasn't there.

He grasped her chin between his thumb and forefinger, angling her face up so she would at least look at him. Accusations lay in those steel eyes, so like her father's, he now saw.

"It felt wrong." His words were soft. Like his bleeding heart any time he tried to avoid her gaze at supper.

"It did? You switched into the role of hungry lordling without fail."

"I had to," he retorted, dropping her chin to plow his hand through his hair. "It's what you told me to do. What we agreed I would do."

"Yes, and it appeared to work. My father did not dislike you."

Adara turned away, moving toward the hulking clothing chest. She freed the laces at the back of her dress, ignoring him. Grahame closed his eyes and begged for patience. He'd *just* made it out of the great room with his neck intact. The Goddamn earl of Bernira was next door and Adara was…he didn't know…moody about him acting his part as instructed?

He felt his sanity slip.

"And how should I have acted, Adara?" he asked, careful to keep his voice low lest someone outside their room hear their conversation. "You were the one who told me to appear as if I aimed high in marriage. To not act as an affectionate husband."

Her fingers worked the laces free, and she was pulling the dress overhead, her back to him. Her under-things were a simple cotton made for travel—God, had they just been traveling? It felt like a week had passed. As if it didn't know his frustration with her, Grahame's cock twitched at the sight.

"I know. And it worked. We will have to be on our guard in the coming days."

She dug in the chest of clothes as she spoke, picked out one of his tunics, then stripped off her day-worn underthings. Without a word she slipped the new garment on.

Adara hadn't worn anything to bed since the first night they slaked their lust for one another. Another spark of anger joined the flame inside him. He ripped off his own tunic, trousers falling to the floor a moment later. Uncaring of her sensibilities, he shucked his underthings too.

"Do you know how long these visits last?"

Her eyes found him as she turned. They widened a little upon the sight of him naked and half-hard. He smirked. A frown hooked her lips.

"They can last weeks. Travel from his keep is long, especially with so many men in tow. This was definitely a wedding procession, bringing the groom and all these people. He was going to strong-arm me into it."

Unease was a leech inside him. There was no way she would be married to the brute out there. Allegiance with the north or not, her father had to know that man would beat her and force her as soon as look at her. Grahame came to her side of the bed, unable to help himself. He reached for her wrist.

"Why are you upset with me?" he asked, softening his tone.

Something flitted across Adara's face before her features hardened. She wrenched her wrist away.

"I simply noticed how easy it was for you to become the man you needed to be. It gave me cause to wonder what else you need to be...for me."

Bloody hell. She thought him skilled enough to turn his feelings for her on and off at whim? To what end? Secure his position? *She'd* put him up to this. The marriage, the plan, all of it.

"Do you need me to show you how good of an actor I am? Is that it?" Darkness layered his tone. He didn't care. Her doubt had hit something in him, a quality he knew he had, one he never thought would be discovered.

"Nevermind, Grahame. Let's go to bed."

He caught her forearm before she could turn, hauling her to him. Shock scored her features for a moment, and Grahame thought of how nice it would be to stuff his cock into her rounded mouth. It would give her something to do other than question him.

"No, Wife. You are angry with me for something *you* commanded me to do." He spun her to face away from him, one hand on her stomach, the other moving from her arm to around her throat. She twisted her head back to glare at him, fussing in his grasp.

"You're right," he said into her ear, his length growing against her backside. She took hold of his forearm, dug her claws in.

"I *am* good at pretending. Fantastic at it, actually. How do you think I was able to make everyone believe I'd be happy taking over the sheep? Or fucking women who weren't you? My ability to lie—to play the Golden Boy, as everyone calls me—is the thing that is going to save our lives. Because, Adara, darling, you can't act for shit. And now that you have me, you're stuck with me."

For all her squirming, she pressed her ass against him, eyes flashing, knowing it drove him mad. That Goddamn tunic was too raspy against his skin. He released her throat to take a handful of material, rucking it up around her waist. The movement allowed his cock to spring up instead of being trapped by her body.

"You're stuck with me," she panted.

Grahame relished the bite of her fingernails. Tunic around her waist, he held her against him once again so the cheeks of her ass could feel the hard press of his member between them. Not wanting to give her any leverage, he bracketed her throat with his hand again, grinding the words they both needed to hear into her ear.

"We are stuck with each other. You call me a pretender, and yet I've never once acted with you. You are the only person who sees through me, as if to see past your reflection on a river's surface. I am the murky bottom. Greedy and ambitious, I may be, but that is only because I knew you'd have nothing less. I am your lord, Adara. But you're the one that forged me. We have always been each other's. We are one and the same."

Grahame let her go, giving her a little shove toward the mattress. Adara threw her hands out in front of her to catch herself. She ended up on all fours, her backside in the air. Grahame didn't hesitate. He gripped her hips and lined himself up with her weeping slit.

"We are," she said, her voice full of command.

Grahame drove himself into her.

A quickly stifled gasp was all Adara uttered. Grahame was glad for it. She was soaked for him, angry in kind, and she pushed back against him as he withdrew. It made Grahame thrust harder the next time, then the next. Her fingers strangled the bedclothes while he created bruises on her hips with the force of his hold. There was a perverse satisfaction knowing she'd marked him with her claws, and he was marking her with his grip.

The earl could refuse the marriage. Could kill him outright. The man could force Adara into a life where she would rather die than live, but he couldn't take away the time they'd had together. The way they molded each other. She was his and he was hers.

Always.

With a vicious curse, Adara seized, clenching around him until Grahame spilled inside her. Fury, anguish, worry, lust burned through him, eating away at any sort of life that didn't include her in it.

When he'd finished, he skimmed an arm up her front to pull her back to his chest. She turned her head, a small grin playing on her lips.

"I love you," she whispered.

The words were so unexpected, so untethered, Grahame couldn't help the full-blown smile that broke across his face. His reaction made Adara laugh, a striking, clear sound that impressed itself upon Grahame's soul.

"I love you," he answered, kissing her.

Though their love-making had been fierce and furious, the kiss was gentle and drawn out, made of all the things they wished for the other. When they parted, Adara eased away from Grahame's body with a slowness that alluded to the next day's discomfort. He fetched a cloth and water, cleaned her then himself and settled with her in the bed.

"I am sorry for my disbelief," she said, her eyes eating him up the way he loved. "I was taught by my mother never to believe anything that was too good. As a child, she would remind me to hold myself apart, for it was the best way to protect oneself."

Grahame settled deeper into the slim bed, offering his arm as a pillow. Adara sank into his side. He remained quiet so she could continue.

"I grew to think I deserved the way my father dismissed me, when Elvin harmed me. I know I told you to be callous. It is so easy for me to believe the worst because what else is there? You've only ever been too good," she whispered.

Grahame's heart swelled. He rolled to the side so he could better stare at her gorgeous face. Gently, he slid his hand to the dip in her waist.

"Say 'I love you' again, please," he requested.

Adara buried herself in the crook of his shoulder, her warm breasts squishing against him. "I love you, Grahame Shepherd. In this life and every other."

Each word filled his heart, strengthening his resolve. There was no telling what the next day would bring. And, despite Adara's reservations, he would lie, cheat, and steal from her father and anyone else who stood in their way if it meant they would remain together.

THIRTY-TWO

Adara

A messenger was sent out in the dead of night. One Adara knew would be gone for longer than she wished if they were successful in relaying what was needed to both Uhtread and Ridley. She had no way of knowing if her promises would be enough to help them. Every day her father remained under her roof was one more he had to decide their fate.

~

"I HAD WISHED to see you wed," her father said.

Side by side, they strolled along the path that stretched from the rear gate down a green slope leading into undulating fields of wheat. His eyes were locked on the bounty ahead.

Bernira was an earldom of strife. Eadric's keep sat close to the ocean's craggy rock face, bereft of usable farmland. Adara had grown up amid rocky cliffs and valleys of cold marsh, unaware of what good land looked like until she stayed with Cecilia that fateful summer. The land surrounding Clayton House and further, into Guston, was some of the best under Bernira rule.

"I am sorry, Father," Adara allowed, keeping her eyes on the horizon.

At the midday meal, Grahame's posture had sharpened when Eadric announced he would take a walk with Adara, alone. Muretta had halted pouring ale for one of the men she'd been smiling with, the jug poised in the air. Hagan had straightened as well, though there was nothing to be done for it. He, Thor, Muretta, and Bhlaine had been banished to sleeping in the stable, and though they appeared tired, none were worse for wear. Adara could not refuse her father's request.

"You've imparted to me the importance of alliances. After Elvin passed, I wished for a husband I could influence. One of the regions, in whom others carried trust, yet one hungry enough to climb. Grahame is influential and well-liked. I have molded him perfectly, which benefits us, the earldom."

Eadric waved a dismissive hand. The sleeve of his charcoal tunic fluttered with the movement. She'd never seen him wear another color. It was as if shades of grey were armor in and of itself.

"You flatter yourself, Adara. You should have known I would not have left you unwed for more than a year. Your mother's death held up the dealings longer than expected. You should have waited."

Adara bit back the fresh wound of grief that surged in her breast. Despite not being close—most of her life her mother had holed up in her rooms, unreachable—Adara wished she'd been able to say goodbye.

Stuffing her feelings inward so her father wouldn't sense weakness, she said, "I understand."

Eadric halted on the path, turning to face the fields below. He drank them in, as if memorizing their shape, the sweep of the breeze across the feather-like tips of the wheat. Adara clasped her hands before her. The familiar lines around her father's mouth and eyes had settled deeper, his skin had thinned with time. Not that she'd ever remembered him being of vital strength; however, this older, more stooped version begged a certain wariness from her. She knew Eadric's physical health had nothing to do with his cunning.

"The priest, Oswald. He is also a Hyrstow man, is he not?"

Adara gulped, remaining silent, for she knew her father was not truly asking. He already knew. Eadric smiled.

"Interesting man, that one. He was only too eager to tell me of Hyrstow's growth, and the close relationship his brother shares with earl Lachlan of Deircia."

Adara's chest tightened. Her father turned, the small smile fixed upon his lips.

"He married us," she stammered.

Betrayal cut through her. Grahame had been right about him.

"I cannot abide by your marriage," Eadric stated in a flat tone.

Adara's breath caught in her throat. His words were so sure. A decision already made. Fire sparked in her limbs, the kind that told her to fight or flee.

"But he did perform it. And the bedding was witnessed."

"By whom? Your men?"

"Yes," Adara tugged the snarl out of her mouth before the words landed. "My men. One of which is your man."

Eadric scoffed, clasped his hands behind his back, and started walking back to the house, knowing she'd follow.

"Hagan was of my keep when he was a squire. He left to guard you when you wed. That was years ago. Though I pride myself on my influence, I know he's likely to have turned against me in favour of you."

"He is loyal because I am your daughter. And I am loyal to you," she protested. "He will testify that the marriage is sound. And I maintain it is a good match for Bernira."

Adara's arm was in his tight grasp before she could blink. Eadric spun her so quickly to face him she barely saw the back of his other hand before it connected with the side of her face. Shock lashed through her. On its heels, a wave of pain. It didn't stop her father from pulling her to him, his hand a manacle.

He spit words in her face. "You know nothing of the pitiful land you claim your husband has rights to. Nothing of the disputed territory other than the problems you've caused after it was reclaimed by Deircia. I was given that land for a marriage agreement after that damned Lachlan stole my bride. I kept the land, but the king saw fit to saddle me with your mother. When Lachlan sent his men to reclaim it, they were under trespass. That land is *mine*. Deircia's reclamation went against law, but you—" he squeezed her arm, taking her face in his other hand, nails digging into her chin— "*you* raided it. You created more upheaval, and for what? You ignore my commands, marry this usurper, and expect me to accept that *you are doing it for Bernira?*"

He flung her arm hard enough to throw her off balance. Adara's toe caught on her heel. She gasped as she fell back, seeing the sky before she crashed to the ground. Pain shot through her elbow and hip as she connected. Before she could scramble back, her father stomped down on her foot to halt her movements. Adara clamped her teeth together to bury the shout of pain that barked through the small bones.

Spittle flew from his mouth as he yelled. "You've caused enough problems, Daughter. Rather than go through appropriate channels, petty squabbles will divide the top half of the kingdom! The land is needed. That is the reason for the Britons. If that Godforsaken Lachlan wants to extend his reach further, I need another set of warriors ready. I'm water to the east, Deircia to the south, and marshy Briton land on the north and west. I will not have Lachlan take *anything* else from me."

Eadric swept his hand along his forehead to rein in a hunk of hair that spilled forward. He drew a breath, turning back to the view of the wheat. Adara curled forward, pressing her hand to her foot to try to alleviate some of the pain that ate at her bones. She didn't take her eyes off him, in case he decided to strike again.

Instead, in an almost wistful tone he said, "Oswald, was it? The clergyman who ordained your marriage?"

Dread curdled in Adara's stomach. She forced strength into herself she didn't feel, got up. An ache like that of a hot iron pressed through her foot as she set it down, and she immediately took the weight off, favouring it. Breaths came heavy and hard, and her fists clenched as she tried to straighten.

Her father continued. "He's a remarkable fellow. I met him as soon as I came to your house. Funny what people will do to get what they want. He assured me your marriage wasn't legitimate. I assured him that such a man of consequence should not be confined to a simple church. No, that man will be coming with me back to Bernira to be involved with a church of nobility. Helpful, helpful man."

"I can assure you, Father—"

Eadric smiled, adjusted the cuffs of his fine tunic. It was more terrifying than any of his frowns. Adara backed away, readying herself to run.

"Your husband will not be at the house when you return. Do not fret; it will be as if he never existed. I asked you on this walk, dear Daughter, to congratulate you on your betrothal to Galan. You wed at nightfall."

ADARA COULDN'T HEAR over the pounding of her heart. Frantic breaths carved a stitch in her side as she ran. She was panting by the time she made it back to the house. Somewhere her father walked leisurely behind her.

"It will be as if he never existed."

Adara's stomach revolted. She swallowed the surge of bile that rose, causing her to pause before the gate long enough to take stock of things. Stupid. She'd been so stupid. She had to get to Grahame. All of it was a waste if he was killed for no other reason than being hers.

Her arm and backside ached from where she fell while every step spiked pain into her foot. She would find him. There was no world in which he'd be wrenched from her so suddenly. Not again. Their fates were intertwined. Pursuing the marriage had been a selfish choice. But they couldn't end like this—not even being able to say goodbye. She had to get to him, had to get out of the house and had to flee to Guston.

Muretta. Thoughts of her friends slammed into her as she raced up the hill to the house. She couldn't just leave Muretta and Hagan, Thor and even Bhlaine and Cook. They were her people. The ones she'd promised safety. Panic clogged her throat.

Adara hobbled through the main gate, past men

congregating in the great hall. She ignored the shout of one as she searched, frantic, for Grahame. Why were there no men in the great room? The hallway? She tore through the kitchens, asking Cook for word, then shoved open the doors to each room until she came to the end of the hall where the door to the dungeon lay. Would they have thrown him in the cell?

Each step down was agony, but the flickering light didn't reveal her husband. Teeth clenched against the flare of pain, she tried to collect herself as she moved upward.

"It will be as if he never existed."

Dead. Dead. Her beloved was dead.

"Goddamnit," she gasped at the top of the stairs, collapsing against the door.

From the hall, Muretta came at her, hands out, face twisted into a question. "Adara, what is it?"

Adara grasped her arms, leaning on her friend. "Where is Grahame?" she panted.

Muretta searched Adara's sagging form, her slight body tensing at the question.

"I do not know. He was riled up about you going for a walk with your father, said he'd keep watch, then the Briton took him by the shoulder and told him he had to stay put. You know men and their posturing. They left out the rear door."

Adara grabbed Muretta's arms.

"Mur, listen. My father is going to have me wed tonight. Told me he was going to kill Grahame. I have to...you must get Hagan and get to safety. See if you can find Thor and let him know. Our people are under attack. We will not be able to escape."

Muretta's eyes widened, her mouth dropping open as she nodded. "Where are you going?"

"I must find Grahame. *Now.*"

Adara shrugged off her friend and darted into the kitchen to grab a knife.

"My lady," Oswald's voice tugged at her as she pressed a hand against the house's rear door. His steps were calm, his hands together as he made his way to her.

"What is it?" She didn't have *time.*

The man's lips quirked upward. He reached out, daring to lay a hand on her outstretched arm. "I thought you were out for a walk with your father?" His fingers tightened on her skin.

"I must go," she said, turning to leave.

The priest did not relent. He pulled her arm to him. "I must be so bold as to say you've made quite a mess for yourself, haven't you? You've destroyed relations with Hyrstow, you've angered your father, and you've endangered a good man. I am not sure that God will look fondly upon your soul when your time of reckoning comes. Though, I would argue that your female mind got ahead of your actions and—"

His words cut off as Adara lifted her knee into the cradle of his legs, hitting the most sensitive of areas. Oswald released a pathetic groan, releasing her arm. Adara didn't hesitate. She shoved on the door, running out to the rear yard before Oswald could catch her again.

She had to find a weapon. Cut her way to Grahame. He could *not* be…

Adara's unspooling thoughts stopped as soon as she stepped into the rear yard. Past the well, men stood in a circle, cheering. The sun had eaten through the clouds enough to pour heat on the dirt. She could make out movement through legs—a pair of fighters or, from the sound of it, a fight where one man was gaining ground.

There wasn't time to second-guess herself. Adara ran for the men, slowing only to scoop up a rusty ax. She grunted as she hefted the heavy implement over her shoulder, before shoving through the small crowd and screaming at what she saw.

THIRTY-THREE

Grahame

He'd known as soon as he was shoved outside what was to happen. Galan had delivered a few good punches. Grahame had given it back as good as he got. Then three of Eadric's men surrounded him with their boots. Pain rained upon him. After their toying, they let Grahame stand, though that wasn't exactly the word for it. He hugged his middle with one arm, bent over like an old man as he tried to focus on the man in front of him rather than all the broken, bleeding pieces his skin kept together. One of his eyes was so swollen shut he didn't think he'd ever see out of it again. No matter; he wasn't going to make it out of the fight alive.

Galan stood across from him with a cut lip. He bobbed back and forth, fists up, a satisfied smirk on his ugly face. Grahame was no fighter. Even with the training Ridley had given everyone in Hyrstow, there was no way Grahame could single-handedly beat the four men that surrounded him. The only thing he was glad for was Adara being gone. She wouldn't have to see him executed. Wouldn't see him be picked apart by wolves. She'd be devastated but would get through it, revenge her weapon as she took whatever her father and that bastard Galen meted out. She would survive. Grahame had never been so thankful for a wife that could be fueled by rage.

"I'm going to enjoy taking that bitch of yours. Show her what a real man is," Galan snarled.

He moved to the left. Grahame tried to dodge, but it turned out to be a feint. A fist plowed into Grahame's middle, striking the air from him.

"You'd better or else," Grahame gasped, as the man kicked at his foot. At least he had the mind to sidestep despite being doubled over. "She'll carve your heart out and eat it if you touch her."

"Speaking from experience, eh?" came a shout in the distance.

Raucous laughter laid atop his foggy mind. Grahame fisted his hands, blinking his good eye against the sun that shone high behind his attacker. Too bright. The man struck with something sharp this time, carving into the meat of his shoulder. The flare of pain hollowed him out, creating a line of fire along the muscle. He only had the wherewithal to grimace.

"My lady is going to gut you," Grahame said, fixing his good eye on Galan.

He hoped they'd have the decency to throw him in a ditch far away or bury him where Adara wouldn't find him. She didn't deserve to see him broken and picked apart by these savages.

Behind Galan, a loud shuffling distracted Grahame for a precious moment. A sunbeam glinted off Galan's upraised blade while a feminine scream of "no!" rocked into Grahame.

Adara.

The Brit hesitated for a heartbeat, turning to find the source of the shout. Abject terror sliced into Grahame. Adara couldn't be there. He forced himself to stand taller, holding his bleeding arm tight against him.

Before he could run at Galan she was there, swinging an ax into his thigh. Galan bellowed as the thick blade sank through the meat. Like blank-eyed sheep, the men stared at her in shock. Adara did not stop. As Galan's hands went to the wound, she yanked the ax back, then threw a knife into his belly. She whirled, her hair a curtain of black death as she positioned herself in front of Grahame, ax dripping, at the ready. Grahame thanked all that was holy that he had the sense to turn so they were back to back. He had no weapon though, with Adara in the fray, he felt as if he could rip the men surrounding them apart with his bare hands.

"I am Lady of this house. You will back down," Adara said in that voice made of steel.

Grahame wished he could kiss her for it. Instead, he had to work at forcing down his rising panic that she was in mortal danger. He bared his teeth at the two men he faced. Both wore the emblem of the earl, both appeared uncertain as to whether their task included harming the earl's daughter.

"Move."

Adara's word held such power. Such command. The men blinked. They looked beyond Grahame, what he assumed was past Adara. Grahame did not dare take his eyes from them lest they attack, but he had a feeling they gazed at the body of Galan behind them. Galan groaned. The sound of him moving in the dirt echoed among heavy breaths.

Adara moved away from Grahame's back. The loss of her made him want to shout. He knew it was a danger but had to hazard a glance over his shoulder to ensure she was alright. She held her ax at the men while she bent to retrieve the knife. She wrenched the handle free from Galan's middle, wringing out a scream of pain. The others' mouths curled upward in distaste.

"Move aside," Adara repeated.

She passed the ax behind her into Grahame's awaiting hand. He almost dropped it as he took the full weight in his right, unable to fully grab it with his left. Blood coursed down his shoulder with the movement.

"We can overlook this slight, Lady, but we cannot let you go," one said, hand going to the weapon on his belt.

Grahame fought down a wave of nausea as he hefted the ax, his training with Ridley settling in. He clenched his teeth and widened his stance, glaring at the men before him.

They were surrounded. And, while Grahame would fight to the death to ensure Adara's safety, he knew she would spill the blood of every man before surrendering. Utter fear for her struck him, as sharp as any blade. Eadric's men advanced.

"Adara!" A woman's voice broke through the din.

The threat of hooves and a male shout echoed through the yard. A horse broke through the men, Muretta atop, wild hair a blonde cloud. Sitting behind her, Hagan swung a heavy sword in a great arc, causing the men to scatter. On another mount, Thor shouted, Bhlaine hanging onto his waist for dear life. In one of his hands was a rope leading Ulrich.

"Back!" Thor thundered again, swinging his weapon. He yanked his horse's reins so it turned in front of Grahame, bringing Ulrich before Adara, boxing her in.

Pain shot through Grahame's leg as he stepped forward. Adara ran at the horse until she realized Grahame had gone down to one knee behind her.

"Go," Grahame shouted, swinging the ax haphazardly to stave off the approaching men.

Of course, she didn't listen. Nearly tripping, she surged toward him. The look of pure panic on her face must have mirrored his own.

"Get out of here," he commanded.

Adara's arm slipped around his waist, hauling his injured arm over her shoulders. "I will not leave you."

He wanted to wring her neck and kiss her all at once.

Together, they stumbled to the horse while Hagan and Thor jabbed with their weapons. It would not be long before the commotion brought the entire house down on them.

At Ulrich's side, Grahame clenched his teeth as he used all his strength to hoist Adara up first. Once saddled, she grabbed for him, her fingers digging into the back of his tunic to drag him up behind her. The weight and twisting caused his throbbing arm to scream.

"Go!" he shouted as he wedged himself behind her, layering his body against hers to fight the sense of dizziness that would unhorse him if he didn't hold onto something. He could take a few arrows in the back for her if it came to that, at least.

Somehow, the rear gate lay open. With a grunt, Adara reined the horse ahead, dashing through. A clash of metal rang behind them while a grunt of pain cut the air. Grahame was too stiff, too reliant on Adara's body holding him up to twist in his seat to see who'd fallen. Instead, he let the ax hang in his left hand while he wrapped his right around his wife's middle, pressing his nose to her flying curtain of midnight hair.

They rode. Over path, field, through tall grasses leading to a copse of trees nearer the river. Grahame remained tense the entire time, trying to make his body larger to cover Adara's back lest the earl's men catch up with them. Pain lanced into his sides with every gallop. The only comfort was Adara's body in front of him. That she was safe, that she was whole.

"Guston," Hagan said, his sword sheathed now that he'd taken the reins, his huge arms encasing Muretta.

For once, the woman had nothing to say. She simply stared at the six of them, her face pale. Everyone's foreheads were slicked with sweat, deep breaths sawing in and out of them.

Adara was already shaking her head. "Hyrstow."

Hagan set his jaw as if holding back words. The sun was a curtain of gold in the sky. They had a couple hours of daylight. Grahame strained to listen for the beat of hooves on the breeze. He wished for the cover of night.

"They'll kill us just as easily as your father's men," Thor said.

Bhlaine looked uncomfortable with his arms banded around the soldier's waist. If Thor felt the same, he didn't show it.

Grahame nodded, his cheek moving against the side of Adara's head. She must've sheathed her knife because when she reached behind her to wrap her arm around his waist, her hand was empty.

"Hyrstow," Grahame insisted, his voice thin. "It is farther, but Eadric will look to Guston for Adara first."

Thor hefted a breath, his eyes searching through the trees that held them. Finally, Hagan spoke.

"Aye. Follow Adara, then. She's gotten away from me to travel to the Hyrstow forest too many times to count."

Only Grahame appeared surprised by the statement

as Adara moved to the front of the party, through the trees and down a shallow valley in the direction of his village. The distinction struck him as odd as they galloped toward the looming forest. His village. Not his home. His home had been overtaken by Eadric. Then Adara glanced back at him, her grey eyes wild, as if fearful of what she'd find. Whatever was written on his face didn't seem to appease her. No matter. As he hugged her tighter, their bodies jostling, Grahame realized he was home. Wherever they went, Adara was his only home.

THIRTY-FOUR

Adara

"Stop!" Adara screeched as she felt Grahame's arm loosen from around her waist. He was slumping to the side a heartbeat later. She twisted, catching him under his arms, using all her strength to hold him upright as Ulrich halted.

Hagan dismounted, crashing through the woods in the dark. He reached up, steadying his hand on Grahame's leg as Grahame faded in and out of consciousness mumbling, "we there?"

"I've got him," Hagan said, his determined expression worn.

It shaved a little of Adara's resolve. They'd been travelling the better part of the night through the forest in silence. Neither Thor nor Muretta gave in to idle chatter.

Beneath the half moon's brightness, the travel had been slow. Creatures scurried away from the plodding horses, which nickered for having to tromp through the dark. Thankfully, their steeds were able to stick to the old deer trail Adara knew.

Grahame had been leaning heavily on her most of the way. She was grateful for the strength in his arm around her, though it had slackened over time. Adara chewed her lip and kept on, burying her worry over his injuries in favor of putting space between them and her father. Adara strained to hear the thunder of hooves, the snap of men through the brush.

"I cannot let him go," she said, a sob breaking through the words.

Grahame tipped dangerously, his legs slack, his head lolling. Hagan held his upper body in preparation to bring him down. Her muscles strained as she clung to Grahame, uncaring of the blood and dirt that stained her clothes.

"I know. I know, My Lady," Hagan soothed.

Within a moment, Thor was there, holding Grahame's leg to offer support. Something warm and wet slipped down her cheek. She sniffed, willing the stinging in her nose away.

"We have him," Thor urged.

Gently, Adara loosened her grasp, allowing Grahame to slide into Hagan's outstretched arms. His sheer strength propped up Grahame enough to bring him gently to the ground with Thor's help.

Adara jumped down as soon as she let go. The pain in

her foot spiked anew. She bit her lip against it. At Grahame's side, she slid her hands along his middle, his shoulders, his arms. In the dark, it was impossible to see his injuries. They did not dare chance a fire lest someone see them.

"He needs care," Hagan muttered, his face cloaked in shadow.

Adara nodded. The bridge of her nose stung with the tears that loomed.

"What have we in the packs?"

"Some food, weapons. A few blankets. No clothing or dressings. Muretta did her best to grab as much as she could."

Adara pressed her lips together. The anticipation of an arrow spearing into one of their backs still haunted her. Despite her father's men not following past the tree-line, no part of her thought they'd given up.

"We hazard a torch. I need to see..."

"Adara," Muretta knelt beside her on the forest floor. She ran a hand over Adara's cheek. Adara wanted to let herself weep. To bury herself in her husband's side and let the forest grow over them.

"Adara, love, we need to keep moving. We can put Grahame over the horse sideways. I'll help bind what wounds we can see," Muretta said, her tone urgent.

Grahame didn't move as Adara put pressure on the meat of his shoulder. Her hands were coated with something sticky. She knew it to be blood, but there was too much of it. Some of it had dried and caked to his clothing but any pressure she applied caused more.

Hot tears spilled down Adara's cheeks. Grahame had to get up. He had to be alright.

"We need a torch. We have to bind everything. We waited too long, he could be injured in more places…"

Her words were frantic things that dissolved in the air. Something that felt like a rock was rising in her chest, choking the breath from her. Grahame couldn't die like this. If she got him to safety, she would march herself right back into her father's clutches just to ensure he didn't go after Grahame again. But he had to survive. There was no world without him.

A heavy hand settled on the back of her neck, soothing in its strength. Thor's voice came next, soft in the night.

"My Lady, Muretta's right. We will dress his wounds the best we can, then we must keep moving."

How could they keep moving when her heart was shattering?

"Listen."

Grahame's voice.

Adara gasped, her hands flying to his chest, her face just above his to catch any word that passed his lips.

"I'm here, Grahame."

"Listen to them," he ground out. "Fix me up; get me on a horse. Keep moving."

His hand found her leg. She took it up, grasping it as she pressed a kiss to his blood-stained fingers. Spirals of moonlight revealed the shadow of a smile twisting his mouth.

"Would be rude of me to die after finally marrying you, wouldn't it?"

A laugh pushed its way through her tears. "Indeed. So don't," she begged.

Behind her, Muretta grunted, the rustling of a saddlebag echoed through the branches. The rip of shredding cloth was next. Bhlaine had taken up the spot Muretta abandoned, his wizened face stricken.

"Please, allow me to help, Lady," her housemaster said, hands outstretched with the cloth Muretta had passed him.

Hagan settled himself behind Grahame and used his strength to prop him up so Adara could bind his shoulder.

"Here?" she asked, praying for an answer.

Something shiny leaked from Grahame at the movement. The metallic scent of blood stung the air.

Grahame grunted. A line of pain appeared between his eyebrows as he grimaced. "Think that kick to the middle might've cracked a rib. Nothing hours on a horse won't fix."

Adara forced a chuckle as she wrapped the material around his shoulder and upper arm. No part of her felt like laughing, but she knew he joked for her sake.

"'Dara," Grahame said softly when they'd finished.

Hagan laid him back down. He and Muretta spoke quietly by the horses while Thor passed Bhlaine a water skin. Adara remained beside Grahame, her hands holding one of his.

"You have to promise me something."

"Anything." She leaned over him to hear better yet couldn't help herself: she grazed her lips along his matted hairline.

"When your father comes, you make sure you say I took you."

Grahame's eyes narrowed to slits as she shook her head. "You must. I took you or you were blackmailed by me so had to save me. Or think of anything else that will soften his judgement upon you. You slayed the groom your father brought. You are powerful in your own right. I have faith you can survive this. You have to promise me you'll survive this."

Adara shook her head as he spoke words that were like boulders upon her soul. "Stop it. Stop talking like you won't be beside me if my father finds us. You and I are bound. We are one. There is no leaving one another, not again. I would rather—"

Grahame's free hand was against her lips before she could say more. His eyes were bright. "You are mine and I am yours. But *if* there is a chance, you must take it, Adara. Promise."

She shook her head against his hand, her lips rasping against his palm.

"You said anything," he said, pushing himself up on an elbow.

Pain flared in his gaze and Adara's hands went to his body to push him back down.

"Fine, yes. I will do it," she snapped. Tears flared in her eyes once again.

He didn't understand. She would not go back to a life

under the rule of her father. She detested the thought of the brutality he would inflict on her. Trying to kill Grahame while she was out for a walk was positively gentle in comparison to what he likely had planned for her now.

Worse, she could not go on without Grahame. He'd forever changed her when they met that summer, and his memory was with her every day after. His teasing smiles, his willingness to go along with her plans, the way his body played hers in a way that made her feel valued and loved for the first time in her miserable existence? There was no turning away from the life Grahame had breathed into her. Ever. They *were* one.

The night held them as they proceeded through the forest. Though it irked her, Hagan had taken responsibility for Grahame after Grahame insisted he could ride. Much to Thorhild's amusement, he rode in the cage of Hagan's arms while Muretta rode with Thor, and Bhlaine sat behind Adara. Grahame dozed most of the journey, commenting sporadically on their path not being the way to Hyrstow.

While slivers of dawn pressed through the canopy, Adara sagged in relief as they approached the section of river they could cross. It was wider than other areas, but held a slower current and had a shallow base if you knew where to tread. Adara knew it well, for it was the way she'd spied on Hyrstow all those months ago. Though the horses were reluctant to cross, they splashed in when commanded. The frigid water was a shock to Adara's feet and legs up to her knees. She sucked in a greedy breath to steady herself. The others did the same.

"If I wasn't awake already, I sure am now!" Grahame called in a worn voice. "Wait. We've been travelling west for miles. Is this how you made it to Hyrstow?"

Adara's clenched teeth morphed into a grin at Grahame's recognition.

"We've actually been travelling southwest. Through the Bernira Kingswood and further into Deircia territory."

"That's how you did it. How you avoided my parents' homestead during the raid. You never even came that way." The wonder in her husband's tone thrilled her.

Adara tightened her grip on the reins as the horse climbed up the river's shallow bank. She remained silent as they watered the horses and devoured a few morsels of bread. Worry as to their reception began to sink into her. Hyrstow's son was returning injured, and she was the one who had terrorized the village. Her father would not look for them there; however, Adara knew she was trading one life-threatening situation for another. How welcoming would Ridley and Yrsa be? Fear gripped her about the throat at the prospect of finding out.

They trudged on with the sunrise, weary. Not long past the river, Adara's head was nodding with fatigue when a voice rang through the woods.

"Halt if you wish to live!"

Grahame

Adara, Hagan, and Thor did not halt, the fools. Not until Branton and Sam appeared from behind a huge oak, their weapons raised. Branton looked ready to murder them for trespassing in Hyrstow territory.

Grahame had managed to lift his uninjured arm in a wave of surrender at the same time Adara shouted, "It is Lady Clayton with Grahame."

"Grahame," Bran had said, concern etched in his tone.

Grahame must have appeared as ragged as he felt, for Branton and Sam shucked their weapons and hurried to him. The story of their journey spilled from Adara's lips, her worry palpable. Unable to unhorse a second time,

Grahame had the wherewithal to ask that they be taken to Hyrstow's hall.

Branton and Sam complied, leading the party past the river to the southwest. As soon as they arrived, Emma, her cousin Ingrid, and Sigrid Tanner helped see to Grahame's wounds. Adara had practically frothed at the mouth at the prospect of the others touching him until Emma drew her away to tend to her. Branton's displeasure lived in the deep set of his mouth.

Through his haze, Grahame hadn't realized just how injured Adara was. He'd seen the cut lip when she saved him, but a limp beleaguered her steps as she went with Emma to the long table running down the center of Hyrstow's hall. White hot rage rushed through him with nowhere to go.

Grahame held still while Ingrid and Sigrid smeared salve on his shoulder and bound it tightly, grinding his teeth through the pain. Grahame's gaze didn't stray from his wife. Too far away, Emma inspected the swelling of Adara's foot, the ragged cut to her lip, all the while speaking in low, soothing tones. Adara's gaze darted from Emma to Grahame, as if trying to convince herself he was alright.

He'd forced himself to straighten and mouthed, "I love you."

Adara offered a wary smile, though something haunted lay in her eyes.

Now, seated on a bench at the hall's long table, Grahame hadn't touched the mid-day meal that had been set out for them. Adara sat at his right, Thorhild on his left, while Hagan, Muretta, and Bhlaine sat across. He felt like a walking bruise, and by the way the others grimaced when they saw him, looked like one too.

At the table's head Ridley was speaking, his fists braced against the table top. Yrsa paced behind him. Grahame tried to follow the conversation.

"...killed her intended husband and fled. There has been no news from Bernira, thank God. I am glad for your safety, Grahame, but you do not know what you've brought upon us."

Ridley ran a hand through his hair, yanking at the ends. Yrsa came to stand beside him, settling a hand on his shoulder, which he patted absently. It made Grahame reach for Adara's hand beneath the table. She glanced up at him, worry lacing her gaze for a moment before she schooled her features into that of a cool leader. The skin around her mouth was tight. She must have been terrified.

"Your earl's steward promised us support, if the time came. Unfortunately, the need for it has come quicker than anticipated."

Ridley's eyes narrowed on Adara. In the firelit room, the man was pure menace, huge and imposing. Adara only stared back, unimpressed.

"Truth. Yet my people did not anticipate having to defend a woman who plotted their demise. We are not ready for a war," Ridley stated, his tone flat. His hair had grown longer, beard shaggier, though he looked better than when Grahame had last seen him. Reuniting with Yrsa had made them both appear healthier, whole.

"One never is," Thor volleyed back around a mouthful of deer. The guard had hunkered down, elbows around his food, as if he thought he'd never eat again.

Ridley's look of incredulity at Thor's lowered head would have sparked laughter from Grahame under other circumstances.

"Be that as it may, we will try," Yrsa put in. Her hand slid down to Ridley's upper arm, tightening on the muscle there. A look passed between them, one Grahame was too lightheaded to decipher.

"You are not bringing this fight to Hyrstow's doorstep," Branton cut in. He stood next to the central fire, hand on his hip, bearded jaw tight. No part of Branton had softened since finding them in the forest. He was a warrior, ready to circle his family, to defend like a wild beast.

Grahame felt the same. As much as he was grateful for aid, people in Hyrstow wanted Adara dead. In his weakened state, it was all he could do to remain beside her, hating that he couldn't defend her properly if the time came.

"Tell them of Guston, 'Dara," he said softly.

Ridley's brow peaked, though Grahame didn't know if it was from the suggestion or the slurred nature of his speech.

"What of Guston?" Ridley asked.

Adara's tone was wooden as she said, "I have influence there. I doubt my herald had enough time to convince others of Hyrstow's alliance, but I hope so. I sent him the same message of distress as I did to you, though I do not know if it made it."

"Will your father come here to find you?"

Adara pressed her lips together then nodded. Branton scoffed behind Ridley. Grahame tried to put himself in Branton's place, but his head felt as if wool had been stuffed inside his ears. He shook it slightly, wishing for the sensation to dissipate.

"He knows Grahame is of Hyrstow. I do not know when, but he will likely pursue us when he finds we have not fled to Guston."

"Even past the boundary of Bernira?" Yrsa interjected. The top half of her shortened hair had been braided back. Wearing a tunic, trousers and leather, she appeared every inch the Viking warrior.

"Perhaps," Adara said. Her hand tightened around Grahame's.

Hagan shook his head over Adara's demurring. "He will. I served the earl of Bernira as a squire before I was positioned as my lady's guard. He hates the disputed lands that Hyrstow reclaimed. He revelled in them when they were his, as his lording over them was a slight to Dericia. If he suspects her to have fled here, he will not hesitate to encroach further. The earls' feud goes deep."

Grahame winced as the deep breath he drew tried to take him down. He'd doomed his family, his friends. His village would be at war because of his wife. And yet he did not regret his marriage. How could he when Adara was all he'd ever craved? Perhaps he and Adara were evenly matched in selfishness for he would not give her up. He could only hope for mercy from his friends.

"Can we rely on the earl?" Grahame asked, referring to the only earl Ridley answered to.

"I do not know. Perhaps not until there has been action against us."

The sound of a cup ricocheting across the ground broke through the room. Branton stood with his fists clenched, fury marring his features into something ugly. He pressed his lips together, glowering at them.

Ridley looked after him for a moment, then steepled his fingers against his mouth.

"I am so, so sorry," Adara said. A waver in her voice threatened to drown out the words but she continued: "My misdeeds are great. The raid on Hyrstow went awry. It was intended to mess up the market. To take Yrsa for my revenge. My intentions were not for undue harm, yet intention does not matter when the actions echo across lives."

Rage was written across Branton's face as he stalked to her. Grahame rose from the table, his arm around her shoulders as she twisted in her seat to meet Branton's fury.

"Shove your sorrys up Grahame's ass, not mine," Branton snarled.

Every muscle in Grahame's body honed against the threat. Branton would have to kill him before he set a hand on Adara.

Bran hocked a glob of spit onto Adara's back. It dripped onto the floor with a wet sound. Grahame was over the bench and Hagan was hauling him back before he knew he'd swung at his brother-in-law.

"She is not worthy of our help," Branton growled as he turned and left the hall.

Though Hagan released him, Grahame sat only when he was sure his friend would not return.

Silence descended as the meal finished. Grahame suffered through a few bites at Adara's insistence while Ridley sat in one of the great chairs near the fire. His gaze remained on the flames, chin propped in his hand. Yrsa settled herself in a chair beside her husband not hiding the way she watched those who had captured her. Finally, Ridley spoke, his voice carrying through the hall.

"We will wait. As much as I would like to send you back to your father, Lady, the dispute between the earldoms over the reclaimed territory is a long time coming. It was given to Eadric of Bernira as an appeasement after Lachlan stole his bride, Cathryn of Wessex. Unfortunately for us, we are the closest tenants. I've long feared the impending battle. We will fortify what we can. Ready the men and station them at Grahame's parents' home."

When he saw Grahame open his mouth to protest, Ridley continued, "It is the closest outpost to Guston. It is where an attack will come from. Grahame, we will move your family into Hyrstow for the time being. I'll send word to Lachlan, tell him of the possibility of trespass on our land. I hope he's obstinate enough to come."

With that, Ridley threaded his fingers through Yrsa's and retreated into the day, leaving them alone.

Grahame wanted to collapse. His body teetered as he

stood, but then Adara was there, gingerly shelving his arm over her shoulders.

"Come, have a rest," she commanded in a quiet voice meant only for him.

The need to spirit her away from the village nearly wrought Grahame in two. He finally understood what drove Branton's brash anger, Ridley's cunning. It was the utter desire to keep their women and families safe and it roared awake in Grahame as he stared down into Adara's tired face. Her damaged lip threatened to split if she smiled, and the way she limped made him wish he could carry her.

"I love you more than all the stars in the sky. Deeper than any well," he murmured as she helped him onto one of the thin mattresses that lived along the wall.

Grahame was grateful the firelight did not touch them there. He tugged Adara down with him and she went, despite the bed being for one. Grahame maneuvered her to the inside, against the wall, so that if someone came to harm her, they would have to go through him first.

Grahame placed a kiss on Adara's temple, breathing her in. Mint and herbs from the salve they both wore stung his nostrils. Her stiff body loosened against his.

"I am..." she started, stopped, took a breath. Her face turned to his, her lips finding his jaw, his chin.

"The love I have for you is my most cherished possession. I know I did this to you and to your people. My regrets are many. And yet I cannot make myself regret you. We are one," she answered, the sureness of her words travelling straight into his heart. Careful of his injuries, Adara kissed him, her lips painting a picture of all the ways he mattered to her.

They held one another as they drifted to sleep, worry lining each of their faces over what was to come.

THIRTY-SIX

Grahame

The crack of the door at dawn had Grahame stirring from a fitful sleep, his body primed to defend Adara, lest someone try to harm her. He ached all over, but the stabbing pain in his shoulder had abated slightly. Silhouetted in the hall's doorway was a slight woman and a sturdy man. Grahame recognised the shapes of his parents within a heartbeat. He gently removed his arm from around his wife in an attempt to ease upward.

His mother hurried to them, her arms open. Tears glistened in her eyes.

"What is it?" Adara asked, rousing immediately. The corner of her mouth twisted down at the sight of his mother and father approaching. Her forearm jutted in front of him, as if to ward off an attack. Love for her flooded Grahame, even if her gesture was misplaced.

"It's my parents," Grahame said, covering her hand with his.

Adara's eyebrows met her hairline. She inhaled a sharp breath, then moved aside to help him into a sitting position. As much as Grahame hated being weak, he accepted the help, though he didn't hesitate to wrap his good hand around Adara's thigh to keep her with him.

"Grahame!" His mother's whispered shout was laden with distress. Fiona Shepherd's grey hair was bound back by a strip of cloth, her tunic pulled tight around the waist by an apron. A trembling smile broke over her wrinkled face.

"Mother," Grahame said, standing to scoop his mother into a one-armed hug.

Adara stood with him, her hand steady on his low back.

"My boy. We came as soon as we could," his mother whispered into his neck, her tears mingling with the dried poultice on his skin.

Her body quaked with quiet sobs, her grasp around him strong. Her lanolin and wool scent, the wiry feel of her—it made him feel like the cherished little boy he once was. Then his father was there, wrapping his arms around his wife and son with a quiet inhale. They remained like that for long moments. When they pulled away, Fiona wiped her eyes with a disparaging laugh. It died on her tongue when she set eyes on Adara.

Grahame stiffened. He knew there was no way his

parents would simply accept the way Adara had raided Hyrstow, taken Yrsa, and forced his marriage. Their eyes were wide, lips drawn downward. Wilfred's hand found Fiona's in unspoken solidarity. Silence grew.

Grahame swallowed his worry over their judgement. Adara had done terrible things. His choice had been to remain with her, so though it felt wrong to have others hate her, he would also shoulder the burden of their feelings. He reached for Adara's hand. She allowed him to thread his fingers through hers, her eyes locked warily on his parents.

Grahame braced himself. "Mother, Father, I am pleased to present my wife, Adara Clayton of Guston. Adara, it is my pleasure to re-introduce you to the only woman who's been able to tolerate me for any length of time, my mother, Fiona, and my father, Wilfred."

His mother crossed her arms across her chest, the ends of the shawl about her shoulders tucking into her elbows. Grahame winced at the stony look his mother leveled at Adara, the lines around her mouth and eyes smooth from her flat expression. Beside him, Adara stood as if her spine had become a tree. Grahame opened his mouth to say something to break the silence rioting around them but Adara swooped low, dirty skirt gathered in hand, her gaze on the dirt packed floor.

"I am honored to make your acquaintance, Shepherds. Grahame has shared many fond stories of your family. I am sorry that I could not have met you under better circumstances."

For a stony moment, no one moved. Adara remained

low with her head bowed, as if offering her neck in sacrifice. Her hand trembled in his.

"Well met," Fiona said, her tone flat.

Grahame's heart went out to his wife as she stood, eyes still downcast. His parents turned back to him, expressions of disappointment on their faces.

Grahame was about to change the subject when a wave of pain hit him, coupled with a rush of dizziness. Adara's arms went around his middle. He leaned on her, grateful for her strength, her love, even in the face of meeting his hostile family. She ushered him to sit on the mattress. Grahame kept his arm around her shoulders, pulling her down with him. He nuzzled an absent kiss into her hair.

The next instant, Fiona was at his other side. She pressed a cool hand to his forehead.

"They said you were nearly dead when Sam found you," Wilfred said, his voice gruff.

His hands were dirty on his hips. Bags lived beneath his eyes. As if struck by lightning, Grahame remembered Ridley was to station men at his parents' and they were to move into Hyrstow. They'd likely been up all night, clearing out belongings and herding sheep.

"Aye, I probably looked like a ghost. Am a bit better after resting," Grahame acknowledged, "And you both? You're to stay here?"

His mother nodded. Grahame winced as her hand hovered above his knee, unsure.

"It's alright, Ma. My arm was shredded and my ribs

feel like hell, but I'll make it through. I'm more worried over Adara."

From beneath his sore arm, Adara turned her face to his in question. Grahame cracked a mischievous grin.

"She's married to Hyrstow's Golden Boy. Handsome, kind, generous; however will she remain humble now that she has the most eligible man in the territory?"

Relief plucked strings in his chest as he saw his mother's facade crack.

A loud laugh rushed from her. "Oh, Grahame, how everyone's missed you."

Adara and Wilfred chuckled, rolling their eyes in unison.

His father let loose a familiar, weary sigh. "I must say, I was disappointed to hear of your marriage. Though, upon seeing the manner in which you seem to care for my son, I look forward to knowing the person Grahame deemed worthy," Wilfred said.

Grahame tightened his grasp around Adara's shoulders and planted a kiss on her cheek. She squirmed, face squished, but a laugh slipped from her. It rang through Grahame like a dinner bell, solid and true. His own shoulders unhitched and, despite the aches in his body, a carefree smile fit itself inside his mouth.

Together with his wife and parents he was truly home.

CHAPTER

THIRTY-SEVEN

Adara

There was no battle the following morning. Nor did it come the next day, or the one following. A dead rat had been left in one of her shoes, Hagan had gotten into a fistfight with one of the Hyrstow men, and someone snuck a dose of something into her food that made Adara throw up for an entire day, but no battle came down from her father.

Adara quickly sank into a routine of tending Grahame's wounds and trying to make herself small. She knew those in Hyrtsow were as tempted to kill her as they were to help Grahame. The outright glares from the men and women were expected. Grahame, however, had no qualms with telling off whoever got too close to her or

Muretta. He'd also begun to take the first sip of her drink or bite of food so as to avoid further poisoning.

Thankfully, Muretta had a habit of inserting herself wherever was needed. She helped with washing, cleaning, dragging a reluctant Bhlaine with her to assist with small farming chores at Emma and Branton's hut. Though his eyes were wide with worry when he left, Adara's housemaster returned unharmed and stinking of manure since Branton gave him the job of cleaning up their animal pen.

Hagan and Thor remained close, but after a few days, Grahame ordered them to make use of themselves and help Ridley and Yrsa patrol Hyrstow's border. Ridley had them stationed near the western woods, close enough that they couldn't easily run back to Clayton House without horse, but far enough from the center of town that they didn't make Hyrstow people uneasy. At night, Adara's people slept in the stable.

A week passed before Grahame's parents' land was burnt. The men stationed there, Sam and Uthrode, came with the news in the dead of night. Everyone was awake and roaring by the time Ridley and Yrsa were roused in their bedroom at the rear of the hall.

Relief that Ridley had the foresight to move Grahame's parents beforehand was a feeling that caught in Adara's throat. They had been distant yet polite to her, despite their displeasure over the marriage. While Sam relayed the sight of the burnt fields, Fiona wept quiet tears. Adara stood near, stoic. While Grahame discussed the fire with Ridley and his father, Adara dared to reach out to pat Fiona's shoulder.

"My heart overflows with regret that I have brought this fight to your doorstep. I am so sorry," Adara murmured, sorrow for Hyrstow a gnawing thing inside her chest.

Fiona looked at her as if she'd grown a second head. Dashing a finger beneath her eye to catch a tear, the older woman whispered, "Thank you."

Disregarding his family's protests, Grahame struck out with his father and friends at dawn to see what remained. The homestead had been destroyed. Grahame returned, paler than Adara had ever seen him. He later described to her the blanket of scorched earth. She'd hugged him, offering no words, for nothing could be said against the responsibility that stabbed her.

Harold Farmer's land was next. It lay south of the Shepherds', near the road to Earl Lachlan's keep. It was sheer luck that the fire had not spread into the trees that overhung the road south. That morning, most began their day while some remained behind in the hall to strategize.

"Eadric is picking us apart," Yrsa spat as she threw her bow on the table. "By the time I got to them, they were horsed. I shot one in the leg, but they still rode away."

Her blonde hair fell in a curtain over her eyes, obscuring her face. Fury lay in the clench of her jaw. Branton nodded, his huge arms crossed, leather vambraces layered overtop of one another. He'd been stationed with Yrsa and Hagan as sentries on Hyrstow's outskirts while Ridley, Sam, and Wilfred watched over Grahame's land to find out if they could see where the attacks were coming from. Others from the village were scattered to Hyrstow's edges, most in groups of two, to watch over and report if the villagers had to flee. Most families had been moved to the hall so Thor, Adara, Awolf, Paul, and Grahame could protect them. Ridley would not chance his people's safety.

"Only two? You're getting slow in your old age," Grahame said with a lopsided smile. It warmed Adara's heart that he had the wherewithal to joke with his friends in such dire circumstances.

"Says the man who choked when I was taken," she snarked, glaring.

Grahame tossed her a wink. He sat at the table beside Adara, elbows propping him up. His swollen eye had returned to normal, though it held a mean, greenish tinge. Adara had worked carefully to change the dressings on his shoulder and side twice per day, and he only winced when he thought others weren't looking.

Adara licked her healed lip. Though she still limped, remaining in the hall monitoring Grahame had given her foot a chance to rest. The pain in the bones had lessened.

"What if we do the same to them?" Branton asked. He held his daughter, Æfflead in one arm, his other daughter, Tatswip in the other. Dark haired Æfflead had demanded he lift her on his return to the hall. As he scooped her up, Branton had scoured his wife's pregnant form then gently taken Tatswip from her. Emma's tired smile was so full of love, it hurt Adara to look upon. With a kiss to his cheek, Emma left the hall to bake with another, stern woman.

Guilt for causing the family such distress in her raid burrowed further into Adara's chest, nestling deep.

"Indeed! Let's burn their fields!" a man named Paul shouted.

He was related to Emma Baker, though Adara could not remember how. Amid the full table, a chorus of cheers rose to the roof. Adara's gaze sliced to Grahame. He was already staring at her, a casual grin fitting itself along his mouth like a soldier readying for battle.

"Those are my lands you threaten," Grahame volleyed back.

Paul narrowed keen eyes at her. His balding head shone under the hall's torches. "Your land does not mean shit if it cannot help us. Just like your little wife."

Grahame picked up a knife, the movement smooth, lazy. He twirled the handle in his fingers. Green eyes narrowed on Paul, and Grahame's smile took on the sharpness of the blade in his hand.

"The people in the lands surrounding Guston are mine. They are just as much under attack as we are, but the difference is they have no choice. Earl Eadric has lorded over them. High taxes, brutal claims on their women, cruelty to their livestock." Grahame slid his ice-cold stare her way for a heartbeat before moving back to Paul. "My wife has only tried to help them prosper. What you see as retaliation will be a move against those who could rise up to join our fight."

"They have not yet done so," Paul said. He spat on the floor, uncrossing then crossing his arms.

"Neither have we. We're playing defense right now. I'd imagine so are they."

"Enough squabbling," Ridley commanded. He stood at the back of the room, stroking his hand over his beard. Adara's heart stalled when he turned his wolfish eyes on her.

"Lady Clayton. You have been rather quiet. Time to prove your worth."

THIRTY-EIGHT

Adara

"Have you allies in Guston? Any who would rise against your father?"

All eyes landed on her.

Adara licked her lips. "I believe most would follow me if it comes to a battle. However, many do not want to risk their livelihood to usurp someone that, if they lost, could come down harder on them. They would need a guaranteed win."

Someone behind her snorted. Paul rolled his eyes, throwing his hands to the roof then turning away. From Grahame's other side, another man shouted an oath.

"We would like the same, though it appears we do not have the option. We must fight," Branton's deep voice drowned out the others. He cocked his head as Adara met his stare, a mocking challenge in his blue eyes.

Adara swallowed around the dryness of her throat, brushing her clammy hands on her skirts. Across the room Yrsa ran a hand through her shortened hair, tossing a look of warning to Ridley he didn't catch. Rather, his gaze remained fixed on Adara, narrowing.

"Fickle allies are not welcome, as much as they are needed."

Adara ground her teeth against the ire that swelled. The backs of her eyes prickled. She would not show her frustration with tears. These people rightly hated her, yet she still had to fight for those who were their adversaries. She felt as if her limbs were being pulled on the rack.

"They are not fickle. They are concerned with living," she said.

"As are we!" a male voice shouted.

She shifted her gaze to the table, to the grain of the wood, choking on her pride.

"Be mindful of how you speak to my wife."

Grahame's voice sliced through the room. It was enough to silence the angry murmurs. Slowly, he stood, claiming attention. The fire's warm light slithered over his strong jaw, the column of his throat.

"Clayton house has arms. It has allies. We have promised reparations to those in Hyrstow who have suffered. I know it will never be enough. We will continue to strive to make repairs. However, this can only happen if we reclaim Clayton House!"

Grahame's shoulders rose, making him appear larger. He braced his knuckles on the table top, his jaw grinding as he allowed those gathered to mull over his words.

"I am Hyrstow's son. We will have our vengeance. I swear it."

Murmurs rumbled through the room. The people of Hyrstow were not simple-minded. As much as they resented her for her role in their suffering, they recognized a forced ally.

"He will!" Ridley's voice boomed around the room.

Adara startled, twisting toward him.

Hyrstow's chieftain had stalked to the head of the table. Arms crossed, a confident smile grew within his trimmed beard. He spoke with such authority Adara completely understood why he'd been such a force for his earldom.

"Adara is Eadric's heir. Grahame, her husband. If we can get inside Clayton House, get to Eadric, we can remake his earldom." He nodded toward Grahame. "You are Hyrstow's son. You will be Earl if we make it so."

The words rang around the room, sinking into those assembled. Every gaze flew to her husband. Adara saw Grahame blanch under the weight.

"I am not..." he trailed off. For once, Grahame did not have a jovial retort.

She knew he saw himself as a shepherd, married into power. Adara surmised the farthest he'd thought ahead was to survive the visit with her father. Perhaps ruling Clayton House with her, if he chose to remain. Granted, that was before her father had attacked.

Ridley did not speak falsely. She was Eadric's heir. And though claiming the earldom was another risk entirely, it was the quickest way to ensure the safety of her people and his.

Another voice joined the hot murmuring of those assembled.

"Grahame is a born ruler," Yrsa said, standing beside Ridley, navy eyes shining. She looked them both in the eye. "Adara moreso. I've seen first hand what they can do together. And if the earl of Bernira has come to shatter the lands of a woman who cares for her people, who knows how to rule, he knows nothing. We will triumph, because we have *her*."

It was Adara's turn for speechlessness. A flush spread from her chest up to her cheeks. Part of her agreed with Yrsa—she felt the innate call to rule and could understand the weight it carried—yet another part screamed her failures.

Elvin had cowed her. Grief had warped her. Revenge had driven her to amass a wealth of wrongdoings. Now, she was nothing more than a discarded daughter, a shepherd's wife. Whatever power she had held was scattered in her lands at her father's hand.

"You think *Grahame* can be an earl? What you speak of has not been done. Bernira must have a cousin, an uncle, that would claim the title if Eadric is gone." Paul's tone ensured the others would doubt Ridley and Yrsa's assessment. It was bold.

"There are none," Adara croaked.

Heads turned to her. She took a breath, her own gaze

finding Grahame's. The doubt in his handsome features caused her heart to go out to him. Grahame did not think himself worthy of much. It was why he put on a jovial front with his friends. Yet he held a quiet strength and natural air of ability that others followed.

Adara confirmed what Ridley wished.

"My father has no relatives. His father was Earl before him and he is dead. His uncles have died, and no sons were sired. My father has kept hold of his earldom with brutal will. Much to his disappointment, I am his only surviving child."

A cacophony of shouts threatened to bring down the high, thatched roof. She stared at her husband and he stared back, unwavering faith in his gaze. It caused Adara to tremble. That faith bolstered her.

Slowly, Adara stood. She looked to Ridley, to Yrsa, even Branton. She pressed her hands to her thighs, willing strength into her words.

"Grahame will be a wonderful leader. He is diplomatic yet ruthless when need be. He understands finances and people. I have knowledge of tenants, food stores, and the earldom. Together, we make a formidable pair. Anyone blind to that is free to leave, though I implore you to consider whether you'd prefer the pair of us or the rule of my father if he manages to take what he wants. Guston, Hyrstow—these lands have a long memory. He sees them as something owed. But what if Hyrstow's son becomes an earl? Bernira would be ours, the conflict no more."

Adara did not allow herself to dwell over the treason

she just spoke about. Rather, she turned to Hyrstow's chieftain, whose mouth twitched upward.

"Adara's right. I would rather have Bernira ruled by one of our own than wait for it to claim us," he said.

The words settled over the others amid contemplative sips of ale. No one spoke for long moments, their gazes fixed on their hands, the table, the roof.

"Let us discuss this amid our own people," Ridley offered.

It was a gesture of goodwill. One Adara was glad for. She backed away from her seat. To her surprise, Grahame threaded his fingers through hers, following.

Outside, the late-morning air was fresh and joyous, a contradiction to the stifling conversation. Bursts of blue and vermillion flowers decorated the path between the huts. Arm in arm, they hobbled north, making their way past the hall to the road that led out of Hyrstow. Several women passed as they went, their attention locked on Grahame. One sighed, her mouth folded in a frown.

Indifferent, Grahame slung his good arm around Adara's shoulder. She wrapped her arm around his waist, her hand landing on his muscled side. His lips traced the shell of her ear.

"What if we remained here? Defended our lands and built a little house on my parent's hill? Your father might retreat and leave us be. What if we simply loved one another until the end of time?"

Adara ducked her chin to her chest. The backs of her eyes prickled at the vision she knew would not come true. She released a scoff, adding to the illusion.

"Indeed, we could have Bran cut new timber, have Ewan build the hut. We could set to work on making babies."

"Aye, I'd have a baby in you by fall. It would be a girl; I've always wanted one, despite the need for a dowry. A girl first, to help soften the four boys that would come after."

A tear slipped down her cheek as a little laugh escaped. She was grateful to have never had a child with Elvin though the thought of not having a baby with Grahame suddenly created a deep ache within her soul.

"And you would take over your father's flock, and we would travel to markets all year long and make so much coin we would never want for anything. The children would grow to know how to work hard and love harder."

Adara looked up to find Grahame's chin wobbling as he, too, stared at the horizon.

"I would keep you in the gowns you love, of course," he said, his voice shaky.

"Of course."

"And there would be no need for war, no need for the earldoms to hate one another. We would be safe. Our families and our friends would be safe. And we would love one another until the end of our days, happy."

They halted on a slight hill before it turned downward into a singed, black field that should have been barley. Adara nodded, unable to speak around the lump in her throat. Grahame cleared his own. He pulled her into his chest, shuddering breaths rattling from both of them. Tears blurred Adara's eyes enough to close them.

"If there is any hope of that future, we must fight. You must become earl." Her words felt like stones she used to beat him with. He'd never wanted that future.

"Aye," Grahame said, his voice thick with gravel, "I know. But, I can only do that with you by my side."

Adara opened her mouth, an apology for changing his life so drastically at the ready.

"No," he said, his tone firming as he cupped her cheek. His thumb trailed over her healed split lip. "You will not say what you're about to say. You think you're so good at hiding, 'Dara. But I know you. You feel guilt over what is required of me. I can understand it—we never thought it would come to this. I was yours long before our wedding day and have been every moment after."

He bent to place a kiss on her lips. It was bittersweet and gentle. When he drew away, his lips were turned upward like a flower rising to the sun.

"I will do what is best for you. And Hyrstow. And Goddamn Guston. I will do what is right, but only if you rule by my side. My only request is that you see that future, the one we just spoke of, as real. No more talk of trapping. No more guilt. You love me with your whole heart. It's you and me. As one. Against everything."

If Adara's heart could have burst, it would have. Her actions had cornered him into that fate. And yet, he didn't hesitate when needed. Grahame would be hers and her earldom's, by his own choice. She had no words. Rather, she let her hands and hips and mouth speak. She pressed herself into her husband with everything she had, wishing her love was enough to see them through it all.

"I'll take that as a 'yes,'" he murmured against her lips.

Adara grinned, her arms encircling him, and nodded.

CHAPTER

THIRTY-NINE

Grahame

"Two men, on the outskirts of town," Sam said, bursting through the hall's door, skidding to a stop at the chairs that circled the central fire. His sandy blond hair was pasted to his forehead, arms wheeling as he brought himself up short.

Grahame blew out a breath, his head propped in his hand. The dregs of lunch were on the table before him. Adara and Muretta had ventured off with Emma, a wary Branton at their heels, to learn how to bake bread.

Grahame was glad Adara was getting out of the hall, trying to make other acquaintances. Though her existence in Hyrstow was tenuous, she was trying to make amends. While most were put on alert to guard their village, she had been learning how to prepare food, had served it to those who ate at the hall's table, worked her fingers to the bone gardening, and somehow had gotten Ridley's wolf dog, Nod, to fall in love with her. The great black beast followed her around as if she had forged the world. Grahame knew the feeling.

"Were they armed?" Ridley demanded. Fires and theft in the dark of night were one thing. Warriors at Hyrstow's doorstep was another.

Sam nodded, his hand pressing to the hall's table for support as he sucked deep breaths.

"On horse, swords, shields."

"I shall find out what they want," Ridley said, moving to his quarters. Yrsa was a step behind him.

"Will you go as well?" Sam asked Grahame.

Grahame hesitated. After he'd returned from his walk with Adara several days prior and proclaimed his intent to claim Bernira, the others in Hyrstow looked upon him with thinly veiled awe. There was no need for it. Their wild plan would surely end up with him dead, but Grahame refused to voice that deep-seated doubt to anyone. He'd been living with that same doubt his entire marriage, only now the scope of it was larger. His need to defend Adara to his last breath was a flame raging inside of him. His friends and neighbors, however, entrusted him with their lives as well. Was this how Adara felt all the time? He did not know how she could stand it.

"I..." Grahame said, dragging out the word. Though his wounds had been healing well, his shoulder still ached, and the thought of riding wasn't pleasant.

Ridley and Yrsa returned after having strapped swords, shields, and daggers to themselves. Ridley carried chainmail.

"Here." Yrsa thrust a sword at him.

Their faith that he would want to join them gave him renewed strength.

Grahame forced a smile he hoped appeared ruthless. "Yes, I am," he confirmed to Sam.

His friend's smile of relief was all Grahame needed to bite back the pain as he hefted the proffered chainmail.

"I'll help," Yrsa said, her tone unflinching. She set the sword down on the table and took the mail, assisting him with threading his arms in first, then laying the rest over his shoulders.

"Where are you off to?" Thor's voice rang out as he passed through the doors. Past the doorway, Isla Dunn was making eyes at Thor's back. He did not notice the admiration when he came to stand with them, his large arms crossing.

"There's men on horses north of Hyrstow. We're going to see what they want. You need not accompany us," Grahame said.

Thor ran his tongue over his teeth then nodded. "Well, I best come with. She'll skin me alive if something happens to you."

THERE WERE NOT two men lingering on the village outskirts. There were thirty. Several were in leathers, others in chainmail. They held real weapons, not mere pitchforks and axes. Ridley and Yrsa surged ahead, meeting the lone man that rode out to the center of the field. All Grahame could do was sit back, readying to race to Hyrstow to warn the others if there was a battle.

"Who d'ya think it is?" Thorhild asked as he reined up beside Grahame. The man squinted toward the field of men, sweat beading on his brow beneath the sun's stare.

Ridley's horse remained steady as Yrsa danced hers back and forth behind him. Surprise lit through Grahame as Ridley pointed at him then waved him forward. Thor raised a bronze eyebrow at the gesture but followed Grahame to the center of the field nonetheless. Despite Grahame's worry, Thor's presence warmed something in him.

Only when he approached did he recognize Guston's tavern-owner, Uhtread. He must have worn relief on his face because the man said, "I'm happy to see you, too, My Lord."

Grahame moved his horse up to Uhtread's, offering a hearty shake with his good hand.

Uhtread didn't hesitate. "We've come to assist our Lady Clayton. Been sent word that she may be within Hyrstow's bounds."

"Aye, that she is," Grahame said.

"Of her own will?" the man pressed.

The line of men in the distance shifted. Somewhere behind him, Yrsa scoffed.

"Yes. We fled Clayton House. Her father aimed to kill me and marry her off to the northerners," Grahame confirmed.

Uhtread hawked phlegm onto the ground as if insulted. He scratched his chest with the meaty hand not holding a weapon while his gaze narrowed on Ridley.

"Friends of yours?"

Grahame swallowed, trying to get his bearings. The last time the people of Guston and Hyrstow interacted was the former raiding the latter.

"Indeed. Ridley Ward, chieftain of Hyrstow. His wife, Yrsa the Viking. They have been of great help to us."

Uhtread's face broke into a smile that didn't meet his eyes. It sent a chill down Grahame's back.

"Aye. Ridley the Conqueror. The one who sacked our farmsteads, pillaged homes with his men. Hurt women. The one whose village we were happy to raid a few months ago."

Ridley stiffened, hand twitching on his short sword. Yrsa had stopped trotting. Grahame kept his eyes on Uhtread. The older man's smug grin told him he'd been aiming low to get a rise out of them. Grahame puffed out his chest, hoping if he came in strong, Uhtread would behave.

"Whatever has passed between our two villages is settled. My marriage to Lady Clayton is proof of a truce. Are you here to aid us?"

Uhtread's eyes snaked from Grahame to Ridley. His grip tightened on the reins, huge shoulders bunching.

His attention slipped to Yrsa. Something akin to a twinkle lit his eyes as he scoured her face. It had Grahame's hackles up, though he forced an impassive look.

"Aye. We are. We stand with Lady Clayton. Though, I will have you aware, we do not take kindly to your people. We will not enter your lands like lambs to be slaughtered."

"Like you did to us?" Yrsa reined up next to them, her lip curled.

Uhtread's grin widened. He leaned forward. "Don't worry, lamb. Yer one I wouldn't dream of harming."

Yrsa recoiled as a laugh boomed out of him.

Ridley growled, his next words coming through teeth. "You shall remain here. No man from Guston is welcome within our border."

"Just our Lady?" Uhtread sneered.

A hawk screeched overhead. The sun climbed. It would be disaster to leave an entire fleet of useful men out in the baking lands.

"Have you tents?" Grahame asked, ignoring their pissing contest.

Uhtread tipped his chin to his chest.

"We will have water and food brought. This is my land. Your men may remain here. We are in the midst of forming a plan of attack. You, Uhtread, will come with us to Hyrstow."

～

AFTER MUCH GRUMBLING from Uhtread and Ridley, their small band rode back into Hyrstow. Joy surged in Grahame when he set eyes on his wife. Back straight, her hand over her eyes to shield the sun, Adara perched on a bench beside the hall. Muretta sat beside her, hands flapping with the story she told. When Grahame dismounted, Adara rushed to him, arms outstretched. Grahame forced back the grimace at her embrace. The pain in his arm skewered him to the spot for a moment.

"Husband," she said into the skin of his throat.

"We have Guston," he said, triumphant despite his discomfort.

Adara's entire face lit with a smile when she looked past him to Uhtread. She shrieked, clapping, before throwing herself into the older man's meaty arms.

"My Lady, I am glad to see you well," Uhtread said as they parted.

"Come," Adara said, drawing the tavern-owner into the hall.

Grahame took a moment to lean against the bench Adara had vacated, sucking in a deep breath to combat the pain in his arm. The chainmail was heavy and he was hot from riding.

"She was worried." Muretta's voice was sharp. Her cloud of hair had been pulled back into braids similar to those worn by Merthe, Emma's daughter. Her usual dress was swapped for a simple tunic.

Grahame blew out a breath. "I had to go. There were unknown riders."

"She's so used to ruling on her own or, like with Elvin, being ruled over. You as a partner are different from anything she's known. She worries when you take off to your doom."

"Aye, and I imagine she will have to get used to it. I cannot balk at my duties, Muretta. Not now. Believe me, I would have rather laid about this afternoon. I did not want to ride a horse in the heat with barely healed wounds. However, next time I will send word to her what I'm doing and why."

Muretta snickered as she walked with him into the hall. When she looked up at him, a tenderness shone in her features. "Good."

Grahame didn't hide his affection, pulling Muretta into his side. "Thank you for being her friend."

Ridley, Hagan, Thor, Sam, Ewan, Awolf, Aeon, and Paul stood around the table while Adara questioned Uhtread. Once word went 'round the village that there was a Guston man present, several more people filtered in, including Branton and Father Chisholm, Head Priest of Hyrstow.

Siege on Clayton House was determined as the best course of action. Ridley had not heard if Earl Lachlan would provide assistance but quick action to halt the barrage on Hyrstow's farmland was deemed of import. Better to trap the earl of Bernira in Clayton House before he could call on more men or retreat. If he retreated, it would be dire for their forces to push up into his lands. They would prepare in the coming days and travel in the evening so as to take Clayton House by surprise.

Grahame's eyelids were drooping by the time Hagan and Thorhild left with Uhtread to relay the plan to the Guston forces. Across the table, Adara rose then came to him, draping her arm about his good shoulder and proclaiming he was to go to bed. They disappeared to the rear of the hall, Grahame thankful to finally have his arms around his wife. As if others were as exhausted as they, the noise of the hall died down quickly.

Adara produced a poultice, helping him remove his tunic and wrappings, then layered the mint-scented salve on his shoulder wound.

"The skin appears as if it has begun to properly stitch itself back together," she murmured, her fingers careful as she re-wrapped the bandage. "Scabbed but together."

Grahame could nearly taste the relief in her tone. He felt it himself. There was something intensely vulnerable about not being able to properly defend his wife in a village where she wasn't safe. The quicker he regained his strength, the quicker he could help fight in this war.

Grahame pressed a kiss to her temple and murmured, "Aye, aren't all of us that? Scabbed, but together."

"Indeed, Husband," Adara whispered as her lips skimmed his.

She tasted of berries and pastry. Grahame threaded his fingers into the nape of her neck to hold her to him longer.

Even if they only had a short time together, he could not bring himself to regret a moment of it. Adara had made him live a thousand lives with her love. And though he wished to live a thousand more with her at his side, he would go to the grave knowing he'd tasted rapture.

350

FORTY

Grahame

It took two days to gather weapons and decide who would travel to Clayton House and who would remain. Another two to collect supplies, instruct wives and sons on tending farms or jobs, and to pray for victory. Most of Hyrstow's men opted to go, though a couple could not bring themselves to fight for the lands of a woman who had harmed Hyrstow.

Muretta wrung her hands and refused at first but finally agreed to stay behind where she would be safe. After a tearful goodbye with Thor and an especially long hug with Hagan, she turned back to the hall. Branton refused to leave. There was no way Grahame's brother-in-law was going to desert his pregnant wife and children. Emma had spent the entirety of those two days baking with Isolde Tanner to make rations.

Travelling with the band from Guston had its challenges. When Hyrstow men broke across the hilltop and saw the breadth of those that raided their village not long ago, Grahame thought there would be slaughter. Adara and Ridley united together was the only thing keeping the seething mass away from one another. Each group fell in with their respective leaders. Grahame was proud to ride beside his wife; he was glad to show both groups of their allegiance.

The glaring sun beat down on Grahame's skull as they made their way into Guston. The plan was to rest there for the evening, to gather whatever extra food stores the village could offer.

"You look about to fall asleep astride that horse," Adara said.

"I am tired," he admitted.

She only stared at him, her rose-petal lips in a neutral line. He simply shrugged, hoping it was enough for her to let it go. His shoulder and ribs ached less, though how they would fare in a fight was a different concern.

"Uhtread!" he called to the man riding behind him. "Is your village able to spare a pig? I know an army such as this will appreciate the strength good meat would offer."

He and Uhtread began a boisterous conversation about meat and some games—a lighthearted night before setting off to the unknown the next morning. All the while, Grahame stole glances at Adara.

She wore one of Yrsa's fine green cloaks, her midnight hair wild and cascading down her back. Lambskin gloves from his mother covered her hands, despite the heat. The slope of her nose, the dewiness of her sweat-slicked skin, the way her legs looked in borrowed leathers—all of her made his mouth water. His cock twitched at the thought of taking her to bed that evening, and when she caught him staring, the coy smile she offered let him know he wasn't the only one with bedding in mind.

Despite their intentions, accommodations were sparse. He and Adara were given a room in the tavern, though others weren't so lucky. Little in the way of privacy was to be had with the main area of the tavern being stuffed with those from Hyrstow. The Guston men were able to return to their homes. Ridley and Yrsa were hosted in Guston's hall, along with Thor and Hagan.

"You need to rest, " Adara said, moving behind him to drape her arms around his throat.

Grahame sat shirtless with his legs over the sides of the small cot that was to be their bed for the evening.

"Aye, we both should," he acquiesced.

Unease laid low in his belly. Adara noticed his hesitation, coming 'round to sit beside him. The tiny bed caved under their combined weight.

"How well can you move your arm?"

"It will be fine."

"It won't, Grahame. Not if you don't..."

"Tell you?" He kept a tether on the prickliness in his tone.

Adara sensed it nonetheless. Her eyes became narrowed slits of silver. He released a heavy sigh.

"I am injured, Adara. There is nothing for it other than time. Complaining won't make it better."

"Yes, but as your partner, it will help me strategize."

Grahame made a fist with the hand of his injured arm, released it and shook it out. Holding onto reins all day hadn't helped. His hope was that siege would mean waiting, and waiting meant more time to heal.

"Grahame," Adara said, her fingers brushing back the hair that had fallen across his forehead. She lightly dragged her nails along his scalp in a way that made him shiver. "I need you to be with me. I am moving against my father in an act that will have us killed if we are caught. I need to know you will be able to stand beside me, to be a united front for the men who doubt me, to show my father that he shouldn't have tried to harm you. You need to tell me if you can't be there. I would rather know now and have you protected than risk you. My concern cannot be split between you and what I know has to happen."

Grahame cupped a hand over her knee. It felt warm and lithe beneath his grip.

"How do you feel about this? Truly?"

Adara blinked, her hand stilling on his hair. Grahame waited. He was learning that his wife was impulsive, yet her actions in the moment sometimes led to her deep regret.

"I deserve to get my house back," she replied.

"'Dara," he chided, "tell me your feelings about our

plan. Trapping your father in your house and demanding he surrender the earldom to us must be cause for concern."

Grahame drifted his knuckles across her cheekbone. Adara's eyes fluttered shut. She drew a breath then exhaled before pressing a kiss to Grahame's surprised lips. When she pulled away, a line of worry lived between her brows. When she did not respond, he pushed.

"I wish to know your thoughts," he said gently.

True to form, she met his inquiry with anger. "You are worried I will falter when I see him again? The way I panicked and fainted after our return from Guston?"

Grahame leaned into her, quiet. He pressed a kiss to her forehead, wrapping his arm around her waist so she was tucked into his side. He waited.

"What good does it do for me to voice my doubt that this is folly? That you will be hurt more or that my father will do something heinous to all these people I've gathered? Worry does not begin to cover the churning I feel in my middle or the pounding of my heart when I think of what is to come."

She bit her bottom lip against the rest of her words. Grahame took her chin between his thumb and forefinger and tugged it loose.

"Keep on," he urged.

She jerked her face away, but after a moment, leaned into him. There was a wobble to her next words. It tested Grahame's ability to just sit there. He wished to fix it all for her, yet an innate part of him knew to be still and listen.

"I am afraid, Grahame. Different from the stab of fear I felt when you were harmed. This is a wave threatening to drown me. A sense of misery that will take me down if I allow it. You've seen the loss of control I have when up against my father. Somehow, after everything he has done to me, I am terrified to betray him. I do not believe he will surrender, and yet all I can do is lead my people the best way I can."

Grahame sowed kisses into her hair, holding her tight.

"I will be by your side. I promise. Focus on your father. I will be there for you in any way you need."

The words were not the salve he wished them to be. He was scared as well, his entire being stricken over the people they were risking. One thing was utterly true, however.

He would be there for Adara. Always.

The next morn, they dressed in silence. When they left the room, Adara pulled him into a kiss that made him see stars.

"I love you. Thank you for listening. For being my anchor," she said before pressing another kiss to his lips.

The men were in good spirits after stopping for the night. Supplies seemed plentiful enough, and they knew they could draw more resources from the surrounding lands if needed. Eadric would be stuck in the house, regretting his choice to have Grahame killed and his daughter married off. He would either leave with his head and the promise to relinquish land or he would not. Grahame had no qualms about his wife's father dying. Not after he'd harmed her in so many ways.

At mid-day Clayton House came into view. A blanket of black conquered the wheat field that had once stood behind Clayton House. Despite the refusal of his mind to reconcile what he was seeing, Grahame noticed the hush that fell over their troop as the property came into full view of the men. The swarm moved, looking more like ants scurrying as their party neared. Grahame cast a look at Adara, then Ridley, only to see their jaws clenched, their eyes locked on the scene ahead.

"Halt," Ridley shouted, yanking on his reins.

Adara's eyes found his, wide with fear.

The fires had been misdirection. Eadric had brought the full breadth of his legions to Clayton House.

FORTY-ONE

Adara

Her father's men were a seething mass among the rear field. It was as if he'd called up every knight in his realm to squash them. She bit back the panic that boiled up her chest into her throat.

"How did he assemble them so quickly?" Grahame asked in a strained tone, reining up next to her. There was not a spot of wheat to be seen.

Before she could answer, Ridley and Yrsa were there. The skin around Yrsa's eyes was tight. Ridley wasn't much better, though he refrained from showing an ounce of fear in front of the men.

"How many?" Ridley asked her.

Adara swallowed. She had no way to know. Her father only briefly made her privy to his forces. She knew more about the breadth of his territory. It was never her job to know the exact details. It would be their downfall.

"I am not sure. His territory expands up to Hadrian's Wall, then cuts down the center of Northumbria. It bottoms out at the Kingswood, however I do not believe anyone lives there."

"Can you guess?" Ridley's hazel eyes were steady on hers.

Adara settled her shoulders, quelled the churning in her middle. She would not falter.

"Around forty knights, though they are likely older men, and their sons. Territory disputes have broken out in the past. Our lands are not as prosperous as Deircia's. Every few years, the nobles fight one another to claim more. It's left few in the way of actual lords. But this," Adara gestured to the mass of people past her home, "he's gotten these men from somewhere. Perhaps they are the northerners. He was trying to marry me off to a Briton prince. They could have been coming for the wedding or to raid, I do not know."

"But you killed him," Grahame said.

"I've heard the Britons are savages," Yrsa offered, her lips curling back in a snarl.

"Said the Viking," Grahame pointed out. His brow was wrinkled with worry, his handsome face cast in stone. He looked stronger, heartier than he had in the last week, for which Adara was grateful.

Yrsa continued without acknowledging him. "Would

they not have conflict with your father if they'd come for a wedding to find their leader dead?"

Adara turned back to her men. Many spoke among themselves, pointing to Clayton House while others sat stoic on their steeds awaiting orders. A fondness for them swelled in her. They had accepted a new alliance and were marching for her. Their wellbeing was hers. She doubted her father cared one ounce for the men he commanded.

"He likely told them the truth. If the prince is dead, it is because of me. He would offer his daughter to the wolves to gain an army. Revenge is an excellent motivator."

Ridley's attention remained on the forces undulating in the far field while Yrsa's was glued to their own sparse band of warriors. Grahame's green eyes scoured her features as if to read her thoughts.

"We don't have enough men." Adara's voice cracked as she spoke, her gaze falling to her hands on the reins. She would not drag these good people into a fight they would surely lose. "I will go to my father. Try to make it right."

"No." The word was impenetrable. Grahame tried to catch her thigh with his good hand. He missed.

"I am the only one who can convince him—"

She flinched when Grahame's shout cut her off.

"Of what, 'Dara? To let your people go? That you had no choice but to kill the man who was going to kill me? He will either slay you on the spot or marry you off to the next Briton in the ranks. I will not sacrifice you to appease a monster."

"Keep your voice down," Ridley hissed.

He turned his horse, a look of concentration replacing the concern etched in his features. The men needed confidence in their leadership. Adara's respect for Hyrstow's chieftain grew.

"How many men would you guess?" Yrsa asked. Her fingers drummed the short-sword at her side.

"About two hundred," Hagan answered, riding up from the group's left flank. He squinted beneath the sun's glare.

"And we have less than half that."

Adara tilted her chin, straightened her shoulders. There was no question what had to be done. She could make a run for the house if she wouldn't get leave to go.

"They're moving," Yrsa said, drawing Adara's gaze back to the house.

Indeed, the main gates were open, men on horse pouring out. Banners flew as the animals began to gallop. With horror Adara watched the warriors shift into formation. The men on horses were the head of an arrow, and behind it, a marching column.

There would be two waves.

"We must retreat," Grahame breathed as Uhtread rode up. Grahame rotated his injured arm, gaze locked on the convening men.

Blind fear threatened to seize her by the bones. Her people were supposed to have the upper hand. The burnt fields, the time to gather forces, was a distraction. They would have been ambushed all along. Adara felt as if she could not draw a breath.

"Too late," Ridley muttered, turning his horse. He galloped in front of the line of their soldiers. Men were already dropping supplies and retrieving shields. Sword belts were slipped on, axes readied. Squinting into the sun, their gazes were locked on the group of horsed men that thundered past Clayton House's gates.

"Adara," Grahame said, his tone steady.

It startled Adara from her thin breaths. There was no time for panic. Only sheer will.

Adara kicked herself into action, moving in the opposite direction of Ridley, calling out to their bowman to ready their arms. When she whirled back, she could see her father at the forefront of the attack, his sword pointed at them as he charged down the hill. She would recognize his helm, a snarling badger, anywhere.

"Weapons!" Adara shouted, her hand diving for her own sword-belt slung across Ulrich's back.

Men scrambled, tossing weapons to one another, while Ridley rode up and down the line, advising on how they would advance. Yrsa threw herself from her horse, grabbing the shield strapped across its back. She secured it onto her left arm in one swift movement, then scooped up her short sword. Shouting commands to fall in line together, she placed her shield up against others to form an interlocked wall, planting her feet. Thor was right beside her. Uhtread, Hagan, Ridley, Grahame, and Adara remained horsed.

"Adara," Grahame snarled.

Adara turned, her breath catching in her throat at the devastating sight of him. Windblown curls pressed his forehead. His cloak hugged his broad shoulders. But it was the haunted shadow in his usually bright green eyes that held her still.

He reached for her, his fingers skimming her knee. Adara's lip dared tremble at the warmth of his skin. A surge of fright hit her. They were out of time. Again. After all the time apart, their reunion, they were out of time with one another.

"Stay beside me," Grahame commanded. He gestured for her to steer the horse beside him.

Hooves thundered. Steel helms glinted beneath the sun, banners flapping as the line of her father's men rode at them. The first wave consisted of around thirty. Each man had a sword and wore some sort of mail. Adara's party looked paltry in comparison. The men on horse did not slow.

"We do not stand a chance," Adara whispered.

Terror for her men, for Hyrstow's, reached up and clasped her throat. There was no way for them to win against such a force. It was her folly that had brought them all there. *She* had incited her father's wrath. If she'd only accepted his decree and married the Briton, all of those with her would have been spared.

"We must stand as one," Grahame said, his voice strained.

It was like a punch to the chest. Adara looked away as her eyes filled with tears. She tightened her grip on Ulrich's reins.

Her mind scrabbled over ways to halt the impending massacre. If she could only reason with her father, give herself up, perhaps he would listen to her. Then she remembered the coldness in his face when he'd shoved her to the ground, the way he enjoyed relaying the news that Grahame was to be killed. There would be no mercy.

"I have to stop him," she muttered to herself. "I've done this."

"'Dara," Grahame warned.

He would be further injured or killed. He was innocent. Hers to protect. And he would *not* die defending her. Adara swallowed. There was nothing to be done other than offer herself up to her father. Perhaps she could halt the massacre. Perhaps she could bargain...

"Grahame, I love you," was all she said before spurring ahead to where Hagan was barking orders.

"Get back," Hagan snarled, his eyes flaring with concern as she rushed to join the line of men preparing for battle.

"No," she growled.

"Goddamnit, Adara! Get back!" Hagan shouted again, allowing his horse to lag as if to force hers to turn the other way. She spurred Ulrich forward, passing Hagan, outrunning Grahame.

A man in black leathers and a metal helm rode at her. He held a longsword, his body tucking in tight to his steed as his gaze narrowed on hers. There was no turning back. Blood rushed through her, charging her limbs. Steady.

Twenty five yards.

Hagan fell in beside her.

Twenty.

She tucked herself close to Ulrich's neck.

Fifteen.

Beneath a mop of grey hair, the man ahead grinned.

Ten.

The man lurched up in his seat, longsword ready to pierce her breast. She withdrew the small dagger from her belt.

Five.

In a motion that felt as easy as breathing, she let the dagger fly.

Men and horses met with a shrieking, whinnying impact, swords and shields clashing. Adara's sword dug into the man's side as she passed. He didn't reciprocate. Her dagger had lodged in his throat. With a grunt, she yanked her sword from him as he fell to the side, sliding off his horse.

There was no time to relish the small victory.

The clang of metal burst around her. Grunts and wails and blood splattered. She reined to the side as another soldier sliced at her leg, missing her by inches. His menacing gaze narrowed on her as she maneuvered. Then he was shouting in pain as Hagan's sword punched through his chest from behind. Blood flecked her legs as the man slumped forward.

Adara clenched her teeth in a grin of thanks to Hagan. His eyes widened, locked on something behind her.

She twisted in her seat, sword up just as metal came

down. The blow fell short of her arm. Adara turned Ulrich, glaring at the horsed man only for her mind to go blank when she saw it to be her father.

"Daughter," Eadric of Bernira snarled, his eyes shadowed beneath his shiny helm.

"Stop this," Adara commanded.

Eadric laughed, a dirty, grating sound.

"You set this in motion, girl. You caused upheaval; you betrayed Bernira. And I see you've brought your own warriors."

A moan of agony cut through the din of metal on wood. Adara forced herself to keep her gaze fixed on her father and not frantically search for Grahame in the melee.

Adara's heart rammed into her throat. Her hands trembled as she said, "Take me and halt this assault. I will go with you. I will do what you wish."

From somewhere behind her, Grahame shouted, "No!"

A grin slid its way up her father's mouth. He kept his horse moving, sidestepping to and fro, so as not to become a stationary target.

"You will come with me, Adara," he said.

Equal parts relief and dread speared her.

The feelings were quashed immediately when her father continued: "Though I will not stop this. These people need to learn their place. You've led an uprising that needs to be silenced."

A sinking feeling heavier than any anchor dropped in her middle. She tightened her grip on her weapon as she frantically scanned the clash of armies. Ridley was unhorsed, locked in battle with two men. Hagan drew his sword from a man's chest.

"'Dara!"

Despair clawed at her. She had to go, had to get her father to *listen*.

"Please," she shouted, her panic rising. "Call back your men. I will go."

Too soon, Grahame was beside her. His leg was drenched in blood.

"Ah, the husband still lives," Eadric said. He spat at the ground.

Grahame was like a feral dog beside her, advancing with his sword raised high. His cloak billowed around his heaving shoulders.

"Stand down," Grahame shouted. Quick as an adder, Eadric spurred forward, swiping at Grahame's middle with his sword. Adara felt her heart stall as Grahame ducked back, his horse nearly tripping on a fallen body.

"No!" Adara couldn't help her strangled scream as the blood-stained metal swiped too close to Grahame's side.

Adara barely thought as she slipped a dagger from her belt and let it fly. The blade lodged in her father's shoulder. He grunted, cold eyes slicing to her from beneath his helm.

"'Dara," Grahame's voice was strangled.

The shift of his gaze to her right alerted Adara to an impending strike. All she could do was twist, hoping her father didn't carve up her other side. Ulrich whinnied as another horsed warrior came at her from the left. She ducked, plunging her own weapon into the man's leg. He wailed, clutching his wound, before falling to the ground. Adara yanked her sword back before it fell with him.

The clash of metal and an oath from Grahame rang in Adara's ears. When Adara whirled back, Eadric was withdrawing his weapon. Grahame's face was awash with pain. She scanned her husband's body but could not see an injury around his robes and tunic. She prayed he'd not been struck.

Adara swore something like pride shone in Eadric's narrowed eyes.

"All my life, I wanted sons. Yet here you are."

Adara could barely hear him over her ragged breaths. The stench of unwashed bodies and fear stuffed up her nostrils. Eadric made sure to shout his next words so they would fall on her like a sword strike.

"You're lucky you are the link to my line. I intend to spare you. I know you likely think you killed him, but Galan lives."

FORTY-TWO

Adara

"How is he alive?" Grahame shouted over the grunts of exertion surrounding them.

Men were everywhere. Some on horse, most hand to hand. The shield wall stood to Adara's right, but it had broken on her left.

Eadric offered a crooked smile. "The Britons are loyal. Their leader is in my care. They are here to lay waste to those who harmed him."

Adara sucked a breath through her teeth as she reined Ulrich as close as she dared. Moving. She had to keep moving. Had to get close enough to her father to agree to stop the madness. It was the only way to end it all.

At her side, Hagan bellowed. Adara locked her limbs in place so she would not look his way. She dug her heels into Ulrich.

"Never. She will *never* go with you," Grahame spat. He jabbed his weapon at Eadric. Her father easily blocked the motion. Sweat slicked Grahame's brow. He was already tired. Yet Adara knew he would fight for her. Would sacrifice himself to save her.

"Aye, boy, she will."

Eadric's mouth contorted into a cruel grin. It called to something deep in her, something she'd seen throughout childhood—her father's cruelty in the face of her resistance. She swallowed over the dry knot in her throat.

"Grahame, I have to," Adara called, her tone ragged, helpless.

How could she tell him she had to own all the ways she failed? The sounds of agony, of metal through meat were enough to tell her how her side fared. Adara narrowed her eyes against the too bright sun. She sucked a breath, steeling herself against the sensation of defeat that threatened to swamp her. She did not dare look at Ridley and Yrsa, Hagan and Uhtread. Her father had too many men. He'd outwitted them. Guston and Hyrstow were to be sacrificed.

If devastation had a face, Grahame wore it when he looked at her. "He will kill you."

"Who said anything about killing you, Daughter? The Brit prince will not care if your face is carved up, so long as your cunt still works."

The disgusting words were barely uttered before Grahame was roaring with rage, slicing at her father's leg. The movement revealed a slip of material poking from beneath her father's arm. There was a gap in the armor between the chest and shoulder plates. Beneath his arm, too, if she could get close enough. With a snarl, she dug with her other hand for the last dagger on her belt.

Eadric deflected Grahame's blow. He parried with a strike that skimmed Grahame's injured shoulder.

"No!" she screamed.

Adara's heart lurched into her chest as Grahame swerved to avoid the blow. To her right, a woman grunted in agony. Adara kept her eyes locked on her father despite her desire to find out if Yrsa had fallen. A man's roar overtook the melee, the clanking of metal stronger, more fearsome. The stench of blood shoved up her nose.

She would not lose everyone, everything.

"You will not take us!" Adara shouted, spurring ahead.

"I will!" Eadric spat.

To her utter shock, he plunged his sword into the shoulder of Grahame's horse. The animal reared back, shrieking in pain. Adara watched in horror as Grahame attempted to keep his seat while holding a weapon in one hand, his injured arm gripping the reins. Grahame slipped to the side, bellowing. He would be trampled.

"No!" Adara screamed.

In a blink, Grahame fell. The beast's forelegs came down hard before it darted away.

For a moment, the entire world stopped.

Her father laughed, the sound awakening the blood-curdling sense of revenge Adara had been trying to leash. Her fingers were strong around the tip of her dagger, her aim true as she let it fly towards her father's exposed throat. His reaction was just as quick. He darted to the side. The blade skimmed the side of his neck. Blood welled. His hand flew up to stanch the flow, but Adara was already moving, spurring Ulrich forward. And, while Eadric of Bernira tried to sidestep, Adara of Guston thrust her sword beneath his upraised arm.

"We will not surrender!" she shouted. "We are *one!*"

Bones shuddered and blood unleashed like a deluge over her hand. Pain rent her father's features in half. He attempted to rear back. Hot blood flecked her face. Adara did not hesitate. She yanked her sword, withdrawing it midway before plunging it into him again. This time, they both screamed as something inside him gave way beneath her blow.

All movement slowed around her, though Adara forced herself to stare at her father as he tried and failed to ease himself off her blade. The man who hated her for being female, who married her off to Elvin. The one who despised Grahame's village, who thought he would own the people of Hyrstow as if they were hogs to be traded. The man who conspired to have Grahame killed. The one who would slay them all, if given the chance.

Blood dribbled from the corner of Eadric's mouth.

Rage and disgust, hope and sorrow lanced through Adara as he groped with faltering hands. Eadric did not look away from her face, nor did he say anything to her.

Adara did not wait for his last breath. She released her sword and hurled herself from Ulrich to find Grahame easing to stand, his face painted with dust.

"Grahame," she shouted. Her frantic hands met with his strong torso, shoulders, jaw. She scoured him with her eyes, panting, "Where are you injured?"

A look of pain slipped across his features, but he stifled it with a grimace. His good arm laid heavily on her shoulder as he pulled her in to kiss her forehead.

"I am uninjured." He pressed the words into her hair, her cheeks, her lips.

"You're sure?" Adara demanded. She was shaking, her hands still trailing over every part of him she could touch. "You went down, and I couldn't see…you weren't trampled?"

Adara suddenly felt as if her mind had disconnected from her body. A rushing sound, like that of a river, took up residence in her ears. Grahame stood before her, whole. She could barely believe it.

"I am well, 'Dara. I promise."

He pulled her to him, engulfing her in an embrace. Adara wrapped her arms around his middle, holding him to her, breathing in the reality that he was alive. Only when she understood that he was whole did a sob ring through her. Grahame clasped her tighter, chanting his wellbeing into her ear. Once she'd breathed in the sweat and sweetgrass scent of him did the truth of her actions hit her.

She had slain her father.

A slow, heart-rending sense of sorrow sucked at her middle. It confused her, the sense of wrong that invaded. Eadric of Bernira was not a good man. He had not been a good father. He would have killed Grahame, yet a part of Adara felt stained somehow.

"Eadric is dead! The earl of Bernira is dead!" Grahame's voice rang over the battle. It was clear and strong and caused Adara's tears to fall.

"Adara," Grahame said, his tone gravelly. "'Dara, look at me."

The command in Grahame's voice calmed the roaring in her head. The battle slowed around them. Metal and blood and pain mingled with shouts for retreat. Hagan was still standing, slaughtering the tide of men that welled against Adara's right flank. In the distance the advancing soldiers halted and began turning back to the house.

"'Dara, please."

Grahame slid a hand along her jaw, gently turning her face to his. Frantic, desperate worry shone in the depths of his eyes. Lines furrowed his brow. His hands shook as he turned them both, walking them behind their line of men, his back shielding her from further assault.

"What were you thinking?" he demanded, his hand turning her chin from one side to the other, inspecting her face. Fury made his words sharp. "You could have been killed. I nearly witnessed your father end you. For the love of G—"

Adara placed her hands on his chest, her heart trying to beat itself out from between her ribs. Grahame kept walking her further back, his strong arms navigating her around the fallen. Their fighters surged forward in a manner that suggested victory. Adara barely heard it. All she could feel, all she could recognise was the feeling of Grahame pressed to her.

"Why do you not care one bit for yourself?" He locked his hands on her hips while his shouted words hit her.

Gratitude that he was whole enough to yell at her pierced her soul. All that mattered was that he was alive. That they both were.

"It's always the same, Adara! You put yourself in harm's way again and again and—"

"We are one, Grahame." The words slipped from her mouth before she even thought to speak.

Grahame blinked, rocking back on his heels as he stared down at her. God, he was so beautiful it hurt. His sandy brows pinched together, his full mouth trembling.

"We are."

"He would not have stopped," she croaked, her throat suddenly aching as a thousand feelings arced through her.

When she looked past Grahame's shoulder, to the scores of retreating men, a sliver of relief made itself known. Grahame's finger hooked beneath her chin to bring her gaze back to his. His jaw rippled with restraint.

"Don't you ever fucking do that again. Put yourself at such risk. Make me think I would have to live this life without you."

"I'm here," she whispered. She barely got the last word out before his lips descended on hers.

Grahame devoured her. If a kiss could have brought someone back from the dead, this was it. The sweep and spar of his tongue with hers warred with the gentle way he held her head in his hands.

They *lived*.

A cheer from their men caused them to break apart, though a small smile decorated the corner of Grahame's lips.

"You did it," he said, awe entering his tone for the first time since yanking her from the battlefield. "God-damn, 'Dara. My little conqueror. You *did* it."

All she could do was nod. Exhaustion made her limbs leaden.

"We need to check on the others," she said, wishing she and Grahame could disappear back into Guston without having to bear witness to the casualties. He nodded.

"You do not leave my side."

FORTY-THREE

Grahame

Blood flecked Adara's neck, coated her right arm to the elbow. Her skin was ashen, her cheeks tearstained, yet Grahame had never seen anything more beautiful. Only when she looked beyond his shoulder, and he saw her face fall did he turn.

Bodies littered the ground.

A small company of their men pressed toward Clayton House, swords and shields low. Grahame had to catch Adara around the waist when she gasped and tried to break into a run.

"Let go! Grahame, let go!" she howled.

Her nails dug into the forearm wrapped around her waist. When he refused, she loosened her grip, pointing instead to the people strewn among the grass.

"Thor!" The name was a sob.

Grahame bent his nose to her hair for one moment—one last moment before grief and rage and helplessness took hold of them again. His wife smelled of dust and blood and sunshine. He knew it made him wretched, but she was *alive.* And so, despite the unrelenting ache in his shoulder, he twined their fingers together as he drew a knife with his other hand.

Men stared up at the sky, forever unblinking, wounds decorating their torsos. Blood had turned into a black river between bodies. Uhtread, eyes closed, had a hand to his chest over a wound. Grahame felt bile rise in the back of his throat. Adara ran past him. She pulled at Grahame, threading them through too many bodies, her hand trembling in his. At the front, straw-blond hair peeked from beneath a bloodied shield. How she sighted Thor beneath the wooden slab, Grahame didn't know. When no one rose up to harm her, Grahame released Adara so they could overturn the round piece of wood. Beneath, Thorhild knelt, as if he'd simply fallen to his knees, his chest to his thighs, hands splayed above his head. His sword lay a foot away.

"Thor!" Adara said. "Rise."

The command in her voice was usurped by the gentle hand she placed on his shoulder. Still. He remained so still. Adara knelt in the dirt beside him.

"Thor, you must rise."

Her voice broke on the last word. She gripped his shoulder, trying to turn her friend's face to the sun.

"Thor, please."

Grahame stepped over one of her father's men to crouch beside her. Tears ran rivers down her cheeks. He steeled himself, placing a sturdy hand on Thorhild's shoulder to help push the man to his front.

"Come on, Thor," he said, more for Adara's sake. Grahame already knew the man's fate but would help ferry his wife's shock to grief.

They managed to roll Thor over, his body butting up against another of the dead. His eyes were empty, staring ahead. A gash at his neck wept a stream of blood while a knife protruded from his chest. Sorrow hit Grahame harder than he expected. Yet he remained silent while Adara's hands floated over her friend's face, cupping it as if to focus his gaze on her. A wretched wail cut from her.

Grahame wrapped his arm around her shoulders to pull her away.

"Shhh, 'Dara. Shhh. He is at peace," Grahame whispered into her hair.

A sob clawed its way out of her, then another. Adara would have bent forward in pain if he weren't holding her back to his front. Still, Grahame whispered soothing nothings into her ear.

Suddenly, she sat straighter, turning to look up at him. Her silver eyes were red-rimmed and wild.

"We must check for others. Yrsa. I heard Yrsa shout in the middle of the fight. Can you see her?"

Grahame ground his teeth and braced himself. He did not think he could find the friend that was a sister to him in the dirt. Knew he could not pull a sword from Ridley's chest.

Grahame rocked back on his heels and stood, the bridge of his nose stinging. He looked to Clayton House where a cluster of their forces had halted at the gates. They were moving back in a somewhat uniform formation. Grahame's fear was subdued. Ridley couldn't be dead. He was the one who would have been directing men like that. And if Ridley was with the men, it meant Yrsa would be with him. There is no way he would have left his wife's side if she had fallen.

"I believe Yrsa to be alright. Ridley, too. Come, let us check for wounded then we must go to the front. They will need us."

Adara reached forward, wrapping her hand around the handle that protruded from Thor's center. She grunted as she tugged it free, fresh tears flowing. Leaning forward, she placed a kiss on his brow then slid his eyes closed.

"We'll be back for you," she whispered.

She twined her fingers with his, her gaze scouring the battlefield for those who had fallen.

Uhtread. Paul. More faces from Guston he'd only met a couple of days prior. At least they were dead. A few of Eadric's men moaned in pain, but when he and Adara assessed the severity of their injuries, nothing could be done. One man begged for death, another was so delirious with pain, he offered his sword to them so he wouldn't suffer. Adara stood by, her face a stony mask of determination as Grahame wielded the blade, striking true. Grahame retched after it was done.

His arm ached, but he picked up a discarded shield

all the same, strapping it to himself. He wanted Adara far from the field but would not deny her victory. Burying their devastation, they ran to the group that rallied against the gate.

"We've been locked out!" Sam shouted as they approached. He appeared as if he'd lived an extra ten years, but at least he was standing.

"Let her through!" a female voice shouted from the back. The wooden gate towered over them, casting their army in shadow. Within seconds, Yrsa pushed through the assembled men. Blood decorated her shortened hair, her face, her neck. There was so much of it, Grahame had to look twice.

"Yrsa," Adara said, eyes wide. Adara reached for Yrsa.

Yrsa simply waved her off, shaking her head. "I am fine. A few scratches. The pigs retreated and barred the entry. None are coming from the back field, as if they've been told to stand down. Is there another way in? We could climb over but with their advantage in number, it would mean death."

"At the rear, too close to the wheat field."

"No." The word fell from Grahame's mouth before he could halt it. "They retreated. We do not have enough men for a full assault. If we go around the rear, the force in the field will pick us apart. We stay with our original plan. Siege. We starve them out. At least we'll have a chance to run if they mount another attack."

Yrsa's brow quirked, the side of her mouth tipping up. Ridley materialized at her side, somewhat less worse for wear. He nodded, relief entering his gaze as he beheld Grahame and Adara.

"It sounds as if there is chaos inside. The death of Eadric was the key." He inclined his head to Adara. She stood stoic against the praise.

"We should wait, Ridley. Their forces could advance and we do not have enough men," Grahame urged.

Ridley issued a curt nod. He scanned the men around him, lips working silently as he counted their number. He called off those pounding at the gate, ordering them back to the area before the battleground. Eadric's men did not reconfigure.

Crossing back over the battlefield was another torture. Those from Hyrstow and Guston found friends and family members among the dead. Adara remained at the fire to help the injured. She saw to everyone herself, either wrapping wounds or offering soft words before she, Ridley, and Yrsa settled around one of the fires to strategize. By nightfall, when Grahame returned from sorting the dead, his ribs and arm throbbed. He only had enough in him to pull Adara from her seat and take her to a tent to sleep.

Beneath the threads of dawn, Eadric's dead were carted off four by four in a wagon originally used for supplies. They were dumped at the front gate. Whether the corpses would be collected by those inside remained to be seen. The only body they kept was Eadric's. Though they didn't want him rotting in the sun near camp, proof of his death was needed. Yrsa wrapped the man in an old blanket someone scrounged from a saddle bag, though

Grahame saw her spit in his face before she covered it. Adara avoided her father's corpse all together.

At the end of the day, they buried their losses. Ridley had asked if Adara wanted them to wait; to bury the dead in Clayton House's small churchyard so that she wouldn't have graves in the field leading to her estate. She shook her head, telling him she wanted the graves in full view of the house so the sacrifices would always be remembered. Later, she shared with Grahame they would build a stone wall around the spot and have a priest bless the area in order to give proper rites to the dead.

Adara's eyes shone with tears as Thor's face was covered by dirt. Hagan, thankfully unscathed, placed a heavy hand on Adara's shoulder. She patted it, offering a baleful smile.

"Muretta will be heartbroken," she whispered.

Hagan nodded, his throat bobbing.

Ridley shovelled dirt with grim determination while Yrsa wiped away a tear.

"They lay in peace, now," Grahame murmured into Adara's ear as rocks were placed over the dirt.

"I know," Adara said, her hands going to his forearms looped about her front.

She sighed, and Grahame swore he could feel the strength leaving her. He turned her into him, settling his hands on the dip in her waist. Adara nuzzled her face into his neck.

"There is more to come," she said, the words muffled by his skin. "I fear…"

Grahame remained silent. Adara hugged him as if determined to never be parted.

"I fear violence will come down on me and everyone here. I killed an earl. I cast an entire earldom into peril."

Grahame tightened his grip on her. She smelled of firesmoke and sweat. He loved it because it meant she was alive.

"You don't know that."

"The Britons can still regroup. My father promised them a union. Stability."

"Then they will continue to be disappointed. We will never give them that."

Adara nodded into the crease of his neck. Her hands tucked themselves up against his chest.

Without a word, Grahame released her, sliding a hand down her arm to twine their fingers together. He led her to the newly erected tent where sleep found them immediately.

The next morning, they awoke to shouts and movement outside of Clayton House. Frantic, they strapped on armor as quickly as they could.

"I'm not staying behind," Adara said.

Grahame crossed the small space, cupped the back of her head, and stamped a kiss on her lips.

"I don't want you to. Yet I will remind you of your promise to stay by my side. We are better as one."

They watched the retreat of the troops from the field behind the house. Tents were lowered, men on horseback moved north. Grahame's mouth fell open as they watched.

"There are still forces in the house," Ridley said.

As the sun rounded the sky, they watched the Briton army fully retreat from Clayton House.

Adara proclaimed she'd had enough waiting. The bodies had been collected from the front gate. It hung open at an odd angle as they approached. Hair on the back of Grahame's neck stood on end as they passed through.

The yard was abandoned. No stable hands nor horses scurried about. No sound emanated from the house. The garden had been picked clean. The party moved to the front door, slow at first, as if the sensation of desertion was a toll on them all. When Ridley pushed the door, it swung open easily.

"Show yourselves!" Ridley shouted into the dark entrance. Grahame swallowed down his rising fear. In such a tight space? They'd be slaughtered.

No answer came from the depths of the house. Ridley's sword remained high as he moved inside, silent as death. Slowly, they followed, Yrsa flanking Ridley's right and Grahame filling the space to his left. Sounds of shuffling came from the kitchens, while low murmurs were heard in the great room.

"Put down your weapons," Ridley said into the house.

They paused, listening for the sound of metal dropping, but none came.

Every muscle in Grahame coiled tight. He angled his body so he could cover Adara's with his if there was an attack. If she noted his movement, she let it slide.

Ridley paused, then nodded, advancing into the great room.

Three men sat at the long table, mugs and a loaf of bread before them. They looked up from their meager meal, no shock on their faces.

One with silver hair and a pointed countenance spoke. "Finally, you've come."

FORTY-FOUR

Adara

The three most powerful landowners in Bernira sat at her table. Men that Adara had met at various gatherings with Elvin, the same men whose fathers were entertained by her father as she grew up. They calmly shared a meal amid a room of chaos. Chairs were upended, wreaths discarded and trampled, the fireplace held the remains of one of her cushioned chairs. Bootprints covered the floor and the scent of piss and sweat clogged the room. The man with a shock of silver hair stood, his gaze falling to Adara.

"Lady Clayton and Lord Clayton, I assume. I am Lord Richard Bennet. Ruler of Bennet Pass, your closest neighbor to the north."

The man's utter calm made Adara's heartbeat

quicken. Grahame turned his body ever so slightly to block her from view. She was grateful for it. There was no reason for these men, these powerful lords, to be seated at her table so casually.

"Aye, I am Lord Clayton. I hope you will tell me why you are supping at my table before I put this blade through you, Bennet."

The other lords, one with hair and beard the color of copper and the other with a drab face beneath a mop of brown, shared a look of surprise before casting their gaze back to Bennet. Lord Bennet's hands rose in supplication as he took a step toward them, a smile pasted beneath his hawkish nose.

"There is no need for that," the man said, halting a little ways before them.

Adara had to hand it to the man for his confidence. Ridley and Yrsa looked as if they were about to string him up by his innards. Grahame was not much better. He glowered at the man, hate rolling off him in waves.

"Myself and Lords Mehghan and Lowry," Bennet gave a slight nod to the seated men, "understand that the earl is dead. His son or brother is next in line to inherit the title."

Adara's lip curled. She placed a hand on Grahame's arm, a silent request to pass. He inched to the side. Adara squeezed his arm as she stood beside him.

"My father had no brothers. Nor sons," she said, her words strong.

Bennet's steely brows rose, though no surprise decorated his face. He clasped his hands in front of him as a smile touched the corners of his thin lips.

"Indeed. Something we advised him on for years. He would have taken another wife to remedy the problem, however, the Lady of Bernira being cousin to the king made the matter more complicated."

"Your point?" Adara snipped. These men had taken arms against her and had raided her home.

"Our point is that you are what we are left with, Lady Clayton. If Elvin were still alive, we'd have a leader through wedlock. Since he is no longer of this earth, we are left with you and the contested man you've married."

"Believing in our marriage and siding with Lady Clayton were options before this battle started." Grahame's voice was sharp behind her.

Bennet inclined his head. "We did not see it to be true until recently."

"You mean, until Eadric was slain by his daughter?" Ridley said. He lowered his weapon, though he did not move forward into the room.

Lowry blinked rapidly at the statement though Bennet had the audacity to appear unsurprised. He steepled his fingers together before bringing them apart.

"Patricide is a sin," Bennet said calmly.

"So is killing one's daughter!" Grahame bellowed.

Swift and sure, he strode past Ridley and Yrsa, halting mere feet from Bennet. The shorter man finally flinched.

"Eadric came at her on the battlefield. I witnessed it.

He was about to end his own line rather than accept our marriage. And for what? To gain the *Britons*? The ones who turned tail and ran after a few days? He put countless lives at stake in order to satisfy his own sense of righteousness!"

Adara had never seen Grahame so barbaric. His shoulders flared as he yelled, eating up space. To his credit, Bennet took the verbal lashing. He stood there, staring up at Grahame, his smile growing. When Grahame finished, Bennet spoke.

"It appears as if you fit the mold of an earl, Lord Clayton of Hyrstow."

Adara stepped forward, fitting her hand into Grahame's as confusion swept his features.

"It's what we remained to tell you," copper-haired Lord Mehghan said, his eyes shifting between Grahame and Adara.

"I do not know what the king will say about this," Bennet continued, as if the other lord hadn't spoken, "but Lady Clayton and, by proxy, you, are the only living candidates for leadership. I would scrabble for it, however, I'm an old man. I'd like to live out the rest of my years in my home without the threat of war looming. I do not condone the rule of a woman, yet Eadric had brought enough troubles to my doorstep as of late. You see, we never wanted the Briton's involvement, yet Eadric impressed upon us the importance of the partnership. And, as events unfolded, we now understand the error of our underestimation."

Grahame's hand tightened on Adara's. "Get to the point, Bennet."

"Our allegiance," the lord sputtered, throat bobbing as he swallowed, "is yours. We have heard rumors of the manner in which you defended Guston. Yours is the house we will honor if testimony is needed. It is your birthright."

Adara tried not to show her surprise but feared it was written in her slow blink as she absorbed Bennet's words.

"You would allow me to rule as earl?" she asked.

Bennet shook his head as he turned back to the table to pour a cup of wine. The look he wore was one of apology. "You are a woman. We cannot support you, though we can support House Clayton, of which your husband is now the head. We can support the decisions he makes, with your heavy influence, I'm sure."

Adara wished the slight didn't hurt. Wished no part of her was contested. But he spoke the truth. It was doubtful anyone would consider her a worthy ruler. That her father's lords were even considering her to have input in Grahame's decisions was a surprise.

"And if I don't accept your support? If we put you to death right here and now for going to war on us?" Grahame snarled.

Bennet's smile was serene, though he retreated a step. "Then we will die by your hand as you try to remake an earldom without its largest landowners. The task will be difficult—nay, impossible."

"And why should we trust you? Why didn't the retreating Britons kill you when they left with Galan?" Adara asked.

Bennet's face fell into confusion before righting. "Galan is dead. I believe you killed him before we were all gathered here."

There it was. Her father's final lie brought to light.

A shout from outside penetrated the walls. All heads snapped in the direction of the window near the fire.

"An ambush?" Yrsa demanded, brandishing her sword at the men.

Lowry shook his head frantically.

"No. The Britons left when they discovered the Briton prince was dead. Eadric told them he still lived. I believe they would have killed him for it. They didn't want a war with Northumbria and Wessex just to gain Bernira land. There is no surprise with us!"

Ridley growled in frustration, backing through the house the way they'd come, Yrsa on his heels. Adara followed. She had to see, had to know what threat could shake them now. Their war band was too few. There was nowhere for them to flee. They would be trapped inside the siege of her own making.

Hagan was already at the gate. He peered through the peep-hole.

"What is it, Hagan?" Ridley asked.

"It's Langley. Deircia has come to aid us," Hagan said. A collective gasp swept through the lot of them as the gate revealed Deircia's flags flapping in the distance, accompanied by a group of knights at least a hundred strong.

FORTY-FIVE

Adara

"To think, after all this time, your brother's scheming finally caught up with him," Grahame murmured.

The grim set to Ridley's mouth did not speak of pain. It did not tell a tale of the bond he and Oswald once shared. Instead of replying, he knelt by the body slumped at the bottom of the dungeon's stairs and placed the palm of his hand against Oswald's forehead. Black blood dried around the wound in the priest's gut. It appeared as if he'd been stabbed then thrown down the stairs.

Adara shivered. Grahame lifted the torch higher for Ridley to see.

"I am sorry for the loss of your brother," Adara said, filling the heavy silence.

Ridley hung his head, as if the sentiment was a burden. "No one else will be," he said, his voice thick.

Adara looked to Grahame who stared at her with a mixture of uncertainty and knowing. He had told her of all Oswald had done to Yrsa and knew now of the role he played in Hyrstow's suffering. Still, she could sympathize with the heaviness of grief for the person you once cared for, even if that person was despicable.

With a quick inhale, Ridley rose. The torch caught a sheen in his eyes.

Grahame lowered it as he said, "I'll have some men come down to retrieve him."

They trudged up the stairs, finished with their inspection of the house. It had been decided to check all the rooms before greeting the Deircia soldiers. Awareness over the importance of the impending conversation weighed Adara's shoulders down. She'd just done away with one ruler and now had to contend with the steward of another. Thankfully, only Grahame seemed to notice. He snaked a hand around her waist and pressed a kiss to her hair. For a blissful moment, Adara sagged into his touch, drawing strength.

Upon entering the great room, however, she infused her spine with iron. She walked straight for the table's head, ignoring the noblemen who awkwardly stood by the fire, then stood in front of the chair her father had placed there. Grahame claimed the space to her left while the others sat with Langley and two of his knights.

"Please, Sir Langley, forgive me for having nothing to offer. The last few days have been quite trying."

The older man nodded. He placed his helm on the table before him.

"Earl Lachlan received word from Ridley that the Earl of Bernira was setting fire to Dercia lands. That there was an impending battle. We have come to assist yet see that we are too late."

Adara polished her nails on the breast of her tunic.

"Indeed."

Langley had the grace to grimace. "Thank you for saving me the work of it. I've also been sent with a message from the earl. It would be in the best interest of the earldom to be absorbed by Deircia."

Rage ignited in Adara. There was no way they'd fought this hard, sacrificed all they had, simply to hand it over to Deircia. Alliances were valuable, yet they were not about to reshape Northumbria. If Earl Lachlan thought he could do so, he was out of his mind.

Spreading her hands, she said, "I am Bernira's heir. Bernira will no longer salivate after Hyrstow. We will remain on our side of the border. I will acquiesce some tax in order to ease the bond between the earldoms. That is all."

Langley's brow rose as a smirk touched his lips.

"Already so generous. So willing to prove you are not your father," he murmured. He drummed his fingers on the tabletop, thinking.

"Do you accept?" Adara demanded.

Grahame leaned on his elbows. "Respectfully, sir, it seems as if you have interpreted my wife being born of Eadric as a weakness. It is not. He was a cruel man, one who honed his daughter into a cunning woman. One with a heart that would see her earldom prosper. I am of Hyrstow descent. We want nothing more than the benefit of our realms."

Langley's eyes darkened a shade, as if he took Grahame's words as a threat. He had more men. If he wanted, he could slaughter them all and plunge the earldoms into further chaos. Heart pounding, Adara pressed for her right to rule.

"These are the most powerful lords in Bernira. They have come to my side in order to aid the smooth transfer of title from my father to me. All of their households know of their pledge to me, and they've sent word to the other consequential lords stating their desire to uphold my birthright. They further insist upon the legality of my marriage to my husband, Grahame Shepherd of Hyrstow. I will not give him up, nor my lands, despite your belief that we are easy to conquer."

Adara did not flinch over the conflated ownership she claimed. To her delight, Bennet, Mehghan, and Lowry remained stoic, nodding along with her assertion.

"Indeed," Lowry said, "Adara Clayton's husband is now our recognized earl. Long may they live, ruling together."

Finally, a laugh like the snap of a branch cracked from Langley.

"I see that you have been forged in fire, Adara of Bernira. And though I plan to carefully oversee the peace between our realms, I am glad that you do not back down so easy. It gives me hope for our future."

Details of the changeover came after that, sparse food accompanying the arrangements. By the time Langley retreated to his camp with Ridley and Yrsa, Adara was swaying with exhaustion.

"You were remarkable."

Grahame was shirtless as he stoked the fire in her bedroom. The bed had been knifed open, feathers and straw bleeding out. Grahame and Adara laid a spare blanket and their cloaks overtop the hole. A makeshift mattress for a makeshift earldom. And, despite her fatigue, Adara watched the ripple of Grahame's muscles as she stripped out of her tunic.

"As did you, Earl."

Grahame's grin was one she wished she could imprint in her mind forever. He ambled over to her, his pants slipping down as he slid his belt from its loops. Adara's attention dropped with it.

"Eyes up here, Wife," he said, his tone low. It made her middle clench. With a sort of hungry leisure, Grahame cupped her face up to bring his lips down on hers. Heat flushed through her. She ran her hands up Grahame's chest, suddenly needing to feel all of him. That was until doubt reared its head.

"Grahame, are you ready for this? I forced you into—"

"If you utter the words 'forced you into this marriage' one more time, I will leave a handprint on that fine ass of yours so angry, you won't be able to sit tomorrow. I am yours, 'Dara. Running an earldom sounds like child's play compared to what we've just been through."

He bent to kiss her again, his hands roaming from her face to her neck, then scraping down her shoulders. His rough palms settled on her bare back, while his thumbs drew lazy circles into her skin. It was enough to make the space between Adara's legs pant with want.

She arched her brow, a devilish smile spreading her lips.

"Forced you into marriage," she taunted, a dare in her tone.

Grahame's eyes glinted with a wickedness she'd not seen since before her father arrived. Then he was bending down, tipping her over, banding one arm around her legs to brace her over his shoulder. She squirmed as she laughed, the sound good and strong and joyous as it left her body. It was shortly accompanied by a shriek as Grahame's wide palm met with the flesh of her backside.

"You monster!" she squealed.

"You must be one as well, Wife. Since we are *one!*" Grahame hollered as he tossed her to the mattress then nestled his hips between her legs. She tried to cover his mouth, but he playfully bit at her until she let her hand fall away.

Then he kissed her, deep and hard, until her soul sang with a happiness that she knew would last forever.

EPILOGUE

Grahame

8 *years later...*

"How fare you?" Grahame asked, a huge smile stretching his mouth.

Fat snowflakes floated from the sky, landing on his and Adara's heads. They had been lucky enough to have fortunate weather all the way to Hyrstow.

"Well," Branton replied as he brought Grahame into a massive hug.

They two men clapped one another's backs heartily before separating, knowing it would be all too soon before they would say goodbye. Grahame pushed those feelings aside. There was no helping their living so far apart. He resolved to be thankful for the few times per year he did see his friends.

"Don't hog him, Dad," Neil said from behind his father.

Grahame chuckled, releasing his brother-in-law. He ushered Adara over the threshold then scooped his arm around Neil's neck, pulling him down to rub the knuckles of his other hand into his nephew's hair. A scoffing laugh broke from Neil as he easily pushed Grahame away. Neil was a man now, as tall as Grahame. To his right, Adara was clasped in Emma's tight embrace.

"How was the trip?" Emma inquired as she let his wife go.

Grahame was already making the rounds of hugs, marveling at how the children had grown. His surprise was postponed by Yrsa and Ridley's children barging through the open door.

"Uncle Grahame! Aunt 'Dara!" Estrid exclaimed as she shoved her way through the throng. Her dark hair fell over her face as she received a reciprocal push from Æfflead.

"Wait your turn," Æfflead said, her voice light yet strong.

Estrid grunted as she tossed her hair out of her eyes but did not listen to her elder friend, instead winding through bodies to clasp Adara's legs.

"The trip was long," Adara answered Emma as she embraced energetic Estrid.

The little girl was practically bouncing. Hanging back

was little blond Bjorn, Yrsa and Ridley's son. He held onto his mother's hand, his large eyes taking in the busy room. Though merely age four, he held the quiet wisdom of his father.

"Let us in!" Yrsa called from behind. "It is freezing out here."

Grahame chuckled as he herded the children toward the living area. Thankfully, the space had grown since he'd moved from Hyrstow. Branton had extended the right wall to make the main room larger. He'd added two bedrooms to accommodate his and Emma's growing family. After the birth of Timothy, they'd been blessed with another little girl, Briony, who looked up at him with wide eyes. Grahame couldn't blame her. She only knew him as a faraway uncle, though she likely heard more about him as Earl of Bernira. Still, he winked at her, ensuring his grin was wide and welcoming.

After greetings were finished, Emma revealed the feast she'd prepared. Sweet buns, ham, a medley of buttered beetroots and carrots, creamed peas, onion-roasted pheasant, and a fine mead spread across the table.

"Emma, this is too much," Adara said in awe.

They settled at the large table Branton had built, ready to dig in after a long day.

Emma's wide grin made something in Grahame sing. She and Branton had prospered over the years, though time was not without struggle. Branton had been a mess when Emma had delivered Timothy, resorting to his withdrawn tendencies as she neared the birth.

They'd had a reckoning when the time came. He'd been better when Briony came along two years later, a surprise for all. Steadfast, Emma had grown her baking business, teaching her daughters, Merthe, Ginnie, and Æfflead baking skills as the years progressed. To see their prosperous happiness now, years after their struggle, was a gift.

"She always makes too much," Yrsa said around the roll she chewed.

Merthe, standing at the side table mixing a concoction of oil and herbs, cleared her throat.

"Of course, Merthe did much of it," Yrsa was quick to amend.

Merthe's lips twitched upward, something Grahame noticed Neil tracked with hungry eyes.

"So," Ridley said once everyone's plates were full, "tell us of the northerners."

Grahame shifted in his seat. He glanced at Adara, who had stilled beside him.

"They are no longer interested in moving south," Grahame answered.

"How? They had a formidable force ready. We were unsure you would even be able to visit, the threat they posed was so great," Branton commented.

Briony sat in his lap, smacking her small hands on the tabletop. When she grew bored, she reached up to tug at her father's beard. He grunted, his eyes widening with the pain. Bjorn covered his snicker with his hand. The action mirrored his mother's.

"Here," Adara said, reaching out, "give her to me."

Grahame had to smother his smile at their surprise when Adara came around the table. His wife held out her hands, and in a light, high-pitched voice asked Briony, "Do you want to sit with me?"

Yrsa nearly dropped her knife. She cleared her throat and took a drink of mead to hide the fumble. Briony stared up at Adara with awe. Grahame had to admit, Adara *was* spectacular in her navy riding dress, the sheen of which screamed expense. The small combs that held her hair from her face were delicate, and the fine shoes she wore were likely more costly than anything in the Cutter's house.

"Well?" Adara asked the child, her confidence faltering.

She glanced at Grahame, her gray eyes unsure. He offered her an encouraging nod. It was no secret that the children preferred their uncle Grahame to his beautiful, intimidating wife. Though he and Adara had tried for children of their own, they had not yet been granted any. It caused Adara to be stiff around them. Formal.

Grahame drew the attention away from Adara by answering the question of the northerners.

"The Britons readied themselves, but our soldiers knew the marshes. They could not invade. Earl Lachlan sent a force, as well as Wessex. Turns out, when we all band together, good things come of it."

Grahame tipped up a shoulder in a shrug. He'd left out the part where he'd kept the other earls in line when land squabbles broke out while Adara negotiated with the Briton king. As much as he wanted to delve into the logistics of how Adara expertly wielded her knowledge and favors for the best outcome, he knew his closest friends were far removed from the struggles of territory. Their life in Hyrstow was very different from the lives he and Adara lived.

Across the table, Briony made her choice. She silently climbed off Branton and scrambled into Adara's awaiting arms. With a little nod from Bran, Adara turned to settle in her seat with a wiggly Briony. His wife's lips twitched upward with satisfaction. It nearly cut him in two, it was so beautiful. Hope shined in her eyes.

"We have something else to share," Grahame said.

He placed his hand on Adara's lower back as a grin spread across his lips. Everyone lifted their heads from their meals to stare. Grahame smiled wider. He could sense Adara pause, taking one more moment to cherish their privacy. Then happiness crinkled the corners of her eyes.

"We are to have a baby," she said.

Ridley's mouth dropped open. Emma whooped, then pressed her lips together to suppress the giggle that sprang forth. Yrsa only offered a savage grin as she leaned across the table, offering her hand to Adara. Adara took it, tears glistening in her eyes. The two women stared at one another for a moment, joy palpable between them.

"You'll be one of us!" Branton said. He came around to Grahame, giving him a hearty smack on the back. "Congratulations, brother!"

Grahame ducked his head, overwhelmed with emotion.

"How far?" Emma asked. She ran a hand over Timothy's head of dark curls. The boy sat beside her, swinging his legs.

"The midwife guesses I am close to half way through," Adara beamed. She glanced at Grahame. He couldn't help himself. Ducking close, he pressed a kiss to her cheek.

"Ah, a spring babe. How wonderful," Ginnie said.

"Thank you," Adara replied, "for everything."

Grahame swiped his hand over Briony's head as sidled closer to Adara. The little girl laughed. His heart swelled with something more than gratitude, brighter than joy.

Even after years of happiness with Adara, he still looked forward to every moment they had yet to experience. Life's turbulence, its utter madness at times, made the good times even sweeter. So, Grahame, the earl of Bernira, kissed his wife again, then smothered his friends in a round of hugs and laughs.

ACKNOWLEDGMENTS

To you, the reader, thank you for picking up my first series. You are the reason I keep writing. Thank you from the bottom of my heart.

Next, I have to thank my amazing beta readers: Stevi, Jody, Monica, and Heather. You helped bring the story and characters to life. Writing is such a solitary process until it isn't. Your feedback was so valuable. Thank you.

To the Accountability Coven! Thank you for welcoming me into sucha wonderful little author community. Your encouragement is priceless.

To my ARC team, thank you for your enthusiasm and early support.

To Tracey, who has edited the entire Saxons of Hyrstow series. I am so glad for your help and guidance. Grammar is not my strong suit, and these books wouldn't be anywhere near as good without you.

To my mom for helping me tweak everything at the end. Many thanks.

To my husband and children. Although my kids can't read these books, I know they are proud of their mom being an author. Your support means everything.

Finally, I would like to acknowledge myself. More often than not, I diminish my accomplishments. This time, I want to shout from the rooftops that not only have I written a book, but I've completed a series. Cayley of five years ago would never have guessed she could produce a book, let alone three. So, here's to me for the hard work and dedication I put into The Saxons of Hyrstow.

About the Author

C.A. Fray is the Amazon #1 Bestselling Author of *The Saxons of Hyrstow* series.

C.A. grew up with her nose buried in all sorts of books. She is a mother to three boys and maintains her sanity by writing tension-filled romances. She has a house full of plants, drinks too much coffee, and loves playing with her rescue pup.

Join her community on Instagram @cafrayauthor or sign up for her newsletter at cafrayauthor.com.

DON'T MISS BOOKS 1 AND 2 IN THE SAXONS OF HYRSTOW SERIES

His Viking Captive

Taken by her enemy...

Yrsa Arkyndóttir has sworn a blood oath to avenge her father's death, but when her clan's Viking raid fails, Yrsa is taken captive by the rugged Saxon chieftain, Ridley. Injured, Yrsa knows she must escape though as she heals, she finds herself fighting desire for her infuriating captor.

Tempted by the woman who tried to kill him...

Ridley Ward is determined to protect his village, yet he cannot kill the impetuous Yrsa. To ensure her safety, he must keep her presence a secret. Little does Ridley know how much the beautiful Viking will test him.

Amidst growing tension in the kingdom and the threat of their illicit secret being discovered, Yrsa and Ridley must come together to uncover the true meaning of obligation, loyalty, and love.

His Saxon Wife

A marriage of convenience...

Heartbroken after his wife's death and overwhelmed by the needs of his children, Branton Cutter strikes a marriage agreement with widow Emma Baker. Despite his grief, Branton's life takes a chaotic turn when the attraction he feels toward Emma is more than that of their arrangement.

A temptation that cannot be ignored...

To escape the kingdom's widow tax, Emma agrees to Branton's proposal in order to save a proper dowry for her daughter. Little does she know that sharing a house with the broken man will test her patience as well as her desire.

While politics between the church and earldom unravel, peril linked to the past looms over the village of Hyrstow. Will Branton and Emma be able to reconcile their feelings in time to ensure their family's survival?

www.ingramcontent.com/pod-product-compliance
Lightning Source LLC
Chambersburg PA
CBHW031739180726
48283CB00005B/1574